WHITE
on
BLACK
on
WHITE

Coleman Dowell

SERPENT'S
TAIL

BRITISH LIBRARY CATALOGUING IN PUBLICATION DATA

Dowell, Coleman
White on black on white
I. Title
813′.54

ISBN 1-85242-160-6

Portions of this novel were first published in different form in
Ambit, *Conjunctions*, and *The Review of Contemporary Fiction*.

First published 1983 by
The Countryman Press, Woodstock, Vermont, USA

This revised and corrected edition first published 1990 by
Serpent's Tail, 4 Blackstock Mews, London N4

Printed on acid-free paper by
Nørhaven A/S, Viborg, Denmark

in memoriam

Tamar Alexandra Colbert
(1962 – 1978)

this book was written for

Bert and Daisy
and is

dedicated to

John Kuehl and
Linda Kandel Kuehl

Was ever dream so crazed as this reality?
—Heinrich von Kleist, *The Prince of Homburg*

Lend money to an embezzler but not to his son. The old man has worked it out of his system but the kid might want to practice on you.
Meredith McAllister, Bonnycastle "Memoirs"

In the land of contrariness lives a black with a white ass.
—From a saying by Sholem Aleichem

part
one

the snake's
house

november

Today is a month from when I would have returned to town. I
had imagined that there would be snow on that December day,
and melancholy, and the greater turmoil of indecision: would I
leave Berthold and try to live in a Harlem or East Village slum
with Calvin? When I went to Partridge House, Cutchogue, Long
Island, in a rented automobile driven by Berthold, I was in love;
that is, I dug and was dug by a man I had known for five months,
give or take a week's respite, as I used to think of his absences.
In the final two weeks before the country loomed as the solution,
I had given in to my fate and acknowledged that I loved Calvin,
though "I dig you, man" was all one could say or expect to
hear. A day without Calvin had come to mean a day of pacing
the floor, of often sick anxiety: what could have happened to
him? for he was dependent upon me financially and emotionally.
Such a man—with a criminal past (eight years in prison) and, it
was poundingly stated, enemies in and obligations to the amorphous underworld—was in continual danger of permanently dis-
appearing. Often when we parted for the weekend he would
say, "I'm not going to make it this time, man," setting me up for
two days and three nights of self-hatred. How could I have let
him go back to that? Once after such a weekend he called early
on Monday, his voice full of the joy of survival, and demanded
to know if I dug him still, as though a weekend could cause me
to misplace the spade!—the relief implicit in the levity. That was
the day he said he was on 110th Street and was leaving to walk

3

down to me, a leisurely twenty minute stroll; that was the day he arrived high, defiant, lying—"I got a job, man!" (he did not have a job, man)—at 4:10. But who, in the throes of digging, reads the graffiti on the wall above?

Thus he began to stay over in the Panelled Room to Berthold's increasing quiet and my increasing vehemence: was I someone to turn my back on a needy brother? Was Berthold after all a racist?

This situation: Berthold's quiet disapproval, my need to be with Calvin, his cannily accelerated insistence that we be together, drove me to seek a place in the country. I called my old friend, Maria, one of the endangered species of great ladies—she had gone to school with Eleanor Roosevelt and though a beauty was very much like her—and asked for her help. By the following midday she had found Partridge House for me. The owner of the place conveniently lived in my neighborhood, a very 'Maria' touch, and by eleven o'clock that night terms had been set, a verbal lease drawn up and signed with a handshake and the check given. On Wednesday night at about 7:10 we were on our way, Berthold driving the rented car. He was to stay overnight and leave at dawn the following morning. Accommodating, terrific Berthold. The day we left he admitted that we needed a separation from each other and said he was not sorry to see me go. He said it nicely.

The afternoon of the day we left, I shaved Calvin's head, revealing a triangular skull, and he shaved mine. There was some sexual tension during the operations, I felt, and a lot of symbolism: shedding literally parts of ourselves that belonged to the city and its illusions, the main one being that we were different, for with a shaven head, the convict's old mark of apartness, Calvin and I occupied the same cell.

We got to Cutchogue, a closed down town, at 9:20 and called Serena Westlake, the agent for the house, who met us on the main street driving a jeep, and led us to the house.

The house: designed by a Name, written up and photographed, a sort of mecca for particular types. Supposedly there was a Zen atmosphere. My first reaction was a moment of panic that filled my throat so I could not breathe. When I could, I attributed it to excitement and fatigue. The high ceilings, twenty-seven feet in the living room, and the, to me, senseless angles

4

were not serene and in its spaces there was yet a kind of clutter making me think of schizophrenia. The room where I was to sleep, for all its skylights and big windows looking east and north, contained a handsome nightmare when I considered my blind bitch, Xan: the bed was set on a platform and to reach it you had to negotiate several steep steps; 'negotiate,' because the steps were crowded with objects, many of them with the appearance of votive offerings set before a buddha. As I discovered later, the platform was practical with storage space underneath fed through a trapdoor. From this room, to the south, a door led onto a little open balcony where one could sunbathe. I could envisage the door ajar, Xan wandering out, falling down two stories to the wide deck. So that one of my first images was of blood and death.

This room was at the top of a winding stair, open, beginning at a landing in the kitchen which featured a fireplace; another fireplace, back to back, faced into the living room. Across a sea of a deck from the main house there was a guest cottage. All the doors and windows in both houses were protected by louvered interior shutters.

Mrs. Westlake, 'wonderful Serena' as the owner called her, was a young woman, perhaps pretty, certainly brusque and nice. Her dirty overalls concealed her body. She gave us a quick tour of the place, joined us in a brandy, and left. I fed us some bad delicatessen food and we all retired, Berthold and Xan and I to the scary bedroom upstairs and Calvin to the guesthouse, to the bedroom that faced the house and the deck with window-doors opening onto the deck. Berthold and Xan, exhausted, went to sleep at once. I, revved up by several nights of insomnia and the uneasy house, prowled.

I finally went to bed but could not rest, thinking of Calvin and what would soon be our isolation from the world that, through its services, had allowed us to 'love' without physical requirements of each other. I wondered which of us would first show the strain of the lack of those services. There was implicit danger in the images that came into my brain of one of us giving way, images that my hyped-up brain could not control. I sought his light, hoping, I think, to use it to imprint my wishes on the unwitting blank plate of his mind. Wishes or apprehensions; I could not have defined which, though self-control had always been my

'stick,' as Calvin put it, meaning, I had always supposed, 'shtick.''
But self-control can be a formidable cudgel, ask the man who
owns one, and my inability to channel my thoughts gave me a
warning foretaste like the hint of almond in the arsenous soup.

I went outside and saw that the louvers on Calvin's window-
doors had not been closed. I stood and spied on him, intense in
concentration, as he cased the place. I saw him open drawers,
paw through piles of clothing. He stood unmoving for a long
time, lapped in the curtains that masked a closet. When I tapped
on his door he came guiltily, a small dish picked up on the way
in his hand. He said that the pebble-filled dish was the only ashtray he could find. I fetched him one from the house, wondering
what he had been doing for the hour, at least, that he had been
in there, for he was still fully dressed. With pleasure he showed
me some magazines he had found, *Penthouse* etc, those beaver
mags dear to the hearts of some men. We said goodnight again.
I went back upstairs to the tiny bathroom off the upper hallway
and found that I could look down into his room and watch him
as he unpacked. I could see one of the nudie mags open on the
bed, to which he referred now and again as one doing research
would consult an open dictionary. I was informed by this that I
would not sleep, that I would intermittently spy. I did not examine the information.

The next time I went out onto the deck I could hear that he
had found a radio, had found WBLS: "Keep it coming . . .
don't stop it now." Calvin was in bed, a cigarette burning in the
ashtray on the cover beside him. He lay under a blanket, one
hand holding an open magazine before his eyes, the other under
the cover, moving. With great stealth I entered the guesthouse
and pushed open his door. Had I expected a prison-hardened
man to be shy about masturbation? He grinned at me, his eyes
dilated with reasonable excitement. Wordless he showed me the
photograph: a woman with her legs wrapped around her neck,
a ludicrous pose. When I laughed man to man he said that a
spread pussy, however it was achieved, was the most beautiful
sight in the world. The connoisseur, he informed me that that
particular pussy was an unusually well-made piece. My interest
waned when he brought his concealed hand forth to point out
the particular beauties of the organ. I saw that his clinical dissec-
tion was mocking, or teasing: that he knew his hand under the

6

covers had been my focus and excitement. I managed some ca-
sualness to throw him off track and went back upstairs and
crawled onto the flat hard pad with Berthold and Xan and dozed.

When the alarm went off it was only 4:45. As Berthold shaved
and dressed I again stepped onto the deck, propelled by a feeling of thickness in the air like fear, and saw that Calvin's light
was on. I could hear Berthold descending the stair. What had
happened in the interval? The loss of time, the first of that symp-
tom at Partridge House, was like a cave through which I had
passed. I imagined that the events, either thoughts or actions,
hung folded like bats above me. I moved out to where I could
watch Calvin. There he was as I had left him, magazine held up
before his eyes, hand moving. As though at a signal he pushed
the bedclothes down and went into the full athletic swing of jack-
ing off. Had he saved his climax for me or was it one of several?
If the former was true then he was aware of my spying. The
information knotted my stomach. When Berthold came onto the
deck Calvin verified my suspicion by bounding out of bed and
going through the little hallway into the bathroom. Berthold,
emerging through the front door, could not see Calvin but I could.
He straddled at the toilet, yawning and stretching and shaking
his cock and laughing. The laughter, unless it was for me, was
idiotic, aimed at some invisible gallery. His stance and the tension of stretching outlined in his legs the maddening, logical maze
of a runner's musculature.

Berthold, sleepy and dear, somewhat bent, walked slowly to
the car as I watched in perturbation, waving, wondering if he
would ever start the car and go. When he pulled away, after an
eternity of the motor not catching, I turned to see Calvin watching me through the glass door. I recall his eyes, excited with an
unusual excitement. I felt that he had learned something about
me whereas I had learned nothing at all about him that I wanted
to know, or could use. But I believed in that dark cold moment
that the hand of power had changed and belonged to another.
My own hands that had held his fate for five months were lax,
inefficient.

I gave him the whitest look I could summon ("There's that
white look again," an expression of his) and went upstairs where
Xan slept too tired to need her breakfast. I held her and slept a
bit, I think. In any case Calvin and I did not see the first dawn

7

as we had planned and when I got up the day was brightening to warmth and the house, all white walls and warm woods, seemed inviting. When I carried Xan downstairs I found Calvin shirtless on the deck and we managed to share a kind of subdued anticipation: six weeks of this! with the Sound pulling audibly at the shore eighty steps and a stretch of beach away.

At breakfast, watching Calvin feed Xan buttered toast with his old tenderness, I convinced myself that nothing had changed.

Around ten Maria arrived to take us shopping. I had not seen her for nearly two years, a time of great turmoil for her, and the changes in her were hard to accept. Her age had stepped up and overtaken her; it seemed to me that she walked behind her age like a child; and her deafness was a barrier. Calvin, dressed in my red jogging suit and a knit cap, was to me a fetish figure. I could not think why Maria did not reach out and grab him. The thought put me on guard against myself.

In the grocery store we were stared at, imperial Maria with two attendants, one bald, the other wearing a red cap and red clown suit, carrying an old dachshund with a white face and blind eyes. We moved up and down the aisles together like an exotic painting, only the shopping cart anachronistic, contained within the frame of our strangeness.

Later, Maria and I had a visit while Calvin went jogging. For hours. He returned, Maria gone, with tales of friendly waves, kindly questions, encounters with children and mamas, even an amiable salute from a police car. That morning Xan had begun to pace, ceaseless.

I cooked dinner while the house turned cold as night drew in. The furnace, we discovered, was on the blink. A half-hour before dinner Calvin said he wanted another walk. I gave him an exact time for dinner and just under the bell he returned. As he came in the kitchen door his eyes were those of the early morning, excited, secretive, inviting some comment. He ran his tongue out and around his lips as though he had just eaten. I wondered if the metamorphosis was night-connected and what part the house played, for I could feel myself changing again. It was as if night in Partridge House was a potion for the skin to drink, labeled Apprehension, smelling of rut. By fighting it I caged my highly sexual response before it broke loose and savaged someone.

8

We had a fire in front of which a mattress was placed for Xan and me, to be our permanent bedroom. With what I felt to be a debilitating effort of will the talk was kept safe, though at times there was the sense of crawling through his allusions, which, like a barbed-wire fence, nicked me here and there despite the caution. But his voice was soft, the music loud, so the nicks may have been self-imposed. When at last he expressed fatigue and got up to leave, I asked him, my relief making the question more of a petition, if 'this' was what he wanted. "More," he said, "Much more." A masterfully ambiguous statement.

I gave him a while to settle into whatever his activity was to be and then went to spy on him. He had closed all the louvers, cutting me off.

One feature, increasingly important to this account, is that the main house had a very good stereo system. Whenever Calvin came in he turned on this machine, invariably soul music, invariably too loud even for something I might have wanted to hear. In addition there was a staticky little color TV on the dining table; frequently both the TV and the stereo would be going at once. When I had visited Jamaica, Long Island, the Sunday before we left for the country, to meet Calvin's wife and daughters, I had heard to my amazement that WBLS was kept on full blast and that they somehow were able to talk around it, but I did not have the technique to listen in this way and much of the talk was mysterious to me.

Our second day in the country was more of the first: Calvin jogging, walking, gone, and when he was there, the noise. I felt as though I kept my head cocked at him like a bird, trying to understand what he was saying and to fathom his insensitivity to me for I would be at my typewriter at times when he switched on the machine. One of his vehemently avowed aims for us was that I would write my novel before we left, a tale in which he would, he was confident, play a part. On this second day he inaugurated his dictatorship where Xan was concerned.

Xan had not slept the second night which meant that I had not either. I had been up with her roaming the grounds and the road from four a.m. When I told him this he instructed me: I should let her roam, alone, whenever she wanted. She would be perfectly alright outside, alone. My demurrals—her blindness and partial deafness—were met with Calvinistic logic. He felt, he

9

believed, he knew. I did not count. He insisted upon taking her down to the cold rocky beach where she sat shivering, unable to tell a direction. He ordered me to leave her alone, saying that she was happy. As though to taunt me, he told me his plans for the two of them, which included long walks on the road, to a distant lighthouse, on the beach where he would sit on a rock and read my new book, just released; and she, why she would be happy with him and *free* (the emphasis sketched the prison of my over-concern), as I would be free and safe in my mind to spin out my writing.

I can't recall what we ate. I can recall spending a lot of time in the kitchen cooking and washing dishes to the tune of WBLS while Xan paced and Calvin drank. At some time in the evening after supper I confessed to him that I could not work to the clamor of the radio. The sound of my apologetic submissive voice haunts me now. To counter this I asserted myself where Xan was concerned: she belonged to me, I told him, my rights secured by over fifteen years of singular devotion; and I asked him, firmly, to leave the decisions affecting her up to me alone. Some details of this evening are quite gone for I had been drinking brandy, a lot of it, neck and neck with Calvin and his gin. I can see us standing on the deck, he in the red suit about to take off for a jog to a town eight miles distant. The night is thick and foggy around us, that combination of warmth and chill that 'clammy' defines. Something is said; he walks to the guesthouse and slams his hand with all his strength against the wall. Earlier he had broken a glass by smashing it to the floor though the events seem simultaneous. What follows is seen in flashes: Calvin in the yard bending over in pain. Calvin standing, his dangling hand hugely swelling as I watch in great excitement. Calvin dressed for town, leaving, gone. I see the figure at the steps, then at the edge of light, then darkness, but there are no transitional steps. Doubtless these placements of the figure involve words as well, perhaps shouted, and perhaps from the seemingly empty darkness an imprecation is hurled ballistically. If so, their absence from my memory could be evidence of self-control. Or, of course, of something else. And I on further evidence suspect something else.

It was late when he got to Babylon and there was no transportation to New York until seven in the morning. He called me, waking me from a drunken sleep, demanding that I get Maria to come for him. If not that, then I must be willing to pay a taxi forty-five dollars to bring him back. I refused to do either thing. He told me, "Somebody will die for this." I hoped it would be he but the loathing words followed the click of him hanging up.

I slept peacefully then, beside Xan whom I had drugged on Valium. I was up, unhungover, and at my typewriter when I heard his step on the deck at 9:15. My instinct led me. I embraced him and wept for his hand, which had been treated in Babylon and was wrapped and in a sling. Later he told me that my crying for him had affected him in a way that he could not describe. He said that when he jogged later he 'did something' he could not tell me about, as a consequence of my crying for him. The sense of nervous mystery invoked by his statement, by the infinity that lies beyond the surface strictures of some *thing,* was, I was reminded, as personal to him as a call is to a bird; I could have summoned as companions to the remark a hundred other such. Instead, I made breakfast for him and sought to soothe him with my actions, or made lunch for him and forgot my work for the day; whatever, they were familiar gestures.

Still, in spite of the matutinal reconciliation, by nightfall we were quarrelling again. All is seen through a veil of booze. The fireside, Calvin once again in the jogging suit. I see him setting out after saying roughly the following: People had been draining Calvin Hartshorne all his life and now he had had enough. When he ran from me again he would keep on running. If I wanted him I would play the game by his rules or not at all. And that included his rules about Xan and the smallest details of my own life upon which he chose to bestow his wisdom—though in my current anger I may be distorting the helpless past.

After his speech he left but soon returned saying that he would not, after all, leave me. Silent by the fire, we drank, I occasionally lurching up to bring Xan back from some trap she had made of familiar things. But when I said that to Calvin—that out of known quantities such as chairs and sofas she fashioned mysterious snares to hold and frighten her—he said, "There ain't no *known quantities,* my man. Rub that on your chest." The set of his chin begged for a fist. We both listened to his words, though, I wondering precisely what they meant, and it was as though he had found a meaning that, like Xan's snares, frightened him exceedingly for he got up, his face twisted, and said that from here on all would be hate. Can it actually have been out of silence that he rose to his feet so twisted and violent? I see him bent over before the fire and his tears splashing onto the hearth in a passion of grief I had never before witnessed. His eyes dared me to offer the comfort I might foolishly have given. He ran off into the night headlong, a fearsome figure.

It was about 1:15 when I heard him in the kitchen and went out and found him with a water glass beside him into which he was pouring gin, and he was still a twisted figure for he was bent over as he poured, trying to ease a spasm in his leg with a kneading hand. On the kitchen counter coiled a length of rope. When I touched it he said he had found it on the road. An interior voice told me, "Attack." I asked if he meant to string me to one of the rafters. After the question I saw that he was mad, or close to it, and that the uncalculated words had been meant to serve to bring him down or make him act. Act. But what action I could not imagine. He went to bed taking the half-gallon of gin with him. I did not sleep again. At 5:45 I woke Berthold and asked him to come for me on Sunday. He had a daylong appointment on Saturday that I knew about. I used Xan's pacing as the reason for my urgency.

I believe it was a mistake to spring the news of our return to town in front of Maria. Calvin's face closed. Maria, taken by surprise, tried to argue with me.

I simply do not recall Saturday night. There must have been food, loud music, and the TV going. There must have been recriminations and threats. Isolated like a signpost in a headlight is his question: Are you afraid of me? For some reason beyond stupidity I still was not and told him so. As though to prove it I slept well. Sunday morning found us having a good breakfast; finds us, for that is where my memory once again picks up; I do not recall cooking or laying the festive table on the deck, though some taunting calculation must have gone into the celebratory air of linen and flowers and best china. As though a curtain had just opened on a play, there we are in the sunlight, Xan on my lap, eating eggs and grits and hot biscuits with fig jam. Calvin's milk, for he does not drink coffee or eat pork, thus the absence of bacon, is amber with brandy; I drink coffee from which the steam, no doubt fragrantly, rises.

Berthold arrived. I, in the sweetness of a day following sleep, told him that if this had been the first day I would not have troubled him to come for me but would have stayed happily on. He said, without implied criticism, "Do you want to?" (Later he said he had feared my return.) Hearing this, Calvin asked me to walk with him. At the end of the drive he spoke earnestly. He told me he was capable of learning, that he in fact had learned, and that if we could stay on he would be what I wanted him to be. If he knew what that was he knew more than I did. All I knew was that my wish to stay on in the bright weather still included him, or included him when he had finished speaking. It seemed that his desire to stay was built partly on the appalling fact that I would have driven him back to the slums, to the humiliation of not being able to support his family, to the danger of trying to make it in the streets, man. His need of the sanctuary sobered and elated me. But the decisive words were those that equated our rough times with the first rocky days of a marriage, and the half-embarrassed, thus fully cognizant, way in which they were uttered.

Calvin and I had a day of talking, walking with Xan, running up and down the beach steps to loosen, and as I said, furnish, kinks. This was to be the first of such athletic sessions that would put me back in shape. Something was said about cutting back on cigarettes and liquor. When we touched in play that was not always gentle, the touches were like those of people who had not yet been but would soon be lovers. I asked myself: if that was part of the new bargain, would I risk it? For beyond the imagined act it seemed to me that there was nothing. I could not see us getting up and going about the business of living. I had of course thought about this before: that in an age and in a city in particular, which gave to pan-sexuality the same importance as the toke from the communal joint, the idea of sex with Calvin carried such a curious weight of irreversibility, as though it would in fact be a real bridge burnt, allowing of no return. But return to what? And there I always, as now, stopped.

Within the clear-surfaced placidity of the late afternoon there was a hidden charge like the effervescence in the soda siphon: a careless touch on the lever and the glass runneth over.

At dusk we built a fire, I cooked, we ate. Dishes were washed, by me, for his ham hand with the movable bone now excused him from chores. The furnace was still on the blink, and mysteriously, for I had not spoken to her, Serena Westlake called and said she was bringing up 'the' heater. Thus she and Calvin had spoken somewhere, sometime. But not that day. He had been mine all day. When she arrived at 9:00 my consternation at her blonde good looks must have shown on my face. She measured me, found me short, and dropped me. She sat on the floor by the mattress. Calvin was in a sling chair by the fire, both of us in robes for warmth, and jeans. She set her gaze on him; it neither swerved nor wavered for the hour and a half that she was there. When I spoke to her the impatience that was meant only for Calvin's eyes, which she hid from my gaze behind the wing of her long hair, was plain to me: I could not see it but I could smell it, that burning odor of contempt that reeks from a woman on the make toward a male not makable. Her clothes—the sinuous blouse, the short sleek skirt and long legs in tight bright woolens—proclaimed her status. If I baited her (and I did) by insisting upon verification of something she had said, or asserted, she questioned Calvin: she needed an interpreter, you see.

Calvin sat beautiful in the firelight, robe falling open to show chocolate skin and muscles that seemed in constant play. I recognized that he was teasing her. I watched her response with less benevolence. For each ripple of his body she smoothed her silk blouse and tautened her breasts. I named the game For Every Ripple, A Nipple. Big and hard they were. Calvin's tongue flickered. I became fascinated, especially by the woman and her exclusive talk to him: if he wanted cocaine, go here but not there and keep in mind that the pigs were especially piggy out here. If he wanted grass thus and so dealer was dependable. She expressed concern for his poor hand. She had said to herself, "Here he is on his second or third day in the country and already he has had to rumble with somebody!" Roguishly she speculated that it was over a bitch. To his credit, though she could not grasp it, he agreed, indicating Xan.

Mrs. Westlake used the word dynamite a lot, and admitted to being frequently pissed off. She had grown up in Washington D.C., she said, in black dresses and pearls (at this I murmured, "Ideal for kindergarten" and was ignored). She thought that her constant state of feeling pissed off ("Incontinent?" I murmured) was because in those days she was surrounded by funky exciting blacks with whom she was forbidden to get down. I wondered if she was really responsible for her words. Her eyes, moving over him, were stoned-looking, needing already, as I did, the constant visual fix of Calvin. Or the eye that I could see was glassy with dreams; maybe the other was marvelously alert and even satiric, but that hidden side of her face, like Mrs. Westlake herself, will forever be as arcane to me as the far side of Pluto; to me she will be eternally in profile.

Forbidden to get down? Come now, Serena!

I had had enough of her and took Xan for a yard walk. When I returned they were gone, then I heard them in the cellar. I stood eavesdropping. There were silences that my imagination filled in. When they came up I was told that they had been searching for something the owner wanted brought in to town on Tuesday. And here another revelation: What a coincidence, that Serena and Calvin were both going into town on Tuesday! Of course she would drive him in, leaving early enough for him to make his appointment, the one I had not been told about.

When she had gone we sat on, Calvin in the chair, I on the floor beside him where he had asked me to sit, Xan pacing. I was vituperative about Mrs. Westlake, though I only meant to be funny. He was her defence. At least, he said, she had not used Greek words as Maria had. Following a chastising silence he murmured sleepily that the bitch was on his side. Something behind the words countered the sleepiness. I shifted position and saw the faint firelight on the moving filled hand within the partially opened zipper. I imagined my hand on his and then my hand alone filled and moving. And then? the old question. Xan cried and I searched for her. When we returned Calvin stood by the fire zipping up his fly. He murmured of gin, of being fucked up, and very sleepily went to bed, upstairs in the main house, now, for he had taken over the platform.

To calm myself I lay thinking how, as a rule, in my writing I chronicle the weather. This is mainly because I see weather as the thread that stitches our lives together or apart. In my southern border state, growing up, I would pray for particular weather: a snowstorm, if the center of family seemed about to give, for in our isolation we could revive mutual interests, such as music and reading aloud, and the fireside would become the necessary focus for even the estranged ones; in the kindly light hateful faces would take on a remembered glow; the storm raging without would make our inner storms petty by contrast. In summer's great heat we separated, I to lie in cold streams with my head on a rock and read; others of us sought out retreats supposedly known only to ourselves—dales and the tops of trees. Thus weather could, for all the silliness of the phrase, 'stitch us apart.'

That night before the dim fire I tried to work my childhood magic. Would a flood keep Calvin from going with Serena? Would a hurricane? Perhaps a freak heat wave would be the solution, the terrible reports of sunstroke victims in, especially, Harlem, that Cynosure (that collection of nursemaids) for the ultimate irate Weatherman. The sweetness of that day's weather and our companionship within it was, in spite of Serena, and Calvin's tasteless behavior at the end, still with me. Our promises of the morning, to change, to learn, seemed sacred to me. Something in me worked to reverse the traditional roles of black and white. I was the nursemaid, he the frequently bitter, because neglected, child. Seeing it that way, I could feel more sympathetic toward Serena, for making a special effort to draw him out. Wilfully suppressing the sexual tone of the evening I told myself, amused, that I was in danger of repellently becoming what Serena said she had been, to make her stay so long: mellowed out. "I got so mellowed out I lost all track of time." I told Calvin what a comedian had said about mellowing: that he was afraid he would go on and rot. He laughed, I recalled, and took this as a good augury. I gave Xan a half Valium and took a half myself. We drifted toward sleep, my hand holding her hind feet to stay her if she were enticed to wander down a darker lane.

Three-quarters of the way down that for me always odd road, I defined for myself the trip, the landscape. It went something like this: Afraid to go unprotected from one world into another, in my preparation for sleep I erect a series of small familiar houses along the road to hold the stages of my unfleshing. In each house I count the window squares and then the panes in the diminishing number of windows as I approach sleep. That is more or less it, but what I recall entire is a thought and a sound that happened at precisely the same time: the sound of a ladder being drawn bumpily up to a high place and the concluding thought of the foregoing: And then you come in and shatter the glass.

I was instantly awake, grateful for once for Xan's deafness for

16

she would have barked interminably at a much slighter noise. I went outside through the kitchen door, which was under the balcony off Calvin's room, and edged my way down steps and onto cold grass until I could look up at the balcony and see the ladder that had been pulled up and leaned beside the door there.

When I went back inside WBLS was loud enough for me to hear it; I had not, in my long leisurely wakefulness, heard more than a faint murmur, like that heard when you press your ear to a telephone pole. The sound was both nemesis and cover. I went upstairs not at all carefully and stood on the landing. The station asked me plaintively to write it a love song, told me to catch a plane to Florida, taunted me with the fact that if I was not in love on Monday I could go it alone. Had lonesome Calvin, regretful but respecting my tiredness, gone by ladder to the guesthouse for something, and back? But why draw the ladder up behind him? And what foresight caused him to place it there? From inside the room moans answered me and exhortations: Take it, take it, Wait, no wait I said. You're gonna git it. Lay still. You're gonna git it. Slow down, mama.

The door stood before me with a handle that gleamed. A turn of the handle. My hand could not do it. Behind the door: heaven for some, hell for others. On one side of the door, songs, commercials, weather, news spots, sex. On the other side, veins, arteries, chest full of puke.

Sometimes the imagination is fulfilled beyond its imagination and a break occurs, a real schism that has to do with the failure of words to define either themselves or other things. When I came to I was sitting on the deck of the guesthouse, huddled in a robe, my gaze set on the balcony and the light behind the door there. Another light caught my eye and I saw that it was sparks struck from the dome of a skylight set in the slanted roof. *The hunter of the East has caught the Sultan's turret in a noose of light.* The sun? The sun. The ladder leaned where it had been. Serena was asleep in Calvin's bed.

I went into the guesthouse and took the telephone on its long cord to the door where I could watch the balcony. I dialed Serena's number. Her husband answered. I apologized for the hour, asked to speak to her. In the long wait I imagined Martin searching the house, not having until then realized that she was gone. When I heard her sleepy voice I did not believe it, then had to

17

and hung up. Had Martin known my voice? Had I identified myself? I still don't know.

Back in the house I walked noisily up the stairs and tried the door. It was unlocked. On the platform a single body lay swathed to the top of the bald head, not just in bedcovers but also in the fur rug off the floor. The night had been bitter. I felt deep freeze in my bones, out for eight hours in frosty weather.

Because he had asked me to, I woke Calvin soon afterward and we watched the rest of the sunrise, mute but, I think, companionable on the windy edge of the cliff.

I got to my typewriter and began writing an ersatz journal entry meant for him to read when I left it lying about. There was in it no mention of the night's occurrences. At least I was writing fiction again. And I had identified something small and fugitive, a tiny mole in the immense tunnel of the darkness that had just lifted.

Calvin sat on the hearth watching me write, an old ambition now being realized. Once he brought me a cup of coffee, another time a buttered muffin, but I did not notice. I was playacting for him, through deep abstraction, a theory I had once explained to him of the mind turning turtle during the process of creation. He had said it was the same in athletics and another bond was forged between us. When I paused to stretch and light a cigarette, startled to rediscover the world, perhaps puzzled by mundane matters, he shook his head admiringly, his eyes a bit too dazzled, and said, "Man, you're laying some heavy shit on me." He turned on WBLS. His mockery augmented my wish for revenge.

Maria brought us a paper and drank coffee with me and left. We read the paper, Calvin in the sling chair and I lying on the floor in a patch of sunlight, my back to him. I thought that his own playacting of the night must have contained a good measure of frustration. To the sound of someone on the radio moaning about ecstasy, I moved my ass. The song was long with a grunting driving beat, like the sounds I had heard behind his door. Remembering the exhortations to lay still, mama, I lay still as though spent. When I got up and stretched and headed for the typewriter he asked if I had to just then. I see that moment now as the proverbial crossroads. I took the other which has made all the difference. I said, yes, I had to.

Serena called, pretending to inquire about the furnace, which had been repaired while Calvin and I ate breakfast. The gesture made, she asked if Calvin would call her later. I said she could speak to him now, and her pause said she did not want to with me listening. I called him. He turned on the radio, listened from midstairs, and came down and adjusted the volume upward, deliberate, retaliatory moves. As though that were not enough, he closed the door upstairs to the telephone room. A long long call. When he came down he was elaborately casual. There was a great deal of consultation of timetables, and a lot of speculation about whether the bitch would leave early enough for him to ride in with her, a great deal of doubt expressed about the latter. He said he could not come back with her because her husband wanted to leave New York late. Another explanation presented itself: Serena's car was a two-seater. I did not imagine she would drive the jeep into New York. I said, really innocent, "Oh, will Martin already be in New York?" Calvin's face told me he knew this was so but he repeated my question, "Oh, will Martin already be there?"

The day turned overtly unpleasant. I advised him to re-check with Serena to be sure she would leave early enough: his errand, he now said, was to sign up, for the first time, for welfare and receive a payment to help out on expenses in the country. I questioned that one both signed and received 'the first time' but did it silently. Anyway, he put off the call though there was a lot of telephoning about bus schedules; he said the printed one in the house had expired in September. 'Compulsive' is the only word for those calls, most of them to Penn Station. Babylon, at our end of the Island, did not answer, he said. In the repetitions I discerned a form of magic, like witchcraft: he was trying from a distance to impress himself upon the city, to be there before he was there. When the line was open and he was talking I envisaged him floating above the city, casing it.

During dinner preparations I started telling him about my Scotch ancestors, a family line that included a number of practicing witches. I said this gift, or whatever, had been handed on. His veiled eyes partially concealed his astonishment and some measure of belief. I related a story involving a great-great-great grandmother, a cockleburr and a ball of red yarn. She had convinced a troublesome neighbor that the cockleburr represented

19

that lady, that it had been given her name and, if and when my ancestress desired, could be made, by having twined around it the red yarn, to foreshadow what would happen to the neighbor soon afterward. Such as, by being tossed into the fire, causing the neighbor to fall into her fireplace and burn up.

I told Calvin that this was simple psychology, that was all, and we cool people were beyond its reach. I illustrated. If I told him that this pencil was him, and if I broke it he would break, would he believe it even for a second? He was silent. I see his head thrown back, his slitted eyes, his tenseness on the high kitchen stool. "OK," I said, snipping the string that held the pencil to the pad, "I name you Calvin Hartshorne and you are in my power." And I slipped the pencil into the pocket of my jeans.

If I leaned heavily against the kitchen counter I would see his eyes on the pocket with the pencil. Sitting down to dinner, in a hand held under the table I snapped a small piece of wood I had taken from the kindling pile and put at my place on the cushioned bench. He stiffened; his cigarette dropped and burned the table's high gloss. Tit for tat I said, bringing the pieces of wood into view, laying them beside my plate. His maimed hand tightened until I could feel the agony watching it. If he knew what tit for what tat it did not lead to a discussion.

Later under the smog of WBLS and the TV I reminded him of the call he was to have made to Serena. He tried her then or said he did and got an answering service. He had asked for a return call. I told him that I could not stand the telephone waking me and he said—how simple the solution—that he would take the phone on its long cord into his room. He did and there it remained. The phone in the guesthouse was now my connection to the world.

Caught in my own game I hid the pencil but folded my jeans on a chair within his sightlines near the foot of the staircase. I believe I saw him later going through the pockets. If so he was clever about refolding the jeans as he had found them.

We had set the alarm for 5:15, the bus to leave at six. When I went up at 5:20 he was still in bed. He was so desultory about preparations that a faint suspicion put down a tentative tendril. My reminders about the passing of time hardly made a dent in his consciousness and another hairy tendril, more tenacious, grew. I finally pushed him out at 5:35, giving him twenty minutes to walk a mile and a half to the bus. When he had gone I observed the well-rooted horrid plant. He was driving in with Serena; Martin was already in New York: Calvin was not walking to the bus but down the road to Serena's where they would fuck until time to leave. I worked myself into a state which was to increase as the day went by.

Serena had meant to pick him up at 7:30. At that hour I called her, insanely expecting that Calvin would answer the telephone. I told her what had happened. She was not surprised enough to comment on it. She asked if she could pick up some things that Calvin had been meant to give her. What things? I asked, not liking his role, assigned by her, as the one to be consulted. A long pause. Oh, a small rug and a lamp. I said, "You didn't find the rug in the cellar," but she had hung up as I spoke. She came, dressed for town, at 8:30. It seemed that the rug was in the trapdoored space under the bed, therefore the search in the cellar had not been for a rug.

Calvin had promised to call me the minute he got to New York. I calculated that, as he was waiting at Serena's for her to return and pick him up, I would hear from him not at 9:30, when the bus was due, but at 11:15 when Serena should arrive. I called Penn Station and got the good news that the Long Island for once had not been delayed. Armed, I waited.

Maria came over to spend the day. I was to use her car for pressing errands while she sat with Xan, then we would have the leisure to bring each other up to date on our lives. She was openly glad that Calvin was gone. When I asked for her reaction to him she said that she was reserving judgement.

At 11:10 he called. The Long Island had been delayed, man; he had just got into town! He spoke in breathless exclamations. I told him, "I know how you got there." He laughed and asked how I had found out. But then the apparent understanding fell apart. I told him that I knew he had gone in with Serena. He said we would discuss it when he got back. I told him that I was not pleased at the subterfuge. He said I kept putting him through these changes, man, and he was sick of it. I asked him to swear on his daughter's head that he had gone in on the bus. He refused, then abruptly swore it and hung up just as the impulse to retract hit me with the impact of a danger sign looming out of mist.

I saw myself in ambush on the edge of an African village. Was I avoiding being taken as a slave or was I there, noose and net, to choose and capture? The smoke curled up, acrid; children played at games they could not name, were summoned to meals called otherwise, as they were called, in the open fearsome air, names that were not their own. They, their parents, the objects around them, the village, were under the protection of a system of double-naming. Would life be called death in that village? A wolf a sheep? No, it would be more complex, no system of simple reverses. A Rosetta stone would be needed to break that code, and immense scholarship to use it. That eagle, talons unfurled above a child: name it, quick! or innocence is lost.

Maria and I took Xan into the yard where she began behaving oddly. The way she used her head was as though she dodged hard punches from an unseen assailant. I was frightened already and her behavior panicked me. I tried to examine her and when I touched her head she screamed in pain. On our careful drive to Riverhead, hurrying only inside ourselves—the slightest jolt, we discovered, would cause her a spasm of agony—I thought about the invisible Bell witch of my youth whose infrequent returns to the place of haunting were only to cause mischief; under her aerial attacks people and animals were said to behave as Xan had behaved in the yard. The thoughts seemed to cast long shadows across the sunny autumnal countryside.

Xan's old vet, who had treated her since her puppyhood alone with me in the country, told us that the trouble was a combination of eye and tooth. She was given heavy doses of demerol and antibiotics and I was told to come back on Wednesday. I could extract no promise, as of old, that she would be all right. The candid man, whom I admired for directness as well as for his great skill, was evasive. Re-hearing his bluntness to others in the past—"Take that dog on home. You got about two hours left with him"—I thought over and over as we crept back to Partridge House, *It's my turn now.*

I could not think of leaving Xan to go shopping. Maria and I gathered the field mushrooms, and wild garlic and onions still flourishing in the warm soil, and I set about making what may have been the original version of burgundy beef before refinement set in. The decidedly unusual rapport that Maria and I had shared since first meeting was encouraged to renewal by the frightful morning, most evident in our avoidance of any mention of Calvin. If we had been separately questioned I am certain we both would have said that we hoped, through the shunning, to make him go for good: two witches working a spell over a pot of wild herbs.

But at six o'clock on the heels of night Calvin walked in. He had several boxes in his arms. I commented on the change in his appearance, for instead of my old suede jacket he wore a new one. Wordless, he tore open a box and brought out a handsome black leather coat which he apparently meant for me. He also had a Mark Cross briefcase. Knowing Maria could not hear when he muttered, he told me that he had bought the jacket for me before I had ruined his day, then we both saw an error: how could he have, if he had just got into town when he called? The deduction was silent on both our parts but might as well have been stated by me, and his accusing eyes were merciless.

The three of us ate dinner standing and though I was reluctant to see Maria, my link with a sane world, leave, she did so, feeling the bad ambience, puzzled and disquieted. Seeing her go, I wished with a certain desperateness that I had told her everything in case evidence should be needed. At the car she held my arms and searched my face. "Soon?" she said, and I knew she was belatedly asking for what I wished now to give. For the first time, I think, the rapport was chilling.

The details following her departure are sketchy. I recall Calvin's vehemence because I had made him swear on his daughter's head. I offered, feebly and shamefully, the story of Xan's pain and trouble, which had come on after the call. I heard Calvin saying, "I go to town for one day and you fuck up my dog." *My dog.* The words and tone made me feverish. I recall his declaration of independence from me, his assertion that he did not care what I did, therefore why should I care what he did? Implicit in this was his projected affair with Serena Westlake. I may or may not have told him that I had not brought him out there for that cunt. I know I thought it. He stormed up the stairs and slammed the door. I heard him talking loudly to himself inside the room. I heard him say, "My daughter's head is more important than *hers,*" and I heard the equation: his daughter's head and Xan's, and wondered, badly shaken, what retribution might be visited upon Xan to make up the sum.

I feel now the urge to take her in my arms and run, to Any-place, Long Island. But, I thought, retribution, like packages from Bloomingdale's, is probably delivered by UPS and Calvin and UPS could have found us in Anyplace.

The sense of fever and the fire so near the bed made me recall the ceiling fan twenty feet aloft, a large old fashioned thing reminiscent of South Sea films. I walked over to turn it on. Upstairs Calvin called out, as though he spoke to me, "If that bitch comes around here I'm going to fuck that bitch anyhow."

I tried then to evaluate the admission—that he had not yet fucked Serena—and to see it as an apology for the torture of Sunday night. I was strongly tempted to go to him and offer and receive amends, but feared that my giving way might suddenly expose me, not to him but to myself, for in a flash like subliminal advertising I glimpsed myself kneeling before him. I took the pencil I had named Calvin Hartshorne out of its hiding place and put it under my pillow. Then I turned on the fan and lay on the bed in wetness and discovered that Xan, helplessly, drugged beyond control, had peed. I fetched a towel and eased it under and around her and lay down with her enclosed in the crook of my arm. Overhead the hum of the fan, like a swarm of African bees, was constantly ominous, commanding one to check on it now and then through slitted eyes, for fear it might be advancing, unmoored by some mad bee keeper.

During one such inspection I saw the slow-motion opening of the big barnwood door through which one could gaze from the upper landing onto the living room. Calvin stood within it, glittering in malignity. The points on his naked shoulders were as prominent as the horns of Moses. Afraid my eyes would reflect the firelight, I closed them. When I looked again the door was shut.

The next day Calvin and I took Xan back to Riverhead in Maria's car. The vet put a tape around her muzzle, and with a sharp instrument began to flake her teeth away. Her screams, the blood, drove Calvin out of the examining room. At last the vet and an assistant took Xan away and hurt her abominably. When they brought her back to me she was missing five teeth, her remaining teeth and gums had been treated, all without anesthesia because of her age, and she was in a shocking state of demoralization. The vet, knowing me, said of course I could take

her with me but he thought a few hours alone in the hospital
would benefit her and, he said, she would drive me crazy with
her cries and protests. I believed him, knowing the distance was
shorter than ever before to that place, and agreed to come back
in midafternoon.

Subdued because of Xan's pain, Calvin and I drove out to
Orient Point and sat in silence looking over the water, which has
the appearance there of the open sea. The blankness of space—
gulls, and one distant ferry rolling a bit on moderate swells—
restored us enough so that when I suggested a little tour of
Greenport he was agreeable. I showed him some handsome
houses but he wanted to see 'where the niggers live, man' and I
took him down the backstreets. The eloquence of his silence
seemed intended to point out the great contrast, but in fact the
'slums' of Greenport are scarcely slummy at their worst; 'disre-
pair' is the strongest word that comes to mind to describe those
houses. But if denied one thing, Calvin, the ingenious, will supply another. I heard him mutter and looked to see a black policeman coming out of one of the houses. In a moment he was
followed by a red-haired woman. I could not see her features
but the lines of her body were elegant. Like a pointing bird dog
that, practicing on a starling flushes a brace of pheasant, Calvin
stiffened beside me, shocked out of playacting into what seemed
genuine, if still theatrical. His hand beat his knee. "That bitch,"
he said, "that motherfucking bitch," and he wrestled briefly with
the doorhandle. Then he lay back with closed eyes and told me
to drive on.

On the way to Partridge House he talked obscenely, though
so low I could not catch it all. He seemed to be delineating the
sickness of whites hung up on niggers, their expectations and
demands, with special emphasis on redhaired women, though
this could be my invention based on his conviction that redheads
are the 'whitest' people. My own hair, now missing, was sandy.
I in turn thought about the problems of queers fixated on 'normal' men, and wondered what it would be like to be a white
woman with a similar obsession, though hardly for the first time.
I wanted to question Calvin about white women, their feelings
as expressed to him in what must be the agony of fulfillment,
and his feelings as savior, torturer, the objectivization of *forbidden*. I longed to take advantage of his vulnerability and tell him

25

about following interracial couples, minutely observing what their defiance could cause them to do, their nervousness, their intensity which nearly always led to gaucherie. I longed to ask him why it was that beautiful black men were always with fat untidy, òr pustuled skinny, white women. But the redhead on the porch had had the lines of a thoroughbred and the cop had been lean and handsome. As much as any of this, I longed to avoid Partridge House and keep driving. But Calvin directed me home.

At the house he began to drink gin.

The wind had risen and we sat inside watching the trees bend, seeing the trees and their reflections in the glass, a double image like our states of mind. As though violently propelled by a tailwind, a small bird flew toward us and struck the glass with great impact, fell to the deck and lay shuddering and twitching. This had a terrifying effect upon Calvin, I could see that, but my immediate need was to put the bird out of its pain. To this end I slid open the glass door and took up the small body. The heart beat faintly beneath my fingers. Viscera oozed from the broken skin at the neck. I hear Calvin's voice now, loaded with more than fear, breathing at my elbow, asking what I mean to do. In answer I take the tiny neck between thumb and forefinger and squeeze as hard as I can, hating the grotesque angle of the head as though it is something I can hear, like an echo.

Had there been, for Calvin's ears, a snapping sound? The pencil flashed like a bar of neon in my mind. It was still under the pillow. I walked to the edge of the wood and scraped a deep grave in the leaves and humus. "No, man," I hear Calvin call, and see him going into the house at a run and coming back with a small box, one of the house treasures. I buried the bird in the box, marking the spot so that I could recover the treasure later on.

As though the words were a funeral service for the bird, Calvin repeated and repeated, "That bird was coming to tell me something when it died." His intake of gin increased greatly; the incantatory words became accusations.

At one point he threw himself onto my bed, his head on my pillow. Calvin lying on top of Calvin. I was afraid he would feel the pencil. A powerful impulse took hold of me, lifted me from my chair, led me to the bedside. I sat by him and placed my hand midway on his thigh. We were immobile except for his

26

thigh's trembling and the tightening response of my hand. He was standing before me, legs spread, rocking on the balls of his athletic feet like a fighter. As though all thought words had been spoken over the months and this was only a continuance, he told me that my only interest in him was centered on one part of his body, that his brain, my man, was something I made fun of, that I thought he had no feelings but was cold and mechanical like a robot. I recalled something that Nancy Cunard, herself hung up on blacks, said about another powerful figure: froid, sec et cassant. I shook my head at Calvin's accusation but saw that he was immensely breakable just then. I won't put a name to my impulse to bring forth the pencil and snap it, slow and deliberate.

When we left for the hospital at 3:00 he was vicious. He told me to stop the car. I did not. He jammed his foot onto mine and nearly caused our deaths. We missed a telephone pole by a millimeter. He informed me that when he said to stop a car, or do anything else from here on, he meant it. I had defied him twice in the past but we would have no more of that. He was taking over the care and feeding of Xan and I could fuck it, he told me. If he had done so earlier she would not be in the hospital crying with pain. And so on. In depriving others, him and Xan, of their freedom, the depriver must find that he has lost his own. I had lost my freedom to disobey or even to contradict my master, Calvin.

When we returned with Xan my own demoralization put me in mind of hers in the hospital. In effect, I too had a piece of tape across my muzzle; I could not speak for fear of angering my self-declared master. My nerves were shot. I was not certain that I could make it through the night. As with the vet and Xan, reassurances were no longer possible.

I called Maria about returning the car. She was too tired to drive me back and asked that I keep the car overnight. I told her about Xan's travail. She said wearily, "Oh darling, don't you think it's time?" "For what?" I asked, feeling a numbness that anticipated her answer. "To put her down, darling. She's old and tired. In such pain." I'm afraid I hung up on my good friend Maria. Back in the house I found Calvin cradling Xan before the fire. The contrast was painful and I told him what Maria had said. I think such a look as his, fixed on a stranger in a lonesome place, would have brought on thrombosis. Looking away, mur- muring, he spoke to something unseen by me, words I could not hear. Turning back to me he asked, "Like this?" His left hand, knotted and scarred, moved to Xan's neck. "Your 'little bird'?" for that was one of my endearments. I could see the violently broken neck, viscera oozing from the massive break.

Then a thing occurred more remarkable than hate and fear and dangerous games. Xan spoke one long clear articulate sen- tence. The tone was human, the sounds were word-length, the rise and fall were those of a speech of protest. I knelt beside the chair and put my head against hers. Calvin put his head against ours. Gently the three of us rocked in communion.

In the spell of amity that followed I told Calvin earnestly that I was in a bad way, that I could not write, that our constant dis- agreements had taken their toll for I had hallucinated him watch- ing me last night. He gave me an enigmatic look and went for the gin. When he came back, as though discussing the lightest of topics, he asked: if he left for good could I write in that house? I said I believed so. He said, o.k., he would leave. Flippantly, as though hope played no part, I said, "Bye."

Humming at his work he set about packing. I waited for the joker in the pack. Even when he had brought his bags down and set them in the kitchen I did not believe he would go. He passed and re-passed me with a kindly abstracted look. Upstairs again, he rang Serena (WBLS for once mute.) I heard the greeting and then only, "Yes, very bad vibes." Coming down again, he told me that Serena was picking him up to take him to the nine- something bus. Then he sat on the raised hearth and asked if we could talk.

Did I respect him? Fervently lying, I said I did. What was my main worry then? I told him that in addition to my inability to fulfill my contract for a book or even a story, I was worried about money. His phone calls to New York—so many, with the phone in his room; I could hear him murmuring at night. He looked distinctly frightened, which frightened me. I rushed on: and the breakage. A Mexican dish, a good goblet, the fancy poker; and there was the cigarette burn on the table. I told him his violence made me afraid for the house, for the windows and skylights. He could always surprise me. When he said "And this is respect," I was surprised. Perhaps it looked like condescension to him.

After a silence he told me that he did not want to go, that

though his respect for me had lessened 'too,' he was still hung up on me. Maybe in spite of myself, he said, I had opened his nose: "That's an uptown expression." My despair must have been visible, it made him urgent. He asked if I would receive him back from New York if he could guarantee me a lot of money which we would share. Welfare? I asked, needlessly spiteful. Cold and dry he asked me, "Don't you know by this time what I do, man?" Hadn't I noticed what part of the paper he read first? (a mystery, still.) His hand opened and bounced as though he tested the heft of some mass there. He told me that he was a hit man, that he took out contracts on lives, that he was going to New York to kill his first white dude. I was impatient: He had just made up his mind, had he? had he picked out the dude? for until the discussion and the question we had settled down for the evening. Was a death by contract something like spontaneous combustion? I wanted to know. He told me he had a weapon in his briefcase and went upstairs. I heard him dial and ask for his brother, Ibrahim, then leave the message: Tell him his brother Calvin will be in tonight. And I thought: the leather coats, the brief case (the weapon), the gifts he said he had bought and carried to his daughters in Jamaica. All bought with money advanced against another's life.

I lay on the bed with Xan. Was it Africa I saw behind closed lids, or the jungle of the city, or the snaky swamp Calvin and I had made out of submerged intentions and wishes and needs? What we had accomplished in just a few days was the opposite of landfill; the morass sucked and pulled between us; within it elongated forms undulated, more hideous for being without details; overhead shrikes screamed; on its periphery hyenas ferreted through rectums for steaming guts.

I heard Calvin come down into the kitchen, heard the long gurgle of gin into a glass, then back up he went, another phone call. Whispered. Something about it was idiotic as though he giggled in whispers. Another call, this time shouted: I'll kill you motherfucker. Another trip down, more gin. I went out to face him. The briefcase leaned against a kitchen counter. Looking at the bulge I said, "Is there really a weapon in there? What kind?" and touched it. I was reeling down a vista of louvers ajar, ricocheting off them as Xan in her blindness did. For God's sake, Calvin. Motherfucking cracker, I was not to touch that briefcase.

Then a ludicrous change of tone: Trust him. He would be

back to me that very night, before dawn. Trust him. He embraced me, gazing at me earnestly. Slowly he brought his face to mine. I saw the pink tongue unfurl, felt it between my lips soft as cotton then muscular and hard.

When he had gone my mind regained the power to observe and speculate. He had taken the briefcase but not the luggage. Since his talk with Serena at least an hour had passed.

I went upstairs and rang the woman. "Were you going to pick Calvin up?" Again the long long pause, the woman a very slow study. Yes, she had waited for him but he had not come. I told her, "Listen, I know your sympathy lies with him but I have to tell you about my fear, about my fear for this house. The breakage . . ." She interrupted. Two people who had a . . . certain . . . relationship were equally important to her. For no reason I could name I interjected, "Calvin is straight, Serena." But she stayed on course. She could not take sides. She could be neutral and a friend to us both. I insisted, "But the breakage!" and then I heard the click on the line. Yes, the blood can run cold. I said to her, "Right," and hung up and went down and out to the guesthouse. In the semi-darkness of the vestibule, standing by the telephone, I found him. Once he had said to me: Don't mind my shouting or anything I say at the top of my voice. Just mind when I get very quiet. He was very quiet. He looked darker, quiet and coldly black. His eyes shone icily.

He told me, the movie cliché justified and horridly new, "You shouldn't have done that." Starting out covered in chills I told him, "I had to mention the breakage." He followed. I did not turn, I could not have turned.

In the kitchen: "Now I can't believe anything you say ever again. All these months of trusting you, believing what you said. All that shot." We sat on kitchen stools. I told him what we had said, Serena and I, every word, emphasizing my defense of his manhood, understanding now that interjection, the awareness of him that was nerve-deep, blood-deep. I told him that when I heard the click of his picking up the receiver I had hung up, though I understood that the sound had been of him hanging up first. He had anticipated the call and had stood in the darkness waiting for it, the red light signal that indicated the other telephone was in use.

Knowing the importance of strict accuracy, still I handed him a test. I said I had scolded Serena for not waiting for 'my friend, Calvin.' His gleeful mockery failed him the exam. *"My friend, Calvin."* But he did not care about the lie. He told me, "That day when I came back from Babylon and you cried, I couldn't believe that soap opera. I said, I don't fucking believe this." I told him I had cried because he had hurt his hand for me, because I had made him do it. I said I could not remember what I had said then, but it must have hurt him. (And recall in this instant what it was. He had told me very earnestly that he felt I belonged to him and I said, because he was leaving me to run in the night, that he was very wrong, my man.) He shook his head. He would never believe me again. All those months of shit. White people's shit, my man. (And the repetition of 'my man,' in my mouth in memory and in his now, reminds me that it can be a scornful address in prison, as bad, if correctly used, as 'Rub it on your chest.') I asked him if his waiting in the dark for my call to Serena had been an act of faith, and the sophistry made us both laugh. He said he had gone to call her to come for him and had heard my voice. The explanatory lie, ignoring the red light on the phone, was very polite, as was the tone of his next words: "My man, I've hated every minute out here with you." "Every *minute?*" The hurt was real but I pushed it and my act caught him, I could see that, and it gave him pause. After all, as he would point out, it was my world and he was lost in it, in its gestures, nuances, lies.

He left the house. Did he watch me? Did I relax or show some sign, of satire or cynicism or want?

Reentering the house he stopped in the storeroom. When he came into the kitchen a hammer was tucked under his arm. He was pulling on a pair of gloves. "I have to kill you." I turned and walked into the living room and lay down on the mattress beside Xan. He told me, "First I'm going to kill her—" I nodded—"and then you. Then I'm going to town and kill Berthold and then I'm going to kill my mother. She hung up on me tonight. Four times. I called her four times and she hung up. That bitch is going to die."

I had a sense of freedom, to be, to say, without thought of consequences. I asked him, not knowing where the words came from, "Was ever dream so crazed as this reality?" Only now do I identify them as Kleist, and the context. When he stood near me my hand stroked his leg. Whatever I said or did, he did not appear to notice. At times we spoke together. My own words are mainly forgotten—apposite quotes, I imagine, coming out of some deep bin without identification—but I recall all of his. He told me how my death would affect others, dwelling on Berthold's loss, guessing my guilt in that quarter. My book would be successful, he told me, but somebody else would get the money. If it went to Berthold he bet Berthold would refuse it, seeing it as blood money. Even under the circumstances that was a curious remark. I vaguely wished for time left to fathom it. I told him, Too bad that he had to kill me before he could be included in my will, and the clever bid for a stay of execution seemed to touch him. He agreed, Too bad. Sometimes I lay, sometimes I stood. If I wondered what his arm felt like I grasped it, or measured his waist in my hands. Xan was comatose.

He asked me: Do you want your brain to go first, before I mutilate your body? and he tapped me, hard, on the head with the handle of the hammer. Or did I prefer the mutilation first? and he tapped me, hard, on the kneecap. I decided it should be the brain but kept my decision to myself. Several times he removed my glasses, asking my forgiveness, saying, "I have to do this." When I asked, why? the answer varied: because I had opened for him doors that nobody had ever opened, then closed them and took away the keys. Or: because I had made him swear on his daughter's head. Or: because he could not ever trust me again. He said to have me alive and like everybody else was unthinkable.

If the urge to murder could be compared to a stream—the thought to the font and the deed to the union with the sea—Calvin and I shared islands in the stream, in the three hour journey, where mutual rest was allowed, where one smoked and played the do-you-remember game, all the highlights of our courtship relived and heightened by the fact of there being no future for us except, for one of us, that powerful profluence and coherence with the deep.

But finally I looked at him and saw how ugly he was, how devoid of charm like any common cocktease. I took Xan in my arms and faced him. When he started for me, hammer drawn back, I said, "You're going to have to kill me from behind" and went around the free-standing chimney and was met by him, then back the other way and was met by him. He took my glasses off again and lifted the hammer. I turned my back on him. In that moment I wanted more than anything for the blow to fall. Then I turned and snatched my glasses from him and put them on and told him I would die looking at him and seeing him in all his stupid ugliness. Then, because it was all at once unendurable, I cried out, twice: What an EXTRAORDINARY thing to do to another person. On the second immense outcry he threw the hammer on the bed and flung himself after it. He wept and shouted into the pillow. I believe he said, "Kill me, man," over and over, but the words are buried in that pillow. He shook in a throe like epilepsy. His hands clutched the pillow, beat it, slid under. In a moment he was sitting up with the pencil in his hand. He looked at it quietly, smiling a bit, and said, "Calvin Hartshorne, I condemn you to death by fire." He broke the pencil and threw the pieces into the flames. Entirely calm, he lay back.

With Xan, I lay beside him, his leg and arm touching mine. "Do you trust me enough to sleep with me now?" "Yes."

But I lay awake remembering a time on the farm when I had found a snake and a toad in primitive congress. The toad was partially swallowed, the snake too far gone in passion to try to move. I took a stick and forced their separation. The snake, hissing, went into its hole but the toad sat there covered with narcotic slime. With the stick I prodded it until it moved, but too sluggish for me and I picked it up in disgust and put it far from the hole. Sometime later, propelled by certainty, I went back to the spot and found the toad, recognizable by the undried slime, once again beside the snake's house waiting.

The application of this memory to Calvin and me was so striking that it must have left my mind and settled in his, for he got up from the bed and moved away, then came back and reached down for the hammer. He stood beside me for a while then went upstairs.

The next morning early I went to his room. No ring of fire swept the horizon. The plate of the window retained no image of the apocalyptic event.

When it was over, in a drugged voice he told me how he had psyched himself up all day to do the job in town but had realized that if he had gone he would have been killing me. He said the 'act' had been to bring himself down. The confidence was, I

33

think, well-meant, but I had a look at the future with the hit man and my skin, still touching his, seemed to shrink, the skin's voice crying out, "No! Help!" Seeing my slime on him, I gagged. For a moment I could not, I think, have identified us accurately.

We returned Maria's car that morning and stood in her driveway talking. That is, I talked and Maria assessed Calvin and me. Her scrutiny was demanding and I think hostile. I saw a look pass between Calvin and her that was competitive and more. Whatever the 'more' represents, Maria won; Calvin looked away first and then bent to stroke Xan. In a moment he was standing with Xan in his arms, wordlessly asking us to notice something. Xan was bleeding from the right eye, the socket overflowing. The eye seemed preternaturally recessed within the bloody envelope. Riverhead was out of the question. We got her to the local man, semi-retired, a distance of a few blocks. After examination he said that the tumorous eye was shrinking and would have to be removed. He spoke rather placidly of the operation, describing how the lower lid would be drawn over the upper and stitched. Maria and I, in deep communication, agreed not to mention just then (we were outside; Calvin, trancelike, held Xan in his arms) that the doctor was notorious for bad diagnoses. How did Maria divine that I meant to let the prospect of surgery point to the solution for me?

Back at the house I told Calvin that I would not let Xan's eye be taken by a country doctor, that I would go with her to New York and get the opinions of as many specialists as there were. In his horror, greater than mine, he forgot that I had deemed Xan's old vet in Riverhead the greatest animal surgeon in the world. He agreed to the return and I did not say that I meant it to be for good, no matter what. The hammer floated before me more realistically than it had last night, appearing like a ghostly bridge, and then Lady Macbeth's dagger, and now it would become a slimy cock; but last night it had been only an abstraction like 'freedom.'

The vet had given me some viscous matter in tubes, to put into Xan's eye every three hours. Before the applications the eye had to be washed in a solution, perhaps saline, that caused her pain. Along about the third ministration, Calvin rebelled (he on gin, I on brandy). I said it had to be done and he could fuck it, and I slapped the counter for emphasis. While Xan shivered Calvin and I set up a counterpoint that echoed up and downstairs: Fuck it (fuck it) fuck it (fuck it), with hands slapping railings and door jambs.

I believed I should not try to sleep that night and took a dexedrine. While I was making an effort to prepare dinner, Calvin came in and straddled a stool. His gaze, when I could take it, was speculative. Out of a long silence he said, "Maria wasn't talking about Xan. She was talking about herself. She wants me to put her away." I can't imagine now what kind of response I could have made. If it were this minute I could not make any. I cannot hear my voice, only his: "If anybody puts that dog away, I put them away—that vet, Maria, you. That dog's going to die a natural death."

He was drinking his gin in orange juice. When he was out of the kitchen I poured the gin, nearly a quart, into a fruit jar and replaced it with water and hid the jar in the storeroom. I knew it was dangerous, that if he took the bottle to his room, I, the house, the countryside, were in real trouble. I drank the rest of the brandy at a great clip.

At dinner I tried levity, telling him to observe how much I loved him (saying the word), because I was giving him his favorite food in a slightly different form. It was a tuna fish casserole. He maintained that a healthy pussy tasted like tuna fish, that if it tasted otherwise on first cautious sample he would not eat it. Unable to help myself, for he did not respond, I asked him to speculate about the taste of Serena, saying, ". . . because now you'll never find out, will you?" I wanted his admission of sex with her so that I could close that door, too. He left the table and went to bed, without the gin bottle.

It was my turn to roam the night. The dexedrine and brandy, and the nips of gin, now, had overexcited me to the degree that I felt I would do anything for an antidote. At the front of the house I could look up and see Calvin lying high in the window on the platform. He was not reading. WBLS was not audibly playing. I wanted to seize a flowerpot and hurl it through the window, climb a tree and howl at him through the jagged aperture, raging with primeval sounds to rouse him.

When I reentered the house I heard Xan crying in panic. It took me some time to find her. She had wedged herself between a massive sofa and the wall. The slight outward angle of the sofa

35

had encouraged her to burrow, then caught her in its trap. I pulled her out by the tail, a hard mean yank. When her smothered crying continued I threw her on the bed and myself after her and took her throat in my hands and squeezed. The long old body struggled, the white face gleamed lemur-like. One eye was glued shut with the ointment; the other, milky blue, seemed about to pop out. When I released her she lay still, but breathing.

In the dawn I called Berthold and told him that he must come for us. I told him nothing of the personal horror, only that Xan was threatened. He agreed to come on Sunday, leaving me the prospect of two days with Calvin and myself.

In the mist and dripping of trees, I set out for the Westlakes' cottage. Going there down the fog-ragged road, I kept looking back, certain that Calvin could see me, would take a short cut, would listen under windows, wait for me in the mist. At last mortally afraid of him, a chill took me, bent me double and rattled my teeth. In a foetal position, I lay beside the road, burrowing into a mound of leaves like a grave.

When I knocked on the Westlakes' door, Serena, dressed, let me in. I asked to speak to Martin alone but she said he was still asleep. If so, he was restless because I could hear him moving behind the thin door. I asked her, "Do you trust me?" and she had to nod. I told her about Calvin, the weapon in the briefcase, the hammer, his profession. I recall her eyes watching my trembling hands; I believed the corners of her mouth would have liked to smile. She understood funky exciting blacks. Did she envy me Calvin's courtship? Maliciously raising my voice I told her, "Last night he said about you, 'I'm going to fuck that bitch all over this house.' " Her head tucked down, whether to conceal excitement or shame, I cannot know.

Going back up the road I had the thought that Martin might not have been the one in the bedroom, that it might have been Calvin. I hurried around to the front of Partridge House and in the contradictory light and shadow of dawn reflected in the window, I thought I could discern him.

He was still sleeping when Maria came to take me to the vet. Once there it was discovered that Xan's eye had dramatically improved, that the third eyelid had lifted and the vet could see beyond it to the cataract, that there was no tumor, and that continued applications of the antibiotics direct in the eye every three hours could effect a cure 'of sorts' in a couple of weeks. The bleeding, it was now seen, had come from the ulcerated cornea.

But I did not tell any of this to Calvin. I let him overhear a faked call to Berthold and when I came downstairs he had, it was plain, accepted his dismissal. Reading each other's minds we could agree that dismissal was what it was. Once again he was helpless and I powerful with Maria as confederate. I had confided in her, going to and from the vet, and watched the burden of my story treat her unkindly. I had made her promise not to leave me alone that day.

Once she had written to me: "Leaning somewhat precariously on Rupert Brooke, 'If I should die, remember this of me' . . . that there is an area in my life that you made warm, brilliant, beautiful and kind beyond anything else I have known." But those were other days.

After a time of staring at the Sound, that he had professed to love, Calvin came in and said he would pack and go to town that afternoon. Maria, as was natural, asked why he did not stay and enjoy the country air for the nearly two days remaining. ('Nothing,' I had told her, 'must let him suspect you know' and her words were perfect.) When he said that he must go, she kissed him lightly. "Like you," she said, "I rush the end of pleasure."

We drove him to the bus and watched him onto it and the bus gone. Only then did Maria ask me, "How did I do?" and the question was terrible, and fatigue overcame her, so that I had to drive us back to Partridge House. There in the twilight I saw that I could not spend a night, or two alone. I could imagine Calvin returning, and the sight that would greet Berthold on Sunday. The sight of my natural death.

I stayed with Maria for two nights. On Saturday we cleaned Partridge House and returned the key to the Westlakes. Serena said on the phone to leave the key on the doorstep and I understood her need of the discretion. After my cowardly call on her, when I asked that they keep watch on me, there had been no phone call on any pretext nor had their jeep reconnoitered the road. Sometime, at my leisure, I will examine the possibilities implicit in the ladder and the trapdoor under the bed. I can already imagine Martin concealed there, by design, reacting to the turmoil above, a curious ménage à trois.

On Sunday Berthold came for me at 12:20 and here I am.

Today, a Tuesday—it is 1:11—I sit behind a barricade of instructions to the staff ("If my mother shows up on a stretcher and I have not warned you, don't even ring the bell"), beside a telephone that I will not answer unless a code is used, the code known only to Berthold and my editor. But there have been no calls since I returned.

I would like to know that Calvin is dead. For once, it seems that somebody else's life is in my way. But even as I type those words their meaning evaporates.

Speaking yesterday to the owner about the breakage, for which I will pay, I did not mention the camera. Before Calvin came for me with the hammer I heard a crash and a long whirring. Later in the evening I found my smashed polaroid. The whirring was of its taking a final picture. What was on that film? The foot of a murderer? Or the face of a maimed and terrified boy, whose mother had hung up on him four times, and whose 'best friend' had just betrayed him and was, further, taking away his puppy?

I believe such sentimental thoughts do nobody any good.

Once, describing my penchant for criminals, especially black ones—no, Calvin is not the first—a friend called it 'nostalgie de la boue,' a racist remark I thought, blacks seen as mud. Now I amend that, with apologies to whomever, to 'nostalgie de la mort.'

I have just turned on WBLS to accompany my peroration, to open the lines to you, Calvin, to entice onto my cockleburr your veins like a skein of red yard. Patti LaBelle is having a breakdown, a performance like a modern Ophelia, "Now That I Don't Have You," chilling and authentic.

Calvin, I ask you now—and if this is slave talk, if this is humble, try to fuck it. Which of us was the snake? If my saliva points to me, what about the slime of the streets you brought into my life and smeared on me, hit man? Which of us has the nostalgia for death—the killer, or the one who loved, without knowing his profession, the executioner? Do I hear your reply, "You know it now, man?" Well. So. If, loving still, I am forced to be the apologist, your turn will come. Rub that on your chest.

december 15

A curious month is passing, one to be preserved in a museum lit only by candles. The parts should be kept in glass cases in which the flickering light will confuse the eye, so that what is within and what is outside is not ascertainable. This preserved month will be like that dawn window behind which I thought I could see Calvin lying high on the platform bed, a figure on a catafalque, swathed, with the reflections of trees mounded over him like funereal wreaths.

I am infected. Fevers rise and fall in me as predictably as tides. If the sequence is orderly I can enjoy fever but in this sickness there is an undertow, a riptide named Calvin. As the month advances toward the solstice, the period supposed to be 'halcyon,' days of calm when seabirds are able to nest on the waves, the turbulence, striking irregularly, confuses time and place. This year New York is like a city above the Arctic Circle with its daylong twilight. When night falls there is scarcely any change, and I wake, or rouse, into the feverish undertow not knowing if it is noon or midnight, if this is New York or Oslo.

I keep from Berthold the extent of my sickness. Tonight we discussed Christmas plans as though our annual party will occur, and perhaps it may. Berthold told me that he was glad to have me with him this Christmas. "Where would I be?" I asked. Quietly he told me that he had been afraid I would, by now, belong to Calvin. This shocked me, shocks me. It tells me that he was not taken in by my lies. How will this affect our future? I seized the opportunity for a quarrel, a little one, but it has allowed me to bring my pique into the Panelled Room, which is also known to us as The Sulk Box. I lie writing in Calvin's bed, on Calvin's sheets, which I would not allow the housekeeper to change. On the top sheet there is a patch, still starchy and puckered, roughly round, of Calvin's essence spilled in sleep, perhaps; at least there are no visible masturbation aids in this room, though he might have employed one of my old bank statements showing a particularly large balance. I have wrapped around my body, like a hair shirt, Calvin's old 'traveling blanket' in which he used to sleep on any floor or couch he could find for the night. He left the blanket here when we moved to the luxury of Partridge House. This object is rough and holey, an old army relic. Did he really sleep in this thick shroud in the steam of Vietnam? He said so, and said that the holes had been shot into it. He did not say whether by the Viet Cong or by someone he had dug in that place.

In his blanket, in his sheets, looking at 'his' view—I recall him saying low-voiced to Serena that from his window he could see the George Washington Bridge—I am trying to imagine what the nights were like for him in this apartment, how he felt about me on the other side of the wall, sleeping, Xan between us, with Berthold. I try to see him casing the room and closets, the chests and small boxes on the tables, with professional stealth. I wonder what he learned of me from old check stubs, from letters written to me by people of varying degrees of fame, the letters destined for library collections around the country—from interior evidence, written for that purpose and so useless to me then and now. This is the side of me that most intimidated him, not because of the condition of 'fame,' always relative and he had never heard of anybody I mentioned, but because of the language of what he called my world: Maria using Greek words, some of the letters in other languages, which, I want to tell him tonight, I can not read without dictionaries.

Trying to see the room through his eyes, I wonder if he guessed at the value of the Nepalese objects smuggled by a friend, six small, ancient figurines that if properly sold could have kept him in bread for a long time. Or perhaps not for very long because this was the man who had learned the tastes of an Arab oilman through drug dealing when he was barely in his twenties. ("I'd take a kilo off Nicky Barnes, step on it three times . . .") At the height of that career he was pulling in around thirty thousand a week. In my contemplation I begin to see why he was so unimpressed by my small offerings.

Fever such as mine can be a form of self-pity. I think of it as the body warming itself in lieu of another body to perform the service, a role Calvin never assumed. Twice we had lain down together when the heat was extraneous: firelight and residue of murder the first time, and shame and desire the second; and both times our flesh was cold. But the riptide is Calvin to the life, trying to snatch away the comfort of my fever.

In his sheets, in his blanket, I can re-hear his tales of Vietnam, improbable enough to contain some truth: the Cong's cover strafed away, a body shot from a tree kept floating aloft on a blanket of bullets until the game palled—his word; he had certain elegancies of speech that would make me double-take. 'Fisticuffs' is one; I had never heard anyone say that word and it may be my imagination that he spoke of fistic heroes, one of which he said he was in Vietnam, a light heavyweight.

Tonight I think that my sickness is really because he has not tried to blow my cover. The coded telephone never rings, my friends apparently under the impression that I am still on Long Island. I believe the alerted staff are aware of anti-climax, and laugh at me. Calvin, killer trained by the government, respecter of nothing, liar to all, has kept his word to me: "When I run from you again I'll keep on running."

41

december 16

Today I made a cache of things Calvin left behind: Magic Shave, that sulfurous concoction designed for black men's hides, his track shirt with the number 42 on it, his toothbrush, a big jar of vaseline that he would slather on himself after a shower to prevent, ease, counter the white residue like salt deposits that afflict him in cold weather. Going through the boxes as he must have done, I found a cache of his: some packages of Bambu and a bag of seeds winnowed out of an ounce of grass, which he called 'urb. I put these things in a drawer beside the bed where I intend to sleep from here on. An interesting fact: when I had amassed the evidence of Calvin and laid it out on a table, Xan came to the door and stopped at the threshold, sniffing. She held her head so high that it was perpendicular to her body. Her assessment was thorough, her conclusions definite: she turned and went away. I followed and found her pacing, the morbid activity that stopped the day we returned from Partridge House. I tried coaxing her into the room using as a lure her favorite biscuits, with no success. Only when I had put the objects into the drawer by the bed and closed it could I entice her to stay with me, but nervously. When I put her in the bedroom on the big bed I could feel some large relief emanating from her. Thus I must sleep here alone for the duration, whatever that means.

With excitement, I sense that her perceptions are showing me something remarkable: that Calvin may have left these things by design. A year or so ago I was involved with a black Spaniard who had escaped from a Puerto Rican prison. He was a practitioner of a kind of white magic—I can't recall the Spanish word; so much for his indelible stamp on my life. But I can recall my emotion when I found a stash of his—a string of beads that he had placed in a covered tureen that we never use—and recognized their intended purpose. The next time he came, I was wearing the voodoo beads. But I won't go into that scene, our last. Obviously I survived.

Calvin is much subtler. The string that holds his essence together is psychological and, I imagine he thought, unsuspected. But that was before I had confided in him the long string of witches from whom I am descended. I wonder if, the night of my confession, he thought with some fear about what he had given me, what tool he had left here for me to use against him if I should be able to work out the puzzle. Without Xan, who is by this time my instinct. The thought has brought me up short. Her instincts that have become mine in fifteen and a half years, have saved me time after time: the hitchhiker at whom she growled until I put him out at a crowded service station, just before the long stretch of road through woods, his face, in that last glimpse, enough to scare you to death. Like louvered doors ajar, the events of salvation project into a room and I go reeling down them, propelled by Black men, saved by Xan. If she leaves me do I perish? I see even her pacing as the means to get me out of Partridge House, away from Calvin. And now, blind and deaf with only her instinct left, she thinks he has returned! In these effects he has left himself here: hair, teeth, his athletic stamina, his skin. Even, in the Bambu and grass seeds, a history of black music, sex, pleasures.

I have just taken my temperature. It is 104.6.

december 18

I was unable to write yesterday. I stayed most of the time with Xan in the bedroom. She was like an ancient link with sanity. I performed two experiments on her, or rather the same one twice. I came into the Panelled Room and opened the drawer that holds Calvin, then brought her into the room. The first time she was a sleepy heavy weight in my arms, too barely awake to be called really conscious. But she soon began the sniffing and when I put her down on the floor she made her way as hurriedly as a blind dog can to the door. The second time she was alerted and struggled in my arms, slippery as a seal. It took several biscuits and many caresses to re-win her confidence. I am quite frightened.

Last night Berthold worried the fact of Calvin's silence as Xan used to worry her rawhide chew sticks. I can't help feeling that he thinks Calvin and I are secretly in communication. This is a first payment of the wages of my lies, his trust gone.

Today the owner of Partridge House left with the doorman the telephone bill run up in the short time Calvin and I were in her house. Wrapped around the bill was a sheet of paper on which she had drawn a large elaborately decorated exclamation point. The bill, for less than two weeks, is nearly two hundred dollars. There are calls of an hour's duration. One night he had placed twenty calls to New York. Listed here are the times, durations, telephone numbers; except for my three calls to Berthold, a couple to the owner of the house, and one to my editor, all the numbers were dialed by Calvin. For this record, Ma Bell, thanks.

I have just copied out the numbers on a sheet of paper which I have put in an envelope and mailed to my lawyer. The sealed envelope I put into another with a letter saying, "Don't open this unless something happens to me, or to anyone close to me." Tonight I will do some telephoning.

december 19

Kept my word. I counted the numbers and have allotted myself just so many per night. I have the irresistible thought that I am like someone in the nineteenth century reading the latest installment of "Oliver Twist," which has just arrived by boat on these shores, stingily meting it out to make it last, excited but self-denying. For in my mind there is always the murder, the impending murder—not Nancy's but the one I prevented, which may by now have been accomplished. And there is the thought that I may one night speak to someone who was willing to pay Calvin to take a life. Or that I may even speak to the intended victim, preserved still by me. One conceit is to dial the number at the time given on the bill, at the hour and minute Calvin had done so.

Last night a woman exclaimed loudly, "Calvin Hartshorne!" and I speculated about the magnitude of that mistake. What suspicious husband or lover had his suspicions confirmed by that exclamation?

The second call was answered by a child. When I asked who it was the child giggled and said, "This is Lisa!" Lisa is the youngest of his illegitimate daughters. I carefully crossed her from the list, the care needed because of my shaking hand that might have crossed out by mistake a potentially valuable connection.

december 24

I convinced Berthold that it was o.k. to visit some friends. He likes to be around children in this season. He has taken Xan, our child, who always has her own stocking and gifts under the tree at the Weisbergs'. The telephone sits alluringly on the bed. I am dialing.

A long call. An authoritative female voice demanded to know who I was and I answered truthfully, compelled by the authority. She was Calvin's mother. At my name her severity lessened somewhat. She had read a book of mine. Yes, I had waked her but she imagined writers never knew what time it was. My book was true to life, though. She had told Calvin it was exactly the way some families were, and advised him to read it, but he never had, as far as she knew. She thought he was too cowardly to read it. He was in there, all right, that troublesome son was Calvin, the one that couldn't love anything, the one that preyed on his family until he had bled them *white*. Naming the unattractive condition, her voice sounded satisfied. Well, since I had waked her up she wanted to ask me a question. I had written in the front of the book: To Calvin, with admiration, faith, and friendship. She wanted to know if that was just a thing a writer put in a book for somebody or did I really mean that 'faith and admiration?' If so, she wanted to know how and why. I knew about his life, didn't I? What he had made of it? He liked to talk about it, to anybody who'd listen. If I did know, how could I write 'admiration and faith?'

Behind her words I heard her belief that whites encouraged blacks in their criminal activities to keep them down, to contain them behind the walls of prisons.

Defensively, I reminded her that Calvin was a fine athlete. She snapped, "What's he doing with it now?" I said, well, that accounted for my admiration, anyhow, the discipline he had once had and could have again. And the faith was because I believed he *could* have it again, or hoped the word might lead him to think so and act on it.

She may have heard the disillusionment under the words, or perhaps I sounded paternalistic. Whatever it was, it stung her to attack her son more vigorously. "Calvin don't want to do a thing he's qualified for, which isn't much that's legal. No, he wants to be president of something." What pain was she feeling to say such things on Christmas Eve? And I heard his voice saying about her, "I'm going to kill that bitch."

In the finality I heard that she was about to terminate our talk. Hurriedly I asked if it was true that she had refused to take him in, once in the spring when he had nearly had pneumonia. That had been, up to that time, the hardest of his tales for me to swallow. I had paid for a room for him, for he was living in Central Park after some nights spent sitting bolt upright on a chair in an apartment that was an all-hours shooting gallery; he said if he nodded off some junkie would steal his shoes. She confirmed Calvin's story without any discernible regret but I could feel her withdrawing before the white man's eternal judgment. I apologized for the impertinence and asked, as casually as I could, when she had last heard from him. She said he had called her one night just about the same time I was calling her, and woke her, and she had hung up on him. Three more times he had called and she had hung up, one call coming right on the heels of the last. I was terribly tempted to tell her that that was the night he had wanted to kill me, had tried and failed. I wished she could share the burden. But we said goodnight civilly enough, with a holiday good wish. I hated to terminate the connection with the mother of my addiction.

I have saved a long distance number the way as a child I saved a piece of cake. It is in Massachusetts. Some ancestors of mine were involved with Cotton Mather there. In my horsy family we had a joke about the stake race. A small tape recorder is running. My excitement is repulsive.

I've just replayed the tape. I hear my voice identifying myself as Calvin, duplicating his "What's happening?" as "Wha's hannen." The man is fooled; the guarded voice drops lower still, a sexy voice. "Where the fuck are you, man." The spittle around 'fuck' informed me of ominous anger, of obligations not fulfilled, and in my anonymity I was (am) afraid. My distinctive voice—pejorative in this case—can't effectively be disguised. I can imagine the man hearing me, however improbably, on a radio talk show, one of those obscure stations where jazz and minor public figures alternate their flatulence, and tracking me down. Or at the least describing my voice to Calvin. Feeling the anger thicken at the other end, for the pause has (had) been a long one, I prepare to hang up. Before I do, I hear myself making a kissing, sucking noise, another insult for Calvin to have to account for some day, and the beginning expletive at the other end, then the click that cuts him off.

december 26

Berthold and Xan and I had a sort of Christmas dinner yesterday, some food he ordered from a local restaurant. I don't know
what it was; it tasted like glue. Xan, after a taste, retired huffily,
perhaps dreaming of last year's Christmas goose. We played
something of Benjamin Britten's on the phonograph by way of
celebration, a choir of castrati as far as I care. My mind was on
Christmas Eve night, exclusively, and Berthold watched me too
much, too closely. He spoke of other Christmases, joyous and
extravagant, and said, again and again, how glad he was to be
with me. I really found this curious. I endured until I could en-
dure no more and came to bed. I listened then as I am listening
now, through an earphone, to the tape I made on Christmas
Eve. After the call to the Massachusetts number I called yet another, a male voice again, one that I would have undone, would
undo, if I could. I suppose by this I mean that I would kill it. The
voice is coyly sympathetic: "You lookin for him too?" and explicit, "I sure wish he was here now, that sweet devil" and I feel
an interior tearing, like paper, and visualize the membrane as
something like lamb fell that will, before I am done, be covered
with rents.

Lying in Calvin's bed, in his blankets and sheets, I hear his
vow to me: "I never got down with no dude, man. Not even in
the joint, man. I always found me some pussy somehow." Librarians, dieticians. The uniqueness of being dug by such a man.
But what about this nigger queen whose voice I am hearing, the
queen you called from Partridge House and spoke to for seventeen minutes only four days into our country idyll ("I just want
to be isolated with you, man, in a shack or a tent, I don't give a
fuck.").

Now I see, as I did not on Christmas Eve, that it was a Saturday night, the one I had meant to be our last together before the
reprieve on Sunday. Thus practical Calvin had only been lining
up a place to stay, a familiar bed for which he had formerly paid
in a familiar currency. The queen's voice told of remembered
sex, a feminine huskiness serving as its evaluator, the yardstick

of its heat. It was probably from the queen's bed that that 'sweet devil' had called me on weekends to ask if I dug him still.

That night, under his blanket, in his sheets which I had not allowed the housekeeper to change, I held up before my imagination like a copy of Penthouse the image of Calvin and the queen. With the queen he was uninhibited, as hot as though the other body was a woman's, and his contempt for the bitch fed the flame. This was the kind of queer to whom he blew kisses on the street with me by his side and described a moment later, with veiled eyes and secret smile, as a creep. These men would be 'jailhouse pussy'—librarians, dieticians.

He rode the queen all night in my dreams, a pornography so excessive as to act like a cauterizing iron to the core of my jealousy, the core like the hard pit in a boil. At intervals in the dream I would ring the number, listen, hang up, as though I could for a moment interrupt and thus prolong the brutal therapy. But at the dream's heart, which I could not touch, there was a wrongness, a lack of fulfillment, like the contradiction in The Stones' "Satisfaction" where the words deny the efficacy of the beat. I left the figures mechanically slapping together and roved around the drug-smelling room, irritated, lost, frustrated, pushing aside the blackened spoon and the candle stubs, the saucer of roaches, the tourniquet and needle, asking myself what it was I had come to find. And the slow seepage of the reply, cold blood from a dead wound: A rope, a gun, a hammer, a razor. The tools of satisfaction.

At dawn I read the extent of Calvin's power on the thermometer: 106. But I did not tell Berthold. I told Calvin, This is the closest to death you have brought me yet.

I am dialing a number.

january 1

I took the tape recorder with me to the hospital. I recall clinging to it. I think I recall Berthold trying to take it with some force. I definitely remember his eyes looking for it each day he came to visit me. Why? I believe all will be answered in time, but I want very much to know the fascination this object holds for him, whether it is like mine. And why. There is not much to transcribe of the last call, the one that landed me in the hospital. There are some whispers, some pauses. The other voice holds a terror at my question, "Is Calvin Hartshorne there?" that reaches into me and squeezes my life. It is a Spanish woman. In a whisper she asks several times how I got her number, an agony of repetition that leaves no room for an answer, as though she questions herself. Calvin's first white dude. Her husband. Maybe this broken voice had managed, by lying, wheedling, threatening, promising, to extract enough money to afford Calvin's services.

She and I cling to the wire that connects us, fused to it and each other by high tension. While we cling we possess galvanic life; to let go would mean to drop from the wire dead or maimed.

"Listen carefully," I tell her. I imagine the pressure gathering in her throat to make some great sound. The pressure is matched in my blood and I black out. On the tape is what occurred during my faint: "Hello hello hello. Please. Please." The sound of hanging up. The piercing sound of Ma Bell's voice, a mechanical Lorelei. Then silence, the death of the siren.

What nags me about this, what is trying to get through? A message on ether. I asked Berthold to put me in the hospital and he did. I asked for a room with no telephone. I also asked for a guard to stand watch at the door in the night but this was taken as a part of my delusion, my madness. Berthold was most emphatic in his refusal to indulge me, saying in his Germanic way, "Nonsense, nonsense," the words said briskly, meant to have the effect of an airspray to kill the germs of paranoia.

Writing this account now, I recognize that my prolonged fever came from madness. I handle the telephone bill like an artifact of that journey into the hot country, as though insanity were composed of detachable parts, not memories but things with bulk, like Calvin's jar of Magic Shave. The concoction and the telephone bill will go down the incinerator.

Still, something puzzles me and nags, a voice, no doubt, calling from the hot country before I get too far away. To leave that place is to leave, to abandon, Calvin, in whose touch and breath and glance febricity lived. The 'cool' stance is essential to febrile Blacks, otherwise they would incinerate themselves. Another contradiction. To understand Blacks everything obvious must be reversed, including perhaps this obvious statement. Once, at the edge of my beginning obsession, I wrote *Trust any darkskinned person you meet on a midnight corner before you place a gram of faith in the ice-hearted blue eyed Anglo-Saxon.* Was 'trust' a code word for lust? As one of the ice-hearted blue eyed, truly warm only when running a fever, I let my search for warmth obsess me and wound up in the hot country alone. Can the heat I looked for in black skins ever be an innocent comfort? I think that is a very southern question.

Berthold, an Americanized German, is puzzled by the bond between blacks and southerners. He says it does not make any sense for the oppressed and the oppressors to cleave together. When I tell him that it is the same as with him and his Jewish friends he is, properly, I think, impatient: these are not really things to be talked about; they should only be felt and pondered. Blacks, he says, were never 'forbitten' to me as Jews were forbidden him in his youth. But the bond is similar, I have told him, being roughly and deeply based on shame and a sense of something lacking in oneself that the other possesses. Yet he rejects me and the bond I offer the two of us. He is attracted to Jews, he says, because of intellectual capacity and a common culture, and the implication is that what he possesses the other possesses, whereas with me the opposite must be so. And once again I accuse him of being a racist.

That scene has been repeated too many times to count. Concerning you, Calvin, I tell him that this time it is different. How so? Germanic intonation deliberately stressed. I tell him, your subtlety, your—but he does not let me finish. Flatly he says, "I have never met an unsubtle Negro. They are breastfed subtlety. It's how they have survived." He says he is not, anyhow, talking about Blacks and me just now. He is talking about me and criminals, and you are a criminal. "WAS," I shouted that time. "Calvin WAS a criminal." And I asked him, "When you pay money back to someone or to a bank, are you still a debtor? Calvin has paid, goddammit." Words, of course, that were uttered before Partridge House.

It was after that argument that he began to withdraw. When I was in the country he never once inquired after Calvin. It was as though I were there alone with Xan. Has he the capacity to wipe, literally erase, someone from his mind? A mental hit man. It is very odd to think—I don't know what I was going to write. Something occurs to me, the nagging has paid off! In my account I wrote—I have just checked this—'my three calls to Berthold.' I made only two. It was Berthold who called me each day at 6:30. One call was made from Partridge House to this apartment at 2:30 a.m. Checking dates I see that it was the night of the hammer. Calvin and Berthold talking together, less than a minute, a seventeen cent call. It's as though I can hear the voices on the ether for a moment. Calvin: "I tried, but I couldn't do it." Berthold: "Keep trying. Use the gun." An exchange robbed of possibility by my poverty. The extent of my poverty shows in that remark which also impoverishes Berthold. But its graceless-ness allows me to glimpse a reversal of the idea that could hold some truth: that in his darkest moments Berthold may have thought. But I cannot set it down. It is my sick mind, not his. Still. Why was he so drawn to the tape recorder and why did he try to take it away from me when he thought I was helpless? It's as though I were saying that even the best of us whites (Bert-hold) will violate our own codes of ethics, and the civil rights of others, in the ceaseless effort to de-mystify blacks, or pin some-thing on them. And again I can hear Berthold: No, not 'blacks.' Only Calvin, who is a criminal. He tried to kill you, did he not? Surely any tactic to isolate the facts surrounding that incident would be permissible?

My Xan came into the room and like a comment on these scrib-blings vomited on the rug. I have cleaned up the puke, she is resting beside me breathing stertorously, her neck curiously thrown back as though pointing, for the chest is behind us, at the drawer that contains Calvin's fragments. Is he permanently inside her skull as an object of fear? as he is within mine, and as an object of desire, and God, or whoever, knows what else. While I have pursued witchcraft, madness, and behavior that at best is barely lawful—the telephoning, to name one activity—what has been my goal? If I am trying to draw him back to me, I don't know for what purpose. My nostalgia for death is now vastly tempered by a desire for life. I could say with Desdemona, "Kill me tomorrow, let me live today."

If I think of physical passion, as Calvin thought when he said I was only interested in a singular part of his body, I see again his triangular phallus, the most weapon-like cock I could imagine. From a small head it descends to a monstrous base, a splitting wedge with the force of his muscular body acting as the sledge hammer. Given the one opportunity to observe it, I did so, minutely. From the base, which my large curved hand could not encompass, there grows to a depth of two inches a sheathe of coarse hair, its purpose to conceal the killing thickness of the instrument, which has to be eight or nine inches around. (The engorgement for me, a dutiful act of blood to repay me for trying to kill me, may not have been his 'best.' Who knows what circumference a red headed bitch might make him inflict upon himself. How much effort for a peacock to lift that huge showy tail!) This base he has always concealed from me, when pissing in front of me or walking naked from the shower, by enclosing it, at times with an air of parody, in the safety of his fist.

It seems as though that pyramid-base is his cornerstone where a secret inscription contains his essential key. It's as if he was somehow able to develop by will such a weapon between his legs, as he developed impervious fists by sitting on a curb and striking the pavement day after day, week after week, a ten year old boy at the outset, in a process of wound and heal, until calluses formed within calluses and he wore what he termed 'natural gauntlets' of scar tissue and cartilage. By what arcane rituals, I wonder, using what secret family recipes, was his manhood distorted. One can imagine the head tightly bound to impede growth, and stinging nettles or worse applied to the lower third to cause blistering and swelling, and the occultation of the coarse hair constrained with oils of snake and castor bean. Veins that normally show and swell and throb during tumescence have had to, on Calvin, forge deeper channels, leaving the black marble unmarked. Only the slight oiliness of the satin covering on the hard ovate testicles—holding them, I told myself that at last I fathomed the expression 'hard balled'—lent lifelikeness to the otherwise carven-seeming genitals.

I am sexually unmoved to think and write of Calvin naked below the waist, for I cannot visualize the living moving muscles of his thighs, the center of my curious desire, without seeing what ominously overshadowed them, literally a case of 'heavy heavy hangs over your head,' almost literally a case of 'phallic symbol' like something erected before a temple.

Can the brain really control? My pulse is fast, I can hear my heart, my own genitals, symbols of nothing, swell, tighten, lift, all in spite of my knowledge. The sound of my breathing horridly fills the room. I am choking to death. Something is wedged

It is as if some of the capsules taken daily contain actual iron filings. Attracted to the magnetic brain they rise and settle in the head. In the night the heavy head can barely be lifted from its pillow. The search for something is conducted head down like a bull stabbed by picadors. Like any wounded animal. Except that in her woundedness she became a long necked bird, her head, her neck arched back until the top of her skull nearly touched her spine. The sound of her efforts to breathe filled the rooms. For six hours she struggled with lungs that must have been like concrete, with air that must have been as heavy as crude oil. When the effort became too agonizing she would somehow manage to bark, a series of pleas. Once when Berthold was out of the room, in a ghastly reflection of a night at Partridge House the effort was made to strangle her. She gave way. Her relief could be sensed. But it became too much to die and once again the long old body struggled for release, the release that would mean prolonged pain. Miraculously it was as though the concrete lungs had been made flexible by death's close passage. She drew breath, shook herself as though shedding the nightmare of the long struggle, and for a minute or two her breath came easily. But once again her head snapped back, the top of her sleek skull parallel to her spine, and the agony recommenced. The first faint death rattle like an echo from a deep well brought pleas to her to let go. She was held, her tortured thrownback head on a shoulder, her muzzle kissed. An effort to draw forth and hold the backslipping tongue was rewarded with a sharp bite. She died with blood not her own in her mouth.

She had been left alone in rooms, in beds, while lust was pursued. Lust was being written about even as death crept up and took hold of her. It is that memory that fills the head with iron, a process of indirection: the effort to forget is fusing the brain cells into a solid mass at the center of which would be one single bright memory, the gold nugget buried in the rock. This is the search that has occupied all the nights of the six months since her death. Once found the perfect moment would endlessly repeat. But nothing good or beautiful or transcendent ever repeats as horror does. Xan has ceased but her death continues.

But she cannot be bidden goodby in public. Her memory cannot be sullied by public tears. There is no fitting epitaph to grace that small grave. And there comes a time when we must put it aside.

part
two

There comes a time when we put it aside. Our spells are empty and so are our lives when spent crouching and mumbling over relics of the past. In the theatre we can re-create something dead that we long to see in motion again but the joke is that the actors who are re-forming our pasts for us draw their energy from sources so alien to our needs and the impulse that made us set them in motion, that it is as though we had rebuilt the house of our childhood out of materials imported from an asteroid. The actress playing at mama's agony over the death of a child can move us but if we could see the image inside the skull of her technique we might even be revolted.

In the months of mourning the only respite I could find would be in lonely remembrance of morbid sexuality, which led to an eccentricity more extreme than any suffered by me before. This was partly manifest in the polemics of writings later found in desk drawers, boxes, hidden from myself and from Berthold. In the hiding I found more witchcraft, though what the spells were meant to do in the long run I cannot now recall, as I cannot recall writing these sometimes hilarious diatribes. Hilarious to me, though I suspect that Berthold, carrying on his back the weight of liberalism, might be coldly horrified. Three examples should suffice.

"When the numbers of people in a city grow so great that their detritus exceeds the capacity of the municipal waste baskets, do not increase the numbers of waste baskets; decrease the number of wasters."

"The emulation of enemies: fairies aping women, feminists inventing the parody called 'the macho woman,' murderous Israelis indistinguishable from Nazis."

"Negroes, under the influence of whites are, at least in the more easily distinguishable traits such as cleanliness, style of dress, elegance of speech, a greater reluctance to lie, a willingness to work—invariably improved. Whereas the opposite—whites influenced by Negroes—carries the opposite effect. These white negroes become addicted to drugs and indiscriminate sex, dress in a lurid manner, tend to smell of dirt and rut, lie easily to their fellows, whom it would appear they hold in contempt, and speak in the Negro's debased language which is composed almost entirely of sexual epithets apparently aimed at the white race."

Toward the end of July I received in the mail a card with a

great balloon face on it and the printed inscription YOU'RE OUT OF IT. As a believer in signs I took this to mean that I had returned to normal and the inner message—OUT OF THIS WORLD—could not touch my optimism, nor did the fact that the card was unsigned cause any anxiety. Berthold could have sent it, or I could have sent it to myself, both hopeful and desperate. It did not matter. That it acted as a catalyst was all that concerned me and I gave it my full collaboration. I made a little grave-box of the pieces of Calvin and tucked him to bed in the storage room wrapped in his blanket. It was like the burial of the bird. I said to myself the incantatory, "Calvin was coming to tell me something when he died." But I knew he was neither dead nor out of my life. Now and then I would imagine I could hear him scratching to get out, like Madeline in "The Fall of the House of Usher." I wondered if this were a psychic communication telling me that he was locked up again.

Berthold could not convince me that Europe held any solutions for me, and he traveled there alone. Once he was gone the extent of my loneliness struck, and it was as though the horizons caved in like a parachute and one floundered in billows of a smothering sea. Clearly I had been given up by my friends. Looking out the window I could see the city across the reservoir and could scarcely recall when life had been centered there, in theatres, bars, restaurants, discos, and the complex of buildings at Lincoln Center.

I had been re-reading a book called "Pygmies and Dream Giants" for reasons not too obvious, though I think my main reason was some half-remembered identification with the Zambales and their ideas of reality. Looking at the city across the water, it was as though I looked through their eyes, seeing it for the first time. I imagined how they would approach each building individually, sensing the spirits or demons that would have to be placated with offerings of tobacco, rice, hair, before they could move on. I think I saw a parallel in the things Calvin had left; that his witchcraft was not to ensnare me deeper as I had thought, but was meant to free him from my demonic grasp.

About that time I came across a line in another book that said, more or less, that we have to like what is because that's all we have, and this seems to me to be sensible, worth adopting. I do not read into it that we should lie back without making an effort to change what is to something more to our measure; obviously the effort would also be 'what is.' To this end I moved out of the folds of the parachute and called up many people and set in motion a social life for myself. I was pleased to see that my friends had waited for me, after all, and that I was welcome back. Of course they were curious, which lent a spice to my presence, at least for a while. Some people professed to find me changed. One, a Russian woman, found me 'deepened.' The hardest journey was back to the source of the deepening, to the obsession that had been sweeping me past the buoy called Paranoia into the hot southern seas of insanity, when Xan's death throes changed my course.

To go back there is to see her as sacrificial, her life for my 'sanity.' The quotes are justified: I wonder if Calvin has left a mark on me for the canny to try to read like hieroglyphics in Black English. The thought does not belong to the category of reason but rather to racism and anti-reason. So perhaps does my suspicion that the two words are not necessarily synonyms. Who can deny that to trust the Germans as a nation is stupid, or that Americans in the mass are cretinous, or that Arabs are greedy and frequently filthy, and white South Africans murderous? The daily assumptions on which we function are largely racist yet hardly anti-reason.

To bear me out, at the gatherings I had recently rejoined I became aware of an underlying motive in the questioning that was like a fugitive small animal. One night at a dinner party the little animal came out and joined in the conversation. I recognized it when I heard myself saying provocatively that out of ten of my friends, at least six were black; because the statement was untrue; since Calvin I had given up the attempt to know anybody at that end of the color spectrum. But the remark was offered as a challenge to a smugness that must have been stated, I can't recall, and was quickly taken up. Where, my hostess sensibly asked, were these blacks? for she was an old friend, as she said, and she had never met any of these people. I said they were window washers, ex-criminals, criminals, delivery boys. She responded in a flat voice: Oh. All males. It was disingenuous of her. She 'knew about' me but the rest of the company, strangers all, did not.

I saw the two birds flushed with the same stone. Blacks and

queers. The old conundrum: that in a city teeming with every kind of liberation, a city volatile with Rights issues, it was still o.k. in some circles to deplore blacks—looting during crises—and to be, with more subtlety, at least in the 'best' circles, anti-queer: Anita Bryant *put into context* (the shrillness of that declaration demands italics)—the context of her ignorance, her low background, her simpleminded fear—could be gingerly understood; or the First Amendment was called, yet again, to the side of bigotry.

It seemed that I had learned over the past months to be more direct, had learned to attack without a pretense of manners. With no manners and a lot of pleasure I said that I preferred the company of blacks because with them I was never bored. I said this was unique. I watched the reactions of the company, sensing somewhere among them a glimmer of sympathy which I could not isolate. I thought my hostess spoke for the majority, for their defensiveness and non-comprehension, when she said, "I think your reason is because, in contrast to their problems, your own would tend to disappear!" Then from the general conversation there arose the explanation of 'nostalgie de la boue,' someone this time quoting Lawrence in "Lady Chatterley." The consensus was that people like me misused the under-privileged. I did not argue.

This talk occurred before dinner and during the meal I found that one woman, seated across the table from me, wished to isolate me for her own purposes. My bad habit of never hearing names put me at a disadvantage with the redhaired woman until I recognized in her simplicity of manner that I could ask her who she was without risking offense. Her name was Ivy Temple, a marvelously resonant name to me, which made me look at her more closely, seeking, I suppose, the shadow of her name: the classical building hung with vines, the arcane rituals within. Out of the company, when we were introduced, she had protruded for a moment because of the red hair which always brings Calvin into my mind. But during the drinks and conversation she had tended to fade for she was silent and, I had thought, uninteresting.

By the way she effected our isolation at the table, I saw that hers had been the glimmer of sympathy glimpsed earlier, and this brought about a close scrutiny that divulged the following:

she had been quite beautiful, and still was, but the beauty was veiled as surely as though it peered from a tangled growth of vines. She was dressed in the amorphous peasant garb that many women had adopted that winter—scarves and boleros and layers of tissue-like material; I remembered that she was wearing heavy boots, laced and cloddy, which had helped turn me against her when we met. But in my prolonged, probably rude, assessment I could see that her clothes were good in the sense of having cost a lot and that the gypsy bangles were real—real gold, real amethyst and jade. Her cloudy red hair had at one time been seriously mistreated and had never fully recovered, and her skin, basically fine-grained, hinted at exposure to the same ruthlessness. But this was all very subtle and had to be grubbed for, and her mouth, slightly smiling when I got to it, was so vulnerable that I felt embarrassed for grubbing so openly. When I looked into her eyes, offering what apology I could for casing her as though she were in fact some lonesome temple in a wood, I was startled by their clarity and resolution. I thought that the latter was like that in the gaze of painted saints; that such resolution is hard-won, is like new fire springing from old ashes. Something about her inspired such thoughts and I supposed that she had what was being called at that time 'charisma,' but that she had learned to veil that too, so that one had to look deeply to see who she was and who she had been. In that moment I felt related to her as though through blood ties.

By then I was thoroughly aroused and the thought made me try to judge her sexual effect. The evenly divided company, we were fourteen, had in addition to me six other men, all, I assumed, straight or passing for the evening. Ivy had sat silent during the pre-dinner chatter; no one had tried to bring her out. Would I assume from this that her allure was slight or that it was known that she was taken? In my own arousal there was mainly interest in learning what had informed her mouth and eyes so differently, and of course in finding out what her interest in me was based on. Then I looked at her through Calvin's eyes. What occurred was singular. A sexual current ran between us as vibrant and strong as any I had felt with him. Her eyes drew the current to her, widening as though to receive it on all the available surfaces, and then it was as if she deflected the force by an act of will. I shivered and saw that she did too. We acknowledged, actually nodding, what had happened. Then each of us turned to others and opened conversations.

We did not talk again after dinner and when she left she left alone. We had been odd man and odd woman. (Later, this observation was to afford us a good deal of amusement.) That night, lying awake in the Panelled Room—for a different reason now; Xan haunts all the other rooms—I put the moment through analysis. That current between us had been a current of blackness. I was convinced of that. She had seen Calvin in me, had opened to receive him and at the last second had decided against it. The rejection was non-violent, not bad-tempered. It was thoughtful, resolute, thorough. And of course intriguing.

Over the next few days I saw that nobody since Calvin had engaged my thoughts and speculations to such an extent. And before Calvin, in strictest truth there had been only Berthold and Xan, and thus by the company I was shown that I had loved him and must one day look at the love without prejudice.

Therefore, before I met Ivy for the second time she had taken a position in my life that made our future intimacy inevitable.

She told me that if I had not tracked her through our hostess she would have come after me. Ivy, the huntress.

Although our uncovering the nature of.our bond was highly interesting to us, I will not detail it here. If this were an opera those meetings and divulgences would be the recitative and I have always, like most common people, preferred the arias.

Herewith, Ivy's lonely song with an occasional line of melody from the basso, the Confessor.

ivy's
story

They met in Selma. She was the first white girl, he said, that he had ever talked to freely and for more than a few minutes.

Ivy was not so inexperienced with blacks, though in New York she had worked with them impersonally, taking and sometimes giving orders. They were all part-time workers for the Cause. With each other they were cool and did not question the others' lives outside headquarters. But in those days hostility was reserved for the Establishment and there was little or none of it in the coolness. Humor would sometimes flare, but, as she told Eager, it was always bitter and exclusive; and sometimes a black man's eyes would register her in a certain way and she would return the scrutiny, a kind of politeness, even when tinged with desire; but the interest would be dissolved into the urgency of the work and if there had seemed to be a promise between them it was never kept.

When Eager introduced himself to her in Selma she said automatically, "Are you?" and saw that the joke on his name was not a cliché after all. He took the question and gave it undertones that she had been too tired to give it, and the fresh sexuality revived her somewhat. She felt dirty and cynical by what she had observed: white woman, black man, deep south, boom. It was happening all around, too obvious, too much like an achieved goal in some instances. But she felt Eager's allure nonetheless.

He was a bit under medium height, the blackest man she had ever seen, slender with bulky shoulders, a bony face, deep-lipped, and like all the blacks he had dazzling teeth as though he chewed constantly on bones. Her second question to him was resentful:

"How do you stay so clean?" because his denim pants, thinned by washing, white-blue, were spotless, as was the denim shirt, sleeves folded up in deep creases, a style she had seen only in rural places.

His eyes stared at her with a boldness that seemed partly nervous. He told her that he had just finished work an hour before and had gone home and washed up and changed clothes. He said, "I'm clean all over" and she saw his eyes flash victoriously as she took his meaning. Curtly she said, "I'm not," but if the words were meant to be discouraging they had no effect.

Irresistibly, because of her resemblance to Susan Hayward, I saw her with a smudge on one cheek—Miss Hayward after fighting a forest fire in Canada—the smudge and a few damp tendrils of flame-colored hair pointing up her remarkable beauty.

Their function was to sit down on the wet steps of the Courthouse and hold their positions in the face of the animosity of townspeople gathered around them as though, she said, to witness the feeding of wild animals. Through the epithets and growing wildness she and Eager talked tranquilly. When they were singled out, perhaps because of their calmness, as 'the redheaded bitch and the nigger' Ivy would sometimes study the crowd with curiosity, unable to understand that particular fear of theirs. Eager, assessing her reactions, himself inured to the virulency, which was a condition of his life, saw—as he later told her—her genuineness in that respect and was able to relax with her. She saw no reason to doubt him, she said, for she was secure in her reasons for being an activist. And here she smiled with a grimness that aged her.

After the beatings and jailings of the day were over, Ivy and Eager, however unaccountably, found themselves free and unwounded, though sopping wet from the firehoses. As though their comical appearance were appeasement enough for the remaining spectators they were allowed to get to Ivy's paint-splashed car—Eastern license plates enough to encourage the paint—and drive away. Even the tone of the sexual remarks was almost good-natured: one man said the hose would be needed later on to separate them because niggers got hung up like dogs on white women, and his companions only laughed. Ivy, shooting a concerned look at Eager, saw the tailend of a grin. She related this with furrowed brow, puzzled that he could share that kind of humor with his persecutors. I said gently that they were all men; but she did not, perhaps did not want to, see that a more ancient enmity made her the sole target of that dirty joke.

What she did see, and she said this with a bitter laugh, was that the remark and all the ones preceding it made it somehow a matter of honor that she and Eager should become lovers if only for the night.

Lying on her leather coat under a high sky crowded with light, they exchanged childhoods, finding, wilfully, similarities. The isolation of their childhoods—she islanded by water and he by the threat of fire—seemed to them deeply similar, and was, in the reaction it evoked, for both had retreated further into themselves as they grew. She had had an early memory of a place not confining, which was the mainland where she was born and where she had lived until her parents' divorce when she was six; the divorce brought about her mother's return with Ivy to the island of her mother's childhood, the old homestead. Eager had no such memory, but a root of belief in the existence of another kind of mainland grew in him because it was necessary. Both of them had dreamed of getting away. Ivy had managed it through her mother's re-marriage to a rich New Yorker; together she and Eager would see to his own release, which was partly effected already in her person.

I was blunt: You mean, I asked, that after one sex experience you committed yourself? The would-be clinical question was so loaded with my prurience that we both laughed, shame-faced. I had held hardly anything back in my recountal of Calvin and me, and she felt that as a burden, but still she resisted me. I thought: Ah yes, the big mystery of man and woman is always going to be withheld, thus voyeurs like myself. (And made it even more mysterious by censoring 'black' and 'white' from the thought.)

All she told me was that she had fallen in love with Eager during the night and that the love was returned. She was dogged about that, a naive narrator of her own story, for the doggedness signalled too much that was to come. But it put me entirely on her side.

Eager took her home to meet his family, a more dangerous undertaking than love in a field. Insanity reigned about them in the surveillance of townspeople and deputies from other parts of the state. "Surveillance," she would say, still trying to fathom the need. It was a revival of the old 'paterole' of slave times. Eager taught her a song from those days, handed on like an heirloom in his family, a song that was all innocent surface, something like a child's counting song, and horror, at least for her, within, though Eager said they had sung it as children as they played.

> Run, chillen, run,
> The paterole will get you,
> Run, chillen, run,
> It's almost day.
> One chile ran
> And one chile flew
> And one chile lost his Sunday shoe.

The hatred of the official patrols—if self-appointed, still official in that place—could be viewed in the light. But it was the back-roads, the dark lanes, that were patrolled by the weaponed psychopaths, and Eager's home was on the outskirts in the traditional southern niggertown. Ivy muddied her face and put her hair up under an old felt hat, feeling, she said, like a sexual adventuress, for the gestures, however necessary, seemed like clichés out of a kind of low picaresque literature featuring slumming society women.

"Nancy Cunard in Harlem?" I asked, knowing only the rumors, having read nothing interesting or definitive. "Not at all," she said with some acerbity. "She was a lot more than that." And added, low voiced, "And Crowder (her black lover) was undersexed." Such minutiae, certainly not common knowledge, pointed toward what could be a heroine in her life, as did her acerbic defensive tone on Nancy Cunard's behalf. The photographed Cunard eyes, I recalled, were obsessed-looking, mad and at the same time as staring and cold as marbles, opposite to the resolution and clarity of Ivy's gaze; but both women had bright hair.

Ivy said she piled her bright hair up under the old hat for she could imagine a black person seeing it as the initial flame set to black dwelling places. Squeezed between Eager at the wheel of her car and another black man reckless enough to run the gauntlet, they somehow made it.

Inside the house, Ivy said . . . "Wait!" I cried. "Are you going to skip over all that—the trip, the danger, your feelings?"

She said, "You sound like a television reporter at the scene of a disaster. 'How does it feel, Mrs. Garcia, to look at your son's mutilated body?' " which cut off my questioning, though I suspected her of melodrama; no gauntlet, if survived, could be as bad as viewing the maimed body of a son. Still, in the silence, I admitted to myself that I knew nothing about it at all; and that it was axiomatic that a certain kind of survival could be worse than another. Just as a kind of death, or method of death, could be worse than another kind. But without her testimony I could not know about psychic wounds incurred in southern places; in eastern and northern places, yes.

As though she read my thoughts, including the mild sarcasm, she said, "Well, we were stopped more than once and things were said and done but there was no blood and the scars don't show to the average naked eye. That's long ago now and not really the point. People were killed for much less than we did but that's not the point either." She touched me and called me an endearing name, for the first time. "Darling, this isn't an effort to make any sense out of all that. It's just a story about wanting, and getting, and losing. Sort of." We ate and drank for a while and then she continued.

I realize that I have given us no locale or locales for the recountal so let me say that they were numerous, ranging all over Manhattan, through restaurants and theatre lobbies and on park benches and riverside walks and ferry rides, through roughtrade bars and the most notorious disco at the time and a cluster of joints around 110th Street when the story got to that section. But if the effect given is that we were suspended in a kind of limbo that too would be accurate, for this country we were traversing had not yet found its cartographer and its roads and monuments were unnamed, thus, in a way, nonexistent.

Inside—she said—Eager's home, which he referred to as 'the homeplace,' she was sorry that she had come. The family did not speak beyond the introduction, neither to her nor to each other. The silence was ostensibly on account of the television going but she felt that if she had not been there they would have talked through the programs. Most people did. And the machine sat loudly spewing out commercials aimed at middle class whites and the episodes tucked between the commercials like indifferent afterthoughts featured no black characters. She imagined that her presence in the somewhat crowded room must seem to them as incomprehensible and silly as much of what they looked at, but they could at least turn the television off. She asked Eager to let her go, to excuse her, to allow her to leave alone. She said that if he had let her go then she believed she would have driven the first leg of her journey back to New York that night, would have started the car and kept going, leaving her possessions behind.

The reason, she said, was because, sitting in the bosom of that family in sudden alienness—her term; it conveyed a sense of shock—she had a look at herself in relation to them and their poverty, which looked to her like a skeleton polished by the rain. It made her so sad and helpless in an unfamiliar way, that she could see herself causing further impoverishment through continual sorrow; that it would be like removing one clean bone at a time. Until she had gone there with him she had imagined herself taking her place beside Eager's mother in the kitchen, that the gesture would have been simple and right and accepted. A man brings his girl home, she puts on an apron and peels potatoes. The two of us sopped up her irony as though with pieces of new bread.

She abandoned her attempt at exegesis, as she had that night in her mind, giving it up as too complicated, saying only, then and now, that her money, if she had given all of it to them, could not have wiped out or changed her thought, which was "I could never live here."

Sensing her need for me to ask, I put the blunt question: "Could you have lived in such a place with a white man you loved?" and received her almost grateful reply, "Yes." American history was in the syllable. She asked me, a formal tone, if I could have lived with Calvin in that tent Calvin had spoken of. "Calvin wouldn't have," I said, and then, knowing that I would have tried to live there with him, I did not know if that made me better or worse, though I at once felt sure it was the latter because of the stirring of my genitals at the thought. Ivy, physically in love with Eager, still could not have been hypocrite enough. At least not at that point in the narrative.

When she left the house Eager went with her. As though to emphasize all of their woes, Ivy tried to take him to her room in the boarding house. Because of her thoughts along such lines, on the opposite side, so to speak, for the first time she felt the impact of such a gesture on bigots for it was as if she occupied the stunned brain of her landlady. The woman was utterly speechless, as immobile in her shock as if a rattlesnake slowly reared up before her, standing for the strike. Eager was not only apologetic, he was compassionate toward the woman and said that he had been asked by "Miss Temple" to move something heavy in her room. Ivy saw that she had endangered him further and probably his family, for the woman would report to some-one, if only to her large sons, giving Eager's description.

When Eager left, Ivy and the landlady reached a quick and mutual understanding: Ivy would leave and at once.

She found another place a cut below the former and in a day or so it was clear that her reputation had followed and caught up with her. Her next move would have been to share a house with some girls who were little better than whores, the groupies of the Movement who serviced all colors though they openly preferred the black men, but to have done so would have been vicious to Eager. She considered buying a house and realized that to have done so would have been vicious to just about everybody in Selma.

"Weren't there any nice people, any sympathetic Alabamans, in that place at all?" I really wanted to know; it felt imperative that I should learn and that she should remember if there had been. I thought it was pathetic that I should recall at that time the policemen of Cutchogue waving to Calvin.

"Of course," she said distantly, "but they weren't interesting to me. Any longer." I saw that she was offering me her growing obsession as it grew or had grown.

An obsession cut as abruptly short as her narrative; she said it came, the need to leave Selma and Eager, precisely as one wakes from a nightmare of paralysis and to exorcise the dream, vio-lently flexes one's muscles and runs about the bedroom: it hap-pened after lovemaking when Eager once again teasingly called her "Miss Anne." She did not say why and I did not ask, but she said she believed it had gone beyond teasing. In that mo-ment she decided to leave at once and did so almost as a continual gesture along with getting up and dressing, a long series of gestures that led to her pulling out of Selma in her paint-splashed car before dawn came.

Had Eager tried to stop her? No. She believed that he was glad, not to be parting but to have a breather, to be freed from their growing notoriety. She said if such notoriety went on too long it became like a monster child that could not be abandoned; that, to prove it had not been murdered, it became necessary to feed it publicly while the world watched the unnatural growth.

Ivy took her time driving back to New York. She took detours and had a look at the part of the world that would make her into a criminal for loving a black man. She stayed in motels and wrote to Eager those midnight letters that she compared to the mournful cries of trains.

She looked at him without the encumbrance of his presence, trying to evaluate the essence that had made it him and not some other to have thrown her off, or on-course.

He had a triumphant laugh, as free as an animal safe in the darkness. He moved with authority, twice his size inside, a hidden giant. His mind was logical and undogmatic. His past had not forced him into being or seeing as a stereotype. His skin had a ferine odor that proclaimed his self-ownership. His soft-eyed interest in her, once he had relaxed out of a certain bravado, was a thing that wore longevity like a hide. He would not bore easily. Familiarity for him would carry sweetness. For and with the one woman. Which she hoped to be. She was certain of that. She was eager to know him, to touch and see and taste and hear him and sense him, in a milieu that did not infer criminality in the public clasp of their hands, and imply it in a hundred, a thousand ways.

And just where was that place? She did not know and told him so in her letters. New York was better, she told him, but they would be stared at on the streets. And followed. She knew. She stared when she saw black and white together, she thought it was because she was aesthetically pleased. She told him that she had never consciously speculated about sex between interracial couples. But probably would now, wondering if what they had was equal to what she and her lover shared. She hoped, she told him, that he did not mind her frankness. And felt that her honesty was ennobling, that it ennobled them both, necessary to counter what had gone on the last few days of her overlong, she admitted it, stay in Selma. Overlong because The Cause has been subverted, The Movement was bereft of any action on her part. Her letters begged him to take up each point she presented and level with her without fear of injuring her pride, or whatever, the important thing, their love, was inviolable. She told him not to be afraid to be frank.

Altogether she wrote him five letters on the way to New York and two more from her apartment.

His letter to her arrived a week after she got home. It stunned her. It was many pages of lined tablet paper filled with the words of pornography. He had ejaculated on the final page and stuck in the copious glue of his body a tightly curled patch of pubic hair.

She tried to summon the loving face, the reticent voice. What she had of him was an expression of the crude cynicism she had witnessed in other black men in Selma, the exceptions, not the rule, who knew why the white bitches came south. In those cases traditional roles had been reversed and the men had become the cockteases, often so explicit in word and action that she had been repelled. Those men had boasted that only one white woman, an eighty year old anthropologist, had remained unfucked, though the reason was only because she wanted it that way, they said. Eager had been her antidote to those displays of public randiness and she, his; or so she had thought. But reexamining her collection of memories she found that only the sexual ones loomed, altered and distorted by the letter. These words were what he had been thinking at the time.

Deprived of the man she had fallen in love with she fell back onto what was left, the thought of the hard smooth black body. It haunted her. She wondered what clues she had given him to what she really was. Feeling the urgency of her midnight letters, she glimpsed beneath the words the thing that he had found. "Be frank," she had said; "Don't be afraid." Here was the result.

Trembling with tension she wrote out a wire to him begging him to come to her at once.

A week later when she was nearly mad she received a second letter like the first but lacking the visible climax and its withholding was an act of gross teasing like withdrawal at a crucial time.

On the way south she was given two speeding tickets and a violent tonguelashing complete with obscenities. What she was and why she was traveling hard was visible upon her as it was upon her paint splashed car. The roads under her tires and the highway policemen whispered the same thing: white bitch.

Eager was the same man she had left, tender, loving, considerate. Her sexual wildness amazed and pleased him but he seemed innocent of knowledge of any connection between her frenzy and his letters, which he humbly called 'love letters.'

The complex mechanics of her visit were recalled after the fact the way dreams are remembered, with difficulty. She put up at a quiet rooming house on the outskirts of town, posing as—but she could not remember her pose. She had changed her appearance in some ways but in trying to pinpoint how, other than piling up the red hair and always wearing big hats and sun glasses in public, she would become confused and her mind would supply earlier pictures of herself with mud-darkened face. She had glimpses of meetings with Eager: a country churchyard, a warehouse where he may have worked, but all was drained of focus by her monomania, which was the pure physical act of sex as Eager alone performed it. She could recall commands to him: "Tell me what you're going to do to me; tell me what you're going to make me do," and saw from a safe place, finally, that she had been trying to reconcile the language of the letters with the man who wrote them. She saw that she had believed the two men were different and that it had been a stranger who wrote to her.

A return to the way they had been was effected, she believed, without Eager's knowledge that he had been for nearly two weeks a figure of pure fetish to her. She had used him as any unleashed Southern woman might have, as an object of lust and hatred and fear. During most of that time his parts had mattered but he had not.

When she left Selma the second time it was clasping something valuable, a talisman against future obsessiveness, for they had discussed living together and the possibility of marriage. She understood his refusal to come to her as a dependent and had never presented to him the argument that ran around in her head, having to do with the inherited money: that she had not earned it either. But it was an argument, probably socialistic, that eluded me as well. As though to answer my unspoken comment she said that she knew that of all things, prejudice and fear included, money educed the most irrational responses. This had been summed up for her by one of her acquaintances in the Movement, who said that in view of Ivy's money it seemed especially commendable that she chose to work for causes. The woman said further, or so it seemed to Ivy, that the reason most of her co-workers slaved doggedly to change ugly laws and habits was because they were too poor to travel and exploit other poor people in Marrakech, Capri, Taormina, Mexico.

Among the beneficences of Ivy's mother's estate was the apartment between Fifth and Madison in the 70s. It was compact and quiet and chic. It had been decorated by a well known man who had taken the color scheme from a small Matisse that was the apartment's treasure. It was a cheerful place to come back to. Ivy thought that Eager's black ivory skin would look even warmer and more desirable against the yellows and oranges, the Mediterranean blue of her bedroom. Her mind would place him there naked on the counterpane sea and trace his outline marveling at such perfection. At no point was he indecisive, at no point negative. Angles, hollows, protrusions, all lines of his body were strongly made, the caster of his mold a Rodin among potters. She would linger in her mind at the arm cavity, the curve that flowed on a long clean muscle into the chest. She made a curious embroidery on that theme: the arm cavity, she said, where she buried her nose, feeling surreptitious, for it was like the cave where his manhood dwelled.

She recalled his body as she had first seen it, clothed, and a little later, wet-clothed, so that the lines of it had been more visible through the clinging denim. She saw herself eying him under the eyes of watchers of Selma, as they walked to her car. She saw again the smooth thighs working under the cloth, the hardness of buttocks and the deep valley of his back. She saw that she was the aggressor for he had not returned her intense evaluation though her body had been as revealed by clinging material as his. But when she tried to recall the moments leading to their first love-making, she could not, and so remained in the dark about who was the instigator, and comforted herself with the thought that the need had been mutual and instantaneous.

In self-dislike she wished that she could dredge up an image of Eager putting a hand on her breast. At times the thought of his assaulting her, because of his strong desire—a hand rammed under her skirt, a brutal clasp that she could not have withstood—was all that would suffice to calm her.

At this point in her story I could see that her belief in a purer love, whatever that might represent to her, had been at best illusory and wondered if in her reliving she was aware of the contradictions, but as the tale was unfolded over many meetings I began to think of it as a psychoanalysis, primarily hers but I was catching glimpses of myself that shamed me.

From the beginning our friendship had had its center not in ourselves but in the Black men we had wanted and desperately needed and lost; so that our talking was, more than anything, therapeutic and thus impersonal, a statement that seems curious but bears its own proof. I imagined that when she had left me, or I her, she would keep rehashing as I did the events spoken of, and the next time around would add details that were necessarily contradictory. As therapist-recorder, I could see the long line that, I imagined, did not interest her, totally forgetting in the immediacy of her narrative that years had passed since her affair with Eager and only I did not know the ending.

When she had been back in New York for twelve days with no word from Eager, she stopped going to Headquarters. She slept leadenly through the sunlit fall days, waking to dusk as though only various shades of darkness were endurable. In her waking hours she began to speculate about other black men, wondering if Eager was unique beyond the customary uniqueness that love was supposed to bestow on the beloved. She could not judge whether her growing curiosity about other black men cheapened him or her. Longing for his first letter after her return, she came to think of the letter as Eager himself and hoped without shame that it would be precisely like the other first letter that apparently had changed her life. Bluntly, she said, she wanted his come on the paper.

Beyond shame, she said, she went to fetch the other letter that she kept in a purse, the only place she believed might be safe from her housekeeper's prying. And there, she said, being suddenly gay and brittle, perhaps acting the part of someone beyond shame, there she found a gratuity from those Greeks who still rule our lives, whose gifts we may be wary of but cannot refuse! A slip of paper with a name, a number, the designation "Drawer B" and an address. The past lying in wait like the pupa of an insect beneath the earth, waiting to hatch and become the future. She remembered how she came by it. A black woman with whom she had worked briefly at Headquarters had given it to her, saying that if she ever had the time or inclination to write to a prisoner, here was someone. Ivy could not recall if it was a relative of the woman's or what had prompted her to make the gift. The Fates, she said, generally cast a veil about their methods. But, saying that in that instant she recalled them accurately, she amended the woman's words to "If you ever had the time *or the need* to write to a prisoner." In any case it defined more clearly the role of The Fates.

She wrote to the man, Jack Roberts, that night. She felt that the only tone was spontaneity and she told him that she felt like a prisoner herself; that if he wished for or needed mail as badly as she did then they could be of use to each other.

Waiting curiously for his reply she found that the burden placed on Eager's silence was lessened. The prisoner replied with exemplary promptness. The reply was reasonable, literate, grateful without being excessive, and not too interesting to her.

"Yes," he wrote, *"I'm in prison but don't be shocked because America is a prison. Man does what he has to do, to survive. I will spare you all the ills-of-society sermons for now. Prison life is terrible but not like it was, say, 30—40 years ago. They are a little, just a little, more liberal. I pass my time by being in the college program."* The letter ended *"May the wings of peace be with you in your moments of solitude and meditation until we meet again."*

She responded without much enthusiasm, answering in a fairly perfunctory manner his few questions about her hobbies, profession, and so forth. Preparing the way for her withdrawal from the lukewarm exchanges she mentioned that she might at any moment have to leave for an extended tour of duty. She said that she was living then almost without thought, that all her responses were visceral ones, and that she simply felt that to write tepid letters to a man who sounded white did nothing for her. The curve of her mouth when she said those words was so full of self-knowledge and amusement that we went on and laughed together. Again, she had given away some of what was to come but I felt relieved, like a reader being given an intimation that

Little Nell does not die in the next instalment, the lie allowing them to be peaceful until the boat comes in.

The main interest in his second letter was the next to closing paragraph, which read, *"I'm tired of the 'diplomatic' lies that surround a relationship. Let's be real with each other or nothing. I know we have much to offer each other, mentally and physically."*

Her responding letter was warm in tone and she enclosed a snapshot, asking for one in return, saying simply that when she spoke to someone she always looked them in the eye and having a snapshot was the next best thing.

On a Tuesday the post brought her two letters, one from Roberts and the other from Eager. Eager's letter was calm, unpornographic, a love letter conventional in her old terms. It threw her. She had believed him when he said the other letters were love letters, believing that that was the convention for blacks in love. She had been willing to learn the lesson as she was willing to learn his language. Instead he had learned hers in the deepest sense, had known all along why she had come tearing south, had calculated her journey and called her there with his essence smeared on the paper. In the new letter he was teasing her in a different way, playing another game with her. She compared the two first letters. Once she had raged because he had not written her the cool sappiness of his latest effort. Watching herself as she might watch in a mirror a person concealed from her direct gaze, she saw herself bend over and lick the letter's final page. Under the dried surface reactivated by saliva there was a sweet liquidity; she watched the reflected woman raven it.

She had paper and pen ready to write to Eager, as cold and deceitful and above his head as she could manage to be, when she recalled the other letter. She said, I thought pathetically, that her forgetfulness of Roberts' letter had been proof to her of Eager's continued importance, but I could see that she was already lost at that point, had passed the last outpost of a certain kind of honor and finally was, in her cliché, beyond shame.

I should say here that I was allowed to read all of Roberts' letters to her, and to copy what I wanted. Therefore these excerpts are exact, grammar and spelling the writer's own.

Dear Precious,

What did Adam do before Eve got here? He could not even have a wet dream. Last night I slept with your picture between my legs up under my balls and it must have been like Adam's first night with his woman. From the evidence on the bed I came all night long without even a pause. I pulled off your blue silk panties with my teeth. Would you kiss my thighs as I kissed yours, eat all of me with wildly surfing tongue as I ate you?

Precious Pet,

It was lovely to hear from you once again and to know you're up and about. I sent you a card which you should have by now. It's the best I can do at the moment, because if I could I would have send you flowers. What I want to send you I can't send through the mails (smile). I want to send this sweet black dick and have you suck it like a lollipop. I'm sure it will make you feel better. I would put my dick in your ass like a thermometer and take your temperature. Your ass (pussy) would feel the hardness of my nerve and feel the hot sperm of pleasure. You have become very close to me and I want us to be happy. Every minute that we can spend together I want to spend with you. I want us to do all the things lovers do. Hope you don't give any other stud any of that pussy. Just having fun (smile). That delicious body of yours is enough to make any man want to stay home with you. The soft music and the love talk is quite heavenly. I like to fuck slow so that I can really enjoy the pussy and that you get satisfaction. The first nut I bust with you will be fast because of my inactivity and the anticipation that I can't express. You can understand. After that everything will be cool. I can't wait to feel your sweet lips on my dick and having your delicious juices filling my mouth.

. . . I'm more liberal in my thinking than when I came in here but I'm still revolutionary. Until this present government is changed I will continue to fight. (For present substitute white racist. You are my woman and I can level with you.) Words are more deadly than violence because they last. Ask any nigger. When you start exposing those people in Washington they want to make deals to keep you quiet. But I won't be quiet. . . .

79

. . . *The New York School system are not meeting the govern-ment standards in feeding the children. What's happening to the $65 million that supposed to feed those children? Look in City Hall, look in Gracie Mansion for the answer. See all the fat cats getting fatter while their women have to go to Fat Farms to keep skinny. The children's lunch money is going to work the greed off the fat cat wives. I can't think about this any more. My mind becomes like a weapon trying to blow up the world.* : . .

. . . *Prisons is part of imperialism and neo-colonialism . . . A few years ago there was mention a baby boom by the Blacks. Why? Black was growing so rapidly until there was no control. So, they said. Can you guess what they did. They introduce sterilization. Why sterilization? A genocide of a mass of people. Just like the Indians, their damn near extinct.*

In the second month of their correspondence:

Dear Love,

While sitting here in this world of non-action these few words pressed my heart. This lonely cell is trying to vacuum my emo-tions that I have left in my body. Each night I read your letters, sometimes many many times to capture that erotic stimulation that I so badly need. My aching lions crave for that release of pleasure. I visualize the softness of your body and the sweetness of your lips. I long to feel the touch of your fingertips traveling the length of my body. And to have your tongue explore the secretive parts of my ever aching man's body.

Please, don't think I am foolish. I don't know if you've ever wondered what its like to be a man and go without sex. It can hurt like a cold knife in your hot regions. That's why a sexy letter from a loved one is helpful. It gives him a chance to release that sexual anxiety. You've seen those girly magazines such as Hus-tler, Penthouse? Those are the dreams of many in here. Me, I like to see a nice pussy but a letter is better. The last letter I got from the outside was four years ago. Prison can strip a man of his physical endowment.

You have become a missing link of love. You see I have not known the love that impales my inner-being, that which I know exists in my aching heart. I have never been truthful in my life than I am at this moment. I am in love, a love that knows no boundaries. You have become that person I want to love and live with the remaining of my years. Seeing your picture I said "There is my love in her glorious manner." And I see you and feel you with your legs over my shoulders and your pussy spread wide. I will fuck deep and hard for me and lite and shallow for you. I know about the clit and how to use it with my dick, not just with my tongue.

Here's what I see us doing together: jogging, the theatre, sightseeing, parties, take cruise up the Hudson to Bear Moutain. How would you like that? I'm not concerned with what you can do for me financially. I am Sagittarius and I'm quite independent. At least I try to be. At times through life it's necessary that a person seek assistance. I know I must work to sustain my own being. You do for me what I can do for you. When you are sick I'm there, when you are happy I'm there, when you need a strong man I'm there.

Baby you never ask me but my dick is thick, not too long, maybe seven and one half inches. I'm still trying to get the flick for you but its a lot of redtape in here. Here's my picture for now: I'm 5'10", weight 175, medium to husky built. Sometimes I wear an Afro but mostly close cut. My complexion is chocolate. My asset is my thighs. They are big and strong, I guess because I did some boxing in my day. My eyes are brown, my hair is black, my lips are natural for a Black man. They are kisseable (smile).

In the meantime think of the day when we will be in each other's arms, kissing and loving. Let me end this letter until we meet (spiritually) again. I will kiss your picture and visualize your beautiful pussy. Sleep warm my woman.

Apparently written on the same day:

My dear Pet,
As an afterthought I felt I should send these few words of endearment. While sitting in this world of inaction I had a vision of you and these words were revealed to me. You were walking

toward me surrounded by the morning mist. Your whiteness was that of a glowing halo, shining bright, and giving off vibrations. You were tall and statursque in physic. Your lips were as soft as cotton. I noticed your nipples were protruding and they were hard. How I wanted to suck your hard nipples and make you moan and scream. It would be pleasure not pain. Physical pain without pleasure is no pleasure at all. I would never do you any harm. You are my love, my woman. To kiss your eyes, your hair, and your neck is another pleasure, my ever wet tongue making you jump and moan. Then to travel down to your navel and tongue your buttonhole. As you will get to know I can do wonders with my long thick tongue. I was taught the art when I was twelve years old by an old lesbian. My sister taught me how to deal with a woman.

By this time your pussy should be good and wet. Then I would proceed to stick the head in, slow, until you get the feel and then inch by inch I would proceed on my way to higher pleasures. Oops!!! I would pull it out and start again, lingering at the gateway until you begged then I would plunge it to the hilt. I would fuck your pussy deep and hard until you came and then I would come. Then we would rest in each other's arms. You are like a rose that blossoms in the Spring. Sleep well and keep your pussy tight.

. . . The Indians are the rightful owners of this country. They were peaceful people until the British (Europeans) came. The Indians showed them how to cultivate the land. You know all this but let me tell you something you don't know. Your great politicians of that day were nothing but slaves, murderers, whores, thieves, just like today. They were misfits from other countries. The British killed and took the land by force. And then they set up their own shop. The idea was freedom for all but in actuality it was just for them. Who was the founding father? He was thief. So this country's based on corruption. How can you have a land of liberty when you have a nation enclosed within a nation?

The designation communist, socialist, and capitalist may suggest social doctrines that differ but these forms are all based on economics period. The revolution has died because those with the monopoly on the economy have bought off the Revolutionists. I have always been a revolutionist because I was born with a leash on my neck. As Mao Tung would say, People who came out of prison can build up the country. Misfortunate is a tool of people's fidelity. Those who protest at injustice are people of true merit. When the prison doors are opened the real dragon will fly out. . . .

When I was young I had the misconception of white people because of the distorted history. I had felt all whites were responsible for the evil deeds that were perpetrated against the Blacks. But an incident happen while I was in reform school that changed my views somewhat. This white boy was about to be sexually assaulted and I came to his assistance. You should have seen the looks on the Black guys faces. They wanted to kill me. Well, anyway we became good friends and he told me a great deal. I seen him on the streets a few times but that was long ago. I even went to his house. At first his family didn't like me and then he told them what happened. Eventually he was raped on one of his bids and it hurt me when I heard about it. He became a drag-queen. He looked good (smile). In essence there are some good and concerned white people in this world. Just as there are some bad Black people.

I grew up on the Lower East Side of Manhattan, Lillian Wald projects. But the neighborhood was good then. I believe its called the East Village now, and stinks. When I'm home I go there just to reminiscent. That's my solitude. When I'm out could you and I go there together? My family moved to Jersey in late '57.

My favorite places to hang out were Bon Soir and the Round Table uptown. There were others but I can't remember their names. I went to the more sophisticated places as you can see, houses that catered to the discreet. I was never one for 42nd Street.

What are your views on a threesome? Mine are tolerable but only if the other person is a woman.

Baby, please, can't you write me a filthy letter? Don't you trust me? p.s. The radio came today!

After talking to you on the phone I had to rush back here. I'm longing to fuck the shit out of you. I want to dick you so far that it comes out your throat. I want to feel your lips on my balls and

*your tongue in my ass. I want to suck your nipples until they
bleed. Say to yourself "I love that nigger" and don't mind the
slang word. Slang is for the purpose of talking over white folks.
I feel that torture of mind and fire of body that only you can
bring on. I want your white body against my strong black body
and feel myself just fucking the life out of you. To make you
climb the walls, scream for me and to call my name like somebody crazy. You are my slave. You will do what I tell you to.
You will lick my ass and eat my shit with pleasure because I am
your man. All your life you have waited and looked for me and
if you say otherwise you're a liar and liars will be made to suffer.
Forgive me pet let me say all this without hard feelings just to let
it rush out like my come because even when I say bad things
they are an act of love baby, can't you see that?*

There was a progressive tone of brutality in the succeeding
letters, hardly a letter without some threat, often veiled, though
sometimes as fearsome as the declaration "I will cut your heart
out if you breathe." My interpretation was that Ivy had begun to
write the filthy letters he had begged for. There was clearly twice-
monthly communication by telephone, the maximum number of
calls allowed him, and from the letters written immediately following the calls, the tone—on both sides?—was solely and dangerously sexual. I wished to know about the calls but they came
under the same rules as those governing my reading of the letters: that she would not under any circumstances discuss them.
Any inferences drawn were my own. I did notice that however
violent the letter, there seemed nearly always to be a gentle,
restrained and actually painful closing, as though Roberts were
consciously and with great physical effort crawling out of a hell-
hole. Another frequent occurrence was his 'thank you' for money
orders. I skimmed over those parts as being too close to me and
Calvin: Ivy, like me, paying for her brutalizing. I wanted very
much to mention this, just in passing, but respected her wish.

She resumed her narrative in this way:

Longing for him (Eager? Roberts?) in all ways, I began to see
him in others.

At dusk on Madison Avenue, halted by a red light and the
press of traffic heading uptown, she saw on a rolled down win-

dow a deep brown arm, sleeve folded up onto bicep, silver watchband, silver signet ring, large pale nails beautifully trimmed, and these were fragments of him after the fashions of New York had transformed him. She tried to imagine what lay at the end of the driver's journey uptown and faced squarely her failure: she had no idea, as she had no idea of the lives outside of Headquarters of the blacks with whom she had worked. But in those days, pre-Eager, she had not even speculated and blamed the fault on the hard and often debilitating work. She was inwardly informed that the lack was a great fault, a grievous fault. Eager had told her that blacks knew about the lives of whites from centuries of working inside their houses, so that an ostensible lack of curiosity, with which they might have been taxed in retaliation, was only familiarity. Therefore the famous lack of communication was the fault of whites, was her fault. Hadn't she, after one look at the way Eager lived, said "I could never live there?" And she was supposed to have been one of the different ones.

The man wore a thin pale blue shirt with several buttons, under the loosened askew tie, undone. His jacket was folded over the back of the passenger seat. The throb of jazz from the car radio was like his visible heartbeat, the strong steady pulse animating all of him. Aware of her scrutiny he turned the music up, turned himself up for her, and moved his jacket to the back seat making room for her. When he had gone, the screeching takeoff a comment on the white bitch, she imagined that she had run around and wrenched open the door and climbed in and that the abrupt acceleration had flung her nose-down onto his jazz-driven thigh. The virtual impossibility—she would have been jerked backward, not down—and the slapstick image did nothing to lessen her yearning for the spicy flesh that would have been beneath her nose. She said that the yearning was not something that masturbation could have calmed.

When the early post next day brought a letter from Roberts she tore at it, needing what was inside, and said that the analogy was heightened by the strips of scotch tape sealing the letter, which gave it something of the look of a glassine envelope. But she was doomed to go without her fix. The letter began "Dear Sister" and explained that the correspondent was writing without Jack Roberts' permission, that the address had been 'coped' while the writer was on a visit to Roberts' cell, when he, the writer, had been invited to read some of Ivy's letters.

We were in Ivy's apartment during this instalment of her story and she left to fetch the letter, leaving me to savor what her feelings must have been like at the revelation that her letters were shared.

Here is the bulk of the letter from a stranger:

Let me tell you something about my sexuality. I just became a participant in oral and anal sex with men since last year. Of course I have more feminine looks and ways now then I did then. However the experience has been valuable. Honey, let me tell you that I looked so young and subtil in 1963 until the Warden called me and asked me why I looked so young. I say maybe its my diet. I don't eat any pork or pork substances. You know what these people done? They tried every type of aggravation known to cause me to look old. That is one of the hundred and one reasons all my communication was blocked. These people wanted me to grieve and beg as if I was guilty of some crime. Honey I don't usually speak of the lowness of anyone let alone the dead but this is necessary. I did not commit the murder they locked me up for but still you should have seen that black hogg they gave me life for.

I mention health and pork. I don't eat it nor smoke because it just put those devils into you called trichina and they disease and destroye the health and beauty tissues.

Sweet, I had a marvelous time just today. I got some loving and God was it great. He know how to make a woman come alive. You know how loving relieves depress, stress and strains. All the sense passages and sex passages are stimulate and sensational channels to release the pressure in the mind, spirit, and physical bodies. If one doesn't have a woman to control his sex than one must have a man and likewise for women. Tell me honey have you ever got down with a woman? That dumb masturbation is a fair substitute but its not good enough. You know what, I have enjoyed heaven when here in prison. Heaven is all around us. What we have to do, Bill, is stop using intoxicates and eating unclean foods. Bill, I know that God is good and good is all of us. Everything is God! All evil is the devil. So be good that you be God (smile). I feel we are sisters in the sight of God.

The letter asked for Ivy's response and must have included some papers for it ended . . . "return the enclosed, otherwise I can't write anymore."

This man would have been one of Calvin's librarians or dieticians, jail house pussy. The implication seemed clear that he was getting from Roberts what Ivy could not. I wondered, as she probably did, if the purpose of the letter was to make this known, though the motivation seemed to be the wish to correspond with a sister, 'sister Bill,' apparently.

"Did you answer?" I asked her. She shook her head. "I saw him." "Saw?" "Him. Both of them. I went up there." "To prison?" "Yes, to Greenhaven. In Stormville, New York."

It was her story. She told what she wished to, withheld what she wished to. I admit that I was often frustrated, longing for details as bald as Roberts' descriptions of fucking. It was not just prurience; I insist upon that. It was also a hunger for knowledge, knowledge of the way Blacks see us whites, see us differently as women and as men, as we see them, male and female, differently, a historical weight pressing upon and distorting that vision as variously as cataracts and belladonna. But she withheld here, and inundated there; and it was her story (and yet mine; in part 'ours' in the large sense but I detest the coziness of 'ours').

She said that she wrote to Roberts and asked if she could visit; his enthusiasm was equivocal, enough for her to determine to go. (She thought of Eager as someone now 'safe' from her, to whom she would return when madness was curbed or spent. She was obsessed and wilful about it in rare rational moments: she said that when it left her momentarily she felt deprived of warmth as though her coat had been taken from her in freezing weather.)

She wrote to Roberts again, telling him that she would visit. She had decided on the following Sunday—it was a Wednesday—so that any letter telling her not to come or to postpone her trip would not have a chance to stop her. As she wanted all of the experience, not just fragments, she determined to take the special prison bus.

She got to the Port Authority early, expecting to find a few oldlooking parents, grim and uncommunicative, and a few young wives, hurt and garrulous, all images from the movies of her adolescence. The bus would be only partially filled, the driver possessed of a kind of sarcastic cheeriness.

What she found was a place packed, teeming, noisy beyond her experience of anywhere, and entirely black, or 'colored,' for there were some Puerto Ricans of sallower complexion. Everybody carried something—packages, baskets, babies. A bus, unannounced, rolled into the loading area and a kind of panic ensued; the doors between the dock and waiting room hardly withstood the onslaught. People pushed so close to the bus that the driver screamed to them from a window, using the harshest profanity; a white man, she said, who talked black. Crushed babies cried on rising notes of fear. She saw one or two young babies held aloft, hovering symbolically over the trampling herd, screaming in the futility of their momentary safety.

Bus after bus, four, counting the one she finally got onto, pulled up to the dock, was threatened by a horde as the horde was threatened by bus driver and grounded personnel. She said that finally all she could hear was 'motherfucker,' as though the word comprised a language with meanings controlled by intonation. When she at last boarded a bus it was in fact partially filled and she remembered that the last two had gone off with people hanging in the aisles like blackened carcasses of beeves. She sat alone, hearing no confession and offering none. The only person who gave her a look beyond a passing glance was the white bus driver who studied her from time to time in his mirror.

The autumn day turned hot toward noon. She had been an hour in the bus terminal and the trip was two hours; and then the bus turned onto a side road, traveled around a hill, and in the distance she saw the building and walls of the prison. She said that for the first time in her life she was profoundly aware of how different one thing could be from another, and that what she thought of was the depths of the difference between the sight of the prison rising in the distance over the fields, and the sight of Chartres rising over the wheatfields in France; that though the images came together in her mind the purpose would seem to have been to indicate, if not define, the word antithetical. She felt there was meant (her submerged mind trying to send her signals) to be a further application that would 'clear up' something for her. But that it did not and only much later, perhaps a year or more, did she return to that remarkable impression and try to fathom it.

There was a welcome calm in the huge reception room, occupied only by some officials and the people from her bus. The room was oddly cheerful, some touches of bright colors in the seat coverings, the big windows looking out at the surrounding hills and gentle slopes. She got into the line of people being checked in and heard that it was necessary to give the number as well as the name of the inmate being visited, and searched frenziedly through her purse for one of Roberts' letters, convinced ahead of time that she had not had the foresight to bring one. He had not said to, and she had not. Instead she found the letter from the 'sister,' number and all, and when it came her turn she simply presented herself as his visitor, rather than braving it out about Roberts. And, she said, all this was done without a thought of motivation or what lay beyond. The only thought she had was that the sister would not be called because Ivy had not been put down on the books as his expected visitor. But she was passed on and went through the security system and the bells rang loudly. She was noticed, then, by all those to whom she had been a contemptible white shadow on the bus: that one, the red headed honkie, trying to smuggle a piece in to her con? But it was soon cleared up—the buckles on her pumps—and she left the building on an ebb tide of anticlimax, swept out, as it were, by the once again indifferent crowd.

She found herself outdoors again, crossing a grassy alley from one building to another. Entering the next building, seeing the barred doors ahead and the exceedingly watchful eyes of the guards, she was afraid, though she said that the word was quite inadequate unless all fear included the idea of premonition; or, she said, perhaps recognition was even closer. And yet, despite that momentary, powerful surge of déjà vu, she realized that she now had no idea of what to expect; her movies had already let her down. Could she at that point say that she had changed her mind and go back into the reception room and wait, or better yet, go out and wander away over the hills, running, after the first few careful steps, toward the hidden horizon? A matter of factness about the people in her group let her go on. They had clearly gone beyond the bars before and returned to the world. God knew how many wearisome times for some of them, nor how many times—years for some, lifetimes for others—they would do it again, until *out* and *in* were the same. Or did the difference increase with repetition and the sickness and the longing to turn back, until one day one did turn back and never again returned?

They went through one set of barred doors which were locked behind them, and wound up in a space, all of them crowded closely together, that Ivy imagined was like a cell, locked doors behind and locked doors ahead. And then she and the others were admitted one at a time into the visitors' room, the visiting room, and she was relieved and unaccountably disappointed to find that it was like a coffeeshop on East 86th Street: horseshoe-shaped formica counter, visitors (customers) on the outside and prisoners (waiters) on the inside; machines stood around the walls from which one could get coffee, softdrinks, candy bars, and cigarettes. There was a lot of light in the room, streaming in from windows set high and barred but that were large and clean. The sole barrier between the people was the waist-high counter. The only thing that really distinguished the room from a coffee-shop was the raised gallery beside the entrance on which armed guards sat.

The room was hardly occupied, no more than a dozen couples. Where were the teeming masses, willing to break something and themselves and their babies to get here early? Eavesdropping, she learned that there was a picnic in the Yard.

She had not known what to expect once she was within the barred place. Anything, everything could happen, or nothing. In spite of her ruse perhaps her sister would not be available, or had a visitor and was attending the picnic.

She sat looking around as one by one the visitors were rewarded by the appearance of their loved one; she assumed the love because she wished to, to counter her own impulsive presence, her own false credentials so to speak. The imminent appearance of one of the prisoners was signaled some time ahead by the clashing of inner bars and gates, hollow sounds like something heard in a cistern. She saw by the analogy that she had dredged into her past as a child on the rural island, finding there the iron bound cistern cover upon which she had used to lay her ear, listening to the mysteries within, thinking of Jokanaan sealed in a similar place until Salome summoned him forth and caused his death.

Nervously she listened to the inner clashing which had resumed after a brief respite and then was aware that someone stood before her. She was perfectly fearful, in her phrase, when she lifted her eyes. The man who stood before her, above her, was large, large-boned and somewhat overweight, and intensely male. The waves of maleness overcame and shocked her. He was medium dark and wore a moustache and long and full sideburns and a goatee. She heard someone calling a name— "Jack"—and realized with a double shock that it was Jack Roberts looming above her and that it was his visitor, a woman across the room, who called for his attention.

"Ivy" he said. She nodded and he was gone. She was still shivering when another figure presented itself, a tall thin man with a sad black face and a handclasp of great warmth. "I couldn't believe it," he told her, and explained that his only other visitor ever was his mother, who was no longer young and could only make the trip a couple of times a year. He had been in Attica most of the past five years, which was closer to his home, and would probably be there again, he said, but. And explained the mechanics of transfers to her but all she recalled was that in the other prison it had been likely that he would be murdered. The day you got in prison, he said, was the day your real troubles started, hard as that might be for a civilian to believe.

She had determined before Tony's appearance that she would not turn and look, not once, at Jack Roberts, or at the woman who thought enough of him to visit, whose impending visit, in fact, had probably been the reason for Roberts' reluctance to encourage her own. She concentrated on her friend and was gradually glad that she had come because he was, as he put it, woefully lonesome for a certain kind of companionship. He told her with a sweet shyness that in the old days on the outside when he was straight he would have considered it a great privilege to have made love to her. He was astounded, he said, by the perfection of her beauty. She found that murmurs and occasional sympathetic pressings on his hand, held to her palm-up, sufficed for her part of the exchange. She wondered if he knew that Roberts was in the lounge. Would they not have shared her letter announcing her arrival?

The person sitting beside her got up and so did the prisoner, and they moved away; she heard the clashing of the gate as the visitor departed and the inmate was returned to the cistern. She said that she would not have left at that point for anything, would have chosen, if it was all the choice there was, to stay locked up, because everything was floating, nothing was defined. As though in response to the thought, to her bidding, the place next to her was filled and the place across the counter was taken also, and the new arrivals were Jack Roberts and his woman.

Tony was openly aghast. She saw in his demeanor that he had indeed written to her clandestinely and that he had not known of her impending visit and believed she had come just to see him. How was he, Tony, to explain this to Jack? to whom he said, "Man, I thought you and your wife were going to the picnic."

"Tony, Tony, Tony," Jack said and once again Ivy saw how real such movie clichés could ring, for each repetition gained in undertone, and then in a voice that demonstrated his power to imply, to inflect, to frighten, Roberts said, "Later, man." In a conversational tone he began a recital to the woman across from him that was like his letters to Ivy, a litany of sexuality, a description, minute and uncommonly skilful, of what he wanted to do to her. And in the telling, did so: to his wife and to Ivy and to Tony, the only one of them, at least in a long time, to have experienced at his hands and mouth and body what his words were extraordinarily duplicating.

Ivy said that in that two hours' nearly non-stop performance by Roberts she completed her obsessional direction by understanding that she would plunge into the drowning pool of unalloyed sexuality, that she was, at least in reference to her old life predicated upon service, quite lost. What she had in mind, or in body, at least that day, she said, was the thought of receiving, of being serviced like any animal in heat. She said parenthetically that of course she and Tony did not sit there silent, but that whatever they said left space for Roberts' words to penetrate and that the very act of accommodation was entirely sexual. Tony aided Roberts by saying things that seemed calculated to bolster what might be flagging energy, such as pointing out Ivy's resemblance to the young Susan Hayward and then rising or descending to the level of specific praise to her visible parts and speculation upon those parts he could not see, dwelling upon her upper legs. When he went too far his eyes asked for her censure or understanding and received always her complicity. Three people at the counter knew perfectly well what was being enacted.

Toward the end of the visit, for Roberts' ears she asked Tony to pass her address among his acquaintance, saying that she very much enjoyed writing to men in prison. She thought of trying to extricate him from future wrath by inventing a reason to be visiting him but knew it was futile and thought that perhaps he might reap some real rewards for his audacity once the punishment was over, if indeed punishment was not part of the reward.

Answering her request for pen pals, Roberts said to the woman across from him, "I don't know why you're trying to stretch your acquaintance. You got what you need." After a moment the woman said, "You're not talking to me, motherfucker," and stared at Ivy until Ivy returned the look. On the woman's face, then, was written the whole story, from having had to summon her husband to her side to the changed seats. Roberts had probably told her that he wanted to sit beside his friend to whom, she now recalled, he had not said a dozen words. When she had it all straightened out she got up and left without saying anything. Only to return, following a hubbub at the door, to fetch her husband, because the inmate had to leave when the visitor left. He knew that but had taken the few moments, ignoring Tony, to try to impress himself further upon Ivy—who said that if he had managed that he would have been inside her: he took her hands and bent to them on the counter and placed his tongue in the center of each palm. Then he said "You write" managing to entreat and menace in the same breath, and walked away. She watched him, trying to imagine the force of the outstanding thighs, to gauge his weight on her, as her palms tingled and uncontrollable tears ran down her face. She said that the only thing that could have satisfied her then would have been her murder.

After a time she managed to ask Tony, "Will you be in trouble?" and he said, "Nothing I can't handle." "Tell him the truth," she said, "that you wanted a sister." Tony nodded. She said,

"He wouldn't hurt you," and Tony shook his head, smiling. Through her jealousy she said, "He needs you." Tony said, "Uses me. Not as much as I'd like." And with a kind of whimper the visit came to an end.

She was apprehensive lest Roberts' wife should be waiting for her or might get on the same bus and if nothing else stare at her for two hours, but it did not happen that way. From the window of the reception room she saw the woman get into a car driven by a man. In the way she slammed the door Ivy read a finality that was more satisfied than not. The automobile was a good one, the man at the wheel was young and obviously accommodating, and Roberts' wife did not give the impression, in bearing, clothes, solicitude, sorrow at parting, that she would make a convincing Penelope. And now, the door slam said, she was free, for she had found him out in infidelity with another woman, another white bitch, even in prison. Excited by him, Ivy felt sure that he had specialized in white women and could imagine that such men wore a special sign for the seekers or the initiate, just as women like herself must be marked in some way for black men to see.

Ivy gave me Roberts' letter to her after her visit and it was more of the same, of a striving for hotter and hotter imagery, which was an impossibility, so that underlying the words was a real despair. I understood, as she did, the intelligence Eager had displayed when he wrote conventionally after pornography. Roberts' letter was filled with such futile expressions as "My dick is hard as a tire iron" and a desire to make Ivy ". . . comey drunk, drunk with wanton lust. I want to fuck you in your eyes, ears, nose, anything that has a hole. You are calling for my dick, a lonely voice in the night."

By that time she was beginning to receive letters from other prisoners:

Dear Aphrodite,

It is with the strength of my Blackness and the everlasting beauty of my mind that I compose for you this writing of tranquillity. Hoping that when you receive this scribe it finds you in total harmony with life and rejoicing as well. Before I move forward into this deep conversation I'm bringing you I will like to

94

express my deep appreciation to you for the happiness you brought to me in showing your concern in me. Thank you! Well, sweet potato, I been in prison four (4) years. Yeah! baby, I know that's a long time. You would think I killed somebody or something. I got knocked off for a robbery and my first one at that, aint that something. You know how when you are young growing up and a bunch of dude will pull up with a stolen car and tell you to hop in for a joy ride and you not really wanting to get in but everybody stars fast talking you. So you hop in. And the next thing you know you are behind BARS and that don't mean you are a criminal. This bid really hurt me and I never had a real friend nor any family. If I woulder had some family then I woulder not got this much time in court. I really want to get into my life with you because I know it is a different one but special. I bet you wouldnt believe me if I told you I been look all my life for a lifetime relationship with somebody. As you know now I got busted at a very young age so I didn't have a chance to get into sex but I'm fresh and ready to learn. But don't get me wrong, I'm no chump though I coulder been somebody in life and still can with your help and more than anything 'love.' I know you must have a man already but I want to ask is you check me out and you mite want change your life style because you and I know presidents change every four (4) years and I only need one more vote to become your new president (smile). I am what you would call 'fine' looking in the soulful world. I am a Golden Brown color with a big afro and a nice sexy smile and my build is top knocks. I am a 'pro boxer' and also a master at kick boxing. I am very edacated and have been to college since I been down. I love kids! When I get out which is next year and become successful with the help of somebody sweet I want to put it all in "kids" by teaching them how to "box" also counciling about crime and any other problems that they mite have so that they wont have to go through what I am going through.

Greetings!

I received your letter today and I must say I am very intrigued with the contents of your letter. Well let me give you something a little bit more concrete in reference to myself. First of all I'am severing a four year sentence in her for assult. I was personally

95

attacked inside of a nightclub by a intoxicated man that I never saw before in my entire life. I was tried and convicted by a very unjust and impartial jury of beaurocratic assholes. Can you imagine being sent to jail for self-defense but since this is a very bureaucratic system and animalistic society that we as people are forced to live in I'am never taken or personally surprized by any of their ruthless tatics. It really and truly hurts me deep down inside everytime I stop and think why I'am here. Especially since I'am not a violent natured individual. I personally don't like fights or any other forms or acts of violence. I'am a very warm and over sexed fun loving very sensitive vegetarian. I'am addicted to the art and beauty of love, nature and the freshness of the out doors. I love music especially hard rock and soul and occasionally a little jazz. I also like to travel, horseback ride, ski, read, read, read, read (bookworm). I have no personal hangups whenever it comes to sex in the 'raw.' If it's all night its all right with me.

Right now I'am personally financially embarrassed. But just as soon as I get some money I'am going to take some sexy flicks of myself and send you a few Okay. If you have a flick of yourself around the crib and you feel like you want to let me check it out feel free to do so (you better. Smile) I've got much more that I want to tell you about the life and times of me!

As soon as I finished reading your tasteful letter I sat down in heat and just pictured the two of us off in a very warm and secluded intimate spot somewhere fucking ourselves into a full state of oblivion.

Well I think I better move on because in relating my feelings to you I'am starting to work my very high powered ass up into a sexual fit of want and desire.

If you would like to send me some money it must be in the form of a money order. Well its now 5:30 a.m. and I must say to you that I'am very tired and sleepy. I really don't want bring this letter to a close but eyes are heavy with sleep and closing. But I will most definitely write again real real real soon.

Hi. My name is Louis. I'm a Scorpio, 5'8'', 170 lbs, black hair, brown eyes, liberal minded and very affectionate. I been incarcerated for 3 years now and I have 2 years more to go *before I go to the parole. If I may be so bold and say my dick is smoking right now, you know 3 years without a nice piece really can get to a guy. I want stick my 9½ into your steaming pussy.*

Thank you for writing again. I find myself thinking of you so frequently. It's like I recognize some familiar quality in you that I can't exactly put my finger on, and it's almost frightening. Although common sense dictates caution in me I find that my rational judgement is being met by overwhelming odds (what real defense is there against the truth?). Some people come to you as imposters whose only desires are to find out what goes on behind these walls, not really giving a damn about the person that they are writing to. But I'm not an animal in a cage! I'm just a man like their fathers, brothers, and sons. I'm capable of loving and want very much to be loved.

But convicted of 25 to life for murder, I'm alone swimming against the current in blood alley, Urban Fascist Amerika. Try to remember how you felt at the moment of your deepest dejection. That is how I feel all the time. I'm on my last nerve, baby, and that's being worked to a frissele. I need help desperately baby but I no longer know how to ask, or who to trust, or where to turn.

There were no other letters from this last man in her collection. I assumed, going by my own reactions, that she did not reply but whether because of shame and guilt and fear of inadequacy, and just fear in the face of living death, my own responses, I cannot say. After reading that letter I felt a sickness and disgust that kept me from seeing Ivy for some time. A final sentence, imprinted on my mind in the duration of an oblique glance, may have been most responsible and I include it here with a feeling of great self-loathing, as though I were responsible for Ivy and all obsessional people who open doors that should be left closed by some of us.

"I am a very warm blooded young Black man who at least four nights out of a week before falling asleep visualize or fantasize having someone's soft lips prest to mine, moreover, a passionate kiss until I can feel my heartbeat in my manhood."

On Madison Avenue the familiar arm on the familiar window, the jazz on the radio, the gleam of teeth behind the irony. She went with him into the clangorous, cool-warm Harlem cavern, feeling life quicken into an arch, an entranceway around them so that looking back she could see the gateway dwindling to a speck as they sped on, the black man's lazy insinuation the new entrance toward which she turned.

She went with him into the apartment, jazz greeting them from the turned-up stereo: left on all day? Wife or lover just departed? They shared the ritual of the joint, which he left with her, and soon he came from the bathroom wrapped in a towel, gleaming with steam. He lay back on the bed and directed her eagerness to seek his out by doing this and that, to awaken and warm it if she could. He called her Miss Anne and she was pained and degraded by the slowness of his arousal, for which she had to work like a nigger. When it came it was a cold thing; even the flesh was cold. With Eager she had thought constantly about warmth, had told him, "I have been cold all my life until now." The stranger would have worn the words on his chest like a medallion, dress-up jewelry for Small's Paradise, a gag. And finally, in spite of her efforts and interim hope, there was failure. He told her why, laughing at her a little, too relaxed for much cruelty.

On the Harlem street she wondered if he had not been jubilant inside at his freedom to turn her down, Miss Anne observed and discarded, for he was still a Southern man, a black man from the deep south; at least with her. Eager had not won that freedom and had had to take her for his pride, to feed the myths. Or had his last letter meant that his freedom had been won?

Her failure seemed too large for her to bear. When she was spoken to on the street she responded, took the sips from the joint in the doorway, was humped against the wall under the eyes of a child on the stairs. The incident meant nothing to her beyond the relief at being wanted by someone accessible.

She sat in her apartment until dawn reviewing what she thought of as her case history. Sometime during the night she wrote to Eager a loving letter, which she did not post. She said that she felt beyond the reach of goodness and that he had come to symbolize goodness for her. Seeing my hungry look, she said that Jack Roberts had come to symbolize the opposite. That was the

98

night she told Eager goodby. She read his last letter to her, which told her of wells of psychological awareness of her and of a fitting contempt. He had treated her like a whore once, as Jack Roberts was doing now, and it brought her running to him. His last letter, by being the opposite, was meant to drive her in the other direction. Obediently and how eagerly, she had complied.

But in her reexamination she had stopped too soon, jumping from Eager's cleanness and comparative purity to his discovery of what she was. On her own behalf she must go back and find that swaggering man who had told her why he had come to the sit-in at the Courthouse: to find a white girl looking to change her luck. He must have told her so. He was honest. And she, dishonest, had refused to hear him until too late. In view of the irreversibility of the changes in her, the expression 'change her luck' tore at her like a prosthetic hand. All her noble thoughts from the beginning about the two of them flapped around her head, torn, foul curtains ('Baby, write me a filthy letter') that had concealed nothing, which only the artificial lighting had caused to appear other than sleazy.

That night she evolved a theory: that the purpose of life was only the weaving of a shroud out of illusions; that when the self-lies made a perfect fit, mouth and eyes covered to all but prescribed sights and slogans, one flash of knowledge showed the perfection of the fit and that flash was death. It seemed logical that the quicker looms should belong to the ideologues, people like her, for she had come to believe that the very stance of an ideology, the position assumed to accommodate it, was like putting on a mask. Speaking to Eager's letter she told him *I am not ready for that flash*.

In her one reference to a letter from Jack Roberts, she told me that the flash had seemed very near because of something in a letter that she received the following day, and destroyed as one would destroy a snake about to strike. Thinking of Calvin and his half-stories of the underworld that did not recognize prison walls, I knew that her fear was perfectly justified, that Roberts could assassinate her while sitting in his cell, by employing someone like Calvin. By employing Calvin. Though, and there was some large comfort in the thought, at the time of Ivy's story Calvin was himself in prison.

Staring at the dawn flooding her street, blood-red, from the distant river, she thought of the incident in the hallway and experienced as she had not done at the time the logical degradation of the act and saw that it was merely therapeutic. She could imagine for the first time that the degradation and the therapy could be extended into a kind of absolution. Even the thought contained grace for she laughed for the first time in a while. It was hardly the first sex act performed in a hallway and the man had been no tramp, if that mattered so much; he had been clean and hot and had even said 'Thank you.' She could feel his soft beard on her neck and the large soft tongue that in her remembrance felt friendly. The degradation had been in her, not in him or in the act; but there must be others who would be glad to get to her and 'degrade' her, because she was Miss Anne; and in degrading, serve her, as blacks had always served whites. Unwittingly? She wondered if there was a white person on earth who could answer that.

She was suddenly and extremely tired, so sudden and so extreme that it looked to me like an old reaction to an old trauma. Reluctantly leaving her, I thought how very much our 'sessions' resembled psychoanalytic ones, except that we were both, too frequently, patients. It was her story but could become mine without notice and violently; and I often took my dreams to her as one takes them to an analyst, dreams that had been brought on by her story. As I put it, ". . . by your tale."

That night I dreamed of Calvin. I went to him and found him with his face heavily bleeding. He said, "What are you staring at, motherfucker?" I wanted to cry out but said softly, "It's like something in a bad dream of *mine.*" He gave me a look of contempt and sarcasm. I said defensively "I don't want or expect anything!" He said, soft and menacing, "You expect me to let you *help me.*" The knowledge he held was like a weapon. I was afraid and left him, afraid to say, "It's not *your* gratitude I want. It's *mine,*" because the confession of something he already knew would be *the last straw.* In the dream all the italicized words were seen as well as heard. Ivy and I decided that something was saying to me, "This is true in two senses" and then that it had application to two sensibilities, hers and mine. That was it, she said, I had just been anticipating *the next piece of her conte.* But what stood out for me was Calvin's ". . . *help me.*"

Following the revelations of the blood-red dawn she made arrangements to move. She took a room on 110th Street with a view of the Park. Why not 125th Street, in the heart of the country? But she told herself that she sought a different kind of violence and she did not propose to perish of claustrophobia, thus the window on the Park. She closed her apartment, telling the superintendent that she would be away for some months. She gave the staff their Christmas checks in advance. One by one she closed doors behind her, through telephone calls to friends and co-workers and letters to the few family connections who might check up on her. The letter to Jack Roberts was written and posted, giving as the explanation a trip to Europe that would keep her on the go for six months to a year; she instructed the superintendent to return any letters from prisons.

She saw herself embarked upon choppy midnight waters and tried to name the journey. Her Scotch grandmother had called any stream a race, and she saw the perfection of the naming: The Black Race. If it had boundaries, she could not visualize them. She believed that when she set out the race had already merged with the sea.

october 28

I, Ivy Temple, being of unsound mind . . . settled in (should be in quotes) by bringing my first pickup in here. On the stairs, man in tow, ran into the Puerto Rican woman who, with her husband, runs this house. She nodded, I nodded, my man, I guess, nodded and we passed on. At the landing I glanced back to see if she was watching the Gringa and the Negro. She was not. Now, that's a lovely attitude, lovely indifference. Whether the Señor will be so accommodating I can't say but will of course find out soon enough. I think men always turn and look out of, if nothing else, a kind of sexual jealousy. I was interested to see that I was afraid after the man and I got up here. My room is still so impersonal, not much to draw courage from. I'm not one of those women who under any circumstance would or even could move around with pictures and objects in tow. Add to that reluctance the perfect (an ironic word here) awareness that I must not keep valuables lying around up here. East 110th Street is not the South Bronx of course but then my pursuits are not exactly Greenwich (though probably quite Greenwich Village. I haven't had time to find out). I wouldn't be surprised if my neighbors were teachers and artists, respectable people without much money. But. In the night there was a lot of racket, as my grandmother would have said, and a kind of siren call of jazz from the Park, a saxophone, I think, to let me know that I am indeed 'far from home,' because both racket and saxophone went on until after three o'clock and if anybody called the cops they didn't come. I think though that I'm in a world now where a cop is the last thing you call; where, even if you're a school marm, the cop is the one to beware of, the one who'll empty your purse, plant a joint on you, cop a feel, demand fellatio in a doorway. I listened to such accounts with just one ear at headquarters the past two years, wondering, I guess, if what I was hearing could really be true. These were respectable looking women with whom I worked, women with good clothes and faces full of character, talking with rage about this SOP mistreatment at the hands of cops, white and black, though mainly white when the encounter was in a deserted place. I got the impression that black cops would mishandle blacks if there were white observers, especially white cops, but were more considerate when it was, as my colleagues would say, one on one; and that the opposite was true when the cop was white. This would seem to demand an ergo: if you want to know the true nature of a cop's attitude toward you, face him in an isolated place.

My 'room' is actually two rooms but the big sliding doors that once made it so have been taken out and their niches, or slots, stuffed up and plastered over and painted in. Now the rooms are separated by a kind of frame. The house is old and solid, thickwalled as a castle, which shows in the window embrasures, inside shutters also painted in. It's a temptation to dig them out and sand them down and wax them, old domestic impulses that I suppose will have to go, like the urge to fill the frame between the rooms with hanging plants that would thrive in the good indirect south light—ferns with long trailing ivy, spiders and spathiphyllum. When I was writing the names of those plants something said to me out loud, "What are you DOING here?" and I was afraid, the way I felt when I was inside this room with my first Harlem pickup. It seems to be fear based on a lack of identity. There hasn't been time enough to establish an identity in this place. All I have, or seem to have, is a motive, and this comes rushing in from a long time ago: like the motive to invent for myself a twin when I was between the ages of ten and nearly fourteen. I told strangers and other unknowing about my twin, whose name was Red Rowan. I wrote a song about us that I sang in a mysterious manner. That was my one fantasy phase. (Until now?)

> "Two sisters there were
> Red Rowan and Ivy
> And one grew as straight
> And as tall as a tree
> The other wound round her
> And brought her to sorrow
> For Ivy's a strangler
> A strangler is she."!!!

What will I call these men? 'Customers' certainly won't do. I don't have a license. Subjects, as in experimental? Victims? I can't even call last night's 'my' pickup because I was his, and I could tell from start to finish that he thought I was quite a coup. A professional man, written all over him, nice corduroys, sweater, loafers, heavy framed spectacles, a good-looking man with the irony that is my catnip in his eyes and the corners of his mouth. A polite exchange began it, along the Park side in the early dark, well lighted over there where we met and stood but pools of darkness around us. The leaves, wetted by the afternoon rain, gave off that smell of dried apricots. I asked him if he didn't think apricots defined the smell. He hesitated then his eyes flared and he said the smell was like a woman to him. That opening move, which led to thoughts of rut and estrus, two clinical words that I think are sexy, essences rising from the impacted leaves, made me 'his' pickup rather than him mine.

It was interesting to me to notice, after this exchange, how I relaxed and settled into the play and how much the central event was edged with something like regret, like frozen regret. He and I seemed to bob in a pool edged with the thin ice of regret that would provide no support when you were ready to clamber out of the hole and onto land again. I suppose it's called pre-coital depression because it was plain that if I would he would, and his half-certainty about me, though it was more like three-quarters, gave him a pain that I could see. My conviction was that there was a tightness about him that last night anyhow only I could rub into comfortable looseness. That if he left me and was able to make love all night with Lena Horne, some part of him would still be constricted and that it was my whiteness that drew the strings so close, that shrank tendons and congested veins. He gave me such a look. I shook my head at him just before we stepped into a deep tree shadow which hid our features for a moment and when we emerged I said "This is just too nice to cut short. Will you have some coffee or a drink or both?" "Where . . ." he said, dots included. I nodded across the street. "I've just moved in." I said, ". . . and it's cold . . ." dots included. Then when we got upstairs and were closed in together I was afraid. *Afraid.* If Red Rowan and I were the sides of a coin and she the cold one then we both were in this room last night, spinning, taking precedence. I wanted him, she didn't. I wanted his touch, she feared it. When he made a move she wanted to scream and there was a moment when he saw this clearly and his reaction shamed me, not her; I saw in his eyes the beginning of 'cocktease.' I told her GET OUT and did something overt and was glad. (*Something overt.* I touched his crotch). I was glad he was the first, glad about my body for both our sakes and my responses to him were not phony and I was glad that I was able ("Did you make it, baby?" poignant words; they shouldn't have to have it verified) to make it that way and that way and then another way. Glad that the sensation of him making it ditto ditto ditto was so good. The launching of the craft on the dark waters with three bottles of champagne!

Then he went home to his wife. He didn't say so but I knew. Otherwise he would have asked to stay overnight.

november 1

Today I bought a television set. I am disheartened by the act for two main reasons. I detest the feeling it gives me as though it were post-1984 and the machine were watching me rather than the other way around. And I think, about 98% certain, that the machine was stolen. But I was so amused by the man's spiel. He said, "I am letting this go at a ridiculously low price" with the most ludicrous intonation. Maybe I was flattered too because he addressed me as 'sister.' We made the deal quickly. When in Rome. And he became at once just a black man carrying a TV set home for a white woman, honorably employed and so forth. And if there was a criminal in the case it was, just as suddenly, Ivy. I justified the purchase to myself by saying that I needed a noise screen, and TV is the most conventional. A phonograph might have done but I don't like any music, not really, though I can tolerate jazz. And that's a crux of sorts, because the night before last the lonely saxophone became an army of drums, called, I think, bongos, the most nervous-making sound I can think of just now. And later on from the same direction there were screams. I've had, too, the chillingly practical thought that I should after all have something that can be ripped off in case it is ever that or my life. The salesman brought the machine up the stairs for me and into the apartment. I asked him to be very quiet because my husband was still asleep. He had no way of knowing that there weren't other rooms and in one of them my big tough protector.

But why, Ivy, not him, the purveyor of hot goods, as your new temporary friend? You've come to think, haven't you, that there's no such thing as an unattractive black man?

Yes, to the last question, and to the first: because it was full daylight, we have our principles, and our obsession is operative (by decree) only after twilight. And something about the man, the very young man, suggested junkie to me.

Now, just as importantly, what did you suggest to him, do you think? Isn't the answer to that a bit painful for you, more perhaps than just a bit?

Yes. Yes. I suggested only somebody able to pay for a stolen

TV. I meant nothing to him. His eyes didn't care what I looked like, his nose did not take my scent, his ears weren't interested in some subliminal voice, his mouth did not suggest or hope. His hands were busy with the TV and anyway did not care to roam.

Was it then, when you saw that, that you invented the junkie?

Yes. His indifference was like some shaky handwriting, hard to read.

Aside from the junkie possibility, and there is always that possibility up here, what other reasons can you think of? Why not queer? Your sister Tony let you know that even black men can be queer! And he called you sister.

Well, he wasn't. I could tell.

What I mean is, why don't you invent, even wildly, rather than face the truth that there are black men who don't give a goddamn about white women?

Not even pretty ones, not yet twenty-four years old and in love with the male half of the black race?

Yes. Oh Ivy!

That's all a little silly but not much off-course. He can't be called a failure because nothing was tried, but it's probably true that he wasn't interested in me, not even before my invented husband. Who was invented only after I had been inside the building alone on the stairs, isolated in the hallways, with a black man who didn't show any interest in me. This lets me, or forces me to see, that what I want, also, is to be wanted, that that is or can often be an end in itself in times of fatigue or necessity like during periods. I still want the right of refusal. Is that just female or a clear-cut definition of white bitch? 'Miss Anne' could be as deep inside us all as our DNA, which is AND backwards. Miss And. And Therefore to give her her full moniker. (And therefore) the cockteasing, refusal, by the man, accusation, beating, jailing, the rest.

If as I seem to be saying no white person may ever look at a black person without the weight of history compressing that look into an unbearable density how can I propose to go on as I am going?

Because I am a white bitch. And I want. I think I must have for a while. I must find out how long.

Find out how?
By doing. What I'm doing.
You bitch.
I said it first.

That building next door I've just found out is a halfway house for criminals on their way to freedom.

november 10

When I asked him what his name was he said Chester Field and I saw that he was looking at the package of cigarettes on the table. To myself I said O.K, not a bad idea, and though he didn't ask for my name I told him that it was Agnes Day. The way he hid his smile said plain as Dei that he got it and was probably sometime or other a Catholic too. I had a peculiar feeling about him from the start. He was old enough to be my father, a gorgeous man the color of light tobacco with features like an Indian, though more Aztec than, say, Chippewa. Deep folds in his cheeks, like Dizzy Gillespie's, so I asked him if he played the trumpet. He used to. The question and his surprise at it broke some thick ice. Up until then he had looked at me as though I visibly carried some virus, what I am coming to think of as *'the'* look. I am horridly drawn to it. I was one of three white women in the bar. One of the others was a beat-up object, dirty and streaked and sad, an old empty November rain cloud lying low on the horizon sucking up dirt instead of water. The other was a whore who let everybody know it. As sorry as these sisters were, they were what gave me courage, looking through the window, to go in, my virgin experience in a black bar. I had cruised the place for days because it's my neighborhood joint, and when I finally went in I think the bartender knew me from my peering face at his window more or less nightly. But back to the whore. She could have killed me. Her eyes slashed my stomach open, cut off my breasts, threw acid in my face. The other one looked like she was viewing something distantly; she kept squinting at me and there was a great sense of space between us. I'm not often fanciful and when something like that presents itself it can be powerful—I mean the two impressions from the two women. The whore's attitude was plain enough; she thought I was competition and I saw her look around for my pimp. Her's came in later and apparently ordered her to get out and hustle it, and she left. But before she did she watched him eyeing me and I felt some pity for her, for several reasons. She was as she would have said, I imagine, hung up on him. And he was a slick man, marcelled hair, or whatever it's called uptown, manicured nails, knife pleats. And alas, sexually magnetic.

As soon as I decently could and in a tone that I hoped was decently low but would still carry I confided in the bartender: I was new in the neighborhood. My husband was in prison. Greenhaven, at Stormville. To his question, was my husband a black dude, I nodded. To the follow up, how long had we been married, I murmured that we weren't actually married, the drug rap had come soon after we got up here from the south. From Selma. Selma was the only southern town I could describe in detail if it came to that. But now I see that I had brought Eager up here and laid a drug rap on him and put him in prison as a long act of retaliation: ever the white bitch, subconsciously or unconscious. Selma is an inflammatory name still and the reactions were various. The bartender acted as amplifier, repeating the most interesting or pertinent facts that I gave him. It seemed to be crucial when he asked if I was a native of that place. I started to deny it, to mention the work in Civil Rights; and thought that to admit to being southern white in Harlem could be dangerous. And still I did; I said yes, I was from Selma. Would he ask the whereabouts of my accent? But no. And though the atmosphere did not become warm with approval, I was not frozen out. I thought that to invent more that night would be to strain my powers, never all that considerable. And then Chester Field came in and I recognized him as what I meant to have and saw that it would not be easy. To all of them, including the whore, I had to present myself as someone just seeking the warmth of black company as a way of being temporarily less distant from my black love.

I've sat here an hour since I wrote the last sentence, just looking at the paper, wondering why it is so hard, so confoundedly hard, as my grandmother would have said, to set down the truth. On a pad by my side are attempts, abandoned in two senses, employing, to be prissy, the most basic terms. It's an odd feeling to be embarrassed when you're all alone inside your skull. There must be some watcher in the head to whom we defer and apologize when we can't. I offer apologies and copy out one of my doodles and will pass on hurriedly:

I wanted Chester Field but I also wanted the whore's pimp,

wanted him to fuck me, wanted him to want to fuck me, wanted to be in his stable.

On the official page it looks innocuous. Many, probably any, women can admit to having wanted to be a whore for a man, to be hurt by or for him. Throw in 'love' and natural childbirth is part of that ambition realized. I assume part of the pain is sexual, that some of the screams are those of a masochist in heaven. How much of a woman's part of the marriage contract is simple masochism? How many choose to enhance it by practices within practices? These are the questions of a naive woman who, until a couple of months ago, had only been aware of one sexual position and that mainly by hearsay. This can be blamed on my self-confinement to nineteenth century writing and my grand-mother's influence, though she was realistic in all particulars but the one of sex. My mother, on the hunt for a husband, was too busy to instruct me, and maybe the missionary position was good enough for them both. At least in that position the lovers are face to face.

Chester Field made me turn over. The humiliation was at first remarkable, impermissible. We got to that position without ex-changing more than a few dozen words. We walked from the bar silently, up the stairs like enemies, I felt the usual fear and self-hatred inside the apartment, we undressed. And then the order "Turn over." I did, not knowing that he meant to mount me. I thought, I don't know, something naive, something stupid, such as a massage. And when I felt him pushing between my legs I was so shocked. I thought he meant to practice sodomy on me and fought and tried to turn. And was pushed and pulled about and molded like so much silly putty, les mots justes. Abasement was the object and the accomplishment. He pushed my breast down until it was impossibly flat on the bed, my face, my breast, my lower chest to the sternum pushed and held down and the rest buckled up, pulled up, held up for him to shove into. His two hands on me, one pushing, one pulling. Complete humiliation. I could feel my face burning, an oddly prosaic detail I see in the circumstances, as though with blushes I tried to nor-malize the ludicrous. Which did not remain ludicrous for long.

From impermissible to working the streets for him, I see now this second, is a small step and if I ever see that whore again I'll tell her I know how it can happen.

So I've managed to set down some of the truth in spite of me. Others of the doodles on the page are nearly insane, I think, a distance I had to travel to get to where I am. The word blood shows up a lot on that pad. Is that just normal for a woman, whose life is periods, cycles of blood? I escaped all those considerations by being political. So today, perhaps, I am a woman.

Chester Field stayed two days. The time with him was as real as a dream and lasted nearly as long. I was aware of operating on many levels, an awareness I've only had in dreams. I thought at one point, "I could go back home now" for it seemed that I had found what I set out to find and accomplished what I had meant to accomplish. I see us now, the two of us, and it's as though I view us through the rents, jagged and hanging, of some *material,* which, blowing and shifting and writhing, occasionally resembles viscera. It's as though I were inside myself, inside the outraged tubes leading to my womb. Surely we are not meant to be so continually occupied or we would all be nymphomaniacs. Just now I see the entrance to myself, as cold from where I stand, or lie, as the entrance to limbo, an aperture jagged with icicles, around which winds howl. But inside (now) there is no weather, nothing but the peelings of old miseries, the rinds of old toothaches, old heartbreaks, the scent of the subtle rotting of old hatreds and envies. And I feel those aches as his, as his deposits in me. And in some shame I remember how warm I was a lot of the time, how warm he made me, not just hot, like the time he finally kissed me and I could feel his surprise, I thought I could feel his surprise at the sweetness that let him kiss me and kiss me. He probably kissed in sardonicism, his face twisted, watching me writhe and glow like a kid whose cold papa is suddenly kind. I remember the Elsie Dinsmore books in my grandmother's house, that sadistic papa the only one I had as a child!

Is it possible for a black man and a white woman to provide mutual warmth, or does first one and then the other leave his/her deposits of venom in the receptive and unsuspecting warm flesh? Can we be both bite and antidote, venom and hartshorn?

I bit Chester Field's shoulder until I tasted his thick salty blood.

As if that was what he had been waiting for he got up and dressed and left.

Another long pause, more doodles, among which I read and copy out: This journey may be more complicated than I had thought. Or more desirable than I had imagined.

We did not talk in the slight interims. Nor bathe except in each other's sweat. There was some food, skimpy and medicinal. I hope what we gave each other was somehow not inconsequential.

november 18

Since the last time I wrote in this book I've had five men. The super's wife no longer looks at me on the stairs and when I spoke to her back this morning I think she took on a little speed. Maybe she was thrown off because I was alone! Her attitude poses a snobbish question. Is her disapproval that of a moral woman for a puta or for the quality of the gents the puta fetches along to her room? I admit that quality has fallen off since the first fella, sartorially at least. I remember his nice corduroys, his polished loafers, his equally polished professional air. The pickings of the past eight days have been from the lower echelons, guys you would not mistake for profs or docs or even shyster lawyers. Clean, yes, but I'm not talking here about clothes. One of them had on a tee shirt that was redolent of about a week's wear. But I could make a generalization about black men based on my knowledge of a dozen or so of them, a ratio that Nielsen might find respectable, considering how many men an average woman fucks in a lifetime, if the product being rated were not so louche. I am reaching the point where understatement is the only way to achieve an effect. . . . The generalization being that the truth about black men is opposite to the cliche about them. Eager, for instance, straight from work without a shower, was spicy, tobacco-y, though he didn't smoke, and so clean otherwise you would have eaten your lunch off his belly, and I did in a manner of speaking. Does the reference hurt? Yes, but not as much. If I were writing this with a fountain pen my tears would not censor it. And so it is, has been, with all my men, my cats, dudes, niggers. I don't know how they do it but under the most neglected clothes I have found bodies like warm marble, like the bodies of Greek athletes after their oiling and scraping: clean down to and into the pores, clean under the balls, clean between cheeks as hard as unripe melons. Ladies, putas, Mr. Nielsen, there is nothing, there are no things, more superb than the bodies of average black men padding the streets in cheap sneakers and shapeless clothes. I have sampled randomly and I know. And the brain? you may well ask. And I may well reply, I haven't got a single clue. Maybe there's where they keep their dirt. I do know, and

114

not just by Eager's teachings, of the contempt there, off which I have learned to feed like a winter bird at a suet ball. And that contempt is for the lot of us honkies, no exceptions. What I suspect is that no exceptions could be made, that the condition is endemic. Is not this why the militants are asking for a separate nation, a black Israel within the borders of this country? Think of all the blacks in America in two or three contiguous southern states, surrounded by whites, the negative image of cities in which, like Manhattan, the centrally-dwelling whites are surrounded by the (always) marginal blacks. And one sees that one race will always at least metaphorically imprison the other, and going outward or inward it's possible to arrive at one of the properties of 'love,' in which there is not, can never be, equality, although the weight of inequality can shift about: the mother loves the child more than the child loves the mother, then the weight shifts and the yearning kid follows the indifferent dam bleating unheeded. And in the great maybe terminal love affair between white and black Americans, it's the whites now who follow and cry, scared shitless of Rap and Stokely. And little Ivy, self-chosen representative of all lonesome honkies and whities, is trying to fuck every black man in creation, trying to take them into herself and

november 21

Three days ago when writing here was overcome by bleakness.
I was frozen by something. It was as if my nerves died. My
grandmother used to say, too often for a kid to hear, those terrifying words, A goose just walked over my grave. Yesterday
minus two, flocks of them walked over mine and more geese
wild and honking flew above. I lay here that first night thinking
of the Island homestead, a very November place it occurred to
me; the house itself could be the house November lives in all
year. These are love words. I loved the house and I've always
loved November. Thinking about the house and Grandmother,
my mind crossed the ferry as I used to do to go to school and I
thought about Cayce Scott for the first time in years. He was the
only black in our school for especially gifted kids. And I thought,
was he the only one especially gifted or the only one whose
relatives pushed him forward, or just what? We used to smile at
each other but I couldn't dredge up one memory of our talking
or fraternizing in any important way. If self-defense is needed, I
can't dredge up a memory of anybody else at all, not a name,
not a face, so Cayce is, whatever my limitations, unique, like his
name; until I saw it written down I thought it was spelled Casey.
What did we study, how did they draw us out, what became of
us all? My fascination with anthropology—to hear Grandmother,
you'd think it began the day I was born—was the reason I was
there, and a certain gift for analysis, practically abandoned; and
a certain snobbishness on the part of my mother which said that
though we were divorced and had to go home again, I should
not suffer what she termed the troglodytes at the local school.
And my grandmother's ironic eyes and attitude toward everything informed me against, about, the future. Did she mean to?
I found her, her type at least, beautifully preserved and presented in the person of Mrs. Moore in *A Passage to India*. Au
boum. Those sounds were all around Gran; her daily passage
was to the hollow echoing cynical sounds of the Marabar Caves.
But of course unlike Mrs. Moore she did not die of the exposure
to a shockingly alien hideously familiar Something but throve
upon. Yes, like a winter bird at a suet ball taking in the guck for

the embedded seeds yet from the guck the body manufactures the inner vest to keep one warm and prolong life. Just like me and the contempt of my lovers. I've decided that's what they are. Just lovers. Embarrassing, this thing of salivating between the legs. Do men?

LATER

The salivation was not as I had thought lascivious leakage but painful period. Thank God. I was too scared to write down that I was scared. Salivation = salvation in this case.

N.B.

Walked around the lake today and looked back as though I were going to keep going and never return to 110th. Noticed how the glassed-in top of the halfway house looms over the Park. I wished for binoculars to see if men were moving around up there. Funny how it dominates the landscape like a symbol for all Harlem.

november 23

He followed me down the street. When he got close I could hear him sniffing. I don't know why—Grandmother, are you listening?—I was not scared to death but I guess part of your information about the future was meant for just such times. I recognized something I didn't know existed, and led him here, and let him feed on my blood. I gave suck to a baby who half the time, probably more than that, starves, and dreams, and sniffs out mothers and is, he said, mainly rejected as a creep or worse. After my little vampire child was full he became a motherfucker, considerately putting on a valorous pose of macho man though I didn't need it. Didn't need a grow-up son. Like a fresh cow with her calf I'm keeping him by my side if I can. And for those inhabitants of my skull who are disgusted I remind them that fresh milk is also full of waste matter. The hired girl on the Island used to turn the teat up and shoot a stream of hot strawy milk into my mouth.

While he sleeps, his stomach contentedly rumbling, I'll add this confession, that I have tasted on his mouth my own blood and think it's sweet and wholesome. I can hear retching rabbis all across-a dis land, puke sounds coming out of the doors of those mikvah parlors where vile woman is forced to purge herself. I recall a small red-headed Aussie friend who told me about becoming a Jew in New York, about being dipped in foul waters and proclaimed no longer a shiksa but pushed nonetheless out into the freezing cold day to be got rid of, memory of her and her problems and all, and herself walking along the street, old matter freezing in her hair, wondering to herself: I am now a Jew. What does it mean?

Maybe my sleeping boy has an arrangement of teeth like the . . . is that thing called the spaleen of the whale? which lets him sieve the briny fluid but inversely. I'm sitting up, blanket tented over knees, writing this, and he lies with his hand cupped under my dripping faucet and it's like a man who has barely made it across a desert to an oasis and even when he sleeps must feel the slight trickle of life on his palm. When he wakes up I'll please him like a good mama with a treat. I'll straddle his face and try to give down what I am trying now to hold back. I just had a funny sweet image that when my period is over he will leave me high and dry. Quite high. For the record I really dig herb. This dude has turned me on in more ways than one. I want to ask him not to leave me but know I'll change my mind. I want to tell him about my contentment but know it's connected with some mothering idea in this bleeding. There goes that flock across my goddamned grave again writing in the dust of my mound their strange webby message about my secret for contentment and my fear of that secret. But I have not been afraid of my boy not even when he told me that he had just when we met been released from next door. He said "I been halfway for so long now I want to go all the way." A fountain myself, I had an image of the halfway house as a fountain supplying a steady stream of thirsty men for me.

november 30

I finally met one of my neighbors, a black woman, former school teacher. We are on the same floor, our rooms separated by a warren-like twist of a hallway at the end of which, I discovered through her, is a john shared by all on the floor except me. Those whispery comings and goings that I had thought were other putas like me, those numerous flushings, are now explained. I have never met or observed anyone else on this floor but imagine that I have been observed or else the Senora Super has flapped her gums about me. Last night there was this peremptory knock on the door, at which I had two thoughts: Eviction; and, the cops. And then a third: You've changed a lot. I opened the door a crack and saw this rather gloomy face above a tailored dressing gown. The face said, "You read Santayana?" and when I said I didn't she said, "Maybe you're right. Look at this." She shoved the book at me, finger marking a line: ". . . *her freedom from prejudice never descended to vulgarity or loss of dignity.*" I think I looked at her with my mouth open. I thought the remark was foolish and wondered if it was some kind of message to me from her. She asked me to read the line out loud and I did, and heard it go from foolish to pathetic, like the sort of English pronouncement that says no gentleman wears a brown suit. Seeing my face my neighbor said, "Making both descents I'd call Mr. Santayana a silly Spic." She took the book from me and flipped a page or two looking for some more proof. I asked her to come in and she did, still absorbed in her search, and sat down, still absorbed. She gave a hearty snort of disdain and read, " 'It never rains but it pours.' This from a self-styled philosophe. A figure of speech vulgar, undignified, inaccurate and irritating." At which I said, pointing to her, "School teacher?" and she said, "Former. I now collect unemployment and slights, wherever I can find them." She gave the book an openhanded slap. "I used to read and admire this mother. You know how much of this crap Blacks take for granted?" The Blacks was so capitalized it was like a fanfare. "Philosophy that says racial prejudice is wrong unless the idea of equality gets in the way of dignity, and it always does." With an effort I dredged up something that might interest her. "I've always wondered how Jews can read George Eliot—" But she interrupted me with a forceful kind of finality: "They've had their turn. Now it's ours." She spoke as though I had gone deaf. "I mean it's our turn to gather all the slights and try to get all the privileges. There's never enough of that stuff to go around and we want it all."

Moving on we touched on Leroi Jones. She called his cry for lampshades out of Jew skin 'just tasteless hyperbole,' saying in explanation, "He's a poet." And the violence growing out of the Student Non-Violent Coordinating Committee? The 'N' was needed, she said, to make the razor sound of the acronym; at least SNCC was an honest sound, which put the committee one up on all the honkie groups full of lying words and sounds. I thought that she must have been a good teacher and told her so, and wondered, it was in my tone, why she no longer taught. She answered the tone. "I was sacked. They threw a sack over the political firebrand spouting Black Revolution at Julia Richman. The firebrand went out the door but it didn't go OUT." We laughed, a silly thing to record except it was the first time I felt we were on the same side, in her mind. Before that she had been on the offensive and done very well at it, and I had had to take the other position. She said "That was early, when there was hardly any Movement. Just a turd or two floating around in the pisspot, to hear it talked about. Now they've all got their Black Studies, but I wouldn't go back." Instead of asking why I stupidly told her about my Civil Rights work, or started to. This aroused her barely napping sarcasm. She spoke to herself but plenty loud enough for me. "They always tell you what they doin for de niggahs."

But I had learned to be smooth about my stupidities, having fallen over that hidden wire many times before. No matter how on guard you want to be or think you are, there always comes too soon that wish to ingratiate oneself, to say, "I'm different" and try to offer proof. No matter how long you wait to make such a remark it's always too soon. I think it must be weird to them, like a crow stepping out of a bunch—I remember that a bunch of crows is called a murder ! Stepping out of a murder of crows to side with the scarecrow. They've tried to scare us off too many times and been misled too many times. Now they believe us about as much as the scarecrow would.

I pause and read that series of statements. I still believe them.

She didn't stay too much longer as if she got what she came for. But I saw her this morning across the street walking a cat on a leash and realized that I had seen her many times before. I let her wave at me first and then returned it, but no more. No smile, no extra waggle of my honkie fingers. Last night when she had gone I wondered why she had sought me out with that particular quote and tried to fathom the message. The message has been delivered but who can read it, that sort of thing. There were, I decided, two possibilities. That she thought I was vulgar and without dignity. And that she thought I wasn't. There's my current philosophy: yes, and no. I'm not capable of the subtlety of 'maybe' nowadays.

I'd planned to go out to a bar but stayed in, too tired or too naked for a pickup. And here I am again, scribbling, trying to think of something besides a black body letting me use it. I'm afraid. This afternoon when I thought about tonight's pickup, planning how he'd look, how he'd be, I had the wish to be hurt by him. Before I could stop myself I had dreamed up this large thick hand slapping me. It's as if that's the only way I can feel used, instead of feeling like the user. But that's a bad direction. And what small weak voice is passing judgment here? I think it's Red Rowan crying out of a tangle of Ivy. I wonder if I should chuck all this and go back to the Island and find myself before. Well o.k. Before I die. At least I ought to know something about the disease and the body it's eating up. I wonder this now most of the time: am I a criminal? Are my impulses criminal, is it criminal to live for the illicit, is the halfway house responsible for these thoughts. Every day now I go into the Park far enough to look back and up to that building with its glassed-in top looming over the Park over the city over me. If I went back to the Island and carried the new woman and matched her up with the old girl, putting one on top of the other like paper dolls, would anything jibe? Have I developed angles beyond the ken of Red Rowan? But November's ending even while I write. So long Nov. A quiet night in Harlem as your ember fails.

december 3

He's gone but not out of the building. I'm sitting by the window checking on him. I imagine him casing the other floors. If he comes back and knocks. But I won't write about that. My husband I told him. Nightwork. Home soon. Black, yes he's black, I said. A big mean dude man. So better vamos hombre. No not us. Just you. Finally went. A Puerto Rican negro. Lips laid back, teeth like white rock on a beach, a man man. Get out get out. I thought it then and pray it now. He said nothing on the street, just smiled, sexy beyond belief. I thought he was American. Then up here I heard the three words in English "You soak me" and saw Jack the Ripper in his eyes. The whore killer. Strangle me while I'm soaking him. Some of them commit religious murders, that's what they used to say at Headquarters. That Spanish men can be stranger than honkies and blacks put together. A combination of machismo and the bloodiest fanged Catholicism. Not defanged like ours and Italians'. God, if I'm going to get everything I think about I've got to find a way to stop thinking. Or think PEACE. And God will send PIECE. I told him I hadn't understood what he wanted and I illustrated, awkward and virginal. I swore that I thought he lived in the same house as me. I said anything, he understood nothing. Except about my husband. I got him out the door at least. But what is he DOING. My pencil just ripped the page the way he would have ripped me. Big hands, big slabs. Dream come true, right? He's on the street now, thank you God! Saw me watching. Somebody's going to get it tonight, this morning. Because of me. Now he's going. What a sexy man, what a sexy walk, what an almost sexy death. In disgust I record my heat. Does the whore practice self-abuse? She does.

december 15

The night of December 7th I went out and came back accompanied. And he was accompanied though I didn't know it until three days later. But I recall speaking to him about the day of infamy. And paid the price for pretentiousness. The stain on my underwear like snot. The burning when I pissed. I thought I'd go on and rot or infect Harlem. Clap gets rid of a lot before you get rid of it. It knocks out culture and ambition and all niceties and manners and hope. I was just a leaking hole that stank. I ate over the sink like a big canine bitch and licked my fingers to get the last of the crud on them. Finally went to a clinic, name and location supplied by my I assume contemptuous neighbor but that's an assumption. She was cool. Sat in the crowd of black men and two black women, one of which I think was a man in drag. Finally my turn and got the penicillin and pills. The female nurse, black, told me "Y'all got your own clinics downtown" and I told her a black dude gave it to me and saw she wouldn't mind if the syringe was full of cyanide. I told her the dude was my husband, sort of, and that he got the dose from a black bitch. She stabbed me with the needle. I thought, let her have that much. Be generous, the way that motherfucker was generous to you. Spread it around.

I think I've been changed. I think there's a stain I'll never get to, to scrub at. I thought I'd come out 'the other side' changed, enhanced, when I moved up here, as though this life was like mescalin which Huxley said would always constitute a religious experience, *unless*. That cherry bomb of an exception. Unless the taker of the drug was paranoid, in which case one entered hell. I don't think I've entered hell but I'm stained and all the perfumes of Chanel and all the douches of Arden will not clean this tiny twat. I think that I carry now, to all the men, a mental stain and that it's uncleanable and evident. I think it's possible to look at me and see that for a couple of days I was eaten with gonoccocus which could as easily have been a spirochete. Could I survive a chancre? Cancer. Crab. I'd like to write a lot about this but afraid of being eloquent which would be like perfume to cover slime or wigs to cover lice or rushes on a floor to hide the shit. Still doggedly I say: this disease is part of my black experience but not exclusive to it. As the nurse said, there are clincs downtown and they're just as full. Though down there somebody of my *class* (snarl) gets privately treated. White history is swollen with Venus's disease though the female histories are generally veiled. Isak Dinesen, a hopeless case before she knew what her husband had given her for a wedding present. Nobody's ever implied that she infected her lover, the English flier, but he died in a crash and who's to say it was not deliberate.

To put it down in basic black and blue (written on blue paper) any girl who fucks twenty-five men in forty days—not twenty-five times but twenty-five men—is a statistic herself, subject to tabulation, no more protected than a number or an item or a datum. To say that I never even considered this possibility just puts me down as a dumb number and saves me nothing. And now that it's over, seeing that it isn't over and never will be, I'm glad.

december 20

I went back to the bar tonight where I met Chester Field, one of my first nights up here. I remembered the whore and her pimp and the other woman, the beat up old object who looked at me so funny. I remembered thinking she had looked like somebody peering through the wrong end of a telescope. Tonight the whore and her pimp were not there but the old object was. She told me I reminded her of herself 'a little while back.' I wasn't feeling all that kind and I said it must have been more than a little while back. I said that I was twenty-three and how old was she? She told me she was eighteen and laughed like an old toilet cistern, all clank and wheeze. If I could have pulled a chain and drowned her I would have. Her breath was so foul blasting across the table that I asked her if she ate shit for breakfast and she said "Black jism when I can get it, same as you." The world crawls with things like that, like her. And it rubs off. The bartender, who'd acted like my brother before, lumped us together, said if we couldn't get along we could get out. I said "Don't you remember me?" and he said sure he did but there was nothing to prove it. I just hate that, that somebody might not remember me. I sat on a stool and ordered a drink, then offered to listen to his troubles. I said you have to listen to everybody else's troubles so come on, now's your chance, I'm feeling generous. The way he said Not tonight showed he thought I was offering something else. A slobby nigger like that! Dammit! I told him, I don't think you black at all, I think you trying to pass. A few laughed which was nice but when I got to the door a while after he suggested that I might feel more at home someplace else. The old cunt made a sound and I thought I would run over and crown her with an ashtray but saw she was crying in her beer.

december

Looking at the entry made some time back I see one of the dangers of my kind of life. I recall that in Swedenborgianism evil is an oblique angle and I see it as a door ajar, the door of that barroom slightly, not welcomingly, ajar, and along its oblique angle slips a person like a shadow who has been slighted or scorned, concealed and abetted by the angle, and the angle leads to a trough which dumps the person into prison. The act by which prison is conjured—the murder of that old babe or of the bartender—becomes incidental. What is important because inevitable *beyond a certain moment* is that the slightly ajar door of the barroom leads directly into the prison door. Two operative words are 'slightly' and 'slight,' representing conditions . . . But I don't know how to continue. There is a brutality in the tone of the last entry that spells m,u,r,d,e,r. I wanted to crown the woman but if the crown is heavy enough, as heavy as a bottle or a big ashtray . . . How often the men I wrote to in prison expressed disbelief at where they were and what put them there. I was guilty of thinking then 'oh yeah,' going by Jack Roberts' statement in an early letter that 'There ain't nobody guilty in prison.' He wrote that in bitterness equal to its sarcasm.

I see that a big danger for me is, what I'm going to call, falling into myself, and the closest I can come to an explanation, and this after a lot of hard thought, is *a lost objectivity*. I had, have, the belief that as long as I keep a dated record I am in control. I think dating of events and sanity—which I believe is as close to objectivity as, oh, a needle and thread—are closely interrelated just as dates and freedom are. That's why prisoners and slaves are often lost in a kind of dateless void. Which means that keeping a journal in a way of holding onto freedom. In my grandmother's Scotch language, this record, these recountals, would be called condescendence, which leads to the thought of condescension: was it condescending to myself and others with the disease to talk about the levelling properties of the clap? Does a bad cold or the influenza level? They're all infections, got, chances are, from close contact with another person. If the snotlike discharge is able to take away culture, and grace, and all the other

127

victims I claimed for it, then blowing our noses or spitting up phlegm could lead to isolationism of the individual, and a bad case of catarrh could bring on the end of civilization. Well, if that's not successful satire it still has a point and in my case the point is that if I hate being put on the same level as the man who infected me then I hate the man and I hate Harlem, which according to Coreen Lassiter the day I asked her for a clinic, is 'dripping with VD.' And it must follow that I hate blacks. And none of these things is true. The only hate I've felt was for that beat up old dame in The Spade Cat, because she didn't believe I was twenty-three, because I reminded her of herself, because she reminded me of me.

Sex and disease and drugs are always mentioned in the same breath like a.b.c. What a lesson. What a directive.

december-january. a reconstruction

As Christmas approached and passed, Ivy moved further uptown in her nightly forays. At first she dressed well and took taxis but later on she walked and was indifferent to what she wore under her heavy coat. Winter was early and cold, rising from the Harlem streets like a sheer black mountain but on its lower reaches it was snowless so that there was a lot of extra irony uptown in the ubiquity of "White Christmas," a song aimed at Ivy by several men who collected the rewards of daring to dream.

But she wanted to give so much more than they asked. Gratitude led to tears and to cries of "Use me!" Part of the abandon could have been traced to alcohol, for she was drinking a great deal during her searches, but she did not know if alcohol or the cry was responsible for the inhibiting effect on some of her lovers. Sometimes the effect was outright failure which made her so sorrowful that she drank in the daytime to forget, to soften the mourning that came with the knowledge that no one wanted to own her.

On rare sober days when lucidity was also vouchsafed her—lucidity no longer a concomitant of sober, which generally meant only a logy interim period of regret that kept her from sleeping off the hangover—she was able to see herself, but without humor, as a stray bitch looking for a home, one knee instead of the many to lean against, one hand to lick. She said that she was, not always vaguely, frightened to discover just how many men would have taken her role, which was the role of service and subdominance, black men who, after all their terrible history, still wished to be owned. At the time of her defection from the Movement, many black militant men were demanding subservience of their women to the extent of forcing them to walk behind their men with lowered heads. But she felt completely certain that no militant would have her, and despairingly sure that if one could be found, in the darkness he would practice the most abasing apostasy which should be kept secret from the world of daylight and role playing. She would lie daydreaming of herself in a dashiki, moving softly in bare feet about a kitchen preparing food for her man which she would then serve him as he sat and she stood; then herself eating alone, the morsels left by him, knowing that when the housework was done—. But the daydream was always spoiled beyond that point by a confusion in the roles. She would see herself lying waiting on the bed and he would appear through the curtains with his head in a turban bearing a tray, laid for her, before him. Or heavy, bearded and very black, he would speak in a whimper like a mewling child asking a favor, and she would feel abandoned, floating anchorless on a nameless sea.

One day when The Hawk, as they called it uptown, was fiercely swooping and shaking her windows, a southeast wind with rain and ocean in it, she got quickly drunk and lonesome but the thought of the wind at her back as she cruised the streets, its beak tearing at her legs and ankles and the dry rattle that sounds exactly like stiff old wings flapping, made her decide to stay and seek companionship in her own sex. It occurred to her drunkenness that Coreen Lassiter, being a black woman, could tell her about black men. Whether she would, was another thing. At Headquarters, that place at least a thousand miles away, the women she worked with had been evasive in front of her and even prim, not like the white women who talked of little else with such candor that Ivy was appalled and wondered if she would ever want to experience what they talked of so cynically. Their descriptions of individual genitalia had seemed especially hateful to her; how could you want and hate something, at the same time and so violently? But her naiveté was not so deep that she could not imagine that this was the way men talked of women and their parts.

When Coreen Lassiter opened the door Ivy told her, "I'm drunk and woefully ignorant" and hoped the remark would be somehow interesting. Apparently it was not and there was no warmth in the invitation to come in.

The room was plainly a Headquarters of some kind. It was laid out in corridors of pamphlets, magazines, and placards, on a stack of which the cat lay looking at Ivy with uptown eyes.

In the way that Ivy's present life tried to disclaim her background, so did Coreen's quarters dispute the cliché about the cleanliness of black women off whose floors the fastidious could eat their dinners. If a piece of food was dropped on those floors the wise would let it lie, as Coreen had done: a sandwich had scattered like a disreputable purse its contents in the dust, where paw marks showed how the cat had played with a crust of the bread. The plaything now rested at the end of a trail like those left by the moving rocks in Death Valley.

Coreen said that when Ivy had done casing the joint, maybe she'd say what she had come for. Ivy apologized for disturbing her, if she had, but did not offer to leave. She half-thought that if Coreen was edgy enough she might tell what Ivy wanted to hear without its having to be asked for.

Ivy said that she had hoped, after Coreen's visit to her, that they might have got to be friends, and did not mind telling the lie. She felt that she should have blushed at Coreen's disbelief that the tired words had actually been said. Coreen told her, with a compensatory flatness, that she had come over that night for one reason only: to get a closer look at Ivy. She said that everytime she had seen Ivy before, Ivy had "either been cruising the waters or bringing home the fish." She observed her visitor for a moment and then said that there were plenty of white men in Harlem "not all of them looking to change their luck." Ivy said as smoothly as her condition would allow that there were plenty of black men downtown, too. Coreen asked, "Not looking to change their luck? Is that why you're up here?"

Ivy said the room was cheap, which wasn't a lie. Coreen said, not at all nicely, that it wasn't cheap to her, that she couldn't afford those two rooms and private bath. But that somebody black might be able to if Ivy was not 'squatting' there.

Ivy thought the remark was not only inaccurate—'squatter' meant something else entirely—but sophistical: the room had been empty, and people, as she told Coreen, were moving out of, not into, New York. Coreen snapped at her not to be condescending, saying "You know perfectly well what I mean. Those rooms might be rented to somebody—" she was savage—"*upwardly mobile* who could finally afford a window on the Park." She said they wouldn't be slumming, like Ivy.

Ivy was thrown off by the accusation and sat repeating, "Not slumming. Not slumming." She wanted to tell Coreen that it was the opposite, that she aspired to black men, though she couldn't say why or what she deeply meant; and an avowal that it was 'not just sex' needed much more thought to back it up and bolster its emptiness than she had given it, though she kept trying and the veil kept falling between her and it. If she told Coreen that increasingly she just wanted to lie with the man and cry, what would she get for her troubles, for her 'condescension?' She also wanted to ask Coreen for a drink but didn't.

"If you're not slumming, I don't know what the hell you are doing. I mean," Coreen said, leaning forward menacingly, "is the whole purpose to fuck more than any whore in Harlem?"

Ivy felt very white, and brittle like a sheet of paper; Coreen bore down like someone writing with a heavy hand. She told Ivy that Ivy was famous, that she was one of the sights of Harlem, that they had names for her on the street that Coreen wouldn't let pass her lips. And while Ivy was trying to recover Coreen hit her with, "I guess you over you dose? You better be. I saw you reel in another fish last night." The bad English was contemptuous and added to the threat.

Ivy got up in a hurry heading for the door. Like The Hawk at the window there were two other presences in the room called Assault and Battery. Coreen had big hands, big shoulders. Her impulse to maim was communicated to her cat, which stood up, back arched to spring; and then it was extending itself in a low stretch like a salaam.

Ivy saw then that the pamphlets were titled in English and Arabic and had the impulse to ask Coreen if women took Muslim names too, and what hers was. But she told Coreen, "I'm sorry" and made it a blanket apology for her whiteness and for being an infidel and any other rap Coreen wanted to hang on her.

Then she saw and felt Coreen look right through her, right inside her and beyond to her purpose which could have been standing behind her like another entity. It was the look of a mystic, of someone entering a trance. She seemed to exude from her body exotic odors that veiled her eyes like the fumes of incense. Sleepily and heavily she said, "Why don't you sit down and be comfortable. I'm going to tell you about black men."

coreen's
story

Coreen said that no white woman ever could get it right. She said that loving dimmed sight further and clouded it the way hate does. The speech was measured like introductory bars of music; behind the words there was the visionary's attempt to alter, to make incantatory ordinary speech and summon winds of vast change. In the effort, which seemed partly drugged, Ivy could see that Coreen loved, too, and that it was probably true about clouded sight. There was a power to what she said that connected the two women as though they served a common god, Coreen the sybil and Ivy some lesser but essential handmaiden. Coreen's timing was impeccable, for just at the point when the measured speech, for all its power, must have brought furtive thoughts of playacting, of overdoing, she segued into a more serviceable matter-of-factness that allowed Ivy to assume the purely passive role of listener without feeling that it was forced upon her.

Coreen spoke of the men in her family, her father and five brothers, and what had become of them. To some it would have been a recital of outrage, of justice miscarried to what would seem to be the point of fantasy, for it was a total refutation of the meaning of democracy, but Ivy was keen to the nuances of truth and she seldom doubted Coreen as she told of humiliations on the way that belittled that word's humble root.

Coreen and her sisters had all managed University educations but two of her five brothers had managed prison, one had managed death, one 'got away' to Europe, and one was getting along *just fine* in Atlanta as a Tom. It was easy to see that Coreen would have preferred death or prison for the latter brother; that, to her, he was the failure for accepting and living by the rules of the white world.

Benjamin Lassiter, Coreen's father, was a fisherman in South Carolina like his father before him, taking his living from the rich waters and thus managing a measure of pride that, according to Coreen, was his greatest legacy to be left to his children. She said with a fierce bitterness that she would always, always be puzzled by his inability to pass it along to his sons, for if they had received it as he had from his own father, they could have bypassed, over and over until safe, what she called 'the mouth of hell.'

But circumstances let her father be lured up north, to become a scalloper, when the boys were all gone and Coreen's sisters were in school and Coreen was teaching. Her father and mother took a small house on an island in Great Peconic Bay. And Coreen named the island and caused Ivy to lose contact for a long shocked while, because it was the island where she had grown up in her grandmother's house, the island from which she had daily taken the ferry to go to school in Greenport. Returning to the present, she had to ask Coreen to repeat what she had been saying.

Coreen's parents had moved to the island and rented a small house near a harbor (Mussels Harbor, Ivy guessed, for it was the traditional scalloper's harbor) and invested in a boat and equipment. The scallops were plentiful in Shelter Island Sound, Gardiners Bay, Little Peconic Bay, and all the inlets and creeks and harbors that made the seabred southern man feel at home. His equipment was bought second hand and though he repaired the large flat boat, caulked it and repainted it and made it seaworthy, he was not too bothered to find it half-submerged one morning. He threw a winch on her and hauled her in and set about repairing whatever the damage might be.

It took three sinkings for him to get the message. But it did not stop him. He took to scalloping at night, knowing the waters by that time as he had known his native sea, and in the darkness his boat was shot at and voices told him that one nigger on the Island was too many and they had one already. The 'one' referred to was the man, also from South Carolina, who had told Coreen's father about the rich waters and convinced him to begin his life again in a place without memories of his vanished sons. The man had a job as overseer for a large estate. To the disgust and ultimate fear of Coreen's father, he also fucked every white woman he could get. On the frustrated island where the men tended to obesity and drunkenness, the woman-harvest was nearly as copious as the scallops. He was a big man and intimidating—'a mean motherfucker'—and had the powerful backing of his employer; and though his dogs had been shot at and one of them killed, and though he was harassed by telephone and by the police and had continually to buck the insolence of waiters and bartenders who did not want to serve him in the island restaurants and bars, he told Coreen's father that he had chosen to live there and he was going to live there and if he died there, of anything but natural causes, he would take some people with him. So Coreen's father took courage and stayed on and tried to work and was shot to death.

Coreen's brother who died was also shot, back in South Carolina, by a policeman who swore that he was threatened with a gun, and the gun was produced. "It was his," Coreen said, "he always carried that piece. He hated cops, white and black, and they should have left it there because everybody knew about the piece and the hate and the combination was enough. But the cops invented a whole situation to justify the murder; had it taking place where some trouble was likely to happen at any time, where he could have been found just about any time. Except he was carried there by the cops after they shot him. And everybody in town knew it, black and white, judges and lawyers, and the white woman he was with when they got him. She was prominent in town, old as his own mother, and had been paying him for services ever since he was a kid. With her—and he wasn't the first one though he was the first to die on account of that particular white bitch—with her it always started out by hiring a kid to run errands, mow the yard, weed the flowerbeds; she liked to get 'em at about age 13 or 14, so by 16 or 17 they were broke in. Marsh was 19 when he was killed. He hadn't turned out like the others, willing to shut up and even out, when they got too old for her. He was a wise mouth and wanted more than she was going to give to any nigger boy, and I guess, I surmise, that he threatened to go public about her. Anyway she set him up and they got him and she didn't even have to go through that old bullshit of crying 'rape' or 'burglar.' They killed him in her room, mopped up the gore, took his body to the trouble-spot and shot him again. Not one bit of this was really suppressed. A five year old kid could have told you the whole story including the blood in the police car that was older than the blood at the 'scene of the crime' and the different times the two gunshot wounds were inflicted. Blood don't do more than seep out of a corpse. It just didn't make any difference down there. Marsh was just another dead nigger who'd outlived his use to some white.

"There was talk that the others, now grown men, who'd serviced the old woman, were going to get a northern lawyer and lay it on her in Court, just break the town open, because she wasn't the only one, she was just the most notorious. Southern towns, big and little, are running sores with women like her that prey on black bodies. Everybody knows about Mister Charlie and black girls and women but hardly anybody outside of the south knows about that side of Miss Anne. They know about the 'rape' cries and charges but they don't know about the thriving industry that prostitutes black boys and gives them a whore mentality when they grow up."

She came out of her trance for a moment and looked at Ivy with the old animosity of an hour ago. "I don't think they pay you," she said, "but do you pay them?"

Her question was like mind-reading for Ivy had been thinking of last night's fish that Coreen had spied her reeling in, and his demand to borrow fifteen dollars, which she had given him. Now she was seeing the episode superimposed over the dead body of Marsh and round it all like the black band of mourning was the idea of the basic training, the early orientation to think of one's body as negotiable.

Ivy answered Coreen in the negative—no, she did not pay the men—but saw that the answer was no longer interesting, that Coreen had withdrawn behind glazed eyes into her memory.

Marsh was Coreen's baby brother, the next to youngest child. Below him there was a girl, Sudie Mae, and above him sister Lou Ella and then Coreen (Coreen Anesta); then came two boys only eleven months apart in age. They had grown up as twins, sharing with each other but not with brothers and sisters, staying apart as much as they could and maintaining secrecy about what they did in their long hours, and days, as they grew older, away from the homeplace. Coreen was in teacher's college when they were put in prison.

About them she said, "They were city niggers, even in our small town. They Georgia Peached their hair and Nadinola'ed their skin. They wore slick zooty clothes, sharp shoes. They bopped, man, when they walked and talked. They were twenty-five, the oldest one not yet twenty-six, when they made the Big Time, as one of them, Elston, put it. Nelson, the other one, wagged his head and laughed. That was when I was visiting them in the pen. 'Did you?' I asked them, meaning armed robbery, their rap, and they told me 'You'll never know' and laughed like a couple of goddam fools. I got mean with them, pointed to their prison clothes and said, 'Man, some threads!' Said I couldn't see their shoes for the steel between us but I just bet they were two hundred dollar alligators. But I couldn't faze 'em. All I know is what the Courts know: the evidence was circumstantial. No money was found and no weapons. But the robbery was committed by two black dudes and my brothers were the only black dudes in the vicinity of that hick store, and the owner 'identified' them in spite of having said that the robbers had Afros a foot tall and my brothers had their conked hair. The Court allowed as how the Afros had been wigs and a half-assed search was made to find 'em and somebody even came up with a kind of wired contraption that some wigs are built around, all blackened from the fire that had destroyed the synthetic hair. Never mind that this was found in the backyard incinerator of the only hairdresser in town. The case was put on through the Court like grease running through a goose. It was like the door of our home was pressed against the door of the pen and those boys couldn't go anyplace, once they left our house, but to jail. That's the mouth of hell all black boys have to pass and re-pass and try to keep from getting sucked into."

Ivy recalled in a dream that evil was an oblique angle, a slightly ajar door. Seeing her abstracted, as it must have looked, Coreen said to her bitterly, "I'm not telling you about *my* family. I'm telling you about all black families, about why there ain't enough black men to go around, because what death doesn't get the prisons do, and in between times there's drugs; and white queers and white women to skim off the cream."

She asked Ivy, "Where's all the cream now? In the Movement, right? Never mind about Black Is Beautiful being on all lips. Half the Movement is shacked up with or married to white bitches, and forty percent more are on the prowl for at least a Jew Princess though the dream incarnate, if you can believe this, is a southern WASP, a blonde cunt who'll make slaves of them and cut off their balls. You see what really gets handed on. 'The evil that men do lives after them.' "

She went off course into a history of blacks and whites in the Movement in Harlem, while Ivy thought about what she had seen in Selma; how the liveliest and loveliest of black activist women were passed over for white females with hardly anything going for them in comparison. She had thought then that if northern women were to be evaluated in the south by those white activist representatives, then pustules and smells and bad breath and teeth would be the acceptable norm. They were almost anonymous in the uniformity of their unappetizingness, which may have been, Ivy thought smugly, why she, good skinned and redhaired, was so frequently picked out for vituperation. She was the only one they could positively identify. But never mind the self-accolade. She was high on Coreen's enemies list, that was plain.

Coreen was silent, watching her. Ivy said, "I know," agreeing with the last thing she had heard Coreen say. Coreen told her, "I doubt it, Miss Anne," and then, as though afraid Ivy would make another dash for it out of renewed fear, soothed her with a gesture and a half-smile. She went on—from where, Ivy would never know:

"But Nelson and Elston's Georgia Peach and Nadinola were just coverups, to cover their stink the way a dog kicks dirt over its shit, because in the world of the white motherfucker, a black man and stink are synonyms. I mean the dirty-minded buttermilk-smelling honkie man whose biggest hangup, even more than black men per se, is that he could never fuck his mother." She told Ivy that that was what the word 'motherfucker' meant: white; that when blacks called each other that they were calling each other white and that was why the term was so loaded. She was so sincere that Ivy suspected a put on, like the sincerity of the man last night who, asking to borrow fifteen dollars, said to her, offering his collateral, "Do you know what it means to just have your word as a man to offer?" His manner told Ivy that he couldn't be trusted with her television set or even the phone. If she were asked (she thought with an inner smile) what she had learned about blacks in her time among them, she could say with conviction that when they were most sincere, watch out.

Coreen was saying ". . . because a black man can and will fuck the white man's mother and like as not get paid to do it!" Looked at that way, it afforded her the respite of laughter and she made the most of it. Ivy, to whom the allegation was tragic, could not have laughed. Coreen's laughter was fathomless to her in the two senses of being measureless and incomprehensible. Ivy tried to imagine what it would feel like to discover that your mother had paid for her sex and then what it would feel like to be a white man, a racist, especially in the South, and make such a discovery. Did the woman who caused Marsh's death have sons who knew about her? Was such knowledge part of the underlying pain of the southern white man? that agony so acute that nothing could dull it, that caused the continual effort to find forgetfulness in steady drinking and violence and denials of birthrights and civil rights and blood connections; and resulted in courts so corrupt and a police force so ruthless that they were known and feared around the world. Though the World, hardly qualified to throw stones, could find nothing to do about it. She thought of Chaney's death and burial beneath the dam, and the two young men who, because they were with him, had had to die: Schwerner and Goodman. Even in the Movement, the latter two were spoken of in a breath, as martyrs; she had heard references to the atrocity that omitted Chaney's name altogether.

The World knew about all that, as it had known about the lynchings and abuses, and it formed committees and carried banners and got up collections and it never brought about any changes, not until the past year or so; and the sacrifices that the blacks had made, in heroes and Sunday School children alone, for the modest gains, threw a fence of spiked irony around each word said or written to try to prove how the Old South was finally changing.

And that was just the south. Before the militants lay all the other directions of the compass, which in the case of Black Rights comprised as many as there were degrees in circumferences, 360 directions to have to take, trying to affect consciences and effect change. Like weathervanes, on the roofs of each direction there were set devices pointing northeast and southwest, the storm directions; and in the houses of each direction the barometers were permanently set on TEMPEST.

Coreen did not seem to mind that the laughter had not been shared. She continued with new-found leisure, reciting from the familial log of decay and betrayal.

Brother Cornell, the next to eldest son, was someone about whom people said, "What a pretty man" without the *pretty* downgrading the *man*. He looked something like Stokely Carmichael except his eyes were wider apart and he was darker and his nose was not so sharp; but tall even before puberty and lanky in the way of athletes, with a special something the French called *je ne sais quoi,* Cornell's language now! But that was jumping ahead. As a kid he had had a quick wit that was not mean, and he was unswervingly good at his books. He worked hard helping his father and in his spare time he read. He was in advance of his school mates and the members of his family, because of the incessant reading. He could make out just about anything written in French as though it was a native gift, though his pronunciation was shaky, and he pondered Latin, sure he would find the key, saying his one sure sentence over and over, Ad astra per aspera. He read books on how to do things and could construct and maintain just about anything you could think of. He installed running water in their house and made them a bathroom, scouring the dumps for the parts, the toilet and sink, the piping and the rusty old tub, which, when he had finished with it, was fit for Martin Luther King. He listened to operas on the radio, considerately turning the volume low until his mother asked him if he thought the music was too good for the rest of them, and then they all listened until, Coreen said, the other children just could not take any more and they piled on Cornell and 'brought him down.' Except, she said with satisfaction, they couldn't really, not in any particular. He *prevailed.* One thing she recalled about him with great pride, now, was the pride he felt in being black which showed in his movements, his grooming, his speech. He took the white culture he wanted and could use and made them parts of a wholly integrated *black* person; in his mouth, Shakespeare was a black writer. And, she stressed, before Afro had a meaning in stylish lingo, as far as she knew, Cornell was wearing a modest Afro of his own and him only twelve or thirteen years old. A fine example for Nelson and Elston, except that they didn't take it.

Early in his teen years, Cornell discovered girls and there was always one to whom he would be steadfast and true until he replaced her with another. By the time he was sixteen he had the reputation of lady killer and lover, and, Coreen said emphatically, that was not hyperbole; his girlfriends were definitely getting fucked and because of this he had to go afield to find them because no parents in their neighborhood would put up with him courting their girls. This gave him an aura that brought him a lot of attention from females of all ages, and he took on a little swagger when he walked, literally a 'strutting cock,' and he cultivated a hard-eyed look that could give even her a thrill, a 'well, are you going to or not?' attitude that became fixed, immovable, so that he was turning the by now famous look on male and female alike.

Savoring the prejudice of her remark, Coreen said, "One of the *fruits* of that attitude—which, after all, was based on a deep sexiness—was a, oh, *man* visiting from Memphis. He was staying with the Mayor, no less, and ran into Cornell and his Look around the Courthouse Square. It knocked the wind out of him. They talked, Cornell and him, and then he followed Cornell to find out where he lived, and just settled in for the, I guess you'd call it, courtship. Instead of going back to Memphis when his visit was over, he took a house in the best neighborhood he could find close to ours. Every time Cornell went anywhere there he'd be, in his car, on horseback, walking, riding a bicycle. It took him almost a year to get Cornell into his house. They had a fancy dinner served by people Cornell knew, the mother and sister of kids he went to school with, who brought outside as much of the story as they could, so everybody either knew what was going on or, having the facts, still couldn't figure it out. These servants told it that he offered to teach Cornell French and Latin, and some of the dumb ones said that was real nice of the white folks, to take an interest in Cornell's education. At least, it was something for his mother and father to hold on to."

Coreen did not know—she guessed nobody but Cornell and Jamison, the white man, could know—how long it took from meeting to seduction and what that seduction comprised; and, in fact, what their kind of marriage meant in a sexual sense. She

141

did not know if Cornell had become a homosexual or if, when it was duty time, he just lay back and got sucked off. Whatever he did he must be good because the man, Jamison, took him first to Memphis and then to New York where they lived awhile, and then on to Europe where he bought a house and where he and Cornell settled. She said, with a kind of satisfaction that contained its own antithesis of regret, that Cornell was master of a house in the French countryside and of an apartment on a grand street in Paris and of another house in Verbier, Switzerland, where he and Jamison went for two months each year to ski.

In the roundabout way that such stories have of reaching back home, she learned that her brother was called Corneille by the French, whose language he spoke with classical precision, and that the originator of the story that finally reached her had been present one night when Cornell's entrance into somewhere, a theatre or a nightclub, had been applauded. For her own reasons, which she soon shared, she said that she tried to see him coming into that place like Mohammad Ali, a macho entrance with hands clasped over his head. He wrote to her and to their mother but never once had he proposed, or apparently even considered, coming back to take part in the latest attempt at gaining black liberty. He was way up in his thirties now and she couldn't help wondering how much he had changed and sometimes had chilly visions (which she had tried to counter with the Ali-entrance) of him standing and walking and talking like a faggot. But it was faggot, old style, that she had in mind, the kind Jamison was or had been, all languid gestures and languid nasality, all bitch and a yard wide. The people who called themselves queer nowadays were getting rough as cobs, dirty beards and hair and black funky talk no matter what color they were. The whites looked like hillbillies and the blacks like hardened cons even when they weren't. She did not think the one was preferable to the other; both sucked as far as she was concerned, when she thought of Cornell looking and acting either way.

And yet her tone was mellow, which caused her discernible regret. She did not want to feel mellow about her brother's fortune because of its source, and Ivy did not think the perversity was what rankled, but the whiteness. Coreen verified the thought by harshness. "Whatever bad thing he is he can thank the white queer. If he's got anything good left, any of his old self, he can thank his roots."

She touched on the eldest brother only briefly and caustically, saying his solution to the problem of being black and carrying a stink had, once upon a time, been the only solution, that or death: to become a yes man, a shuffler, a Tom. He lived segregated from his rights and said, or pretended to think, that that was the proper way. His gold tooth flashed in a shit eating Tom grin when he talked about his 'good white friends' who treated him just as good as if he was one of them. The last time he pulled that on her she told him, viciously black, "That's because you *is* one of them, mothafuckah" and left him to his deaconhood, or whatever it was, in the Church and his tokenism, and his, she was convinced of it, eventually lonely life filled with all kinds of retribution. She disclaimed him in one way but could not in another, for he represented too many Blacks, Blacks without pride, which after all was only a sense of self, too afraid to seize their identities and with that, their rights. But now was the end of that line; when the present Toms died off there would never be another one allowed to live. What was being born into each family now, in place of the Toms, were killers, white haters and Tom haters, a crop of black avengers who in the near future would display their harvest.

Ivy was accustomed to the polemics and listened instead to the subtlety with which Coreen used the word black. When the person referred to had her approval or love the word was verbally capitalized, a small explosion of sound; when the opposite was true, she deprived the word of its capital letter, a little act of violence that was always effective and always bitterly savored. Coreen had not used it as merely descriptive, as in 'a black ribbon' but Ivy was sure that even then the usage would not be neutral, that the ribbon must carry some additional weight for having the fortune or misfortune of being black.

She wished she could discuss this with Coreen, just two educated people discussing a point of usage, and saw in her wish that she approached the tired sentimentality of a bad hangover, a kind of hangover she experienced with increasing frequency. She would go from a visionary drunk in which sight and hearing especially were abnormally acute, to a sentimentality that tried

143

to temper itself (despite her) with what turned out most often to be pedantry. Her lovers were sometimes impressed (or put her on and down with their pretense) and sometimes they laughed at her. But it did not stop her feeling that her discovery was important and must be discussed. As now: this subtlety of which she was thinking was there whenever a black person spoke English. In their mouths the language regained a lost passion, the kind with which it had been invested from the time of Chaucer, a passion that had died or gone dormant in America, in common usage, by the first of the 20th century. Supposedly the passion had been preserved in rural places, southern and downeastern; but here, here was its true survival and revival in the black speech of politics, of jazz, of Harlem.

She tuned back in to the slogans and clichés of the Movement that Coreen was now mouthing, in itself a sentimentality like that trying to push out of Ivy's skull, and the similarity, and the refutation of her 'discovery,' made Ivy laugh out loud, a laughter incongruous and insulting and, she knew with despair, absolutely unexplainable: this laughter following the horrors Coreen had, for whatever reason, shared with her?

Coreen lunged and Ivy backed and filled, the dance of incomprehension taking the two women around and around the room, pamphlets and magazines, placards and bumper stickers, and the cat, flying before, below, around them. Ivy feinted and cried out "Please!" many times, while Coreen yelled at her, such things as "Some Sister is going to slit you from tongue to twat," calling her names the meanings of which Ivy could only guess at, affording her a curious relief in thinking that the street names Coreen had told her about could hardly be worse. And as they dodged about, and some of Coreen's blows landed, Ivy still managed to think that the name-calling must be a great relief for the other woman. They blew out of her with the force of bad canned goods that in the middle of the night wake the household by shattering to smithereens the Mason jar in which they have been seething with gas and botulins in the hot closet. The thought was again so funny that she laughed, again. And Coreen landed a serious clout, so square and potentially killing that both were horrified. Even the flying cat froze. As her face swelled under her own nursing hand, Ivy left the place in silence deep and

144

dark and reeled through the twisting passage and once she was in her rooms she passed out for a while.

Throughout the night there seemed to be taps on her door, more pats than taps, but she did not stir except to get more ice that, by morning, had reduced the swelling greatly, though the discoloration of a deep birthmarklike bruise seemed enough to permanently derange the melanin. All through the night she thought about the life stories and their culmination. She had taken a long trip with Coreen, one that included in its itinerary the island of her childhood. She saw Coreen's father trying to live there and dying for his attempt to be a man, and saw the big man who survived and refused to leave, who stayed on and did to white women what he had been broken in to do in the south by aging Miss Annes. He had got away but carried with him the acquired taste that could still be dangerous. She too had been broken in, in the south, and got away with a dangerous taste for which she had recently been maimed, an acquired taste that she could not obliterate from her senses, not even if she sanded herself everywhere as criminals sanded fingertips to erase identification.

Like a fraction of something, an image in a shard of mirror, Ivy glimpsed that her constant sex, which all the street knew about and talked about, was still a clandestine act for it was performed without permission or sanction and it still broke laws. Therefore it was the blackest thing that she, a white person, could do.

She questioned herself on the subject of 'justification' and answered as though she were Coreen: I don't have to *justify* anything, mother. What I have to do is stay alive until—something—breaks. I mean (she said she said, feeling her nearly broken face flare up like a dormant fire) until there is a breakthrough.

That night, hurt by a black woman to balance, she felt, the hurt to her by a black man, seeing herself, fractionally black because of a dogged lawlessness, trying to take refuge from her pain in the exercise of an analytic ability gone rusty, her childhood's equivalent of counting sheep; in a perhaps mature or maturing, or black, exercise of irony, she dedicated her bruise and her fucking, midway in her career, to Eager's proud memory.

Ivy spent Twelfth Night in a hangout for pushers on 118th Street. It was a place new to her and looked so gala as she passed that she peered in the steamy tinselly window thinking that probably not one person inside knew her reputation or had ever heard one of her street names. She was enjoying one of her good drunks, of which the optimism was a part, having begun to drink with the ceremony of taking her wreaths from the windows and recalling childhood tree-dismantlings that were never gloomy times because of her grandmother's sense of occasion.

Before she knew how it happened she was being drawn inside the bar out of the cold, invited by men and women alike even though all of the women were black. Since Coreen's warning she had looked at all black women carefully wondering which one carried her death concealed in a sleeve or a pocket or purse.

But the women, perhaps because of the holiday mood, were kind and often flattering. There was none of the menace she felt coming from whores on the street, though it was impossible for her not to see that many of this bar's customers were indeed whores; making out in fact rather well and on the premises. In company with a man they would disappear and after a time return only to repeat the disappearance with another man.

By the time she had become aware of the nature of the transactions and the real cause of the frequent trips of pairs of people into the back where, she discovered, the restrooms were, she was flying too high on wine and grass, to which she treated the bar several times, to make judgment.

It seemed right that in the early morning hours of Epiphany Ivy should be taken, just a bit apprehensive, into a brightly lit toilet where her arm was prepared for the needle.

As her companion, one of the friendly women gone suddenly businesslike, prodded her arm for the vein, Ivy felt the arm become detached and thought that she could leave it with the woman and go away and that what happened subsequently to the arm could not affect her. That detachment of the arm was a preview of the heroin experience for her, during which all but a small apparently impregnable chamber of her brain would be cloaked in indifference. Part of what she chose to forget lived, unfortunately, in that vigilant cell so that she was never able to give way entirely and forget and nod off.

What was begun in the early hours of Epiphany replaced to a

large extent her addiction to sex, one drug replacing another, and for many months, nearly every day at first and then more than once a day, she sought out her fixes as she had sought out her men. Occasionally the connection would connect in another way, or she would get down with another junkie for the comfort of the hard body, but sexual fulfilment did not happen very often for either party. She would tell a man that she liked to be held while she dreamed.

And in this, for the junkie community was glad to oblige, she found her truest comfort. After the fix she and the man would undress and lie on their sides facing each other and Ivy would nuzzle at his hard chest until she latched onto a nipple and there she would suck, warm and barely conscious, as long as she was allowed. Even when the junk had worn off she found that she wished to go on sucking at the male breast and her hands would knead and pull at the warm skin rather frantically as the disordered world returned in bits and pieces, reassembling itself like a jigsaw puzzle on which corrosive things had been spilled.

Those were the times when the man would want to attempt sex and would sometimes succeed; when he would want to do the sucking at her breast and because she loved him she would tolerate it, but soon enough she would suggest that they go and get a fix, her treat, and she dimly saw that the purpose was simply to render 'him' acquiescent to her eager, breast-seeking mouth. It no longer mattered who or what it was, did not matter about age or condition, muscularity or shade of color or cleanliness. None of the old nuances of erstwhile proclivity lingered to haunt her. It was just that while she pulled and kneaded and dreamed, she was safe, and she sensed love without being able to define it, the way a small creature must, by smell, texture, taste, the movement of breathing, the twitches of dreams, arms to hold, loosen, tighten, hands to smooth and caress and pat, and deep voice to say, as likely as not, "You're something else," and laugh at her without passing judgement, though the deep sounds could to another small creature have been borborygmus and come from the belly of a parent. Once in a lucid dream that contained some of her old interest she imagined that she was a joey, the embryonic marsupial, which had endured vicissitudes of climate and terrain and chance, blindly and with blind instinct, until it found the nipple where it clung unshakably.

But she was not unshakable. The pressure of the arms and the urgency of the deep tones could change and an appendage, not a kangaroo tail, could poke between her legs. This was so wrong that she could have cried out and would have if it had not been for the vigilant cell where memory willy nilly persisted. But for those months of many dreams and bodies and sleep, she was reluctantly sexual, reluctantly, as a man would have it, a woman.

She had the most trouble with trying to relate how important pieces of the world managed to lodge in her mind. The closest, she said, that she could come to it was to think of a bullet with a picture attached being fired into a deep cushiony mass of jello, some pictures being The Supreme Court ruling that any poll tax is unconstitutional, and that picture is dated in her mind, March 25, 1966; another, without a date, is the Alabama primary with blacks voting in large numbers; and there is a large static image of a large static gathering in Washington, a rally of some sort; and a double-image that remained double after time and dates were sorted out: of James Meredith being shot to death and Martin Luther King being stoned in Chicago. Occasionally people shouted at her as if she were to blame.

She was aware of summer passing, arriving and passing, by the swelling and diminishing population of the streets through which she passed, and by the clothes it was necessary to shed and put on again. It occurred to her that she had an anniversary coming up but could not recall what it was to commemorate, just that it was connected with turning leaves and a smell of dried apricots and a coldness to the nights. But she was so often cold because, paradoxically, the heat was on in the streets and connections were hard to find and warnings were being issued, it seemed, from all mouths at which she gazed, like parking tickets from machines when you pushed a lever.

One night when she was shaking with the cold she went into a bar to try to get warm, too strung out for any prolonged coherence, such as walking more than a few steps. What articulation she had had been mechanical and was no more; she felt the need to be re-wound as though there were a key that the heroin activated, which tightened her sagging springs. Sounds vibrated among the loose wires within her and came to her ears fragmented, unevenly echoing. She got to a barstool and managed to get onto it by steadying herself with a heavy hand on someone. Looking at the hand she saw that it rested on a section of a leg. The leg was missing half itself, stopping just short of where a knee would have been. The heavy leg was encased in denim which was sawed-off and sewn at the bottom. Beneath her tarrying hand the leg stirred and swelled and hardened.

In the extreme candor of her condition she became instantly and, even in the circumstances, unnaturally excited. She looked at the leg's owner to convey the pureness of her passion that was unsullied by restraint of any kind. If he would she would, then and there and with that instrument. The man's slow almost catatonic response was like a mockery of the way she had been but was no more for in the strength of her passion her blood had sprung forth, leaping in her veins as though approaching the precipice of a waterfall, a bloodfall; her quick breathing turned into panting to keep up with the demands of her leaping blood. The man's face was carven, noble. She wanted to hold the head and kiss the lips, drinking from the brown lips that looked like crêpe de chine. She saw his eyes widen and gazed into them, her gaze saying what her mouth could not manage. He slowly looked at her hand on his thigh and then, turning his head, instructed her with his eyes to look at herself in the mirror over the bar. There was an eloquence in the instructive nod that sobered her somewhat, making her wish that he could not see what she saw from the corner of her eye: the ghost of a flash. She could not look at her direct but believed that some ratty old woman from the past stood looking over her shoulder, her ravaged face being reflected as Ivy's own. She remembered thinking that necessity was the mother of intervention too and she intervened with herself, meddled in her own life, and managed to leave the bar in silence. But believing that the silence contained compassion was like a hammer knocking down some final barrier to her fate.

In the cold moonless night she went into the Park along whose flank she had, even stoned, never been able to walk alone after dusk. On the other side of the wall she had sensed knives and garottes, the termini of her kind of wilful, passionate and obscene life. She hurried along the lake where the lights were too bright, the wind too cold for loiterers, drawn by something too dimly heard to be called a sound.

Within the deep sanctuary of an underpass she met up with it, a blob that, before the ordeal was through, had been identified as five men. Walking into them, feeling them close around her, brought one perfect moment, which began with panic that was like a hood of fire; she beat the flames with her arms and called out a name but it was pushed back into her by a nervous hand over her mouth; and then it was as if the hand holding back her words absolved her from having to use language for dissemblance. Her panic ceased.

In the rotation of their use of each other there was ritual and in the pauses separating the cycles there was ritual too, in the sharing of the wine, she taking her turns at the bottles. In their deep cave out of the wind they used each other twenty times. One man came to her only once and unsuccessfully, and she could feel his distaste and dislike. Another was reluctant, though without dislike, and when she encouraged him to please himself he awkwardly hoisted his body upward holding onto some unseen rockledge above their heads, until her face was in the fork of his legs. Ever awkward, he fumbled and went, small and flaccid, into her mouth where he grew and grew satisfied, she supposed, with the effluence of thin wheylike material. When he returned again later she knew him by his smell, which was like buttermilk, a pallid slightly sour odor as thin as his come. She imagined that he was white but what flesh tones there were to discern in the black deep cave were reassuringly dark. One man came onto her again and again, using her and being used coarsely and tenderly, brutishly and with silken grace. She felt that they became a perfect pair, not the beast with two backs but an entwining of mer-creatures in the grotto. She recalled from some poem the playing of sea serpents, could see two undulant black bodies as though she were able, under the influence of the most powerful drug on earth, to stand apart and above and watch herself and her lover. Wishing to see him more clearly and herself in her new body, she thought of going with him to the deep wells of light and bathing there before God.

After the experience with the buttermilk man, when the true lover returned to her she encouraged him to straddle her face and there found the antithesis of the pallid smell in his strong dark purple odor like the color of eggplant, the smell she knew to be the scent of the true black man that was kept secretively, for it was his treasure, his identification, and must be kept in a cavern as dark as the one in which all of them—for now there was activity where the others were, soft sounds—made love.

Under the strong funk of her lover there was another aroma, faint as an ancient memory, once she had blown him, that seemed to become activated or re-activated and she had the sudden, overwhelmingly wonderful conviction that the man was Eager. He had come to New York to find her, had found her gone and taken to the streets! She called him by his name at first under her breath and then louder, identifying herself each time with a sense of ineffable excitement. "Eager Ivy!" she said, a self-definition as well, and he chose to tease her, to pretend not to hear; and yet with the words his ardor renewed and redoubled and she thought she felt her soul return and nuzzle at her and push under the counterpane like a puppy at night.

Coincident with the dawn that split the night's intense and remarkable blackness her euphoria was invaded by something alien and ridged, for which the word 'stickle' came to her as descriptive. The presence was stickling the curiously relaxed air that had surrounded her. The smell of the entity was cold like the skin of an iced melon, faintly reptilian. With that perception the invasion was no longer confined to the atmosphere but shifted brutally to her body, to her morbidly over-used cunt; and before she opened her eyes she believed that what she would find tearing at her would be the immense sawed-off muscular leg of the man in the bar, for which she, like Salome, had lusted, for she had wanted to kiss the immense head and puckered cocklips that were like crêpe de chine.

What she found when she opened her eyes was not a rapist or a lover of the night gone insane. The trouble lay not outside but within. Feeling the beginnings of a hemorrhage with her hand, she saw in the riving light the dozing men and saw that one of them was white though weathered darkly, and that not one of the remaining four resembled even slightly Eager. She wondered if they had a sense of being bound as blood brothers by her blood.

Trying to stand up she realized that she was in a bad way. She said it was like a film running backward to see the men recede, when they saw her condition and heard her ask for help; facing her they became stealthily indistinct like some swift retreating noiseless tide. She thought of Santayana—"Her freedom from prejudice never extended to vulgarity or loss of dignity"—and thought that to drag herself home and up the stairs would exhibit a freedom from prejudice against the five men that would be undignified, vulgar, and impossible.

Waiting in the cold of the first frost she could feel her blood freeze on her. When help came it was black, a black man; she thought he was as brave as any man she could ever meet, to carry an apparently raped white woman across the daylit Park. She could feel him tremble as they approached the street and knew it was not due to the cold. But the brave man persisted, the brave father man. He had a comfortable gold tooth and wore spectacles and she could feel through his good heavy coat the presence of a paunch. On the street she told him, "The halfway house" and feeling his reaction added, "Next door." He supported her all the way up the stairs and at her door she wanted to plead with him to come in and stay with her and succor her through the days and nights of her recovery.

He asked if there was a neighbor he could call to tend her until he could send a doctor, an acquaintance of his, to her, respecting her vehemently expressed wish that no policeman be involved. She was touched by the way he edged up to and around the question of the color of her 'assailants,' an assumption he had made without encouragement from her; she wished to tell him that she and the men had equally been rapists, if the word had to be used at all. She wished, while he held her hand, to tell him at length about her half-conviction that the men had gathered and waited because she had summoned them. But she told him, no, there was no neighbor to come and sit with her, thinking that she would not impose upon Coreen Lassiter again because she could not. She felt it would be impossible for her to impose further on any black person, of any age or sex or attitude, alien needs and desires.

When her savior had gone she 'stood back,' she said, out of whiteness and out of obsession, for to abandon one was necessarily to sacrifice the other. It was simple and complex: to stop being white was to give up the preoccupation with blacks; that was half of the equation that Malcolm X had aimed at and missed, when he defined whites he liked as *apparently* white, or white *on the surface*. He had jettisoned his near-revelation, however, in favor of a continuing cupidity, and it was that greed as much as anything that made his autobiography simpleminded: he had not been able to give up his worship of money and money-based power—his whiteness, his obsession—to pursue the one genuine glimmer of prophecy afforded him. The other half of the equation was of course that blacks, by ceasing to brood on Mr. Charlie and Miss Anne, would stop being black. But many if not in fact most whites and blacks would see such a simple-complex act as self-murder, or, after its accomplishment, might still be able to accuse the other color of murder outright; for, fearsomely accurate cliché, nothing dies a harder death than prejudice, for or against.

Having arrived at that point she had to look at her own coming sacrifice, the end of her sensual life. The thought of a white man in her bed made her cross herself. All whites were devils. She might have gone against her religion but she had thrown it away. *See where Christ's blood streams in the firmament!* That was what it meant to have abandoned your faith, or tried to bargain with it. Grief at the thought ate at her guts and burned her veins. She had never known what the loss of God really implied: that blood and organs, tissues and marrow, being but acolytes in His Temple, would try to rush out and go with the rejected sorrowing retreating God, abandoning the desecrated temple—herself! the Temple of Ivy—to the lonely shingle like any empty carcass or shell on the beach. Her pain was only at the thought, but vicious, a cop with a truncheon, a cracker with a whip, a big dog unleashed by a sheriff. Unmerciful. She tried to throw herself into the fetal position but discovered that she could achieve the stance only by movement as slow as a dream. She was like some unsupported jelly-like thing lying naked on the naked shingle of the world. Like her awareness of the onset of the hemorrhage which had presented itself as an alien presence, she sensed another presence in the room and saw that the door to the hall stood open and by following a wake in the air with her eyes she arrived at the feet and legs of someone and they had something false about them or perhaps they gave off a false odor. The sense of great danger gave her mobility, unlocked her frozen bones, and she moved cautiously so as not to attract attention; but with the feeling of being in ambush, she tensed for the spring and just then into her sightlines came two hands, white, holding a syringe. She knew that the fluid would either kill her outright or would kill her baby that was trying to be born between her tensed legs, his large hard black head tearing with love at her, a subliminal voice saying to her, "Mammy, I need air," to explain the fierce pain it was causing. She had resisted that syringe when they came at her trying to sterilize her, sterilize her man, tie off her tubes. Mr. Charlie's timing always sucked. It was too late now to stop her kid. She would fight with what she had even if the kid was hanging from her womb by its ankles. A little more pain for the kid, a little more pain for her, and then, Great God Almighty we is free! She lunged for the genocide bag standing by the honkie's big feet, hoping to find a piece or a knife. She was aware of the syringe coming at her. It kept swooping in from all angles, determined to make a hit. She had to give up her scrabbling at the bag. Holding her kid in between her legs with one hand she made it across the room to the big ashtray. The room was roaring like caves. Tides. Mobs. When he came for her again she let him have it up side the head and when he fell down she lay down too, to let her kid be born.

Ivy always thought it was a perfect irony and a perfect example of justice that it should have been Coreen Lassiter who found her lying on the floor with the only white man to have been in her rooms. It was Coreen who called the police to come for the two honkies, one dead and one dying. Thus it was Coreen who 'freed up'—one of the phrases she would have uttered with savagery—the rooms with windows on the Park, making them available to some deserving black, Ivy, by killing the doctor who had come to save her, lived up to Coreen's worst beliefs about whites: that they were all beyond any kind of redemption.

But all this speculation was, as Ivy said, a lifetime later, because she still had, before serving her prison term, the endless lifetime of withdrawal from heroin, and the withdrawal from her total delusion that she was Black, one of the new breed of killers Coreen had talked of, and withdrawal from the illusion of having killed one of the enemy.

She said that during that long time her thought was reduced to slogans and every pro-black cliché she had ever heard uttered. She said if she suspected that a thought was coming on she would sit and say "Power to The People" until it went away; or, if she was terribly tired she would just say "Right On" over and over. The most difficult of her withdrawals, and the reason for the attempted blockage of thought by slogans and clichés, was from the belief that she had had a baby. She swore that she had 'birthed' it lying on the floor of her apartment; swore to the Courts and the police whom she accused of taking the child. Her memory of feeding it at her breast was so acute that she could feel—still, when she was telling me twelve years later about the hallucination—each movement of the tiny hands kneading her flesh, and the contented kicking of the little feet somewhere on the great mound of her breast, and the occasional sharp pinch of its gums on her nipple; and could hear, still, the mewling sounds of its happy greed.

Only later could she see that her imagination had made the child so tiny it was scarcely larger than a joey; the other interpretation being that it was woefully immature and doomed. Either way she saw how sadly symbolic it was, this child meant somehow to represent a new black/white race, or just herself trying to be reborn of herself. She had plenty of time, she said, to think about that.

When at last the ordeals were over—withdrawals, trial, sentencing—approaching the prison a thought from the past came to her entire. It was not just a thought but a segment of time intact, of the day when she visited Tony and Jack Roberts at Greenhaven, and the dissimilarity of Chartres over the wheatfields and the prison rising above the landscape had nagged at her. She knew then, on her way to serve time, some of what had been incomplete and puzzling about the vision: there were the antitheses and the likeness of religion and death, crime, murder; but the missing part was due to her inability to know or even to suspect that she was being haunted by the future, her own future as a convicted murderer, though each day the halfway house had repeated the image to her, hanging above Harlem, bidding her remember the prescience, the warning: if she had turned back. But once inside the prison the warning bells had rung for her in recognition. And, she said, 'if' is just another illusion; we have to play out our fates and that's all there is to it.

Trying to hide my profound shock I said, "But from then to now is a long time."

Like the most accomplished narrator she had kept the ending of her story for the very end and all the clues I had read with such smugness, and all the portents and omens I had seen in trivia, were just window dressing. She, of course, had known where she was heading all along and the hesitations, the tentative interpretations that were then taken back (I've blue pencilled a great deal of her recountal) were to keep her from being bored as she told her story yet again.

Having put that down, I see its unfairness and bitchery. I believe that I am her only confidant; and can believe, with little effort, quick change artist that I am, that the fumblings and occasional tergiversations were spontaneous; that at least in one sense she was looking at her story for the first time by seeing it through another's eyes. Of course there was the long-range glance that precludes spontaneity: the Chartres image—but there was not too much of that. I'm glad that she skipped the trial. In doing so she seemed to be saying what I believe: if you're heading for prison, and know that you are, the trial, unless it is filled with great drama and interesting reverses, is the least of the stops on the way; Terminus presides only over the boundaries; in Ivy's case, the murder and the prison; and all the territory in between is no man's or woman's land, and godless.

But there was more to her story, there had to be. As soon as I could I looked up the newspaper accounts of the murder. During Ivy's withdrawals and trials and sentencing the black world that had been her focus had been advancing, retreating, advancing—the most frightening to the white race being the emergence of Black Power. Therefore the murder of one white by another was not given as much prominence as was a shattering story of a black man kicking to death his white dog as a political act on a Harlem street. It was an eye-witness account; the cringing shivering dog refused to try to run away but kept coming back to its master's hand, hoping this time around to find the old caress, the tidbit for a treat, encountering each time the murderous foot. And a crowd stood watching.

There was a brief flare-up, though actually too mild for that, in the sleazier papers concerning Ivy's belief that she had been a black killing a white, but the snide tone of the items reduced the mysterious transfiguration, with its roots running beneath all parts of America, to a kind of low-class joke.

What I found out was that part of her sentence was commuted—and here a perhaps symbolical thing occurred: following the words 'because of' the typesetter, or machine, or deus in or ex machina, went wild and for a paragraph we were given the expletives of comic strips, the #&$#!es of Dick Tracy. If I wrote that this happened in all the papers would I be believed? It happened in the one paper, a tacky afternoon number, in which there was any mention that I could find at all. Later on Ivy told me that the time served was four years but not ever why the sentence had been partially commuted. I still don't know.

I think I had imagined her coming straight from prison, with a stop off at Bloomingdale's for clothes, to the party where we met. The condition of her hair and skin remarked upon in those early writings would have been explained by that dry cell that contained her. Irresistible image here of a voltaic couple, two plates of dissimilar metal producing a current. Ivy or me? No, we are the same blood.

So there was more to her story. I asked her. She told me some but not enough, saying, I thought evasively, that it was as much another's story as hers. And then, breathtakingly, for she had refused to say one word about prison life, she told me that compared to the corrosive effect of some of her experiences in those places—she was moved about, she said—the act of murder had left just a scratch. I saw then what clarified her gaze and made it so pure: a constant burning. Some of her travail, or agony, would never end. And as though imparting a secret message only through its aura, she told me that she had 'finally' got to work among books, graduating to librarian, in a place of minimum security that not only allowed weekend passes but was coed.

Forgetting everything else I searched her face, body, the aura of her secret, for signs of Calvin. She would, wouldn't she, I asked myself but not her, have known his name? If he had, as he said he had, laid her (the librarian) on the floor? And once, in a story that satisfied too well the needs of my prurience, he told of how, as they stood on the moving steps that hook onto a top rail, he had driven his wedge upward into her as though she were a tree to be brought down, and, fucking, had moved them around the periphery of the room, propelling them by his jets, the constant refiring of his revved up engines. These were his images and words. At the time to hide excitement I said, "You're out of your fucking mind," the way we expressed disbelief in each other in times of amiability, and he, biding his time, said "It takes one to know one, my man" handing me as he usually did the ball.

I had said his name to Ivy a hundred times in the course of my own story and she had not reacted. A mystery among others to be looked into. But thinking of him as living, perhaps imminent, I was assailed by jealousy and longing. Longing: in Ivy's solution to her problem, the murder, I had found such sympathetic responses in all my body and the cells of my brain that I was buoyant and could have lifted up and flown. The release, I kept saying to myself, the release. But, to kill a stranger as she had done? And my conclusion was, no, not a stranger; as in other lovemaking there is no substitute for the beloved.

But, like her story, I felt that my story with Calvin had not ended. I cajoled her, and complained, and badgered, and managed to convince her that the project, the book, was worthy and transcended whatever she suspected my motives were. And so together we went back yet again, into her past and mine, with one shock at the onset that made me want to curl into the fetal position, the fatal position, and be sucked back into the womb of the earth.

We got in her car and drove. Pack, she told me, and I packed. She named a time and I was ready. We set out, crossing the Triborough Bridge and enduring the Grand Central Parkway with its piled up wrecks in the underpasses and around La Guardia, and onto the Northern State, the Long Island Expressway, and various new and emerging by-passes, on out the North Shore by the least traveled Route 27 beyond Riverhead. The last time I had come out these precise routes had been with Berthold and Xan, with Calvin plotting in the back seat. Just over there was the village of Cutchogue and that turn to the left would lead to the Sound and Partridge House.

The air was vibrant with memories, all of them good in spite of that word 'plotting' above, a bit of hindsight that, had it been foresight, could not have benefited me because I would not have allowed it to. To quote my redheaded and most singular friend, we play out our fates and that's all there is to it.

As an exercise in pleasure I read out name signs: Peconic, Southold, and down that lane, Chapel, one reached Route 25 and came out beside the Drive-In Theatre. And here was the ferry sign, and here the traffic circle at Greenport around which we swung and up by the monument. Ivy turned onto a street that I thought I knew and drew up to a house and began to park.

I am in terror. Xan is in the hospital in Riverhead and Calvin sits beside me drinking and malign demanding to know where the niggers live man. And we are here and two people come from the house and Calvin mutters and I wish I were dead. More than anything on earth I want to fetch Xan from the hospital and ask her to dig a place for us down under the roots of a tree, to make us a barrow, to let us curl down there together and seal the opening and have been dead for a hundred years, our long old skeletons, wrapped in moss the daylight has never touched, safe at last from predators.

Coming out of the experience I felt as though I were reassembling slowly after time travel, looking around for pieces of myself, morbid and anxious, scarcely aware of Ivy. But two missing parts, two objects of my profound anxiety, did not return and for the absence of one I was grateful. He was in my mind though and when we got out of the car and walked toward the house I remembered him saying "That motherfucking bitch" and he was talking about a redhaired woman on the porch of this house.

When Ivy introduced us, Cayce Scott took my hand with reluctance. I could feel him forcing a surface geniality as though he were living up to some promise. As we sat in his room—one chair, he and Ivy sat on the bed—his eyes kept leaving mine as I spoke to him to seek out hers and question her. Whatever the promise he had given, or she had extracted to allow my presence, it was not on the firmest foundation. As she had briefed me to do at the last moment, crossing the little lawn, I was telling the unfriendly man about my hopes for the book, of telling the plain and sometimes painful truth about—

He interrupted me, using the heavy voice of parody.

"Why don't you say it like it is, man? Say, 'This book is about the fucking of America, the public fucking of America. What you hear ain't America singing, man, it's America fucking, twos and threes and mores, white on black on white, male on female on male, male on male on male on male. . .'." He had left parody for savagery, then eased back and added, "White on black on white. Right?"

His long iteration of male on male made me resentful. I was also resentful at Ivy for having told him something about me and told me nothing about him. It seemed that her penchant for the mystery writer's tricks extended to and included the manipulation of our friendship for the sake of effects.

And was immediately, or almost, sorry. She seemed to be enjoying the animosity between the black man and me but there was no complicity between them.

She said, "Cayce doesn't like white men."

I almost hooted but needed to be a bit more relaxed for that; say about 99% more relaxed. And he, apparently, did not hear the wildness of her understatement, which, if it had been between blacks would have been the occasion for slapping five and giving skin and, a few years ago, bumping hips. He snapped at her, oblivious, "You've explained me. What about him?" She did just that. "Opposite of you," she said, and added, "Like me." And sat there. I admired what she had done for the maneuver itself: what she meant was, if he rejected me now he also rejected her. But the look in his eyes was for me alone, and it was rejection.

Once in one of my least successful encounters I was called by a black man reared to strike 'a white nigger'. An essay written on an allied subject had commanded a lot of attention in the 50s and I wondered if my athletic would-be assailant had read that piece. But when I questioned a more sympathetic black he was succinct: if 'nigger' was low, then 'white nigger' had got to be the lowest. Scott's eyes repeated the epithet.

So there I was, in Scott's eyes a white nigger queer; and in Scott's room from which I longed to escape and quickly. Never would this man be my friend, never would we be even guarded confidants. No sympathy going from white to black man, however extreme, could assuage him enough, for he was one of the permanently wounded ones. And yet there he sat with Ivy, black and white, side by side, hands lightly touching on the bed between them. Not like lovers; like brother and sister, an odd impression, as odd as thinking they were somehow buoyant.

But I would not leave. Nothing but a loaded and cocked gun could have driven me out the door then, because Ivy had brought me here for a purpose, and the mystery of it all including the quickness of his open animosity had piqued me far too much.

Feigning a complacency I could not have felt, I cased Scott's room. It was a pleasant place, littered with living and shiny as to brass and wood. Nice curtains, nice rug, a highly polished dark-stained floor showing the usual veil of dust in the sunlight, faint indeed through the dirty windows. There was a good stereo and a record collection. I saw Eddie Harris side by side with Vivaldi and smiled to think of 'Compared to What' in a baroque arrangement, and suspected, perhaps wildly, that the juxtaposition was deliberate, an almost Oriental gesture on Scott's part to make one think precisely along the lines of my thought; but looking to him for his reaction to my smile, I decided to tease, or anger, him further by not explaining why I smiled. For the best of reasons, at that moment Coreen Lassiter came into my mind and the occasion of Ivy's one painful visit to her room. In the event that I had been wrong to think 'no violence' I decided it was best to go on and look at the man for purposes of future identification.

I looked at a tall man with plenty of brawn concealed in his leanness, a man about Ivy's age, his beauty, like hers, roughened; bighanded, the bones clearly defined in the backs of the hands; eyes almost yellow, slender nose, thick neck; his knee-caps were so defined beneath the thin summer chinos that I could have drawn his legs from hip to ankle (but never the feet; Blacks always have surprising feet). I let my eyes edge up to the crotch area but disciplined myself to look no higher. Could he tell about the restraint? I felt that to actually look there with a full gaze, as I wanted to do, would be almost the same as laying a full open hand upon him.

I tried to judge the effect of my assessment without looking at him direct and figured he had withstood it pretty well. The prolonged silence was as resonant as any I have ever inhabited, but it was not up to me to break into it. I was only a guest in the house of a reluctant host. Let him, let Ivy, carry the old ball, and fall and break their assets. My one asset was my ability to wait, and if necessary, wait some more and appear serene.

I returned to my casing of his home. Over the window and in shelves down both sides there were books, these in my direct line of sight; I could see others in clumps on surfaces in the periphery of my vision. Here the eclecticism of the records was repeated. Kipling and Charles Lamb—

I am well read and I at that time had an obsession. And I saw that I understood the man at least in part, in whose rooms I was, because of the arrangement of his books and the authors of those particular books. I was certain that I could name other authors and books that would be found in that room, without looking. Many abilities based on peculiarities of education appear occult.

In the corner of my eyes Scott stirred and actually rocked, (preparing to make some unpeaceful movement) and turning quickly I saw two more things at once: the rocking came from the waterbed that he and Ivy sat on, too quietly before for me to see that it was one; and Scott either knew that he had been partially apprehended by me or else he was one of those people whose books one does not examine without express permission, withheld from all but intimates, because their books are too privately, even secretly, a reflection of themselves.

The records, the books, the waterbed, even the polished brass lamp and the leather recliner chair on which I sat, had told me a remarkable amount about Scott. On the bases of these things alone I could fabricate a man, a personality, a collection of tastes, a character, that would serve as well in my book as any based on confessions, true or—black, wasn't he?—contrived and exaggerated for the goddamned honkie. He hated me, did he? Well,

163

I hated myself even more. And hated my feigned cool. And I got up and walked to the bookshelves and in passing saw inside a closet whose door was partially open, held open by a regulation black shoe, and in the closet I saw the cop's uniform and the cop's hat on the shelf.

Feigning nothing, feeling shocked, I turned to Ivy. My friend, the convicted murderess, the jailbird, now sitting on a waterbed with a black policeman, the side of her hand touching his. Gentlemen, speak about resonance!

"Sit down," she said nicely, "before you reach for that book. Lamb, or Kipling? Cayce's no more of an injustice collector than we are, baby. And L just happens to follow K."

Did she really say that, that day or at anytime? She was capable of it and knew her man as well as books. Or is this an effort to deflate the Sherlock pose before I have to reveal otherwise, that I am really no good at following up on portentous 'clews,' which, in my case, do not, like Ariadne's, lead anywhere? Why, anyway, should it be surprising that a black cop collects slights to his race if not to his profession (those other books I said were in his collection)? Kipling, in his *American Notes*, is as racist, as loathing of American blacks, as he is racist and loathing of Indians in his Indian books. He was, however, prescient when he said that America would one day have to deal with the freed, multiplying black; as silly as it is to have to point that out; but so many others of his day—white Americans, legislators, presidents—did not share even that bit of obvious foresight.

Before I return to what I think Ivy really said that day, to end the long and pungent silence, I will copy out here what Mr. Charles Lamb—the gentle, did someone say?—mouthed, or wrote, on the subject.

"In the Negro countenance you will often meet with strong traits of benignity. I have felt yearnings of tenderness towards some of these faces, or rather masks, that have looked out kindly upon one in casual encounters in the streets and highways. I love what Fuller beautifully calls these 'images of God cut in ebony.' But I should not like to associate with them, to share my meals and my good-nights with them—because they are black."

Further deponent sayeth not.

The way Ivy really broke the silence, I believe, was to say that

I had heard about Cayce Scott before even though I seemed to think I had not. They had gone to school together, she said, to that special school for gifted children? Yes, that is what she said first including the inverse circumflexion. And then she turned to him and said,

"And I told you, Cayce, at least something of my friend's unhappiness. Two weeks ago, no more than that." Scott looked blank. She said, "I told you about my friend who was in love with a man who turned out to be a hit man."

"Yeah," he said, fairly indifferent. "With Hartshorne."

My heart was shorn then of its beat, even as Scott performed a terrific doubletake and said, "Cal? And *this dude?*"

I could not look at either one nor work up any paranoia about what their glances might be saying behind my back. If Ivy cautioned for decency with grimaces, if Scott semaphored overt distaste and disbelief—these possibilities present themselves only now. I was lost again in a world that had contained Calvin and Xan, though not swallowed by it as I had been less than an hour before; its artifacts were ranged in rows like the trees in a planned forest, made symmetrical by proof that auguries exist, are functional, and that the past can be presaged and thus returned to; and I had simply returned there and from the corridors of its monuments I gazed out, and into the room where sat three people, and was entirely indifferent to them and the time they occupied.

Then, instead of returning to the room and the people, it was as if one of the people came into the past with me, the long sought link, and it was, of course, Cayce Scott who knew or had known Calvin. He made the journey on his own; I did not summons him; and the fact that it was voluntary was evident by the look in his eyes: the man was after all capable of sympathy.

"In 'Nam," he said to me though I had asked nothing. Calvin's grisly stories of Vietnam. Scott could have been one of those ghouls, playing with the dead and dying like rag dolls.

"—seen him since?" some echo seemed to be asking.

Scott nodded, but another sound got in the way of whatever he said, and one was left with the impression that the man spoke Arabic.

"—what?" The echo.

"Abdul hakam latif."

165

"—sorry, I don't—"

"His name. Now. Muslim." I remember that he pronounced it 'Mooselem' with a grim smile. It was the reality of the grimness, its nitty-grittiness, that banished echoes. I came back into the room to a silent Ivy and a somehow receptive Scott.

I said clearly, for my benefit, at least, "Did you say that Calvin is a Muslim?" A nod. "Named—Abdul Hakam—Latif?" A nod, all the while the past, level with other times like words on a page, showed me the Book of Names that Calvin had given me, wherein—

But no. That is in the future, the gift of the book and the kufi, a black and white crocheted cap that Muslims wear; at least, my cap was banded (will be banded) white on black on white. So how could I anticipate the future and say to Scott: "Named— Abdul Hakam—Latif? That means The Arbiter, and The Subtle One."

I don't know how. But Ivy verifies that I did indeed say so. The mysteries that we accept daily, along with our hamburgers and Bloomies and rails of cocaine laid out on mirrors, in fact those very things, are more mysterious than my memory or anticipation of Calvin's gifts, so let it pass.

Scott said, "There's a Muslim settlement, I guess they call it, out there a ways," and his head tilted toward the end of the island. "Just a Mosque and some beat up outbuildings where they live, no more than a handful of them. Involved in some scheme to reclaim a section of Greenport, with Government aid, buy the houses for a dollar apiece and restore them."

Calvin within nodding distance. It was like being told I could hold Xan in my arms again. I could see, not far away, the three of us, Calvin and me bent over Xan after she had spoken a full sentence, rocking a little in communion, like figures in a crèche

In a contemptuous voice I asked Scott, "Has he changed, this subtle arbiter? I don't know what the hell he could arbitrate but he was subtle, all right." Crude, rude, my voice.

I looked into impersonal cop eyes, no more sympathetic to me than his, I saw now, evilly big thumb. Aware of substitution, of really absurd displacement, I still get hung up on that thumb: had he been hung up by it, to lengthen and coarsen it so grotesquely? If 'length of thumb equals length of cock' was true, and circumference ditto, Scott could have earned his fame in the

166

Havana of my youth, that was, pre-Castro, so my thought ran; but it was as if the thought really said 'pre-Castration' and I snapped out of it and apologized for rudely staring. Had Scott answered my question about Calvin? If so, it had been with a nod or a shake of the head that I had missed.

I asked Scott if they had telephones at the Mosque but he did not know. Ivy said, "Would you really call him, just like that?" I said I thought so, and she asked me, why? I said, "God may know. God, I'm tired" a natural progression. Would she be staying with Scott, I wondered, rocking on his waterbed, rocking under his body poised precisely over her on knees and elbows, letting the rocking bed do the thrusting for him while Eddie Harris made farting sounds on his sax and Les McCann tried with growling noises to loosen the lyrics caught in his throat like phlegm? I asked her if she was staying. She and Scott smiled at each other, all alone, it seemed; and, both standing up, she laid her head for a moment backward onto his white-linen clad shoulder, and one of his big hands with the preposterously phallic thumb lay upon her black-silk clad shoulder, and it was marvelously intricate, like looking inside them: white on black on white on black on white. But, lovers? And again there was the brother-sister impression, devoid of eroticism, full of some old sweetness like mutual memories of a playroom on a rainy day, and innocence of everything.

Impossible. But there was a mystery there, a story, the story she had brought me out to find or complete. Who would tell it to me? Ivy had refused before, saying it wasn't all hers to tell, or some such, but tired, I think, of so much narration. Would Scott tell me? I really thought not, contrary to Ivy's plans and her hopes, for me at least. Probably only because he could not bear to spend so much time with me. Would I tell it to myself, basing it on what few facts I could get by any means, making it a tough-cop story? Why not. For Calvin would be in it. Or there at the end. Waiting, there at the end.

cayce's
story

The 11:07 bus was already over an hour late and the ferry slips were dark, the ferries berthed on the Island side. The spilings were gathering black ice rapidly, increasing in girth as Cayce watched from the shelter, pausing as long as he could between turns up and down the meanest block in town.

In summer winos and addicts slumped on sidewalks and hung puking over the railings of the hotel porch, shot and stabbed each other, and nonchalantly took luggage out of the hands of mesmerized vacationers.

But on nights like this they were holed up wherever they could find burrows, and whenever eruptions occurred they were swift and terrifying, like boils bursting: suddenly, into the black coldness, out of doorways, boxcars; and before you could move the sidewalk of cindery railway siding would be running with somebody's life.

Cayce preferred the summertime when violence was circusy, an open spectacle. The hippies gathered then, to watch and sometimes to participate in the trouble, but in the main they were a peaceful lot, grazing and ruminating, full of mild grass. Cayce, young and a pig notwithstanding, was sometimes offered a toke and if the offerer was a pretty girl or, as generally was the case, a girl who might have been pretty once, he pretended not to notice. He had no real sympathy for the smokers, having been one of the handful to resist the stuff in Vietnam, but the contrast between the effects of their habit and those of the users of hard stuff and even winos was too obvious for even a pig to miss.

But he could turn cold when they got political with him. Full of grass they were more than anything else like the twenty-five year old Mongoloid girl who came across from the Island to attend the school for the retarded on the other side of town. Hopefully, her mother brought her across each day expecting something wonderful, a miracle, to occur between morning and night. If that girl had spouted isms at him as the fading hippies sometimes did the effect would have been the same. One reason he had become a policeman was so (he had thought; he really had thought) nobody could try to screw up his mind about what he thought, what his convictions were concerning law, order, and how to make them the same. And whatever the odds or results, he had fought for this country and when somebody gave him the Peace sign he wanted to give it back to them, one finger in each eye.

He hated especially the word 'idealism' in their mouths, because they showed what they meant by marching under the flag of the Viet Cong. The only times he drank heavily were after Peace Marches under Communist banners. Nobody seemed to tell them, the rotten white middle class, that they would not survive one day under Mao or in Russia. Let them march in those places under the flags of Capitalist countries. Observing their self-important revels his trigger finger would give him trouble.

While he was in 'Nam they were all going South, the avowed purpose being to free the niggers, but he knew they went, male and female, to search for fresh black meat uncontaminated up until then by too many white passions. Unlike the north, where blacks were becoming objects of open fetish: Hendrix, for instance, had turned himself into a big black cock to satisfy their needs. He reserved his most profound contempt for those white women who believed they had not been fucked until a black man had plugged them.

He stepped into the wind and saw that the ice had grown at least a foot out from shore. At that rate it would be halfway to the Island by morning.

When he was at the far end of the block the bus pulled up in front of the depot and a woman got out. She was wrapped in sagging dark leather and a bulging totebag hung from her shoulder. He saw her shrug at the driver and imagined the man's sympathetic return of the gesture before the doors soughed shut and the man took off for home.

Doing his duty he moved slowly past the hotel so that any

lurker with intentions to rush the woman could register him plainly. He watched her walk to the chained-off ramp and stare across the black expanse of water. The feeble light over the shelter caught the red in her hair. Cayce's foot crunched on something and the woman turned so slowly that the movement was barely discernible.

"It's o.k. I'm a cop." Feeling leaden he walked toward her. "Ivy. It's Cayce."

An expression so curious crossed her face that it stopped him cold. Beyond the look she made no response. He said a little angrily, "Cayce Scott." Still she moved as though to pass him without a word, which made him wonder if he was mistaken, but in spite of all the changes in her she was not somebody you confused with another person. For four years they had gone to the same school, sat in the same classes, and he had wondered about her and the kind of privacy that had matched in a peculiar way his own, as though the privacy and inner assurance had the same roots in both of them.

He tried a curt and authoritative tone when he said her name again, which brought a slow look of surprise that opened her face up a bit; her nod acknowledged that he was right but showed no curiosity about him. She fumbled for a cigarette and when he lit it for her she offered him one. In back of the filter tips he saw the tightly rolled joints and felt an inexplicable rage to have this explanation of her heaviness and slowness. He wanted to hurt her, to think of something to say that would pierce her to the heart, and could only come up with a phrase so hackneyed it could barely hold together, and yet some cynicism allowed him to believe it still had power over certain types.

"I guess," he told her, "we all look alike to you."

Her face shocked him like cold metal against the back of his neck. For a moment he thought that she would break apart in front of him, fall into fragments like a Mason jar that had survived a fire but crumbled at the touch of a cold breeze. Gazing at her in awe, he was simultaneously seeing the Mason jar turn to glass dust as it had after their house had burned down when he was a kid. Watching the jar he had suspected something about the nature of apparent wholeness, about the illusion of it, and had applied it to what he was learning, painfully, about the inwardly shattered males who comprised his family and their friends.

On Ivy's face he saw something that was like his revelation that day. He put out his hands as though he could with pressure keep her face intact. But his hands still hung by his sides, nightstick swinging from one of them. In keeping with his thought, the betrayal had been inward, of himself.

"Cayce," she said and he took the small victory in spite of the tone, which was as if she kneeled before him. He shook his head to clear it of the fantasy. Like a kid she responded to his gesture: "I haven't asked anything yet! I was just going to say, walk me to the hotel, please," and she pointed toward the fleabag den of pimps and addicts.

"You're not staying there. You can forget that." When she looked surprised as though his denial had been extraordinary he learned a lot about her expectations and now it was his turn to see a stranger before him. The Ivy he had known (had invented, his mind corrected him) would not have set a foot on the hotel porch. She stood still under his assessment. He saw that her hair was coarse and that some of the ends were matted. Her skin looked abraded. He thought that rough whiskers had done that job. The leather coat creaking from her shoulders to her ankles hid her figure but the big boots looked whorish. She was one of his 'types,' all right, whose 'Liberal' response to certain lures was like fish jumping at bait; but in her response she had swallowed the line and gone for the pole.

When he met her eyes again he watched them flicker then settle down to become a look he had not seen for a long time, not since Vietnam. The look measured him, was speculative and conclusion-reaching. It knew pretty much what he was good for, but not entirely, and he saw the look become interested in a way he detested. He wanted to push her down in the snow and cover her with it. He told her, "There's the hotel. I'll watch until you get there."

"I asked you to walk me there. I am a citizen asking for your protection." She spoke as though addressing a retarded person. He set off at once, taking big strides. Behind him a man's voice commanded him to wait a minute, goddamit. He looked back and saw that she had got her whore's boots tangled in the frayed bottom of the cracked leather coat. She freed herself and marched forward. "That's it!" he told himself, for the walk proclaimed her a Marcher. He could see her marching under the enemy's flag.

He found a nasty amusement in thinking about her current problem with him. He was a pig, which from her type commanded one kind of behavior; and a black, which automatically commanded another.

He stopped at the foot of the steps to the rickety hotel porch seeing without appearing to the interested derelict faces of all colors pressing out of the gloom behind the dirty windows. Propping one foot on a step, letting her catch up to him, he said, "This place is jumping with men who'd like to get you in bed. Or on the floor. They're not particular." Whatever response he had expected, her hoarse laugh did not fill the bill. He wheeled on her roughly, for the sake of the past.

"You can't stay here. You can get clap just walking through that door. That's if you're lucky." She was silent. "You know this town," he told her. "Motels are for summer months. But you could find a rooming house." Yeah? something inside said, for she was so trampy looking he doubted if a door would open to her knock. "Look, isn't there somebody you could call up, some old buddy, kinfolks?"

"Buddy? What's that! No, no kin . . . I can't even remember the name of one person on the Island."

He argued. "Even if you'd made it over there, that house has got to be closed up tight. I heard the old lady died while I was away. Sorry." She gave him a speculative look but did not ask where he had been 'away' to.

"I was going to break a window." Then as if all the rest had been a preliminary they both had been onto and here was the nitty gritty she said, "How about your place, Cayce?"

In a minute, soft and with an attempt to be nasty, he gave her another cliché for her liberal response. "Lookin' to change your luck?" and waited for her knee-jerk protestation. She gave him the first clear focused look since they had started to spar.

"Yes," she said.

He was disgusted to feel the stirring against his groin, the easy betrayal of what he believed in. In a minute he fished in his pocket and gave her the keys, the front door key singled out and pointed at her like a cock. Without a word he turned and walked off to the ramp and the black freezing water. Behind him he heard her. "Where?" and his voice jerked out the address. Hearing her walk away was like listening to something in harness.

He imagined her in his room, on his bed, the light of dawn smeary through his dirty window when he went in. Was she pretending to be asleep and did the rise and fall of her breast betray the rape fantasies she had been having since she lay down and smelled his funk in the sheets? How did such a woman, in a black man's room for the first time, feel the weight of the dark lying on her, spread-eagled, touching all the surfaces of her skin? Did she push back the covers and open her legs inviting the night in? Did she curl up tight under the covers, regretful and afraid, in the famous fetal position of passive resistors?

His major confusion was in not knowing how he wished her to be: avid luck-changer or scared virgin. He looked back to the first expression on her face that had brought him to a standstill. He thought that it had been both starved and stuffed, scary and scared. But he saw it now in the light, or lack of light, of her in his room, in his bed: circumstantial evidence that was of no use to him. Looming above her in his mind, looking down on her in his bed pretending to be asleep or zonked out—in the ashtray on the nighttable he placed two then three roaches and a roach clip—he tried her out as she had been, a schoolgirl tight everywhere, shiny red hair, blue veined creamy skin, and then as the hard abrasive woman, coarse and probably smelly, funkier than he was after a long hot gritty night on the beat. The girl was covered to the chin but the woman lay splayed out on top of the covers like a porno queen, spermy and flaccid.

Neither woman was Ivy. Both were Cayce Scott, his confusion. What was actually happening now in his rooms he could not imagine, the failure based on his essential lack of interest in white people as other than the ancient foe, the ofay, as people had said when he was a kid. He knew how to reason out their potential danger, their condescension, and all the ways they could use him illegally, morally illegally; in other respects it was still open season on niggers with legislation to prove it. But what the theories were behind their maybe profound need to change their luck he had not examined beyond the up-front lust.

He looked askance at intermarriages, even at hand-holding between mixed couples in the summertime, an increasing sight as were public kisses, because of the possibility that they just might involve the word and condition 'love,' which he could not see, not even abstractly, as able to suture such a big wound and keep it shut for long. Sooner or later a white word, a white look, an act, and the stitches would pop and love would suppurate like any other sore.

Cayce had learned to be a listener when he was growing up and among the first lessons had been the sexual ones, tales of sexual abuse and misuse told by the males in his family, not without excitement, not without a kind of pride: white women who called into the house the yard-working relatives, the delivery men, the brick-layer uncle; white women drivers who stopped to pick up job-hunting kin plying the roads between potato farms; the hair- and for some dick-raising stories of a cousin who captained his own for-hire fishing boat. The stories rode up from the south on trains and buses, transected the country as unbrokenly as the rails the trains ran on. The progression from first meeting to bed was frozen like a church ritual, beginning with sympathy and concern: the black man must be overworked, over-weary, over-heated, hungry, thirsty; and ending with 'fuck me, nigger.'

Among the younger men the shoe had begun to fit the other foot, so to speak, and the hunted were becoming the hunters, but the nomenclature was equally brutal, the quarry being seen in terms of meat, of bounty, of white female organs to be hooked like trophies onto a belt. In 'Nam he had come across the tribe of eaters, of black men who talked about the taste of white pussy, the goal being to make her climb the walls, beg, scream. He had never heard the word 'love' used; 'tender' was descriptive only of the quality of the meat based on its age.

Straddling the charcoal stove in the shelter he thought about his growing up years without, or nearly without, females. There were aunts, remote and kindly, busy with their own broods. There were teachers, all white at the special school for the gifted he and Ivy attended; and there were classmates like Ivy.

"O.K. Unless she changed her mind and ran, I got a white woman in my bed tonight. Let's have a look at that fact, man."

He watched her after she had left him, walking along the streets she knew, seeing them strange because of the circumstances, because of where she was headed. The town did not have enough blacks to have a ghetto so his room was in a section lapped around by and interchanging with houses of whites; she didn't have to be nervous on that account. But he could feel her nerves jumping. Her footsteps would feel different. Was it because her feet were trying to turn away, to change the direction she had set for them? Supposing they don't manage and she arrives at my door. The cock-key, she didn't miss that, is slipped in the lock very quiet. She doesn't want to make a sound and bring a black woman's face staring at her. Everybody knows how black women feel about white bitches. The key goes in, she feels it like a dry-run of what's coming down later. She hopes? Or she doesn't hope? Let's give it a sixty-forty, twenty points for being scared. She's heard about us, hasn't she, thirteen inches minimum? Now she's in the room, leaning against the door, smelling the nigger's cave. What does she think she'll see when she finds the light and turns it on?

Inside the white female mind there flashed weapons, grease, sex books, Panther poster, the equipment of a shooting gallery—candle, spoon, syringe.

He had made himself laugh and he bent out into the wind again, warm between the legs only because of the charcoal stove. He saw his imaginings as uncharitable not to Ivy but to himself, the mechanism of the black man's self-putdown. Sarcastically, in response to the needle wind as well as the needling thought (one white person's plight and the black extends his alms) he put Ivy once again against his door in the dark and within her skull he put other expectations for the second after lights on: spotless white rug, white velvet banquette-type sofas, huge stereo speakers, well-stocked bar, murals on the walls. He had seen a room like it, a basketball star's pad, in Ebony. He put Ivy outside his door, had her ring instead of use the key, had the door opened by a white maid got up like a Playboy bunny. A party was in progress, sleek black dudes and all white chicks.

He thought the one fantasy was as realistic as the other, if you went to the movies nowadays or watched the box. He didn't know if she did either one. She had been, in school, both the rich girl and the only one really interested in social reform. He recalled her dogged plain-spoken arguments in government class. She had been cool, logical, and unpopular. At times he had imagined that the two of them shared a sense of irony, a close tie never tested.

An outcast was waiting for him, had watched for him from the window of the hotel saloon—a janitor who never worked, was addicted to everything and had a walk like a hyena's. So much an outcast was he that if he had claimed to be one thing, color or creed, the other members would have jumped him and smeared him on the sidewalk for defaming them. If there was one germ he didn't carry in or on his body it was because there was no more room. Sidling down the porch steps he got to the point.

"I seen you give that white woman your keys. You can turn in your badge tomorrow." Said like an order, stained teeth bared in a cautious grin. Shit, Cayce thought, Ivy's given me the chance to off this mother. For he knew a little blackmail was about to be attempted. The creep never gave up, tried one scam after another the year long. This time the honkie was going to threaten to drop a dime—a white woman in the black cop's room in this town, in winter, was crueler than a sizable stash of snow; and the old traditional (honorable) stink would be raised, the great equalizer because they all squatted over the same pot. Cayce tested the balance of the nightstick. Mystical, the way its weight increased when it wanted to see some action.

The creep saw the slight movement and stood back. Cayce knew they were thinking the same thing—that it was easy to scare the man off but how did you stop his mouth? For once he was under the protection of an almost sure thing. There were two ways: counter-blackmail and death. But this side of death a good thing is hard to let go. The man, smelling his own blood, still made an offer: share the cunt with him, a threesome, huh Cayce? The nightstick defined momentum, gathered speed like a kid in a tire swing. A smell came out of the man, this was a night of smells. It was his corruption leaking like gas out of a bag, his letting go his scam like a fart. They always led you to it as though looking for praise. "In the toilet," the object said, "that one that don't work on the second floor? Down inside the tank. Nearly a pound. I got the only key." If a skull could drool his grin would have likened him to one. Death grinning at what is stripping his flesh away.

"Go on back in, man," Cayce said, handing the object a shred of identity that he would never be able to believe in; if he had ever been a man it must have been long ago. The grass was safe in the toilet. Having given the weight, the failed blackmailer would leave it there until Cayce came for it.

Back at the water—sometimes, even in winter, they poked up

176

from under the spilings like rats—throwing his beam down onto the barnacle-like ice, he found some gratitude for the encounter for it had taken his mind off Ivy, though she had been the reason for it. But here she was again and behind her all white woman-hood, and on top of all them, all black manhood. Somebody said that if there were not white women and no black men, America wouldn't have any problems. Right on! he said, appre-ciating it for the first time. She'd have Indians, baby, nothing but Indians. So he figured the wit had been a Native American. Like 'Negro,' you didn't say 'Indian' anymore. Then why not take a leaf from the Black book and go for color, simplify, call yourself 'Reds?' And the Orientals could become Yellows. Then Amer-ica—Blacks, Whites, Reds and Yellows—would sound like what it was, or was becoming: an arsenal of chemicals, of Downs and Ups, of Pills.

Taking a leak, he sent his mind to the room again where Ivy probably lay thinking about him. What if, by mutual consent, she stayed with him for longer than a night? The bathroom opened straight off the bedroom and had a door you couldn't close with a crowbar. What would she do, what would he do, about going, with that bathroom door cracking open and all the sounds and odors? He had never, not even in Vietnam where the women were as casual about crapping as kissing, heard a woman on a john. When his girl—what the hell, his Gook; in spite of being almost as black as he was she acted like a whitie—when she hiked up her skirt to squat, grinning at him, he always gave her a disgusted look and made tracks. Some delicacy for a soldier, right? He supposed it was because of his all-male upbringing that he wanted to think women were or should be something special. Which was why things like porno movies and hard core maga-zines with pictures of women giving head and spreading beaver, didn't just disgust him; they frightened him too. Who, exactly, was representative of real womanhood—the demure young lady in pigtails and white collar on her way to church, or the foul-mouthed hippie, or somebody's gospel singing mother, or the hard core bitch? Or Ivy Temple? What scared him and other men was that they might all be one and the same.

A man, unless he was a psychopath, was pretty consistent in what he was, whether he was black or white or red or . . . well, Gooks were treacherous so maybe Orientals didn't count. But

177

men stood by their prejudices, their loyalties, their dirty or clean minds and habits, and did it openly. But women. There was the possibility that under the white-collared and gloved church goer, the gospel singing mama, was the split beaver, the snake mouthed headgiver. Eve and Lilith. Two sides of the same betraying woman: the spare rib and the cooze.

Men go to work. Women, the wives and lovers of those men, go to visit other men in hospitals, in prisons, men they've been corresponding with, making love to in letters, sometimes for years. The men are in the hospitals and prisons because of other women, wives and lovers, who held out on them, or wanted too much; who wanted too much and held out until they got it. From the bed and the hearth and the house, paths run out, radiate in all directions with so many twists and turns that a jungle strategist would have trouble engineering the return trip. On the way to and from, so much has to be shed, feelings and ideas and needs, that it's like shedding clothes on the way down a hillside to a beach, clothes that the wind can pick up and blow away, so that, coming back, you're always minus something you started out with. Men and women, years and years together, might suspect but never really know the dimensions of the deepening gully between the beds, between the pillows, the easy chairs . . . between the hearth and the beach.

And so by such thought Cayce kept himself reasonably amused and his mind sometimes off Ivy until just before dawn he heard the abrupt and terrific clatter of the ice cutter attacking last night's growth of ice, beginning to clear the channel. Somehow, he couldn't think why, the sound was totally unexpected, the sound of his and Ivy's rescue, if you wanted to look at it that way. If he waited an hour longer, had coffee somewhere, hung out with the ferry crew, when he got back to his room he'd be able to tell her, what? Get up and get out? He could sit by the bed in the one chair and watch her sleep, gently rocking on his water bed. And when she woke up there he'd be and she'd let out a scream. Or hold out her arms and say "Fuck me, nigger."

He could not see himself rousing her and taking her out for coffee. There'd be too many questions about that, wherever he took her. Nor could he see himself just going in and having a bath, which was the way he always ended his beat. Her in bed, him naked, the door between that wouldn't close.

No matter how small the consideration, where a man and a woman are concerned everything is walking on eggs. Make that a black man and a white woman and you could multiply by infinity. Looked at that way, you came right back around to the old problem but with an edge of new understanding.

In school where he and Ivy had been at the top, one of the teachers had called them budding philosophers and he had been stupid enough to believe the woman. He began to see himself set apart, heading for some place high up, so high that it was out of the shit and toil, out of the race issues, and from that lofty place he observed, and then wrote and turned in to the favored teacher, a white middleaged woman, an essay that he still could quote to himself, word for word, any goddamned time he felt pretentious.

The white southerner's attitude toward the Black is an extreme example of the results of dividing man's nature into irreconcilable parts, which are called 'white' and 'Black' not only in the American South. To the white man, the Black had come to represent the worst part of himself according to his religion, which was his lust. If the Black and his brothers were given their freedom, freedom from censorship included, then it would be the same as freeing the worst part of himself, the part which he loathed and feared as well as, in his Black persona, desired and loved. If freed, that side would take over because of its superior strength. This superior strength was never doubted for he did not question that all others shared the Blackness that was precisely and metaphorically the base of his nature. The freeing of so much Blackness would be the end of civilization as the white man had strived to make it since the time when he realized that civilization would have to be the result of the suppression of the Black brute that inhabited each man from the waist down. Slavery was therefore symbolical in its most deeply psychological aspects— the caging of the brute—and the freeing of a slave was an extraordinarily disturbing act. Enforced mass-manumission was like the rape of the world.

On the top of the essay the teacher had written 'Manicheism.' In discussion she told him that to free himself from bondage he would have to learn to look at things from some perspective other than black. He told her the essay was written entirely from the white man's angle. She gave a social and distant laugh and told him, "Impossible." The one word. Going over his essay he found that she had changed all the capitalized Blacks to lower-case.

But it was what he had left out of the essay that the woman was afraid of: that the white man knew if his woman's true nature was set loose the world would turn out just as it had: women giving head in magazines, spreading beaver, screaming and falling down because some singer pushed his crotch in their faces; or, the latest thing, bragging publicly about being dikes. Whichever way they took, the white woman went hog wild.

And Ivy in his bed.

Except she wasn't. She must have been watching out for him because as he stepped onto the porch of his house she walked out the door, leather coat buttoned, tote bag swinging, holding out her free hand. She thanked him. She had had a nice rest in his bed, in his nice room. But to an old Island girl the sound of the ice cutter was like Gabriel blowing his trumpet. The sound, she said, of liberation. When he knew what she meant, why did that bother him?

He did not offer to walk her to the ferry.

As Saturday went slowly by Cayce thought about Ivy as he had with few pauses since 11:30 the night before, but the earlier thoughts had fluctuated among sarcasm, superstition, and, he saw now that she was gone, some concealed but real anticipation: that was the reason he had not let his imagination go beyond his arrival back at his room, or jumped from his arrival to her having been there for some time. What came just after he went in and found her, asleep or awake, in his bed would have been a virgin experience. And for all his antipathy to the idea there must have been some sexual wanting, or curiosity.

Pondering Ivy and himself, he began to take shots of whiskey early in the day, sitting by his window watching the snow fall. They were both twenty-eight years old, both scarred by experience, but she wore hers more openly. What could have tarnished her bright metal, that copper glow that she once had? Teachers said her looks pointed to Hollywood but her brain would land her in the cloisters of a University or a convent. He had heard them talking and then, because he and Ivy were scholastic equals, they would bring up his name and their voices would drop. What had they seen for him, where had his brain pointed?

To the cloisters of a prison? Because good looks on a black boy were probably a liability to start, setting him up for more attention of the wrong kind. A black boy should only aim at 'clean cut' as an ideal, if he could swing it, though he had heard Sugar Ray Robinson, surely a clean-cut man, described by a whitey as All American in a tone of disbelief followed by laughter. Cayce had kept out of trouble by ignoring such things and keeping as low a profile as he could. There was a statistic being handed around when Cayce was sixteen, having to do with the odds against a black youth's living to the age of twenty-one, and another purporting to show his chances of doing so without having been in jail at least once. The former odds were seventy-five to one; those having to do with jail varied but were considerably higher. He fashioned this information into an invisible talisman and wore it around his neck, imagining each escape, and some were extremely narrow, as a groove cut into the metal. He had the talisman still about him, a gruesome mental memento like something brought from Treblinka by a survivor who had notched the days into his own flesh.

When he came back from Vietnam, disaffected and definitely strung out though not, like most survivors, on drugs, he had wanted to prove something to his old teachers, to present himself as a survivor of more odds than even they had imagined, to flaunt himself. But when he got to the school he found it boarded up. Dissolved, disbanded, whatever the term was for the death of a school—to him it was a chunk of his past like an amnesiac's, gone.

Ivy had been so much on the side of what she called equity. Had she narrowed? Something had swiped her. Too much equity?

Thinking that tonight the ice would probably grow all the way to the Island, he got to a certain bitter feeling, as bitter as black ice secretly flourishing. He had been, somehow, rejected. In answer to his nasty question, "Are you looking to change your luck?" she had said, "Yes," and asked for his room. She knew what he meant, he knew what she meant, but when he got home the cupboard was bare.

He instructed himself, forcefully punctuating his words with fist in palm, that he had not wanted to fuck her. That all he wanted was to know what had happened between premise and conclusion. He drank, pondered, steering clear of the parodies of his earlier thoughts about Ivy in his bed. But when he steered clear of parody he lost out entirely, which showed him just how capable he was of putting himself inside the mind of a white woman. If she had been a criminal, or simply accused of a crime, he would have jumped in that skull with no trouble, a goldfish in a fishbowl, in his element. He felt that his affinity with the workings of the criminal mind was mystical. With scarcely any thought, employing only instinct, he could weed out from the law-abiding herd the sly lawbreakers on every hand. Faces behind windshields of moving cars told him about glove compartments stuffed with pot, heroin, LSD, expired permits, doctored registrations; leisurely passersby, sauntering windowshoppers, ruminative dogwalkers, communicated to him their real intentions, indicated just where under the bulky sweater the gun had been shoved behind the belt, or the knife; gestures unseen by others activated his X-ray vision.

When he came back from Vietnam where cynicism had made the GIs equivalent to street criminals, he got in his old Buick and drove. At his narrow end of the Island there was no hope of finding the open country he sought and he went afield looking for it: the country he thought, or had convinced himself, he had left. What he found was shopping complexes and motels grownout of deep concrete, one smelling of avarice, the other of illicit transactions, both smells too familiar from Saigon. To try to imagine grassland and ponds under that sprawl was impossible. He thought it was like psychosis, that mental dredging for nonexistent worlds, and felt that to keep doing so would carry breakdown the way an automobile carried timed obsolescence.

When Long Island ran out he took a ferry across open water to New London, drove for days on end, and at last realized that what he was doing was trying to reach the end of 'civilization' as he had come to recognize it: murder, arson, mayhem, rape, riot, all practiced among 'allies' in an undeclared war, the ugly range of human behavior stretching from misdemeanor through the larcenies to felony. He saw it as he had seen uncivilized Vietnam: mountainous, treacherous, with booby trapped foothills. The expression 'peak of civilization' carried for him the image of the gas chamber.

What he had planned as healing trips of a couple of hours a day ate up time and miles and he began staying over in the illicit-smelling motels, and in the morning would take off again, shooting radially from the town or city and drive until futility overcame him, looking for America, the Beautiful Non-existent, looking for a place where the echoes matched the echoes in the cave of his memory, or matched his desire. Looking back from 'Nam, he had come to believe that such a place not only was, but predominated, and was America. His America. Everybody in Saigon and the jungles was planning some kind of scam when they got back; they seemed to be trying to outdo each other in the scope and outright viciousness, at times, of their vengefulness, in return for the pieties mouthed by politicians and repeated in the newspapers, and the highly publicized lack of support for what many of them, for a while at least, had believed was necessary to preserve American democracy. He supposed his scam was to find a reason, any reason at all, not to join his fellows in ripping off the country that ripped them off; and fantasy was the only way he could do that.

One night he found himself on the edge of Harlem and went on in and found a room, his first time in what his uncles had called Nigger Heaven. The cool man who had fought in jungles and walked down foreign streets admitted, that night, that he was Small Town, that he was Country, because contrasted to Harlem, where he had been was no place.

But he would never share the experiences of that night with anybody. All he would tell anybody was that, that night, he became a cop. The only specific that he gave, reluctantly, to an auditor who insisted rather too much, was that sometime after midnight on a 'weird street' he hallucinated: barely visible at first on the edge of a dark doorway Ivy Temple making a drug connection. He said the glassine bag caught the light the way her red hair did. Then, some interchange of light-rays 'apprehended' her face and revealed the same features he had remembered unaltered except that they were 'hurt.' The articulate man clung to 'apprehended' and 'hurt' as the best words. And then, he said, the eerily lit picture went out as though a switch had been flicked.

He had a dream that night in the Harlem hotel (behind a

heavily barricaded door) that stayed with him in small detail. He used the dream from time to time as a kind of yardstick, mostly against which to measure despair.

He dreamed that he woke to a morning as soft as a keyhole threat. Low clouds cut the city in half, making of it a village of uniform buildings, slicing progress off at the half-way mark. The tower-hives above the fog had no more reality for him than the land-filled ponds, the weighted meadows. To try to imagine the hundreds of thousands of people working above the clouds was to hurt the mind.

He dreamed that he drove out of the city, deliberately observing only the printed directives having to do with speed and other matters governed by law and soon enough he reached a welcome state of disorientation. If he suspected that the river was on his left he would contrive to convince himself that it was on his right, and emerging from a fog-bound pass and finding that it really lay on his right was a triumph of mind over matter, for with the river on his right he should have been heading into the city but was not, the increasing wildness of the terrain advising him of that and no more, for there were no signs or billboards, or, as far as he could see, houses.

The road was good, an unpatched gentle curve along the river, and soon he had it to himself. In a thirty minute stretch he passed one pickup truck and rode for five minutes behind a red-flagged vehicle carrying a load of telephone poles glistening with oil. Pulling ahead of it he told himself that he was leaving communication behind him.

The road rose up and up and then began a long descent that seemed disproportionate; if he had begun at sea level, and had judged the ascent with reasonable accuracy, then, he told himself, the only logical end of his steady decline was Hell.

He pulled up at a neat little landing hung with curtains of fog and waited, unanxious, for ten minutes or so until a rush of water against spilings announced the ferry. Its size hinted at the island's smallness. A question to the ferryman could have settled the matter but he was unwilling to have names and statistics infringe on the true sense of freedom in which he was finally wallowing like a hog in good clean cool mud: what greater freedom could a man ask for than to have his mind clean of 'facts?' These were surely the essence of leavings, of 'small particles broken away from the mass.' And then the definition, that he had seen written out on the fog, detritus of his education, was sucked away by some current, a funnel to the mind.

Land unrolled under the lifting fog, trees grew slowly into woodlands, pocket-mirrors of brightness opened into inlets, canals, and harbors. Houses were sparse, and old. Even the paved roads were modestly paved, patched like quilts, and there were a good number of grass grown lanes and rutted bouldered roads that only wagons could negotiate. No sign anywhere carried a place name. When he wound up on the business street the plain signs were simple surnames: Taylor's, Wainwright's, Wheeler's. And there was a Whaler, marine supplies, he guessed; and a Catboat—bar and restaurant. A service station, no name, with a newspaper rack, empty, outside the door, and the now-glittering harbor brought the street to an end. Nothing said WELCOME TO or YOU ARE NOW LEAVING. No speed limit was posted nor were there warnings of any kind; deer crossings were known and did not have to be staked out. Therefore it was a place that expected no strangers. He could imagine that directional lights were never used on automobiles because 'everybody knows I turn off there.'

He recognized it as a place of familiar habits where quotations over supper tables made personages of everyone: "Bill was saying today;" "Tom swore he'd never seen anything like it;" "Emmy was sounding off about it down at the store." Animals shared: "Old Smoke chased that buck clean on back to the sand pit." If there were two people of the same first name the context of the quote would serve as identification; surnames were never used. Cayce thought he remembered this and a deep sentiment cozied him like fire on an open hearth.

The image of fire spoke to him of food, of clams and lobsters and boiling broth and salty crackers, and beer not too iced up to kill the taste. He parked his car in front of the Catboat and went in.

He ate chowder, clams and potatoes in equal proportion in a heavy creamy sauce with a bowl of rendered salt pork on the side, and drank beer and listened to the small talk of the hunting season beginning in a week, and the unseasonably warm January, and savored the lack of hostility in the eyes of the dark-blond men as they surveyed him from time to time, letting their eyes rest on him in mid-remark as though including him if he wanted to be included. A fire on an immense hearth exploded softly now and then as flames found secret pockets of resin in the aromatic wood; bursts of piney odor laced the barroom like stout in ale, adding to the savor of the day, of the dream of fulfilment which he somehow knew was a dream: they were all white men and he was reluctant to look at his own skin, at his hand, afraid he would find that it too was white. But it was not, and the easefulness was real, and he drifted in and out of contentment that was like bordering sleep, which finally became a deep drowsiness and he moved from his barstool to a chair near the fire. The murmurs of the masculine room were a peculiarly male lullaby and Cayce, asleep and dreaming, fell asleep in his dream.

He came out of the double sleep to see a small figure that he took at first to be a child racing through the room, murmuring breathlessly, a combination of greeting and apology, and just before she disappeared into the galley she gave Cayce a full-face look, electrifying: a face like a cat's with large wanting eyes; a whore's eyes in the little face under the fringe of red bangs. What followed was underscored visibly like printed words: the quiet masculine room was all at once charged with aggression and unrest and so slight a thing as Cayce sitting up from his slumped position and looking around him, nose sniffing at the difference, turned all eyes on him and the eyes had changed, had become narrowed, suspicious, resentful. It was as if in his sleep within the dream he had been picked up and set down in some other place, or that the room had turned inside out and was showing its lining, its own antithesis.

The dream ended there with him in that room. As if dreaming it had settled his prolonged dream about America, it also settled his searching for it and he went back to Greenport and took the necessary steps to becoming a cop. The main result of dream and search seemed to have been that his cynicism had settled into a groove, where 'peak of civilization' meant gas chamber.

From the look of Ivy, she would not have been able to tell him that her experience had been so different, whatever banner she had marched under, whatever cause taken on for a minute or two. She was roughened, coarsened, on dope, and had come back to the old homestead in disgust and bone weary, to die.

Seeing twilight outside his window Cayce sat up suddenly as though called. What? Come back to *what?* and relaxed. He had confused her with himself, confused her return with his own and the dream that set 'closed' to a bigger one. He had survived, a fine paradox, had survived himself and the death of the dream by crawling inside himself, making a burrow out of himself and just crawling down in there and becoming the inner animal. If she did not know that technique of survival he could hand it to her as a gift, if they met again.

As darkness dropped over him like a net, the speeded-up end of the day like a criminal's ruse, so did the conviction that Ivy had come back to die; had meant, an inspiration of the moment, to do the trick in his room, but that part could be very deep and he would think about it later, about what happened once she was in his room to stop her. Maybe it was something as simple as sleep. But his cop's instinct for people made him riffle back through all the impressions he had had of her since her arrival when she, glazed eyed, tried to deny knowing him. That glaze was not, as he had thought at first, from grass; it was the half-dead-already look of somebody condemned; self-condemnation carried the same face in its pocket like a mask to slip on when the time of execution arrived.

The ferry ride to the Island would be slow because the channel was closing its vise on the boat. The pilot, an Italian, would tell Cayce it was like pushing the boat through polenta, then with a grin would change that to 'grits.' Three-quarters of the way across, the snow would become sleet and by the time Cayce, the only automobile to make the crossing, rolled off the ferry, the hill he would have to climb would rise before him like a slope of glass. With nobody to observe or challenge him he would cut across lawns and tack back and forth and make it to the top taking a couple of KEEP OFF signs with him.

Behind him the hill houses would be silhouetted against the sky faintly lit by the town across the harbor. Other houses would loom behind street lamps, fanciful summer houses with intricate masses, like things roused from hibernation by the arrival of the Black Stranger.

Crossing the canal at the foot of the slope he heard the heavy water receiving heavy sleet. It sounded like foliage being strafed. Passing the saloon, the Catboat, beyond the wavery freezing pane he saw a red head, as rare in this place of blondes as it would be in Africa. He slid to a stop and positioned himself so that he could watch through the inadequately serving wipers, looking for her among the flickering motions of pool and dart players and people moving in front of the blazing fire. The double distortion of windshield and saloon window made the scene resemble a bad print of a movie.

Here niggers were not welcome after dark. But wasn't that Dan Coon, as they called him (and he put up with it), the Island's one, determined-survivor black man, bending over the pool table? He lived and fought and fucked here in spite of the citizenry and answered their bigotry by laying their women and the summer girls who, according to Dan Coon, came back just because he was there. About the name he said, "Let the motherfuckers have that much. I get all the rest." Fucking white, as he called it—yelling out to Cayce in passing, especially if there was a white person nearby, "Fucking white tonight, babe"—was not just a pleasure; it was a duty and definitely a political act. When you're in politics, Dan bragged, you've got to reach all the people one way or another. He figured that by fucking their women, many of them, he got to their men, every man honkie of them. If Dan Coon saw Ivy he would nail her to the floor before she knew what was happening.

Cayce gets out of his car. The sleet, hovering above the trees like a chopper, bears down for the capture, swinging ladders as heavy as chains that touch his ducking head just before he makes it to safety. Or to what would have been safety in a democracy. Because just inside the door his undemocratic impulse to flatten himself against the wall like a black cat is pure instinct. Up the line of the bar and to the left the dartplayers pivot in slow motion, the weighted tools of the game quivering in their palms. The mirror on the right, a long ribbon tinted blue, is like a thin mural of living swiveling eyes. A man coming out of the john pauses in the process of buttoning up, wondering about the wisdom of sheathing his one weapon. Behind his back Cayce can imagine the pool players hanging suspended over the table, their cues taking aim at his spine. He tries to let coolness grow from his center like an iceplant, the way he had learned growing up and perfected in 'Nam. But sweat breaks out on his head in drops that feel so big and hot it is as if his pores are being reamed with fire. He turns to leave and the bartender's voice cracks like a rifle: "Yeah? You want somethin' "? The sound, the impudence, hands Cayce back his cool. He turns around, an arrogant nigger cop who carries a big stick and knows how to use it. He runs his eyes over the honkie, very slowly, rejecting what he sees the way he would reject garbage crawling with slugs. Feeling the air heat up with so much hate barely contained, he becomes Mr. Iceberg.

Grating a little the way an iceberg would, he says, "I believe—" slow, bemused—"that you know me." The bartender's face has known him since he came in the bar but he pretends, walking down a few steps and pepping at Cayce like something hiding in the bush. He wants so much to say "Naw, I don't know you niggah" that it is almost sad. If he could just bring himself to do that it would set them all up for the night, neuter the storm, light up the joint. After Cayce had gone they could buy each other drinks and slap backs and harmonize and take pisses together, sloshing and laughing. But on the other side of the water Cayce is a cop with a certain . . . reputation . . . and they all know about it, all see him on his own turf too many times a week, and he watches them give up their dream. The bartender says, as distantly as he dares to, that, yes, he does know him—Scott, isn't it? and Cayce waits, giving off some bad vibes, until the man, losing all of his fat face to the barroom floor, changes that to "Officer Scott" and Cayce acknowledges that he, is, indeed, himself. . . .

Sitting in his room in the dark he watched on his window faintly lit by streetlights the dispersal of his kiddish fantasy, his rescue mission, watched as the back of Officer Cayce Scott wavered and separated at the spine, broke apart and disintegrated in slow motion while the patrons stood shocked and still. One shoulder and its blade seemed to ride up the pane, the other and its arm and elbow slid down and away on runnels of thaw: a brave man gone like his pipe dream.

Who, he asked himself, had that been for, that big nigger act? He had even given the Island bar the name of the bar in his long-ago dream, The Catboat. The child-woman in that sleep fantasy had been redheaded too, like Ivy, and had a whore's face. He tried to recall: did Ivy have a whore's face, last night, this morning, so soon? But found that he could not remember how she looked at all, could see her only as she had been when he last saw her at sixteen. And his failure to recall how she looked seemed like rejection of her, and should have balanced the scale for him—one rejection for another; but all it did was make him sad.

He had not taken a drink for, probably, a couple of hours, judging by the density of the night, and a thick hangover was setting in. He tried to gauge how much of his anxiety, very real, a short time back, about Ivy's having come home to commit suicide had kept pace with the lowering level in his Scotch bottle, one inch from the bottom now, full when he started in on it. If he had actually gone over there and found her, not dead but alive and sooty from coping with clogged chimneys and bad-tempered to boot, what would he have said to her? She would have seen his concern as a cover-up for the rip off of that pussy she had denied him earlier. Was she right?

He tried to imagine them, then, as man and woman engaged in the old struggle, tried to let his mind out full on the scene: a red-headed woman in his bed, him standing beside her naked then crawling in, the first touchings of their skins, the quick breath, the trembling, the tongues, the entrance, the movements, the words, other sounds. But somebody, some fucker, said 'love' and ruined it for him, made ugly scratches on the smooth scene. That word would go from his mouth, if it ever did, into the mouth of a woman with lips more like his and skin more like his and into his ear only from that red-black mouth. No hair would spread on a pillow below him from the head of a woman he truly spoke love to but would rise strong and crisp out of her skull, crinkly and tight as the head on a good chrysanthemum. Then when everything was copasetic, to use an old word, 'love' could be said and the old bells could ring out.

Telephone in the hall, bells ringing into his fourth or fifth fantasy of the day. Landlady at the door. Phone for him. "My, I haven't seen you all day," then "Whew," just partly playing, at the smell of his passing breath. A speculative look at him before she closed the door and left him with the telephone. And Ivy.

"—to thank you so much. Cayce. Cayce?"

Still here. Bad connection.

190

"—copied the number down this morning, wondering why exactly. You know. Why should Cayce want to see me again? But just in case."

Thought about you too. Wondered if you were o.k. Glad you called, Ivy.

"—Cayce? Don't go just yet. Where. You said. Where *were* you? Away?"

He understood. A kind of apology. He told her. Vietnam.

"—Yes. I was kind of involved. Against—"

He didn't say, I know. (Where were you, Ivy? But didn't ask that either.) Liquor pounding in his head like the Sound under their conversation that faded under static, came in strong. Disconcerting.

Let's talk? he asked her and thought she had faded, the silence went on for so long.

In a while she said, "—but no—important—questions? You know?"

Just voluntary info, Ivy. And felt relief too. He felt her going and asked, Where you calling from?

The connection went bad or she mumbled. He asked, Bar? and told her on a bad impulse, I saw you there, in there, tonight.

"WHAT?"

Would he go on and tell her she was talking to a visionary cop? Decided not to and asked again where she was calling from.

"Merry Death." His heart jumped. Then she said, very clear, "Old friend of Grandmother's."

In his relief he asked, Did you get the fires going? and astounded himself with the overly friendly, overly relaxed, almost sentimental tone of voice. He nearly hung up before she could reply. But her instincts were o.k. She said, tough enough, "An old boy scout like me?" What she gave to 'boy scout' was clear; he could see her scouting.

"I can start a fire with two *anything,*" and her emphases said *and I got 'em.*

She let him go with the liberating image of her rubbing together two big crusty nipples, shooting sparks into a pile of paper and kindling wood.

Later that night, with the one sympatico whore in Greenport for his money, because there had been too much about sex all day to go without, in mid-stroke he began to laugh and told her why, though not that the nipples were on white tits, and she laughed too, even as they began to come together. It was late and she liked him and he didn't ask for it on the house; and she contracted with such vigor that she kept him up for yet another time around before they slept.

An uncle had told him a long time ago, when he was barely old enough to grab at the meaning, "Scotty, marry a woman that can cry but fuck one that can laugh." Knocking on sleep's door like a polite kid he asked again just what the real message had been meant to be. The part about a woman who could cry was plain enough—a compassionate wife, forgiving, long-suffering; she'd need to be, the implication ran, married to a swinger like me, and she would be tender with the kids. But the rest: that sex was funny, too? Not many people seemed to know that. The morbid ones that didn't know it made trouble, and starting from that premise and looking around at all the trouble because of sex, you got at just how few people knew that laughter was hot enough to cauterize the morbid matter out of sex. That was one meaning. But had Uncle Will meant, marry a woman that can do both, or, don't marry the woman you like to fuck?

The question was the kid's and not the man's. A private matter between him and himself, between the boy and the man. He wondered if the whore too thought kid thoughts on the edge of sleep, to allow her to incorporate or forget what society called her transgressions, so that she could pass on through the doors and have dreams without a dick in them, something she had to clean like a raccoon cleaning food before she would put it in her. Dreams without dirt and medicine and periodic check-ups and periods of blood.

The men killed in line of duty in Vietnam. The men he could kill in line of duty as a cop. The citations society allowed for those murders.

Only by retreating back to where he had not understood fully what his Uncle Will meant could he manage sometimes to make sleep at all, to slip in before the doors snapped shut, just another set of doors closing in his black face. Sometimes he managed to dream without blood, to dream about trees without leaves ragged from strafing, about kids playing without napalm roasting their hides while their mothers ran and screamed. And all the murdered men and screaming women and kids had skins his

192

own end of the spectrum. Niggers and gooks, bloodkin. Man, why did I do it.

You clutch but you can't catch hold of it, ahold of that moment when whatever had been planted there bloomed in your brain. You try to trace a thin line back through the past, the faintest trail blazed in the jungle, to what could be termed 'the beginning.' You try to see yourself at whatever age, free of all of it, of white and black talk, of any brainwashing whatever, and what you get every time for your hard brain busting effort is heavy sweat pouring off you, soaking the bed, because you can't see that far back, and you are longsighted, man, can see the flies on the shithouse wall when you were less than one year old and being held over the stinking hole by somebody laughing. Can see farther back than that, can see *her* looking in your face and murmuring, you in the crook of her arm, dinner just finished, her fingers plucking at your dress. When you start to grow up they call the brainwashing education; and if you are particularly bright they send you to a special school for very special brainwashing; otherwise your brain might survive them, might have independent thoughts that forge independent actions. You might find out a way not to fall in line. The dude used language like smoke. If I had made a wrong move, asked a wrong question, he could've blown it all away like a smoke ring. One direct question would have done it. Now I'm not saying that that's the first time I've heard the brainwashing while it was going on but it was that really weird thing, something non-existent existing. Better still, something, some thing, that can be in seven places at one time. Microscopic, subliminal. Casual talk up front, laidback, and under there that current, that real voice handing me what could be a life or death version of the old 'shape up or ship out.' A line of graft is what I gather, a set-up of shadowy cousins, all cops, the hierarchy reaching to the very top, to the Commissioner and probably the Mayor, but with smoke talk how the fuck can you tell. The dude himself was a Detective Lieutenant. Black dude. They knew their man, knew I wouldn't even listen to a white man murmuring, plucking at my dress. Sorry mama, but I felt that helpless. We'd just finished eating too. Laid a meal on me, the doubletalking motherfucker. Talked about guys willing to stay on the beat for life, guys who might not have lives all that long to spend walking a beat. And this under-voice began to come through. Asked me midway if I thought there was such a thing as an honest cop, laughing with a toothpick stuck in his teeth. Old Cayce Cool smells the trap in there, smells death in there, and says "Hows about a dead one?" and the dude knows he's been apprehended, got the cuffs on the mother, and it's a good time and a bad time, a bad time because I'm calling him dishonest and a good time because . . . because he's proved again, to himself and all of 'em, that there's no such thing as an honest man. Shit, motherfucker, I didn't crawl in that shit in Vietnam to come back to you, I didn't belly down through all that crap of my whole life to. To. Well, Scott, there's your future dilemma. And there's the past, stereo and bloody technicolor, screams and blood. Take your pick. Some choice you fuckedup ratshit motherfucking goddamned God. Damn. World.

His present. The woman's leg over him. He pulls it closer. She is breathing heavily, a tired overworked sound to which he had contributed his bit by busting an extra nut. Wilfully he thinks about her muscular pussy and big mouth and strong flat black stomach that could hold and push out when the time came a strong kid, a survivor like herself. Like him. He thinks about her cheerfulness when he sees her in the streets and her big laugh that she is always ready to let loose. Uncle Will would have said, Right on, Scott! about the bitch in his bed.

Grateful to have made it through the fear once more, in a friendly vein after so much effort, he changed 'bitch' to 'lady' like all the dudes on television talkshows nowadays referring to their live-in whores as 'my lady' this and 'this lady I live with' that. It was worth the brainwashing commercials just to dig it, to savor the bittersweetness of the fucking of America, the public fucking of America. What you hear ain't America singing, man, it's America fucking, two and threes and mores, white on black on white . . . male . . . female . . . male . . . male . . . male . . . right?

But right now it was black on black, rare combination in a dying world. Winnie's leg on his felt good in the cold night. Her mound, which some pervert had paid her to shave while he watched, was nakedly warm on his thigh. And the bittersweetness of his thoughts cracked the doors of sleep telling him that it was all so bad—the bloody misguided past, the future when he would have to become a criminal or die—all of it was so bad that he had a right to sleep without anxieties, an unassailable paradox.

And (he said the whore's name was not Winnie) just before he slept it came to him why Ivy was so much around edging his thoughts no matter how remote like a picture frame. As he was going through those goodly doors he wondered whether a black man and a white woman could ever be friendly, could laugh enough together to cauterize the morbidity. It came to him how often he had used her image to counter something over the years, in 'Nam especially; that since schooldays she had been another kind of talisman for him, but so close to his thoughts that she had disappeared in a way. He wondered if she might possibly have used him that way, or suspected it about him. He bet she did. Bet that that was one reason she had not waited for him in his bed.

Inside the doors of sleep, watching the light disappear as mama carried the lamp with her, he was conscious enough to know that he felt good.

Reading in my presence my feverish sloppily written speculation about her re-meeting with Cayce Scott, Ivy was subdued. Once or twice she lifted her eyes to mine, which must have been eager, hopeful, perhaps frightened, and gave me looks which were both puzzled and oddly darkened: that look that can be passionate or disillusioned, when the eyes appear inwardly shadowed, the pupils in a state of eclipse, as though heartbreak or desire were an inward moon. . . . The gist of this thought I suppose is that our two strongest emotions have sharp shapes, like discs; and some children collect them like fireflies in jars, to be opened over the years.

When she had finished she only said that the story interested her as a story and she would like to read more of it. Should I, I asked her, show it to Cayce? and she weighed my hunger and said if I would have a copy made of it she would perform that office. And so she did, depriving me of the chance to watch the man read what, for all I could know, he would take as a vindictive act: so much fuck-talk, and the sort of subordinate position he assumed, in spite of me, by becoming the seeker after Ivy's reality (as I assumed, more willingly, the subordinate position in seeking his 'reality').

But what came back with the manuscript—though I had gone on writing in the interim and had more to show by the time I received it back—was a diagram and some scribbled words. I reproduce them here precisely as they are, with Cayce's corrections of my terminology ('cousin,' it seems, is not a cop but a gambler). This is an authentic document.

Division
Dep. Insp.
|
2 Lieuts.
|
18 Patrolmen

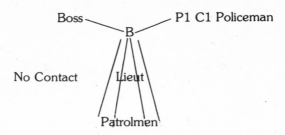

First 2 mos in division cop is not approached. Then when he is, if he says no, he is bounced out. Paper work takes three mos. Man has been patrolman for five mos.

Deal betw cop and gambler = contract
gambler = cousin

Chief of Detectives
↑   ↓
Precinct Captain
↑   ↓
Patrolman

After convocation* Patrolman is made Det. Third Grade and assigned to Chief Inspector's Confidential Invest. Unit.

*This word not verified. Cayce's handwriting indistinct here.

Since I received this cryptogram from Cayce Scott several months have passed, and there have been many revelations in the press concerning graft and corruption in copdom. But I have not attended them too closely; if what Cayce showed me, or tried to, has now been shown to the public, this verification will simply bolster it; if not, then it is probably dangerous to reader as well as to writer and informant.

As of this evening, this writing, Cayce is still a patrolman—not, I am happy to say, a Detective Third Grade assigned to the Chief Inspector's Confidential Investigative Unit.

Cayce and Ivy established a habit of talking on the telephone once a week, Ivy calling from a pay phone until the troublous line to the old house had been replaced and she had her own telephone. Then, they spoke just about anytime one of them felt like it, for whoever called was certain of a welcome; so the assumption is that they both felt like communicating all or most of the time.

But they did not see each other. Neither crossed the ferry for any reason. Winter melted noisily, icy rivulets running down the steep Island slopes, and blocks of ice, sometimes with animals isolated on them, swirled and collided in the Bay and the Sound. In the harbors there was a steady noise of regeneration as spilings and bulkheads and ferry slips were replaced. Marinas led independent boisterous lives of their own as 'Spindrifts' and 'Idas' and 'Sea Sprites' received facelifts, and a sizeable yacht, the 'Allos Ego,' displayed her beautiful skeleton in the boatyard. Then before anyone had had time to notice the transition, trees were budding along the shores on the Island side and leafing out, and the great display of weigela and bridal wreath that ran up the Island hills in pink and red and white profusion could be seen from the mainland as though composed of broad neon strips, so steady was the glow under sun and moon.

Cayce, still on his nightbeat, feeling the slowing pulse of life as the air grew warmer, would stand sometimes gazing across the dreamy bay to the light hung at the tip of the ferry slip and with the sprawling 'mansion' of Greenport sleeping behind him, he would think of himself as Gatsby, with Ivy, most of the time, as Daisy Buchanan, though on occasion when her whiteness or negative side predominated in his thoughts, she would become Jordan Baker who cheated at golf.

A black Gatsby? Why not? Black literature does not dangle any such romantic simpletons for a moonstruck guy to emulate; yearning across silvery water to the far away sound of jazz, no man is going to want to think about Bigger Thomas. And Gatsby, like Cayce at that time, was the passive center around which violence swirled, the eye of the hurricane.

One night well into spring when the full moon preposterously lit the air and water and laid a burlesque runway across the already brilliant stage of the Bay, Cayce saw someone, inevitably, waving, a white arm and hand and a streamer of white cloth, too big to be a handkerchief; a chiffon scarf; and behind that the glimmer of white dress and faint blur of face around which he supplied the nimbus of red hair. How often, he asked her silently, had she stood as he stood, looking across water bright and dark, wondering about him in speculations that edged into the metaphysical?

In their telephone conversations a high place was always given to banter, for it was as if they were practicing so that when they met there might be ease in the male/female repartee that the black/white visual aspect could no longer affect. They were like two people who fall in love through writing letters, so deeply that when they finally meet no degree of deformity in one or both can demand more than passing notice.

(In the typescript of this section, that last sentence is strongly marked out and I know it was Cayce, not Ivy, who censored, though I can imagine her pencil hovering uncertainly over the concluding image—deformity etc., wondering if it is a racist remark. For my own reasons I am over-ruling Cayce as I have done in other sections of censorship, the sole despotism I can ever practice with this terrific independent man.)

Watching the semaphoring arm across the water, not yet returning the signal, in doubt about what the message should be, Cayce said he had a double image-impulse, one fitting perfectly over the other: to answer Ivy's wave by shooting off his gun, and to row her across the Bay in a canoe, the two of them hearing the distant sound of the pistol shots, far, distinct, then the slow reverberant rolling of the air's reaction along the horizon, like time grinding to a halt before reversing.

The image was complex, based on Island history: the first inhabitants of the manor house, a planter and his wife, would send their daughters off to church on the mainland in slave-rowed canoes, and pistol shots heralded both departures and arrivals, signals that the girls had not been raped and mutilated.

It seemed to me that within the confines of the imagery, for the space of a heart tick, Cayce had stopped being both a Black and a man and I see this as a triumph for him, and as the moment of genesis, the beginning of the end in the matter of a solution.

He waved back to Ivy, they waved and waved in the moonlight, and in a day or so one or the other made the trip and they were together again. CAYCE'S BACK AND IVY'S GOT HIM.

The best way to get out of doing anything, thinks Cayce, is to say, "I can't" and the best way to present impotence is with foresight, to bring it up and establish it before another says "Will you." And that is what he does. He and Ivy make a little excursion out to Orient Point—the old hotel was still standing then and serving lunch—and it is over the coldcuts, appropriately, that he alludes to war and wounds and slyly works in a reference to Jake Barnes, placing all these in such juxtaposition to himself that Ivy's eyes widen, then lower to hide pity or whatever ('disappointment' may be included only parenthetically); and Cayce said that in the faint flush of color rising and receding in her face he saw that her youth could be, was being, restored.

He had no way to judge if he was being a martyr or a heel, performing a gallant act or insulting her. But finding out something was more important to him than getting something off, and there was a beautiful paradox in his thought that Ivy was his woman because the possessive was devoid of possession, in the diabolical and American sense—the possession that equals obsession. He also felt smart, really savvy and slick, for having found the one single way to discover if a man and a woman could be friends. By the time the flaws in such reasoning were becoming apparent, he was enjoying life to such an extent that he believed he should back off, but didn't.

For all the things Cayce and Ivy did together in that splendid spring and summertime, substitute a memory of your favorite montage of happiness from a forties movie, with perhaps here and there a bit of up-dating, but no more than an overtone to the: horses, bicycles, hampers, sailboats, motorboats, ferry boats, stout climbing boots and sticks, bikinis, convertibles; a trampoline; a puppet show at the end of a pier (black Punch, white Judy); a shooting gallery—and here one hastens to mention rifles and stuffed toys, though the aura that day of another kind of shooting gallery deepens Ivy, perhaps, and is heavy enough to make Cayce recall his glimpse on a nighttime Harlem street of a red-haired woman dealing in a doorway, and each thinks, for a moment, how difficult it is to learn anything about a lover during a montage, at the end of which waits either a painful goodby or an altar; and in these scenes the wind often streams her hair back and often there are glittering drops of rain on his impervious poll; and if you require it, place around them the screwed-up visages, not just white, of town and country people, like the astounded faces in ancient paintings, gazing at something we cannot see, at beatitude.

And if you have to have it to allow these scenes of sweetness to stay unburnt on the page, let there be some faces with mouths open as in Munch's 'Scream.' It could be that that would be the accurate depiction, the one detail, the one Americanness, to let you know this isn't happening in some Scandinavian country. (Calvin said that what those girls, those Swedes and Danes and Norwegians wanted was a 'New Yawk niggah' for their first night in the U.S. His, if I recall, hungry blonde was named Ingrid.)

One day a severe storm, a white squall for which those waters are famous, caused them to put in at East Marion, by the causeway; the ketch they were sailing had its mizzenmast broken off by the sudden swooping wind that brought with it a drop in temperature of twenty-five degrees in fifteen minutes. To find safe shelter for themselves they had to break into a house and to dry out they had to strip and share a blanket before the fire. Did they not? No romance is complete without a version of this and in their case there would be a special poignancy and one would very much want to have a close-up, especially, of Ivy's expression, to study it with the camera as though that instrument were a microscope, for only under those circumstances and given the added condition of her prolonged celibacy could we be assured of her palingenesis. That it occurred is without a doubt; that is the miracle. That Cayce was her savior is also without doubt for she led me, and I led you, to him. That the instrument of his Godman-like offices to her was not his cock has been, somehow, indicated by both of them, though it must be said that she was not restored by its withholding, either, for then the tool of her salvation would still be that one and I can't believe anybody was ever cured by sexual deprivation, which will prevent the spread of syphilis but hardly purify the blood.

If Ivy's obsession was a disease, compared to which nymphomania would be a surface itch, it was a disease already cultured in withholding and denials and directives, a virulent spread far beyond the reach of inoculations, which otherwise is one

202

way we could look at Cayce's pose of impotency: as a hair of the dog. So what I have, finally, is a mystery, the fathomless mystery of a man and a woman and I cannot penetrate it, and am too embarrassed to try any longer.

The day of the storm they were sailing back from a visit to the Island, where Ivy had introduced Cayce to her grandmother's old friend, Meredith. It had been in the nature of a command performance, for Meredith could still be very grand and issue directives as though all around her were her old business managers to be browbeaten and otherwise intimidated. Something about her encouraged obeisance and obedience, in her old age as in her youth when she had been the youngest concert pianist in the world.

That year Meredith was seventy-nine years old. When I met her six years later she was as tough and resilient as a peach-tree switch, and as capable of cutting through the flesh. Staying with her in the big Island house, a fortress to which many aspired and few were admitted, was her niece, Catherine, or, as the girl amended the introduction, "Your great-great-great niece." Cayce stared at the girl who was as small as a child, his eyes so mesmerized that all three women, Ivy, Meredith, and Cat, felt the current like electricity and were silent. Meredith ended the moment peremptorily, putting herself back in the spotlight through superior willpower, and assessed Cayce in a distinctly personal manner, as though gauging whether any of his individual parts could be of use to her.

Nothing is being copped-out on as we segue to Meredith and Cat, for Cayce is still in the picture and where he is, Ivy is. At this moment—of the story, not of the writing—he has not yet suspected that Ivy, in a slim and radiant person, as reborn as a Phoenix, was everything he hated including the dope addict and the criminal. Still, no need to spell it all out. Sometimes it's best to bow low before the worst has been said and withdraw, for farce can be the hidden overpainted companion of explicitness, jumping out at moments of Truth and dangling a big blubbery tongue.

But later that day, wrapped in the same blanket with Ivy, Cayce may have told her his reason for staring at Catherine, at her small whore face and cat eyes, at her child-like stature: that aside from the color of her hair, she was the girl of his dream whose entrance into the bar, that was called—he must have said with the exclamation point—The Catboat!, terminated his dream of America. He may have said that he was frightened to see her, as scared as though she were his own death; that, nerves standing on end, he had stood there before her wondering how his fate and hers might become entwined.

But given the circumstances, Ivy would then need and want to soothe him out of his fear, smooth it from his knotted muscles that gleamed in the firelight and with the wick of her tongue draw it from his mouth into hers where love transforms poison into cleansing heat. But this would of course end the Paul et Virginie idyll precipitately, and in a very penetrating manner.

Meredith, like her niece, was a tiny woman, so economically made that there was hardly any excess flesh for age to tug at and wrinkle, though her comparatively bulky shoulders, when one saw her without the shawls she favored, gave her the appearance of having a dowager's hump. If she caught you looking at her back and shoulders she would snap at you, "Muscle!" and prove her agility by banging herself on the back with her hard little hand that could stretch and span ten notes.

It took a feat of the imagination to connect her with the portrait of her by Sargent, which was the route you had to take to make a connection between her and the photographs on the chimneypiece of Chaliapin, who had been her professed lover (the profession was hers), by whom she had a child. She met him, she said, when she was eighteen and he was forty-nine. Three years later she bore him a son. Never mind that the biographies failed to make even a mention of her, much less of their child. "They did not consult or interview me" was her dignified response, and her large flexible mouth would become prim with the effort to hold in further observations.

In 1944, when World War II was at its peak, she would have been forty-nine herself. She traveled tirelessly, one gathered from the clippings, playing concerts 'in places that even the dead should fear,' to quote a magazine article of the time. The same article cites her on musical matters and personalities. She knew Scriabin and said of him, "He was a little thin man, a bit off." She told the interviewer, who wrote that she and Josephine Baker were the two most glamorous women the writer had ever interviewed, "Russians won't use the sonata form. Too European for them." And, "Americans go to the opera, to concerts, but they aren't really moved by music. Most of it is European and Slavonic, written out of identification with one country. Americans have many countries but no identification with one, and there isn't any American music except Ives."

The reporter, who admitted that this riled her, asked Meredith, "What about jazz? What about Ellington?" Meredith shrugged and snapped, "Beyond my competence" and continued as though no interruption had occurred. "Ives was a towering figure in many ways but the humor of his music spoils it eventually." "Why?" asked the reporter, perhaps to prolong the interview, and received a reply so emphatic that she had it set in italics to convey Meredith's passion. *"Great music must obsess us. When humor obtrudes, obsession must go."*

The article ends with apparent irrelevancy, "As she violently gestures you notice that in the hollows of her skin the color is of old meerschaum."

Meredith was nine years old when she played her first major concert, in Vienna. When the family got to New York from Georgia, Meredith's mother discovered that she was pregnant and would not go any further. As Meredith's father elected to stay with his wife, Meredith traveled alone across the ocean. She was even then what she came to refer to as 'a tough cookie' and old letters from managers and other people on the business end of that first concert tour bore her out. She would display these letters gleefully for she kept them on hand, on her square grand piano, along with the marked-up personally revised sonatas and concerti and two enormous tattered scrapbooks of her most laudatory reviews. Because of early adulation her need to be the center of any group could take spectacular courses to fulfilment and she tended to thrive, in the long run, on controversy.

When Cayce got the telephone call from Cat, saying that she was calling at her Aunt's insistence to ask him to dinner—her tone implied that she had rather he would refuse—he found himself in the most peculiar predicament of his life. His impulse to call Ivy and consult her instead of some black friend defined the size of the change in his life. He had a curious vision of whiteness: he could see a triangle made up of the three white women and himself in the middle trying to peer through the spaces to catch sight of, or signal for help to, somebody black. But whiteness ran from woman to woman and it was like milk glass, a shiny, cold, impervious, opaque fence.

Grim, he called Ivy and told her, no request, that he would pick her up and they would go together through the hedge from her grandmother's house to Meredith's. She sounded subdued and serious and then he thought he heard something else, some mockery, some humor, in her voice when she told him that she had not been asked, and that you didn't invite yourself to Meredith's. She urged him to go, if only out of curiosity. "You *must* be curious," she said, like a directive, and then really laughed, and said if he felt like it he could stop by and see her on the way home. Her behavior angered him.

the dinner
party

As soon as Cat let him in the door his hostess came forward, the top of her head like Cat's barely higher than his navel. When she reached out her little hand he had no doubt that she was aiming for his crotch and he turned aside. This brought a smothered laugh out of the girl. Meredith's eyes went opaque as though a blue-white milky glaze were spread over her sight. She stood holding her hand out until he took it and feeling a certain power travelling along his arm like a command he bent to the hand as though to kiss it and make obeisance and amends at the same time. His inner voice told him, "Watch it!" so sharply that he sprang back up like a Jack in the Box and looked from woman to woman to see if they too had heard. Meredith told him in a cool, formal voice that she would have to leave him alone with her niece 'directly' while she saw to the rest of the dinner. "Since my cook died I do for myself," and ordering Cat to give the visitor a drink, she left.

From a distance Cayce was able to watch his impulse to flatten himself against the wall. It was like being able to look at an echo. A silent Cat led him into the living room which was fancy with gilt and marble and plain with dust. He saw from the flourish of her behind that she meant in spite of animosity to entice him.

She ignored her aunt's order to give him a drink and sat down, choosing a chair that was facing no other. Her expression challenged him to find a solution. He promptly picked up a chair and placed it exactly opposite to hers and sat down, splaying his legs and giving her the apex of his crotch right between the eyes, thinking "No use in wasting time." Her eyes told him that he had fulfilled some expectation of hers; she looked both smug

207

and mean. He gave her a cop's response to the look, a very slow once-over that was meant to make her squirm. In the process of the assessment he came to the fact that she was a very sexy piece. Her tits made him think of eggwhites: beat until they just hold a peak; the peaks visible through the figured blouse that was alternately modest and see-through as she shifted under his gaze. Now a nipple was exposed and now it was covered by a red shadow of hibiscus. Her navel was not protected by a flower print and he saw that it was the kind that sticks out at you like a third nipple, a tease of a navel. He wondered if she could suck it in and out. He laughed inwardly to think that she would have no problem with lint. Traveling down he found that her miniskirt barely made it to the tops of firm thighs with, in their current open, ready position, a thin line of muscle showing on the inner side—the tailor muscle he had heard it called, a puzzle for years until he had run across the answer: that old time tailors sat on a bench with their ankles crossed and their legs laid out, which put a strain on that muscle and built it up. He had rather think of Cat's tailor muscles gripping the back of a horse that she rode without a saddle. As though she read him, she pressed her legs together several times, leading him to visualize the hidden activity there, giving him the impression that he could hear a faint moist sound.

Meeting her eyes after the journey over her he found them waiting for him, eager for the meeting. She returned the assessment as slowly as he, as subtle as a truncheon, her expression bleeding hot or a parody of heat compounded by malice.

From a distance a strident voice commanded, "I want to hear some conversation in there!" The last word was 'theah' and Cayce felt a cold tingle on his spine. He asked Catherine if her aunt had maybe a touch of southern in her.

"Meredith McAllister Bonnycastle? She's as Southern as a lynching." Cat threw a vindictive look in the direction of the kitchen. He saw that between them discomfort could be turned into a kind of pleasure. He looked at her slightly thick lips that wore no makeup—only her eyes were madeup and heavily— wanting to cause them to say or do something revealing, because he was not going to be any goddamned mouse to her Cat.

"I am too," she said, as though insisting that she was cat to his mouse, then added, "Southern. I'm as Southern as a Geor-

gia redneck. I just don't choose to talk in that shitty draggy way."
Dreamy eyed she told him, "I've never sat and chatted this way
with a nigra man before. I'm not allowed," and in spite of the
phony accent and coy expression that was a caricature he felt an
ancient freeze in his bones. It was like the response to a shadowy
enemy, a silhouette in a jungle thicket. A cracker bitch said a few
words and a man was unmanned. His contempt for himself
brought about thaw and he shared the contempt with her generously if silently. Short of calling her a cunt, out of the blue, and
leaving he couldn't find a word to say in response.

Through walls and rooms the voice commanded again,
"Catherine, I said for yall to talk!"

The girl made gabbling turkey noises that Cayce supposed
would pass for talk to distant ears. His wish to know all at once
outweighed his animosity and he asked Catherine, "What does
she think's going on?" He wondered if the old lady had anticipated Cat's opening move, which was to isolate herself and leave
him on his own.

Cat opened her mouth and ran her tongue around her lips.
As comprehension dawned on Cayce she went on to give a blow
job to a phantom cock. Both of her stubby baby fat hands held
onto the imaginary instrument and her head moved up and down
while her tongue swiveled about the preposterously large circumference. In her mind she was giving head to something like
an overgrown squash.

Cayce wanted to laugh and at the same time to replace the
phantom with the real. He was getting tired of blocked thoughts
and actions where white women were concerned. He told himself that quite firmly. He wanted to pull Cat's mouth onto himself
by the ears, force himself into her as if she were a thick regulation sock, warm and snug-fitting, and feel himself bobble her
uvula, that clit of the throat, until she puked.

He directed some of the brutality toward Ivy. Thinking of her
was like thinking of somebody on another planet though she was
only on the other side of the massive hedge. He thought that if
Cat kept up as she had begun he would go to Ivy at the ready
and go into her and where the fuck would that leave old Jake
Barnes. Trying to cool himself off he thought about how many
baths Lady Brett took in the course of that novel. She must have
felt dirty all the time from a sense of inward filth. He decided

that she would stand for all white women in the world, the one across from him and the old broad in the kitchen. It seemed to him that the room he sat in with the dirty-mouthed girl smelled like a sex bed and when his old hostess came boiling to the door enraged by the prolonged silence he believed the smell came from her too, because the two of them, the white bitches, had finally got a nigger to come into their parlor, baiting the old trap with food. He was just the same as any hungry field hand lured in with the smell of hot grub, as far as these southerners were concerned.

Meredith's eyes stabbed her niece in several places but her voice was honied as she invited them in to dinner, then turned sarcastic on the way to the dining room. "I just luv my gar'lous dinnah party," she said, "my social gatherin." He heard that she was putting him on with the southern talk the way Cat had done. There was no difference between the women except for about a hundred years. He determined to eat as little of the food in this house as he could manage without the insult becoming open. He did not break bread willingly with the Lady Bretts and Miss Annes of this world.

In sight of the table he stopped dead as he had been meant to do. Before him lay a starving black man's idea of Beulahland: ribs and chicken and collards and yams and butterbeans, corn-bread and hot biscuits, salads made of potatoes and macaroni, bottles of hot sauce; and on the sideboard were neckbones and okra, big white hominy streaming butter, rice, a ham whose smell overpowered all the others for it was a long pungent rear quarter of a Virginia razorback. He saw a pitcher of buttermilk and one of iced tea as well as opened bottles of wine. He was sure that in the kitchen were a sweet potato pie and a coconut cake, and maybe some boiled custard and ambrosia because in here in this place right now it was sure enough supposed to be Christmas-time. In the middle of the table there was a big fat cake of butter that must be fresh churned for it wore a design stamped on it that could come only from an old wooden press. Gazing upon the feast he thought of Circe.

Meredith said, "I hope you like southern food," and the ten-tative sound, the sudden gentility, made him want to explode and yelp, like a turpentined dog, in laughter. He thought "Miss Anne wants something bad" and wondered as he sat and murmured and let her pile his plate high if there was something illegal going on and she needed him to hide behind. The Soul feast did not cancel out her whiteness nor neutralize his black vulnerability.

He filled his mouth and nodded to her waiting eyes his approval of the first bites. Catherine ate stolidly and each time he looked at her she managed to do something suggestive with the food.

Meredith talked.

"I'm delighted you like downhome cooking. I'm reduced to doing my own because southern's really all I like and I never never go out anymore. All through my professional years, which means foreign countries mainly, I had a cook, the same girl hired when she was just a little older than me so she wouldn't go popping off of old age and me tied down by contract to some herring country for months. My mouth puckers up like I'd eaten a green persimmon when I think about green herring. All of it I've had to eat to be polite to some fat Teutonic. My liver swells at the very thought of Strassburg. The cruelty of food, the pain of its pursuit, the priority given to obesity! A fat capon, a fat oyster, the fat of the land. There's even Georgia fatwood to make a more sputtering fire! Of course the reverse can be just as bad if fat must stand for hospitality. The last time I went out to dinner in this country, to someone's house, I mean, I was given a salad that was actually growing on a piece of felt, I think it was. It looked like an old hat I used to have, still have somewhere, one of Lily Dache's. The main course of that meal, I swear this, was bamboo, surrounded by these little bitty green pellets that could have been anything but looked like you know."

"Shit," Cat said in a most considerate voice.

Meredith nodded. "Rabbit, or deer. I wasn't, because I was hungry, very nice about it. What I said would make old Smutmouth here sound like Elsie Dinsmore. But—" she said, putting an effective stopper in Cat's open mouth, "I said it in extremity, not just to try to insinuate myself into another's conversation." She gave Cat a bow, and turned to Cayce.

"Mister Scott, I mean Officer Scott, I can be a real despot and a hellion so fair warning. I've had my way for too long and now won't have it any way *but* mine. And policemen do not intimidate me! There's a song I heard in a nightclub, Bricktop's probably, had a line goes, 'Don't call a constabull for this mad one has had one.' In my case that 'one' is a bit off. I never had just one of anything except one kid. I even had two appendicitis operations believe that or not. They left something in there the first time and had to go back in and git it. What they left the second time was, I think, my appendix. I still get these stitches. Yes, Catherine?" she said, for Cat had leaned forward in a very interested manner.

Given permission to speak Cat said, barely containing her laughter, "I bet I can guess what they took out instead!"

Meredith was kindly. "My heart, perhaps?" and held up a warding-off hand for Cat's mouth was open gleefully waiting. "Let us speculate about the nature of your reply and spare ourselves the inevitable disappointment. Of course we are intrigued but not now. When I speak, Catherine, there must be utter silence so that all the notes can be heard! No coughin or rattlin of papers or opinions, contrary or agreeable!" She laid her hand in the vicinity of Cayce's, palm up, as though waiting for him to slap five. She told him with great coquetry, "Catherine and I just have the best old times, don't we sugah!" and continued without pause. Cat's face wore a half-amused waiting look but Cayce noticed that her hand that lay on the table had clenched itself until the knuckles showed white. He anticipated a bitch fight and settled down to eating as though at the dinner theatre he and Ivy had gone to in the summertime.

"Because of my early start at my profession I've been what's being called 'liberated' most of my life. A child prodigy, of course, is something of a slave by nature but I managed to reverse that fairly early, once I got out of my father's clutches. Scott, I was some tough cookie! Try to bite me in those days and you came up with a sore mouth. *I* did the biting and I still have all my own teeth!" Catherine gave an incredulous laugh which made Cayce dislike her. Nobody could have mistaken the big white gleaming fakes in Meredith's mouth for real teeth and it was low of the girl not to let it go at that. He heard how the laugh made Meredith falter in her narrative.

"I always used men for my own needs," she said, sounding more puzzled than assured, but regained her aplomb soon after. "That's supposed to be something new nowadays, they're calling this new breed Macho Women. All I can say is God forfend.

But at least I was comparatively happy in my relations. Now, there's no such thing as perfect anything, Scott, even perfect misery is marred by little glimpses of better times; ask Dante's Beatrice about that. But these liberated ones don't admit that. I watch them on TV straddling all over the place, and what are they talking about? Why, about their perfect misery as human beings, their total former misuse by men, their utter waste as mothers and bottle washers. When it's as plain as the sky that most of them have no talent for anything, not even for rhetoric. And let us skip over how lucky the majority of these bags were to find a man to look at them twice. I think their real misery is in being *without* men, who they've thrown out with the baby and the bathwater.''

Instinct made him look to Catherine rather than to the speaker for the effect of the words. The girl's face was screwed up as though she wanted to cry and now both hands lay on the table-cloth knotted and white as two root vegetables. He admired the way she calmed herself when she saw that he was watching her, the way she pretended that the pained expression had just been her suppressing a sneeze. She couldn't have identified with the 'bag' part of Meredith's description, though there might be a husband and a baby in the background. She turned her lips inside out for him, making a kissing sound, and showed him her tongue. He saw this as a maneuver to cover up the more difficult unclenching of her fists. He felt murder in the air. Meredith had not stopped talking and he returned his attention to her, picking her up midpoint in a further declaration.

". . . all the while the self-referents fall like rain in a monsoon. They would even change language itself because of their puny requirements, their tacky experience! Recall that self-styled philosopher who got a whitlow on her finger and wrote a book about it? She couldn't do much with 'whitlow' her being white and that word being rooted in 'white flaw.' So she researched her subject and found that 'felon' was a synonym and she had herself a book! I watched this dingleberry on the TV and could scarcely believe sight and sound. She had just got back from the ugly parlor and her hair would have scared a cat—yes, even you, Catherine—and her 'philosophical' thoughts were like her hair, in total and hopeless confusion. There she sat, talking about the cruelty of using such a serious word as 'felon' to describe a criminal, a common criminal! Why, she had had a felon on her own finger, gentlemen, and that word had acquired divinity by association! Wanted to get rid of such as 'felonious assault' and as far as I know such a phrase as 'fell on the ice and broke something' and I wish she would, would be forbidden in her new lexicon of the English language. I hoped against hope that doozy wouldn't get a case of the piles and write another book! Well, she's a macho woman and I hear her next project is to change 'hemorrhoid' to 'personrhoid.' Or was it 'herrhoid?' They could adopt it as their emblem and have it sewn on their clothes. Except—though never having seen one—I imagine they, hemorrhoids, must look like little tiny male . . . things."

"Dicks," said Catherine with a chip in her voice.

Meredith was delighted. "My walking encyclopedia! With her around I am never at a loss for words! Well, come to think of it, a little tiny what-you-said looks like a clitoris and *that* would be perfection!"

Cat spoke to her in a voice that sounded grownup. "Let them go, Meredith."

"Them?"

"The white flaws," said Cat, "or whatever." Cayce saw that the two women were in communication before him but he could not intercept the message. He was glad and sorry for the end of hostilities. He had been looking forward in a really nasty way to some fireworks. But eating such food he could not bring himself to finish the uncharitable thought.

Meredith resumed thoughtfully. "But to return to my original premise, which may have got waylaid. I was talking or meant to about this American dissatisfaction with the thing one is by nature. You see it everywhere. It's like a continual complaint underlying the culture, or lack of it. Wrong sex, wrong profession, wrong neighborhood—environment is 'by nature' too isn't it? And you can supply many many more 'wrongs;' just look at and listen to the man on the street. Wrong this wrong that wrong everything."

"Wrong color," Cat said quietly.

"Yes, yes," Meredith said impatiently, then gave Cayce a sly look. "I bet *you* never wanted to be a whitie, did you? You look like a man who accepts what he is."

Cayce thought a minute to keep them waiting, telling himself

'Be cool.' "Well," he said finally, judiciously, "I guess 'reconciled' is the best word. I guess I'm *reconciled* to being a blackie, *accepting of* the knowledge that 'honkie' is just about as bad as 'nigger.' " He paused. "And could be a good deal worse."

"Oh, my yes," Meredith said. "That dreadful word," but she did not say which word she meant.

"What was your point?" Cat asked her as if she really wanted to know.

Now it was Meredith who made them wait. Her voice had no color when she replied. "The American-ness of this dissatisfaction. Everywhere else people fight for the very precious right to be just what they are. Just what they are."

Mockingly Cat repeated, "Just what they are." Cayce thought that knowing her aunt the girl certainly took chances. He envisaged Meredith's hard little weapon of a hand flashing out and knocking Cat out of her chair. He was surprised at the hostile image seeing it as wish-fulfillment for he had softened up a bit toward Cat, his lust for her tempered by an odd little nugget of tenderness. Did he attribute this to the wine he had gulped with the food or to the cliché of the black response to white need? what he had heard called 'the nursie syndrome' by a black revolutionary woman he had known. She had been savage: "Let one of them hurt a finger and damned if we don't drop our banners and even our goddamned guns and wrap the motherfucker up!" She—Coreen, that was it, strapping piece with a sergeant's voice—said that type of nigger was obsolete, that the new batch being born and trained would be without mercy, without stain. She said that black mercy toward whites was the true mark of Cain, apparently not caring that the remark was without even Fundamentalist logic.

He came back from his inner trip to find the women silent and Meredith gazing at him with something very like approval. When she said, "More?" in a peculiarly inviting way he was at a loss until he followed her eyes and saw his empty plate. It was with real enthusiasm that he told her "yes" forgetting about the shame of breaking too much bread with the Bretts and Annes of this world. He told her it was the best food he had had since childhood, when a relative would remember him and make up for having been forgetful by providing just such a feast. To compound the compliment he told Meredith that it was worth being

215

forgotten to be remembered in such a style. He watched the rosy color rise up in her parchment cheeks and thought, 'Why, the old girl's got plenty of juice left,' and told himself that he did not stir where he knew he had stirred, then admitted it and wished that he could let Meredith know that she still had the power. She took his plate and roamed among the dishes on the table and sideboard, filling with a generous but not undiscriminatory hand— a sliver of this, more of that, a dollop out of this bowl, a slab out of that. So that all the while she had been talking she had noticed what he favored most among the dishes. The fabled hospitality of Miss Anne. The way she found out which dish to put the poison in! From the way he felt, it had been put in the wine, to which he helped himself generously, thinking to die a good death. The women made him feel alternately masterful and out of it. Just now he felt masterful and wished he could command Cat to get under the table. You-know-what-for-Miss-Cat-honey.

She murmured across the table to him. He leant toward her words, obviously spoken to be beneath the perception of Miss Anne.

> "Speak kindly to your slave, my boy,
> All things that live know pain and joy.
> Speak harshly to your slave and see
> How sad and shamed he seems to be."

"What are you mumbling, Catherine?" Meredith was amiable as she set Cayce's plate before him. He asked himself, was he in shock at what he had heard, or had he heard it at all? What was the point of that obscene little verse? How did he react—by pushing the table back, he meant pushing the plate back, or—

Meredith sat down and leaned on the table, one arm extended. She told him, "Before my niece came here, whatever her reason for volunteering to come—" She stopped and looked at Cat, then murmured, "nothing falls out of the nest. It jumps or is pushed." It all seemed so odd. Cayce began a laborious effort to bring things into focus. He told himself that he was a drinking man and—he checked—nearly a bottle of wine meant nothing to his constitution and concentration. But what did she mean about the nest? She did not say.

"My trouble is that I was almost entirely alone and given to the kind of speculation that believes it can solve anything by concentrating on it, having, of course, solved my own problems to satisfaction. All the ills and dilemmas of the country, even unto its sexual conundrums. I had perspective—my age, my ancient prominence, plenty of do-re-mi—and I had myself a premise: that in America, Scottie, every single solitary problem, however secret and individual, from guilt to graft to graffiti, is based on black and white. On Blacks and Whites. And that includes the overuse of Black and White Scotch, for that matter." She leaned back from her clean plate. She asked him brightly, "Now, what do you think of that?"

It was Cat who answered. "You're obsessed, you know."

"You *know*. You *know*. How could I not *know*."

She drew with her unused fork a mark on the tablecloth as if she kept score. In a subdued voice, gazing down at the mark she had made in the damask she said, "I often suspect my niece is a racist." Cat's intaken breath did not escape Cayce's notice. "Though sometimes," said Meredith, "what looks like prejudice is really just a lack of sociability." As if to demonstrate the opposite, in a very hostessy voice she continued.

"Seems to me that what we call social behavior might be compared to a series of screens that are unfolded and set up for the comfort of others, artifacts that a host can use to control in a sense the climate for his guests. Good guests return this consideration by not writing graffiti on the screens, or carving their initials there. Or spilling the beans there." He gave an inward shrug; she was still talking in riddles. She said, "Of course if they choose to misbehave—but you must know the old southern axiom along those lines." She gave Cat a very nice smile.

"Northern nigger, ma'am," he said with a full mouth.

"Most good northern niggers have southern connections." The smoothness of her tone was like a paradoxical burr under his skin. She could argue that like any good hostess she was only using her guest's terminology, 'not correctin his English, God forfend!' But he knew she was aware of what 'nigger' in a white mouth, coupled with 'good' especially, could do: the opposite of setting up one of those screens she had talked about. But he would not let her see how exposed he felt, and the cop in him, lulled by food and mysterious talk, surfaced. He would fathom the old dame if he had the powers.

Was she setting up one of those screens? For she changed the subject and proposed to demonstrate an equation that interested her, she said. That was, how cultural and social and Art, as actions and as words, were inextricably entwined despite appearances. She told them that 'cultural' and 'social' are in constant and observable interplay, but between 'social' and 'artistic' or 'artistic' and 'cultural' the interplay and change are not observable at least by the day or week, the month or year. It is a symbiosis best studied, she said, in decades, and she was the only one there qualified to do so! First this one, cultural (social), then that one—artistic—is the leader, the instructor, and never gently, nearly always harshly revolutionaryly (she said). "Think," she said, "of the original reception given in Paris to *Le Sacre du Printemps*—a bloody riot." She was there. White handkerchiefs on canes waving, seats, human and theatre, flying through the air. One couldn't even say 'disgrace.' To say 'human' was enough, and the same thing. She said that cultural and artistic, though symbiotic, are viewed by the other as parasitic at close range. But if you were able to look in decades, this interweaving-advancement-temporary-backsliding could be seen as ribbons of light and shadow, like black and white snakes moving up a road, en amor up the dustless road of Time; each dominant, each subservient. And at last from a serene distance it will be seen that the three—cultural, Art, social, are all the same, merged but still distinct like where rivers meet—white on black on white et cetera.

There was a silence before she said, "But of course there are always exceptions to the long view and in those times and places we get pretty much what we've got today. Andy Warhol. Acid rock. No, the music isn't all that simple and the silk-screened electric chairs aren't just trash." She gave a long hooded look to Cayce and then to Catherine, as though she placed on them the burden of Andy Warhol and acid rock. "But knowing what they aren't doesn't lead to knowing what they are. Except cold. And dry. Dry and cold."

She got up and told them, theatrically desolate, "I am a rain person in a dry country" and left the room with the weight of a successful concert upon her shoulders.

Cayce turned to Cat, woozily aware that he had something to settle with her. But found that he could not recall what it was.

He gave her a puzzled look and she told him, misreading the look, "Don't try to figure her out. She just talks, that's all." She mimicked Meredith. "Nothing *falls* out of the nest. It *jumps* or is *pushed.*"

Meredith came in with dessert.

"Well, Catherine, I see you've finally learned something by heart!" She sounded delighted. Cayce thought, 'She talks in italics and exclamations' and thought they were like a net to hide what was underneath. Still, he had caught glimpses of what swam there, big toothed and sharp finned.

But here was the dessert and it was the anticipated pie made of sweet potatoes and spices but raised to a higher plane by the whipped yellow cream that was served with it, as yellow as butter, scarcely even a relative of the supermarket 'heavy' cream. The generosity in everything she did, he thought, including her insults to Cat and her prodigious number of words, obscured rather than defined her. He had the perception that she was, like the yellow cream, scarcely a relative of the person she seemed to be. But, approval of her prodigality and hospitality notwithstanding, he was growing more alert to the possibility of something: a stash, a weapon, a dirty secret.

He watched Cat lick at the cream in a sullen way. Or was she just introspective? He was bemused to see how he attributed only the most petty motivations and reactions to her unless he was constantly on guard, a waste of time. She was just a young pretty probably vain and rather stupid girl, which could serve as a definition for white middle and upper class girls of her age. Black girls and probably lower class whites, for all he knew, had to hustle too hard for vanity to catch much of a hold, and if you spent your days sharpening your wits there wasn't much room for stupidity either. If they knew they were pretty then they used that as one of the resources, along with youth, to help pull themselves up out of the shit without falling back in it. If they failed it wasn't stupidity so much as miscalculation of the men they had tried to use. He turned his grin at the thought of his prejudice into a grin of approval for the pie and the yellow cream. He saw fully for the first time what had been catching at his mind throughout the meal—that Meredith had touched no food at all. He supposed it had to do with bowels. One of his relatives had worked for a white woman who had to eat all her meals sitting

219

on a slop jar, the food went through her so fast, her remaining guts just swiping at nourishment as it rushed by, trying to retain enough to keep the old motor running for another day. His relative said this condition was common with whites, that their guts didn't hold up like Black guts, living as they did on pap, never swallowing pieces of gristle or sucking down by mistake a segment of neckbone, nor cleaning out their craws with daily cornbread. Did anybody ever, she asked, see Miss Anne or Mr. Charlie chewing on a bone, gnawing away like a hound in the yard to get at the good marrow? That's why their teeth gave out too.

Cayce poured from a new bottle of wine. Miraculously it turned out to be just sweet enough to set off the pie and cream. Looking at the label he saw that it was the grandest Sauternes of them all. Another proof of his hostess's prodigality. He felt sleek within his hide.

As though she had waited for him to finish his rumination Meredith began to speak of 'the man I married for about five minutes' and Cat's reaction drew his attention. Her astonishment told him that the story was new to her.

The marriage had been a business deal (Meredith said more or less reprovingly as though anything else was unthinkable). The man had wanted her celebrity to decorate what remained of his life, for he was dying. In return she would inherit his considerable estate, property in Switzerland and France including a vineyard. She had scarcely got to know the man; he was something of a neuter; no scandal of *that* sort was attached to his name, by which she meant sexual liaisons with women or men, and that curious virginity went undisturbed by their marriage. When she saw his body it was on the beach, a handsome body that was completely, but completely, tanned. But more of that in a moment. He was a competent gambler at the gaming tables and a brilliant one on the international Markets. He had an axiom drawn from the world of business to fit each occasion. For example, he told her, "Lend money to an embezzler but not to his son. The old man has worked it out of his system but the kid might want to practice on you." He was reasonably well liked (in sexual Europe real popularity was based on availability and performance though if you were rich enough a louche reputation could be purchased), his manners were superb and he kept his head shaved so close that she had never seen one wisp of his hair and had no idea what color it was. His essence, however, had eluded her until a moment after his death. "Mainly what I recall of him alive is that seamless tan, very dark and rich. He sunbathed the way he played the market, with all his heart. But of course playing the markets is a highly clandestine thing—who said 'Money isn't made in the light?'—and he sunbathed starkers and I'll be damned if he didn't shave himself down there too. I suppose it was pure narcissism that let him revolve like that patiently without boredom or pain the livelong day under the Riviera sun, pure narcissism like the donkey on the treadmill turning the spit. He was famous on all the beaches of Europe for his tan and his nakedness, nobody more naked then he, my shorn and shaven business partner. The water that day at Deauville was clear as mountain air. We eschewed our private beach for the chic public one—he said he wanted people about. So there he lay under the sun as the hours went and I stayed under my big fringed brolly studying a brand new concerto, Khachaturian's *Concerto for Piano and Orchestra*. It was just out that year, '36, and I was going to play it privately, for the first time on the Continent, before an audience that would have its share of Royalty. In those days you couldn't stumble and fall without squashing a Royal, or worse, a German, one of those living high off the hog setting the tempo for the death dance to come. No I wasn't especially prescient but didn't like Teutonics and thought they carried an odor of decay, even the most beautiful of the blonde women, soignée and silky as crème fraiche, a soupçon too fleshy for their clothes but oh how that drew the men. I was slender, too angular, and wore long robes—was that the year we said 'trig' for 'chic?'—on the beach and bathed only when the sea was private. The concerto I was studying makes use of that mournful instrument called the flexitone by the composer; in America it's called a theremin. I was working, hard mental work, on the last movement, the Allegro Brillante, that contains a cadenza as hard as anything Godowsky, that sadist, ever dreamed up. But in spite of my concentration, the theremin, which does not even appear in the last movement, kept obtruding as though it wanted to seize the lead and make some big trembling statement. An inaccurate statement it would have to be because that is the most unstable instrument in the world, like playing a lightning bolt with your bare hands. It was then I looked toward the stranger I'd married aware that I had been aware for some time of something odd. And saw what the oddity was. He had not turned upon his spit for a long time and was mottled as an egg and all congested looking. What had happened is that he had died, segued from life into eternal silence there in the sun at Deauville, the flowery esplanade just up there, the beach as gay as a carnival, the carriages parading. Standing over him then sitting behind him on the sand, I recognized that 'eternal silence' was correct, and I am no atheist. I saw, don't ask me how, that he had not been tagged for reincarnation or transmigration; that he had been endowed with no renewable spark; that his shell had contained no equivalent of spirit or soul. He was as transitory as the numbers, the figures he had dealt with and now he had been erased. That was all. He was just *not,* any longer. That was what had puzzled me about him, the way he had existed in life like a share of stock, entirely dependent upon the market for his very existence. His meaning rose and fell; his essence was on paper. I saw that 'it' was too specific for the remains on that beach at Deauville. I saw the shadow of a pigeon approach on the sand and pass over him and leave looking like a paper bird being jerked along by a child holding a string."

After a silence Meredith said, "I had him properly buried. He had no family and there was no risk of having to open the coffin."

Getting up to lead them away from the table she said, "Nowadays the risk lies in the other direction of finding the coffin too full. A million coffins full of plastic. They won't even burn you know. At least he, a paper man, could do that."

Very touching, thought Cayce. But how did Deauville get on the Riviera? The old witch changes the topography of the earth to suit herself. I'll bet even Cat, who howls at the full moon, knows where Deauville is.

In what Meredith termed the drawing room Cayce was given strong coffee into which Meredith poured brandy with a generous hand, without asking his tastes. When she poured herself a glass full of the mellow liquor he guessed he was witnessing her little vice.

She spoke generally as Cat yawned and shifted around in her seat, occasioning him glimpses of her cobweb clad glory, the sweet-thatched mecca of all self-respecting Dicks, Peters, and citizens of the land of Cockaigne, cockalorums to a banty. But the humor did not stay his stiffening and he thought about where he was, where he really was for the first time in his life.

Above him rose the house of Miss Anne and he felt that Mr. Charley was there too, harumphing in some upper room. To him the sense of the house was more arcane than religion, than God. The word 'tabernacle' came to him, a word that had scared him when he was a kid because it seemed to sum up what went on behind, under, the pulpit, what it was that gave the deacons in their tall chairs on the platform such power and mystery. 'Tabernacle' could be a machine like the one Ezekial saw whirling way up in the middle of the air. It gave off invisible rays that smelled like the air after lightning and cast blue shadows on the faces of the deacons. (Meredith spoke of the 'genital' nature of summer, and spoke of meeting 'dogs with faces wreathed in hot-weather smiles.')

He was in the house of the ancient enemy, not close to the kitchen where blacks knew how to be comfortable but in the room where 'nigras' were discussed and where their fates used to be decided. The southernness of his hostess seemed to affect him electrically. He was hanging on a high telephone wire, wondering if the next wire he reached for was the one loaded with death. (Meredith broke into his death revery like a raucous old parrot of a standup comic with a one-line zinger: "I've been thinkin about her so much lately but I'm afraid to call in case she's still alive and answers the phone!")

He questioned the assumption that blacks had made in his hearing, that because they had to keep their eyes on their oppressors at all times looking for an escape route or some gap in the wall of the prison, they knew more about whites than whites knew about them. Whites, it was said, were secure in the success of their oppression and never bothered to look or see more than the surface, which was color, though they noticed the satiric behavior that was often called 'cool,' that gave them consternation because they always believed, anyhow, that blacks were making fun of them. (Meredith was talking about The Virgin Mary. "Absurd but so beautiful. See how hopelessly we long for purity even in sex? Even porno stars. But not as much as Bishops.")

To bear the whities out he recalled jokes just making their rounds, jokes that Martin Luther King had made about his white allies, one about the President after his assassination.

The thought made him acutely uncomfortable. He and Meredith ran on parallel tracks for a moment then reached a junction where they merged.

". . . the kind of vision that sees the operation to correct the hairlip wasn't successful, or the silicon injections have gone to the wrong places, or the toothcaps look more like cheese than chalk. When the inferiority of the other has been firmly established they try to become very best friends with the specimen. They run after it, laying themselves open to all kinds of possession, begging to be *used.* That was all in the world that aberration called Radical Chic was about! Have the darkies in and hope they'll do something outrageous, something sadistic! Pretending to be in the same boat with those poor deluded street creatures, wallowing in their 'human condition' like pigs in a sty, pulling the mud up cozily. When one of those Radical Chic-ers cried out 'We're all in this together!' it was sexual perversion—they were using The Human Condition as a kind of Plato's Retreat. Those of us who could not share their vision were forced through those long years to watch in silent loathing their foul partouze!"

The voice was so full of hatred that Cayce made an effort to bring the speaker into focus and when he had done so he asked himself if it was a defect in his vision or was that foam? Was she foaming at the mouth? As though summoned to her aid fog rolled into the room and lapped about her hiding her from view. Looking elsewhere he encountered Cat's hypnotic gaze her eyes floating by themselves in the fog. He was on the other side of the mirror now having waded through the upright stream on his big innocent black feet even though he had seen the teeth. Was he white over here and could that save him? Cat opened her mouth so wide he could see her uvula. The opening and quivering stamen were a cunt, a painted scream, an insect eating plant. He saw himself as a black fly crawling over the edge falling into hot scarlet. He tried to move a hand, a toe, but was caught in the ancient condition of thralldom and would need to beg permission to use his own body. In Vietnam he had first encountered the story of the killer dream, the Bangungut that was said to happen only to Filipino men, the nightmare that murdered the dreamer. His family background was sketchy, just word of mouth mainly; maybe in one of the secret spaces not filled in by meager fact was an Igorot, a Filipino nigger, and he, Lucky Scott, had got handed on that particular pair of funky genes. Because this had to be a dream, he had to have slipped under all the wine and brandy into that subterranean stream that leads to that mysterious realm where each shall take his chamber in the silent hall of death. Cat's mouth snapped shut with him inside, struggling inside the football field of her palate surrounded by the white bleachers of her teeth, riding the high team-back of her tongue toward his reward for scoring, that quivering uvula, the biggest clit of them all. He prayed she wouldn't swallow just yet until he could find a cavity to hide in, snag some old root and hang on. But she was so young! He cursed her youth, her white health bolstered up by phalanxes of dentists who filled any holes they could find. He heard a gurgling and feared it was the waterfall of her saliva gathering upstream. He heard a slurp and Meredith swam into view drinking brandy. How had Cat got them both down? Snaked out a long long sticky tongue and gathered them in, that was how!

Meredith asked him, "Is there much hope for people who can't pronounce the name of the enemy? 'Rayshist,' they say, most of them say. One man on the TV, a high up in some Movement or other, was talking about the 'proverty program'. *Proverty.* You either speak English or you don't. No qualifiers will do. None at all."

Mournfully, seeing where he was, Cayce wished that he was really inside Cat's mouth fighting her teeth and her spit. 'Cause here come de niggah talk yessah. He was about to pay for that meal.

"I'm speaking about Black English so called, Scott. I'm speaking about black education or the lack of it and the ones who withhold it while pretending to purvey it. You know who I mean. Withholding anything the blacks could use but pumping them full of propaganda against everybody else. Like they were raising a private army and keeping it stupid. Private greed and public philanthropy. *You* know who I mean. Public peace talk and private support of vicious wars, private glee in wholesale murder of darkskinned peoples, even their own. *You* know who the hell I mean! Everybody seems to have forgot that they were banished from the world because of a penchant for violence. I wish Dorothy Thompson was still around, *she'd* tell you. I asked one of them before I left, *fled* New York, 'If you can't teach them English why don't you teach them your own language now that you've got a real one again?' I should have told her, 'It's no wonder you can't teach English, you can't even speak it.' All those glottal stops—that comedian what's-his-name who makes all those monologue movies—Catherine, who is that little Jew? Sounds like he's speaking an African click language!''

Cat exploded, jumping up with inarticulate sounds of fury. Cayce, wide awake again, saw that the look Meredith gave her niece was full of very real menace; he had seen it on criminal faces and respected it. But her voice was sweet and considerate.

"I'm afraid she has these seizures, sometimes literally a Cat on a hot tin roof."

"Drop mort," Cat screamed. *"You damned old rayshist."*

Meredith told Cayce, "They all learned something during the troubles. They learned to stand up for Jews and to be bilingual. That is, to talk clean and to talk dirty. 'Drop mort' is clean for 'fuck off' which is what I generally get." Cayce wondered, what troubles—the sixties or World War II? Because the gist of the exchange had been Jews and not dirty talk. Meredith was talking to Cat. "Sit down or leave the room. I will not have you hovering over me like, like some bird of prey. I'm the Cat now so watch your feathers, Miss Bird."

Her authority and menace were unquestionable. All of what she had called her ancient prominence was displayed so that he was privileged to view the mechanics of it: she knew that she was superior, that she was or had been a kind of genius, that power and the using of it was all there was. Cat edged back to a chair and sank down. Cayce thought, poor little kitten, for her moment of fame had been very brief.

Meredith spoke toward Cat. "Now, what is the alternative to blaming the teachers? Does one say, as so many have done and are doing, that blacks are not teachable, not capable of learning? Everytime you turn around there is a new statistic. Shockley, that's his name. And now others." What she was saying and her tone threw Cayce into confusion. She told him, "Ivy told me about your special status at the school. You're clearly an *exception*." She spoke with cold bitterness. "But I don't know why you decided to be what you are. Unless you're heading for more power."

The things that came out of her mouth! He kept silent.

All at once Meredith rounded on Cat. "Can *you* learn, Miss? Are you so superior? Did the Jews teach you anything except to toady? Why don't you demand—demand—?"

Without any transition she had gone from an impressive authoritarian stance to searching for words. But he saw that it was worse than that. Her face was animated not by the fluxion of power but by nerves, tics. Her mouth stretched and pursed, her teeth chattered in her mouth.

"Tired," she said, "so tired."

Cayce expected Cat to bestow on him a complicitous look, to mouth at him a silent putdown of Meredith. But she did not. She looked tired out too. Cayce let his confusion go and went to Meredith and picked her up, setting in motion the small table on which she had put her brandy glass. With one hand he caught the table and righted it but a small box slid onto the floor and discharged a quantity of white powder that he knew was not sugar. Meredith's chair, Meredith's table, Meredith's stash of cocaine. Cat's face, looking upon the accident, was uninterested. She probably thought that it was in fact sugar. He felt the tiny skeleton in his arms, no more weighty than a lap dog. He asked Cat, "Where's her room?" and the girl pointed. He told her, almost in pantomime, to clear up the spilled sugar, to put it back in the box. She shrugged listlessly but did not move. Feeling the weight of the house upon him he told her with hard anger, "Do it!" and saw that his voice made her go limp. In her total laxness there was invitation, he felt. More than that. She promised him whatever he wanted. He turned at the doorway and saw her crawling around on the floor scooping up the spilled cocaine on which, unsuspected by her, her aunt subsisted.

In Meredith's bedroom he put the twitching body in the middle of the great bed that was heaped with cushions of all shapes made of all materials he had ever heard of. Some were so metallic they were tarnished, torn silver-green lace. And real lace and needlepoint, silk, satin, velvet. Listening for some directive from his hostess he stared around him at dozens, maybe hundreds, of photographs, all old timey, yellowed to that shade that used to be applied to black entertainers—sepia. He gazed at strange-grained furniture that was also yellow and saw how even the corners of the rooms were draped with voluminous theatrical drapes that were tied and swagged, hundreds of yards with probably hundreds of pounds of dust in the folds. He stared at the tables, two or three clustered around each chair and sofa, tables laden with boxes, some carved, others set with gems, others painted, and he imagined that each box contained that which he would not want to know about. It was said that every household in the white Southland had a female member addicted to morphine. He had been brought up on that statistic along with others potentially as damaging. He thought about the misconceptions one race had for the other, one more virulent or farfetched than the one before it, and was wearied by the idea of so continual a feud.

The room was so big and high that it had shadows before your eyes got to the ceiling or could assess what might lie beyond the carved screens that cut the bed and ornate fireplace off from the rest of the room. China cats of exaggerated size sat and crouched about the hearth and one, larger than the rest, was in the position of licking its parts, one leg raised straight up, nose plunged beneath tail, the spread-out pink tongue the most realistic part of the uncannily lifelike animal. Beside it another cat stood on its hindlegs with its paws far up the mantelpiece, claws seemingly dug into the wood, and following its movement you came to still another cat sitting on the mantel, neck stretched out, looking down; six big black china cats that would seem to bask in firelight, a comfort to the old lady, cold companions artificially warmed to the touch on a winter's night. Then glimmering above the screens a portrait set high on the wall drew his gaze. His first startled impression of it was that it was a black woman, then Meredith's features emerged from the gloom, forming as he watched: Meredith as she would have been when she married the stranger and watched him die on a beach that was not on the Riviera. He went closer and gazed over the screens at the glamorous painted woman pondering his first impression. He decided that it was the privacy in the eyes that had done it, the wilful veiling that was like blankness but was much more, which he had seen twice tonight in the eyes of his hostess.

He heard her whispering and went to her then bent to her. She was telling him in a dry sexless voice like a bone dug up from the sand about how in sleep another's features would overlay her own so that she would wake up as a stranger and would spend the day trying to find out who she was. Once she said she had discovered that she was Faye Dunaway, had been brushing Dunaway's teeth and trimming her nails. But it was not always a woman nor did it always occur in sleep. Sometimes she was a child, a man, an infant. "I pick up these faces on the street or by looking out of my window, or from the television screen, or even from a memory. And they obsess mine so completely that I have to stand in front of a mirror, as desperate as life and death, and watch myself, force myself to reassemble a piece at a time. As *myself*, and it is like trying to play the theremin without letting the tone wobble. Have to remember who that is, what she's like in all particulars. What her tastes are, her clothes, her memories. It's like if I don't I can't come back in my own body. I stand there and tell myself, *Girl, you are famous. You have been world famous since you were barely nine years old. You don't have to ask who you are. But I do. At those times I do. Have to ask permission to be myself.*"

She turned her face on the pillow and in the reflection of distant light he saw on her cheeks the tears like snailtracks on parchment. He wanted to do something to bring the juice back into the mask. He raised her hand to his mouth and when she looked at him apprehensively he ran his tongue out just barely beyond the rim of his lips. He was asking her permission to touch her hand with his warm red tongue, to let the tongue stand in for his manhood as her knotted little hand, like a memory of a bound foot, would have to stand in for her womanhood, those two euphemisms for what made them what they were. But his tongue frightened her, the red flesh emerging from snuff colored lips. He felt her hand tremble and saw that the trembling, or shuddering, moved her entire body. He let her hand go and she turned her head again on the pillow. But in a moment she said to him, "You like my treasures, I think." He said that he did. She said, "Come back another time and I'll show them to you." He thanked her and turned to go. "My shadows," she said. He had the impression, looking at the now still figure, of a shadow like a cat's back looming on the vast headboard above her.

Passing the china cats on his way out he saw that there were only five now. The watcher on the mantel had gone.

Outside the door he heard her speak and bent his head to determine if she called him or addressed herself. All he could make out was "They won't let you be who." He imagined that her eyes had gone opaque. As though she reassured one of them, she added in her italic speech, *"You are."*

He stood pondering her art or whatever it was that gave her the ability to turn inside and walk down a road and keep on walking, a road so long it could not be seen from a plane or another planet as having terminals. That was what the blankness meant. On the surface she or another like her would seem still attentive, still polite and responsive, but inside she was as far away as you could get and still be called alive. He saw the ability as the sole reason for her survival but did not know why he thought so. It was not a technique that Miss Anne was supposed to know about. Then he recalled the cocaine and felt an inexplicable relief at that explanation.

The lights were off in the living room. He guessed that Cat had gone to bed and felt regret but when he went past the door her voice called to him from deep inside the room. He experienced the by now familiar impulse to flatten himself against the wall, then recalled how he had been fattened up for something and went into the dark room and walked blindly until a hand touched him in the vicinity of the knee. The hand grasped the knee and pulled at him until he was close enough to Cat to feel her nakedness through his clothes. Now two hands loosened his belt and tugged at his zipper. Together they undressed him.

He wanted her to be so good that there was nothing for him to compare the experience to, his first white woman and maybe his last. He wanted something he had had too little of. He kneeled over her then placed both sets of fingers at the base of his cock pressing them deep into the hair, feeling the heavy shaft lean out from the pedestal he had made for it. He told her what to do with her mouth and when she had begun the engorgement he told her, "I want you to touch the fingers with your lips." She gagged at the thought and tried to pull away but he had her clamped onto him and let her feel the pressure building in his thighs. Her hands fought with panic to push him off, her fingers curved around his balls. Then the hands grasped his thighs in a show of frenzied surrender and rubbed at the knotted muscles.

"Touch the fingers." She did.

part
three

white into
black

Scott speaking. Scott speaking. Wheres the rerun button on this. This is edgar cayce scott. That first name should serve to identify me if theres any doubt about the uh validity of this tape in the future. By which I mean the full handle is known only to a few old relatives. Even my social security number is socially secure under the name of cayce scott. As far as anybody knows I was given this name because somebody my mama hoped that I would turn out to be farsighted and a healer. When I pause like this it means make a paragraph.

Having identified myself ill proceed to my reason for buying this tape recorder. Ive got to make some kind of statement that may find its way into print. Into the body of a document that purports proposes to be the story of part of my life the part that pertains to ivy temple. The reason for the invention is given just before the start of whats called cayces story and its ingenious ingenuous based on refusal to spill my guts. Its also unreal as i was never asked to spill my guts. I am quoted accurately at the start. White on black on white et cetera but given a savage that should be in quotes tone of voice and then the narrator takes off into some pretty stratospheric territory killing the engines now and then to justify his invention of somebody called cayce scott.

To him I would say whites have always written the lives of blacks and filled them with enough exaggeration of one kind or another to make some black somewhere sometime step forward and counter the exaggeration with some of his own or occasionally a little bit of the truth. Ive heard this described as a white strategy to get at the black truth which may be like trying to get at the gold in fort knox as far as whites are concerned. The most vulnerable black man or woman or fairly young child is a fortress undreamed of mister horace in your philosophy. But the strategy works to a point because i sit here with a tape recorder running and most or some of what i say into this microphone will be the truth or truthful as i think there is a difference there. You can be truthful and still manipulate. But ill try to level.

I can start this off by saying like david copperfield i am born. But nobody much is interested in the sexuality of a newborn baby and hes too little to deal dope so until he grows up a bit nobody white is going to take much notice of him. The only tragedy is the babys too little to know how to be grateful for that.

But long before puberty the black kid has become interesting to a lot of whites and the ones the black ones that read capital o Orwell must have a special sense of connection with that book. The sense of being watched at all times. Now that whites are being watched by their own machines among which you can place the incumbents in Washington this category is not as black as it was from slave times until now though the reasons are different. The white is watched so that he may be caught in some criminal act. The black is watched so that he may be enticed into some criminal act. If that sounds prejudicial stick around.

I have relatives who are kindly and private people holding on because of what they really and truly believe which is that theres a jordan river which is death and on the other side black and white are going to be the same in the sense of well off and sanctified and all forgiving. Im not saying this is a black perspective. Just that my relatives feel that way. They hold on and talk low and get old and when they cant work any more they pray that their social security checks if they can straighten that out with the government wont be stolen out of their mailboxes by other blacks. You see they blame other blacks mainly the young bloods for all the trouble befalling aging black folks. But in line of duty i have caught one thief in the act and he was white. I worked the other side of the law you might say for expediencys sake and after i kicked his ass i threatened his life. The treatment was so effective he now works a counter in a supermarket a checkout counter that i cant use because when i go through there he tries invariably or did on three occasions to lay some merchandise on me. As a way of showing his gratitude for saving him from a life of crime. In which he persists and in which i am invited to join him by receiving stolen goods. A particularly white attitude and a particular predicament involving black and white. That is that a black even a cop is looked at as an instant accomplice in crime or partner in sex of any persuasion or dealer in dope. Ive had strangers in town approach me and ask me where they could find the stuff man and me in my uniform. Im not saying it doesnt work out a lot of the time. Why should a black cop be different from a white? But it dont work out with me. Ever. And thats how i can observe and pass on what ive observed. Like the divergence of the paths once partnership has been so to speak established.

Take this. A senator is caught making a connection by a network of his own machines so to speak. The dealer of course is black. There are no black senators. Once theyre running for office they are fading and once they win the seat and are glued to it they are white. Remember adam powell and his shenanigans and ostentation. Black folks loved him and said he was beating capital t The man at his game. They were wrong. He underscore was *was* the man. So we've got these two criminals. A senator and his connection. The pusher gets the limit and deserves it. The senator who deserves it gets a suspended sentence. If theres a big enough outcry he might get a few months in a hilton. But these are the same men working identical veins of American opportunity. Their ambition was the same and a key to the good life. One of them wanted to rule and one to deal. Both careers involve promises of purity. The senators purity of motive and the pushers purity of junk. Both cheat the government out of tax money and both make promises they cant keep. The senator cuts his promises to his constituency and the dealer cuts his junk. For each year of reelection the senator subtracts more from his side of the deal until hes sitting in that seat just because he exists. And the dealer cuts his junk by stepping on it with poison one fatal time. Both say fuck the people through what they purvey which is junk and lies. Lies and junk. And then theyre purveying nothing. So finally the two men the white and the black become indistinguishable. Dont say they aint working out the race problem down there in Washington.

Those two men and high government itself are as close as two sides of a zipper. The dealer couldnt deal without the senators help in getting the shit into the country. So here once again we have proof of a solution being worked on and i just dont know why people arent more grateful. For every highly publicized bust of a dope ship theres another one that slips quietly into port under cover of the hubbub and that ones the governments you might say. No matter how high up a white man is nor how religious hes always willing to lend a helping hand to a neighbor regardless of color when it comes to dope. Remember that rabbi bernard bergman. Cat was advisor to presidents. Knew what he was talking about. His pile was started with heroin brought into this country in a torah. His parents brought it in. They wanted the kid to have a decent start in life. It was just a slipup that so many old people died because of the kid. Some of them of starvation. Well he said he was sorry and frankel his judge said the kid had suffered enough and i guess by suffering he meant grieving by the gravesides. Losing his medicaid franchise. So he gave bergman six months in a country club which some people will agree can be punishing if you sit around without exercise and get fat and have to work to take it off when you get out.

Now people are talking all the time about the role of black youth in crime. And again I just wish those dudes in Washington would step on out here and let the public give it what it deserves in the way of applause and like that. Because Congress preserves traditions and one of our countrys traditions is that the whites do all the work and the blacks lay around because the workers have naturally got all the jobs. Congress has got to stay on the ball to see that no proposed legislation having to do with jobs for young blacks is allowed to pass. Exclamation point. Because every few years some joker tries to sneak a bill through and Congress has to you might say wake up and jump on that funky thing like it was a cockroach man. Hey all those black kids working would throw the whole system off its axis and Congress and the Senate and the President and the Cabinet you dig might go whirling off into space. Yeah. I know its simplistic and ungrateful to refer to young black criminality as quote legislated unquote but lets just say that thats one way to look at it and move on. Well id better mention that some of us are convinced that at least some legislators are grieved when seventy percent of young blacks wind up either in prison or dead. Especially since theyre starting to take some whites with them.

When the highest officer in the land was trying to put the

country through his personal shredder a lot of black folks were clapping their hands having a ball watching the circus. Whats the constitution mean to most of them? They were slaves when it was drawn up and if they know anything about the amendments that pertain to them they know that in any practical way theyre just pieces of paper. I heard one black man say hell tricky dick must be a brother way the cats carryin on. Said nixon reminded him of ol adam. I dont know if he meant the devil or clayton powell.

That bunch looked like a tangle of earthworms eating every kind of shit passing tons of it through their bodies daily to keep the soil friable for the governments plans. Watching them this dude said soon there be no laws at all not even agin us. I couldnt say brother you misread the omens. If they get their way there be signs in all the harbors of America saying government property keep off. I mean you hate to spoil a mans good time. Exclamation point.

To whoever or whatever will transcribe this tape. Make a parenthesis here. (I hope its a whoever. I dont know of a black man who aint afraid of a whatever. We all seen too many ghosts. Yassuh. Close parentheses.)

I return to you refreshed. I have walked my beat. I have had my sleep and my dinner. I have had a bath. That clinking sound you hear or record is the drink i am now having. Make that the drinks i am now having. The bottles here. The ices here. The document that started all this commentary is on the table in front of the uh protagonish. Ist. Just having a little joke there. Parachute. Paraguay. Parapsychology. Paragraph.

To put a tag on what I was saying in my sermon of yesterday. Washington refers to people who dont partake or approve of government as the disaffected. I think a better word is the dis capital eye en disINfected.

Now to proceed to this document called cayces story. Theres not a lot id object to or change as a man period. Even as a black man period. At least during three quarters of the dudes speculations on me. Theres a hell of a lot of sexual imaginings which dont i guess redound to a mans discredit exactly. I just wonder how the dude thought i got educated. How i trained for a profession. How i survived his race and my race and the viet cong with nothing but pussy on my mind though i guess thats not fair as he records or invents for me several impressions that are as good as thought. But a man will reveal himself even when hes trying hardest to reveal another man. So lets let the sexual preoccupation stand as self revelation and get on. One thing that interests me about this document is how close the dude comes at times to the quote real unquote cayce scott. Some of the speculations nicked my skin like a real sharp razor. But as the dude says given a mans books and records and furniture to draw from a perceptive person can make up somebody that could pass for a relative of what you might call the perpetrator. Or better still invent a kind of dopple ganger. I see that word like a mans alias rising up off the page and walking out in the world on its own. Doing what the man cant bring himself to do.

So what this dude has invented is close to being my dopple ganger. By which I mean that he does a lot of shit i couldnt bring myself to do. Like pretend to be impotent. I wouldnt want to dwell on that because its a dangerous piece of ground. Racist ground. Make that r a y s h i s t. The old time solution to such a mans problems with a white woman was castration. If they let the cat live. And this impotence shit is like a version of that. But as i said i wont make a federal case out of it. Just express my view and move on. Jake barnes my ass. The sun also sets and it just set on the concept that a black man any longer in this country is going to take to the idea of pretending he cant get it up. Man. Eunuchs went out with harems.

That clinking sound is a fresh drink. As a british buddy of mine used to say in saigon up your giggy with a meat uck. Meat hook. We solved some of the worlds problems together but nobody was listening. In the newspapers we saw there wasnt much about those of us in vietnam. Most of the stuff was about the ones back here who wouldnt go and what they were writing on walls and on signs they carried. I thought about thoreau writing on new york but not with a spray can quote the pigs in the streets are by far the most respectable part of the population unquote. But back in his time pigs werent cops. My brit friend was a mercenary and a really bad dude in the sense of being nerveless and ruthless. His solution to the graffiti artists was this. You paint every enticing surface he said with a pigment that is colorless and odorless and that on contact with spray paint emits for a space of thirty seconds and to a distance of two feet fumes that are powerful enough to knock a person out for at least ten hours. Dig the scene. Graffiti artists stretched out under their master-pieces paralyzed every man jack of them. And he said lorries come along and scoop up the buggers. Now this emission leaves a permanent mark thats invisible except under special lights and if a person put under such a light shows up as a repeater then hes put into the old bailey and smoked like a ham. If a chap he said just cant be rehabed after umpteen times in the old smoke-house then hes requested to execute a mural on a wall of the loo. And that wall has been sprayed with a slightly. Different. Coating. The fumes are lethal and the artist passes over in the can and can in hand to that great white surface in the sky.

My limey friend was a capital are Radical. Some of his ideas anyhow warranted that capital letter. He called himself a radical socialist but the socialist was a smoke screen to hide the blaze in radical. The dude wasnt a socialist or a commie. What he was was a man who believed in continual overthrow and plenty of violence as an example. All on behalf of the people. On a hill at da nang in between fire and the quiet that could be worse we worked out an acceptable government. Acceptable to him and to me at the time. There would be an elected body of represen-tatives and an interlocking grid of foolproof methods to deter-mine the legitimacy of the vote. Once elected they were given a matter of time a few months to show some progress on their campaign promises and platforms or at least some real proof that they were in there pitching at all times. And the limey meant at. All. Times. They were given sundays off and that was it. He said unless they were catholics the chance to make money in church was slight. I always knew england was a long way off but that remark put it in the vicinity of pluto. I told him about the money changers in harlem though all I needed to have said was rever-end graham. He can stand for all of them the ikes and the fal-wells. If within the given limits of time there was no provable evidence of progress the peoples representatives were sent back to their own states or shires or cantons and local holidays were declared. These were to be called straight out capital kay capital

dee Killing Days. And the peoples representatives were exe-
cuted. The effect of this was supposed to be that no mediocrities
would be running for office. Parentheses. (The limey thought this
might be a special hardship on America. Close parentheses). The
office seekers would either be fanatics like the limey and me or
the biggest crooks in the land who had enough huts puh to believe they could get away with it. This had two things in its favor.
The biggest crooks would be up there in plain sight at all times
and the limey said the spectacle would afford some amusement
as one watched the feeding of naked egos more obscene he said
than the dead wallowing in the gulleys drinking blood. He said
this particular pornography was presently concealed from the
people by practically. Prehistoric. Poses. Of piety. But i said naw
we had always had that spectacle back home.

Author of cayces story. You sir yes sir talking to you sir. In the
preamble you wrote to my life or the forward you imply. Well
the way aaron implies the ball with the bat. You imply that my
reason for cutting you down or off or under is because youre
queer. This limey ive been quoting was to quote him again as
queer as a duckbilled platypus. I think he may have been gay
too. A little humor there. My reaction to finding out that hartshorne was your careless lover wasnt because of straight versus
gay. In saigon. But thats over and over there. Still i never saw
calvin in the company of a white. A division but never company.
So my response was to your color in that context. It must have
been a surprise to him to feel something for a white. A highly
emotional dude i recall. He said something one night thats stayed
in my mind. We were talking about snakes and he said quote
they stick out their tongues to hear and we pick up a hammer.
Which is like man trying to kill somebody because they have to
wear glasses to see unquote. Ive thought since that he must have
identified with the snake and wondered if somebody in his life
had taken a hammer to him. Thinking along those lines it seems
to me that people are afraid of things that live in holes not because of the things themselves but because their habitat reminds
people of the grave. Its not too big a stretch to include among
the things that live in holes other people. The ones that live in
slums in the dark and slime among the rats.

Then ivy said. Cayce doesn't like white men. I was sorry she
said it like that. Her timing is generally a fine thing. I dont. Un-

240

derscore dont. I *dont* like white men quote unquote. I dont much dig anything that comes in bunches except food. Maybe my perspective is peculiar. Here are some bunches of things. Planes. Airstrikes. Refugees. Graves. But if you try to hand me anything thats just a mob and a gender and a color except a herd of black angus bulls ill try to hand it back to you. I tend to be a one on one man. Like hand to hand combat. Like two person fucking. Conversationally what the french call tet ah tet. Lets have a little paragraph here secretary or machine because i dont know which.

I wish i could look through this tape recorder to you on the other side but i might not like the expression on your face when i say certain things. And on the same other hand a machine cold and impersonal probably couldnt think nigger if it didnt like what it saw. Could it. Paragraph.

Lets talk a minute about legends. Black and white. One of the biggest is that somebody speaks for the black and somebody for the white. What speaks most of the time for both is hate and hate aint somebody. So what you ought to have and what we need is one on one. Ivy and me. You and me. You and Ivy. Two people even when theyre races. You know how peoples minds are blown when they sense this thing between two people. You saw it with ivy and me and called it brother and sister. And when the black says my brother and my sister hes trying to make all the confusion into a family where it can be dealt with. Only thing is when youre grown up theres no parents to settle disputes. To take it out of your hands and arbitrate. So here we are back to one on one. Start with the capital o One. To an isolationist by which i mean a sniper mentality the sight of two people close to each other can be disturbing and confusing. But suppose its two races and hes included cause nobody is capital e capital ex EXcluded. Everybody is brought in out of the cold air. If you stick out your tongue to hear aint nobody going to grab a hammer. Hartshorne was a one. The loner with the rifle in the brain. Are you a one too? Oh ivy told me there was a dog. A loss like that can hurt a mans life.

One on one. In the view of your document its the on that becomes most important. That somebody wants to be on somebody because that person is black or because that person is white. And in your book when sex is not supposed to work you give us a lets put it this way sexually absent montage. But whats in-between is never faced and you give up and say its because theyre a man and a woman and i cant fathom that. We could let your professed limitations pass if it wasnt for the fact that we then move on to more sex. Some kind of dream fulfilment i guess for cat and me. All i could see for us in your book was a sado masochistic gig. Me batting her around hurting her with my of course huge dick. Parenthesis. (Is there one small or average black dick in your book? I dont think so. So we still got legends to deal with sometime. And incidentally heres a maxim for you. White men have cocks and black men have dicks. Close parentheses.) And i would be calling her all the names id ever wanted to call a white woman right? And her calling me of course nigger and crawling to me inbetweentimes and plotting my death or worse. Maybe there was a pair of shears in cayces future. Making the old impotence pose a foreshadowing. Though i think it was badder than that because of the long dream set up. Cayce must face his fate. Right. Well thats your i guess you can say fictional privilege except now and then like now a man is able to step into his own life so to speak and say unh unh. Unh unh.

I keep thinking about cats thick lips. Not just thick cocksucker lips. Something else was coming down. Goodnight. Sleep tight.

When i was shuffling the pages of cayces story one of the sheets got turned around and i read what was written on the back. Quote. Have meredith mention a gala at which she played the piano to accompany paul robeson. Cayce sees all black references as sops thrown his way. Unquote.

So i went through the story with the pages turned over and found a skeleton with bones that definitely make a kind of mutant. Ambivalence is a good name for the monster. Quote. During sex talk meredith says she has been very drawn to black men all her life, but never had a black lover. And in parentheses youve got quote by play with cat.

Another bone. As meredith explores all the topics during the dinner party of sex and religion and politics though cayce finds parallels to some black thought he also finds such dissimilarities as to be intolerable. So we once again have the desire to find differences creating the differences. Unquote.

And a long quote. Meredith is talking. That slime in the oval office passing the buck so fast in so many directions you cant see his filthy hands. But we know where theyve been. We know he directed every step of the break in and you wait theyre going to kill martha for saying so. The only solution to this is plain. Prolonged public torture. And then murder. Thats the ticket scott. Otherwise these American sheep will just put another one in there and another and another. Can you name a good man that ever sat on that throne? And cayce says levelly warren gee harding. Quote. Her bright eyes appraised him weighing the irony against something she knew. Then she said he was a piece of slime. Cayce thought a moment and told her sure. She nodded and asked does it matter what color slime is? And again cayce said sure. Cat said in a plaintive voice i wish you wouldnt talk about slime when im eating okra. Close quotes.

Priority questions. Why make cayce somebody looking for dissimilarities? He knows what those are. Why make him see all black references as sops? That much paranoia would make a pretty unsettled cop and man we got enough of them. Why give the old woman all the good lines?

From the meeting with meredith and cat on im reminded that ive started reading articles by whites on blacks that were so fine you couldnt believe yours eyes and your heart. And were you right not to believe. Because here come de legends and before you know it youre up to your bottom lip and thats when dont make waves can become a very poignant outcry.

But what youve got going here for old Scott would make a pretty heavy trip. Like the bases are loaded and hes got to carry the bags with him as he runs. Im beginning to think we had better be prepared to take the rap for all heavy trips we contribute to. Thats a primary tenet for my brave new world. A good motto is be prepared to take responsibility. Every man as capital gee God. Why not. At least we would be entitled to our cut of the ego which when you are hungry is all protein. Black is beautiful. Thats pure protein. Like god is love. If eternity is just everything possible in every possible time then god cant be inside eternity and less than eternity and he cant be outside it and more than it is. How can something be more than everything. So god and eternity are equal. And if god is all how can a man be something else. Something set apart and down on his knees supplicating. If god is all then we are god. Be good that you be god. If anything the races are like molecules in the one god eternity which just says that they are part of themself. If we were taught that instead of all that other shit wouldnt we behave more or less in an ethical manner? Including the senator and the pusher and the president and the rapist. If do unto others was finally explained i think those categorys would disappear. If in order to function at all it was necessary to identify positively with the active structure that is ourself. Dig that our. Dig that self.

You see finding those directives that would lay a heavy trip on cayce for no reason that i can see has strung me out. The black hero that youve treated o k is being haltered up for the last act in which his role is to be scapegoat. To make what point? Like the french say man plu sa shanje plu say la mem shows. I dont know if im afraid of that writing because the words could influence my life and make me into that dopple ganger. Im hung up right now on wanting to ask why. Youre inventing this man so for once why cant you. But you may be the realist and i may be the sentimentalist. It may be that to believe a cop can stay within the law not to mention involve himself in the idea of order takes a first class sentimentalist. Because he has also got to believe he can be strong enough and pure enough to go against the system when it comes to his personal justice and not see color. When everything else is unequal including the way you yell halt to a running figure. Even the tone of voice is there in the training manual. Maybe it takes a sentimental square to think we could look forward to an increase in the common ground. A dee em zee make that all caps DMZ between people and races where a common truth could grow. Its been a long day. But hear preacher scott out. What im onto is this. If everythings going to hold it has got to go forward. To go backwards is called unwinding. Root around back there saying this is me and this was me and your like somebody digging in his own grave picking up bones. All you know is the language of death. But is your shinbone more yourself than your fingerbone? Will you settle for your jaw and leave a part of your spine? Every seven days your skin renews itself but if you sit around feeling it happen your nerves will give out. Watch yourself making time and thats a pun and your brain will go. Because doing that is watching yourself die. Everybody has got days when they hold their head to make themself let go of that thing and get on to this thing. Its a growth pain that i bet some son of a bitch would call existential. So its birth too. To keep from watching the process we teach we plant we make love. Theyre all the same. We are all the same. Good night ladies.

The reverse button on this machine is busted which may be a good thing because if i could i probably would erase what i put on here last night. For all i know it may be like the preacher talking in unknown tongues. God. Eternity. Time. Lonesome words. Maybe all time is is a jap tape recorder with a busted reverse button.

Last night on the box another process of reversal which is what most tv is all about. Pure being some piece of chemical shit and nutritious being something as nourishing as a piece of coal. And a womans hair and hair dye and hair spray and shampoo being what its all about in the mid seventies on mad ave. But they slip it to us easy with fuckable broads doing the pimping and we take the shafting without too much of a fuss though our dreams may be increasingly bad. But last night right after god and eternity and time i tuned in the box and there was the autumn of the year which is the most complicated season. There were the trees just showing a hint of their skeletons and the leaves brightly dying and there was a skim of frost on a hillside. And this voice saying autumn hellmans like bond bread talking. See theyre trying to make somebody swallow along with the mayonnaise the idea of sereness and skinniness and even thoughtfulness i guess when what theyre pushing is oiliness and fatness and if you eat enough of that shit real obesity.

And so i pick up the document again thinking about reversals and deliberate obscurity and hidden meanings. Ive read cayces story twenty times and last night i thought this about the writing. Its like the writer runs into a person and deals him a glancing blow and while the persons smarting the writer slips a note in the victims pocket telling him whats going on. But the victim is so outraged about being run into that he doesnt find the note until a lot later.

And so I looked for the note not really expecting to find it actually written down. But there were some lines I had missed hidden in a tangle of words I had read before. Quote. The book is about misconceptions and masks hiding obsessions and masks being removed at some midnight signal revealing some other obsession entirely. Therefore meredith who delivers the peroration and must touch all bases and the like is the ideal person. And must and ideal are underscored.

Now im moving back a little and then forward a thing this machine cant do he said in a macho tone of voice. Quote. Touch the fingers unquote. Thats ok that part as far as it goes and if it goes no farther. But. Studying your methods in other parts of my story i think for the sake of what you would call symmetry you had to be planning something like a scene between the old lady and cat where cat says about me quote well i had a part of that nigger you never got and the old girl lies back and smiles. Just like a cat right. Bringing out their strong family resemblance. Have i touched you yet? And then says like shes talking to her selfself capital t Touch the fingers. And cat says all full of half laughing disbelief quote you overheard us. The old sister smiles again and says did i. So now our black quote hero unquote is taking head from eighty year old ladies. Did he rape her in the mouth the way he raped cat? Or is the old sister just a natural cocksucker?

The grace and frailty of old age can be put to one side where miz meredith is concerned because what you had planned put her out of it in the very beginning. I think the revelation would be presented slowly like in the movies where a leaf tears off a calendar to show time passing but here we dont see sat or sun or a month but the feeling of the word chaos. Peoples minds are spinning back and recalling. Her skin in the shadows like old meerschaum. The portrait cayce thought was a black woman. Cats thick lips. Meredith talking about how capital double u We have to impress upon others that we are. That we are. That we are underscore us. *Us.* Another instance where cayce is too dumb to hear whats being said. And the mysterious remark about harding because a lot of niggers have heard that he was a black man passing. And we have here in meredith a black woman who has been passing all her life. And readers remember her kid by the famous wop singer. The dinners with kings and queens. That she had been the toast of a white world that never knew. I dont say it never happened. I just say that passing as a theme has got to be retired. Got. To be. Retired.

So cayce was not the only one with a heavy trip laid on him. The old woman if you went back to her beginnings had to live a lie. All her long life long. For what reason? Fiction? What people might call a good old fashioned read? To titillate some old or young redneck or some honkie hater? Man you cant have thought about what imposing that on somebody would mean. Nowadays i think this pinkie thing might cause a few snickers. Because today there are black women and men who if they didnt say im black youd never know. But they do say it. You might call this seized progress but progress. But back when meredith had to put on the mask she just might have had to share it with death if she was found out.

Now im writing your rebuttal to all this. Im giving it to you the way you gave me some noble speeches. Quote. Curing is a physicians art not a writers. A writer confined to curative writing is under a handicap and would come to hate it and all who touched it. And if he strayed from the imposed path and wrote dangerously or bitterly he would come to believe that his own deviation could cause death. Unquote.

I believe thats your style my man. Now im writing you in your own language and heres what you say in my book. Quote. I am sick of perversity. I am sick of the lethal scalpel in my hand. I am sick of hate thoughts and death thoughts. I can imagine a healer turning on the world at the worlds insistence. No. At the worlds denial to him of an alternative. Unquote unquote unquote.

Miss machine that sound i just made is spelled double u aitch e double u. W h e w. You see how even in the middle of me writing you man you tried to rebel and create a healer turned monster. You have got to be watched man. Here you go again this time according to cayce. Quote. I have scraped away at myself like an old floor turning up instead of pegs the dovetailing of another time. Only the footprints of footprints of footprints. Turning up ancient shadows of myself unquote. A sympathetic picture for a white man. But i could set you up for ridicule just as easy. You how how easy it is. Like quote a lifetime of me me me like a limited singer warming up for a second rate concert that never takes place unquote.

Now heres meredith telling me on our second visit about discovering a central metaphor that works for her. She said as she got older and it seemed like all she had left was technique she used these images like a well bucket to draw up emotions. Its a triple image she says. The first one is of a man or woman in their sixties asleep on their feet being walked around between two nurses in a sanitorium in switzerland. Put to sleep for two weeks she said a large fat sleeping it being drained of shit and piss by nurses so that when it wakes up it will have shed twenty or thirty pounds of blubber put on by nonstop eating and drinking. The second image imposed on that one is of a big black woman on welfare fat maybe obese because to fill up her belly she eats starch. Not fettuccine alfredo tossed with two golden forks but laundry starch out of a box the way her ancestors ate clay out of a special clay hole. To fill up the emptiness left there by the greed of others. And the third image she said is of all the skinny hungry kids in the world looking on like birds around an empty garbage can. She calls this triple image a palimpsest named his eye is on the sparrow.

One question before we say nighty night and i go to think about your fate. You say i brought on ivys rehabilitation. You say she says i did. But you dont say rehabilitation from what. Im curious to know how you planned for me to take the revelation that quote ivy in a slim and radiant person as reborn as a phoenix was all that he had hated. And in my copy the rest of that line is blotted out with what looks like violence. What did you mark out there for me to discover someday? Is it something that was meant to blow my mind?

Oh man that note you slipped in my pocket has worked up to my brain. This is the paranoid hour when yawning graves give up their dead. Its like falling asleep and catching glimpses on the way of the dream thats going to happen to you. Dozing and starting awake. This doze dream wake is like falling asleep at a keyhole on the other side of which people are talking in low voices deciding your fate. If this machine is a keyhole and i think all machines are keyholes with our fate on the other side then if we could see through to the other side we could read our futures. Capital punishment comes to my mind but the way its spelled is C A P I T O L. If C A P I T O L S decide our future lives then can c a p i t a l s? Miss or mister or miz secretary please when your transcribe this tape make us important with capitals. Give every man and woman and place and thing its uppercase upperclass. Dont let c a p i t o l s even semantically take over because their aim is to reduce us to lower case and then to case histories and then to mental cases and basket cases until finally the process has reduced us to case shot.

Last windup last reel cayce at the bat the last time.

To pull the pin on my capital case of paranoia that could have destroyed me last night i thought about the paranoia of others. I saw that if i ended this story on what might be called a black note people looking for symbols would see it as a projection of a black police state to come. For them i say all it is is a declaration of independence and when i finish somebody is free to rewrite me like theyve been rewriting us for over two hundred years. But given my turn again i decided that unlike meredith and her white husband i am going to trust the embezzlers son. Its not like she said. The old man hasnt worked it out of his system so that leaves the kid like it or not. But a lot has happened to the kid to let me and others like me. Well. Hope is the word i guess. Im basing this on a dream and i am counting on that dream to persuade you or them or us to let whats good stand and get to work on the rest. It was not the dream you gave me man but closer i guess to martins dream.

I go to sleep around dawn and look out the window of my dream and through the window which is nearly opaque with dirt i can make out a window washer floating around working at his trade. He is jet propelled. I want him to wash the ancient grime off my ancient pains. I open the casement that has an intricate lock like the doorlock on a jet plane. I step onto a little balcony that is thickly encrusted with old ice and snow and all the high places around me are encrusted in the same way and i mean high places because i realize that i am two hundred stories up in the air. I call out to the window washer and he swivels in midair in the thickly falling snow away from me and then toward me and in spite of the bitter cold of height and winter this black man shows a bare ass. And that ass is a healthy pinkish white. Not from skingrafts or burns but just because its a white ass. And he comes sailing on a straight line to my balcony roost to wash the crud off my windows so i can finally see out. I step back into the room to let him land on the little balcony and there is a big floorlength mirror there and i see that i am a white man and my ass is hanging out of my clothes and it is as black as it is in real life. Not from frostbite or any morbid thing. Just a healthy skinned black ass. And i think hes been out in the cold a long time too and im going to get some rags and help him clean our windows and i wake up.

Since then ive thought about you and calvin and me and ivy and the others who in a fairly complex way through accent on asses may have made some kind of progress though it may have looked like the opposite. I am finished trying to analyze you and myself and ivy and blacks and whites. Knowing the perils of playing pollyanna i am going to end my section which may be my life the way i would want somebody writing my story to do it for me.

I cant give you back your dog that died and id advise you to get another one pronto. Get another breed if having the same breed in the house would be painful. Dude i know has a terrier and he swears by their brightness and fun and loyalty. And man instinct by any other name smells just as sweet you dig.

Now take your new little dog and go out to orient to the muslim settlement. Youre afraid of what calvin will do to you i think. But he will be expecting to see xan who ivy says he loved and this visual proof of her death will change him in some way for a little while. Soften him or harden him but change him. Take advantage of that. Drive him on out to the point. Sit the three of you looking over the water. Toward your roots man. He says did you get my card. You say what card. He says the one saying youre out of it. Out of this world that is.

Then you remember that card you got the one that had no signature. You realize that he had been thinking about you back then and paid you the only compliment he knew how to which was an unsigned one. One he didnt have to take credit or the rap for. You see it as a kind of i was going to say love statement but maybe you dont want that. I dont know what you do want man. My imagination is not tuned into dealing with two dudes. But he could give you one of those muslim hats. A kufi. Bands of white and black. Black on white on black intertwining. Call it an integrated hat. If it was me and somebody id felt so strong about. Lets take ivy and me. Because i have and i do. And i will. I will take the hand of that person who is not my sister. I would

250

if i were you hold the hand of that person who is not my brother as long as it felt right. If i was you in this scene because of all the game playing and witchcraft between you and calvin i would look for some sign. An omen. If i thought it might be the beginning for us and wanted it to be i would make the time of the year the breeding season of the least terns that lay their eggs on open dunes in beach grass like that right there where the new london ferry comes in to orient point. And id look and see a tern nesting there and it would stand for my hope. If on the other hand i felt like it had to be the end for me and that person and i had somebody back home id forgot in all the obsession. Berthold is that his name. Then id watch a plane draw a straight line across the sky and id think that was the first line of a stave of music and when it was finished it would draw four more lines. And then another plane would zoom along and draw some notes of music on that stave. And then gabriel would fly down and read that music and play that great trumpet solo man the solo i would be convinced the world was waiting for. Because to lose that person after all the hate and the love and the games and the obsession would feel like the end. Make that all caps miss secretary. THE END.